ALEXANDRIA LEE

Kissing Death

Star-Crossed Series: Book Three

Copyright © 2022 by Alexandria Lee

All rights reserved. No part of this publication may be reproduced, stored or transmitted in any form or by any means, electronic, mechanical, photocopying, recording, scanning, or otherwise without written permission from the publisher. It is illegal to copy this book, post it to a website, or distribute it by any other means without permission.

This novel is entirely a work of fiction. The names, characters and incidents portrayed in it are the work of the author's imagination. Any resemblance to actual persons, living or dead, events or localities is entirely coincidental.

Alexandria Lee asserts the moral right to be identified as the author of this work.

First edition

Editing by L. Mariani
Cover art by Darla Cassic
Proofreading by Briana Mae

This book was professionally typeset on Reedsy. Find out more at reedsy.com

Contents

Acknowledgement	v
Kissing Death	vi
ONE	1
TWO	13
THREE	23
FOUR	33
FIVE	45
SIX	52
SEVEN	58
EIGHT	73
NINE	98
TEN	105
ELEVEN	116
TWELVE	133
THIRTEEN	143
FOURTEEN	155
FIFTEEN	170
SIXTEEN	181
SEVENTEEN	200
EIGHTEEN	209
NINETEEN	229
TWENTY	241
TWENTY-ONE	248
TWENTY-TWO	261
TWENTY-THREE	269
TWENTY-FOUR	288

TWENTY-FIVE	295
TWENTY-SIX	313
TWENTY-SEVEN	326
TWENTY-EIGHT	340
TWENTY-NINE	347
THIRTY	360
THIRTY-ONE	377
THIRTY-TWO	394
THIRTY-THREE	409
EPILOGUE	427
Next Book by Alexandria Lee	444
Want more Kat and Dom?	446
About the Author	447
Also by Alexandria Lee	448

Acknowledgement

To everyone who has been by my side this last year, thank you.

Your messages and comments, your love and support, each one helped keep me standing. My readers and friends are the backbone of my strength, and I am indebted to you. You are a blessing, and I can honestly say that through all the difficulties I've faced this year, that I am *lucky* because I have each of you.

This series has been a whirlwind to complete, and I hope you enjoy it.

Kissing Death

"If the scar is deep, so was the love." - Unknown.

For a list of potential triggers in this series, visit my Linktree.

ONE

KAT

Over the last month, I'd had my fair share of waking up in compromising or otherwise unpleasant situations.

And I was getting really fucking sick of it.

My brain flickered like window shutters rattling in the slap of wind. Light peeked in momentary slices before darkness ate it all up in gluttonous chomps. This predatory attack of light and dark went on in an endless roundabout until the battlefield swept awash with a fixture of both.

The phantom weight on my eyelids shed itself to let in some light, only to find a floor of black staring back at me.

And my bare legs.

A groan creaked past the silence as I rolled my neck, a twinge radiating up my spine and singing a song of pain through my skull. *Fuck*, why did everything hurt? My jaw was stiff, my back was sore, and my head was a swollen clusterfuck of confusion.

Fog rolled through my head, pirouetting clouds around memories my brain was fighting to dig free. Heaviness drowned my eyelids back down, the struggle to keep them open as exhausting as the one to remember what happened.

I went to rub my fingers over my sleep-heavy eyes.

My hand jerked to a stop, barely moving.

Confusion mingled through the haze in my head. I tried the other hand. Same shit.

Pain carved into my wrists as I pulled and pulled my hands and didn't stop. The more I pulled, the more I could sense the posture of my arms… like they were slung behind my back instead of at my sides.

The fog hovering in my head was given a swift exit as a gust of panic blew it all away.

Why were my hands behind my back?

Riding the high of panic, I went to stand up or jump around or fucking fly if I was able. Every frantic move was met with resistance. *Painful* resistance.

My arms. My legs. My feet. Nothing was moving but my head and my heart, which was flying a million beats per second.

My eyelids snapped open, a burst of anxiety kicking a gasp to the back of my sandpaper-dry throat. Four walls of black closed me in on every side, the room they were holding together no bigger than the bathroom back in Blake's room.

Blake.

My heart stopped.

Every muscle in my face tied with tension slacked instantly.

His name in my head triggered a reaction of pain—of sheer *panic*. It squeezed my lungs like a stress ball, rapid breathing sucking in and out as I tried to recall my last memory of him and where he was right now and figure out where the fuck *I* was right now.

Or why I was sitting in a chair.

Or why my hands and feet were restrained to that chair by the pinch of zipties.

Or why I was wearing an outfit I'd never laid eyes on before.

Red satin underwear shined up at me in the murky wash of overhead lighting, squeezed between my pale thighs. The satin turned to lace as the design went up my flat stomach in a strip as wide as three fingers across, leaving my sides bare. The opposing materials mixed into one and cupped

ONE

my breasts to create a bra that pushed my tits up to my hanging chin.

My gaze stayed on the lingerie, tongue glued to the bottom of my mouth. All thoughts in my head began moving on an unwilling trek…

Someone dressed me.

Someone took all my clothes off and put new ones back on.

While I was unconscious.

While I couldn't stop them from seeing all of me. *Touching* all of me.

Horror shook the blood in my veins, a breath of realization rattling out. "No…"

My stare jumped all over the revealing lingerie, trying to ignore the writing of my whereabouts woven into its lace and satin designs, spelling out in blood-red letters exactly where fate had landed me.

Hell.

Where my body had a price tag and my life was stamped with an expiration date.

"No…" My breath came out shaky, desperate with denial. *"No."*

I ignored the pain breaking in my stiff neck as I snapped my head up to the ceiling, squinting at the mustard lighting spilling out of the singular light fixture. There was the silhouette of at least six swollen bug carcasses staring down at me and mold the color of soot leaching from the base of the light.

Death was in these walls, permeating the air, sticking to my sweat-damp skin, ebbing its ghostly screams up the pipe of my throat.

"No, no, no, no, no."

I bared my teeth against a grunt as I yanked at my bindings, elongating and trying to twist my fingers so they could slip between the zip ties. A slow-building cry stretched my mouth apart, the pitch crescendoing louder and hotter as defeat clawed at my wrists that wouldn't fucking *move*.

Helpless energy skated over my skin, enlivening every inch of it with tiny bursts of fire from beneath. My chest. The *pain*. My god, there was a goddamn creature inside my chest, moving around in a rampage, hitting bones, smashing against ribs, searing my throbbing heart until the beast finally erupted out in a slashing scream.

The explosion peeled up my throat and splattered the walls of the compact room, its echoes blanketing a wallpaper of devastation over its mold-infested interior.

No. Please, God, no.

How? *How* did this happen?

Blake and I planned *so* meticulously. Something must have gone wrong. I didn't even know if he was okay as I kept screaming and screaming, not knowing if I was crying for help or just crying.

Somehow, even after all the late night planning, the fighting to stay alive and untouched, and the stupid fucking hoping, I'd landed exactly where Heather wanted me. I was *trapped*, and I didn't need anything other than the devil red piece of lingerie to tell me I was at the auction.

To be sold. To be raped. To be hopefully killed soon thereafter.

I thrashed in the chair, desperation numbing the pain embedding in my wrists as my flesh merged with the plastic ties. This couldn't be happening. This *wasn't* happening.

I was no angel, but I didn't deserve this kind of hell.

Horrific images played behind my watering eyes as I continued to yell and yank at my restraints. Images of men perusing my body all tied up on display for them, their eyes beady and the front of their pants tight. They would loom over me as I yelled and pleaded for them to stop and go away. I screamed just the same now even though there was no one in the room with me.

But there would be eventually.

And that's why I was screaming like I was dying.

Because, in the finale of my fucked up fairytale, I was. Death was coming to get me so I could die the same way I lived the majority of my twenty-one years.

Bound in terror I'd never admit to, wishing for a rescue that would never come.

In the middle of wailing at the tragedy of my story's ending, a sound screeched off the walls from somewhere behind me.

Then, *her* voice scraped down my ears.

ONE

"Ms. Sanders, your loud mouth has always been a thing of irritation, but this is extensive. Even for you."

My voice got plucked dry at the appearance of her. Her presence was a black hole, manifesting out of nowhere and sucking down my screams until I hadn't a clue where they'd gone.

All that existed in the room was her. *Us.*

Us, and the stench of hate. Vile, palpitating the air in pulses like a volatile heartbeat, tangling in the empty space in my throat until I wanted to throw it all up. It tickled the back of my tonsils, encouraging a reaction, igniting a fire-hot spark that shocked my voice back to life.

"Are you *actually* shitting me right now?" I craned my neck back to where she was, my temper steaming away any tears that might have been. "What the *fuck* are you doing here?"

"You didn't think I'd miss your big send off, did you, Ms. Sanders?" Soft clicks of heels pounded inside my head with each step she closed in until her arrogant fucking mug was standing in front of me, poised with disdain that only she could wear so well. "Seeing you bound and stripped down has been a personal achievement I've been dreaming of for some time now."

Slowly, she inhaled through her nose of manufactured perfection, dropping a thoughtful look down my body. A goddamn twitch triggered at the corner of her mouth.

"It's every bit as satisfying as I imagined it would be."

"Funny," I cocked my head and ruthlessly let my venom spew. "Your husband said the same thing the first time he fucked my brains out."

That smug smirk of hers vanished like the mirage of victory it was.

At this point, I'd be in denial to think she didn't know the full extent of how sick I was for her husband and how sick he was for me. She knew every sordid, infectious detail of our affair. Of our *love.* It's why I was here. It's why she sent Mr. Smith for me.

It's why I was about to die.

Rubbing her snotty face in it was all the ammo I had left at this point.

The peak of her upper lip twitched. "It will always baffle me how you convinced someone like him to lay a finger on someone like you."

"On. Inside. It's really semantics at this point."

My windpipe narrowed in reflex to the squint of her viper eyes. "Is there any situation where you won't milk the opportunity to make a heinous joke?"

"Why? Does it bother you that I'm funnier than you?"

"A woman's job is not to be *funny*, Ms. Sanders."

"Oh." I bristled back in the chair, batting my eyes extra wide. "Oh okay. So, is it to be a two-faced liar? Because I think I missed that memo at last month's women's meeting."

An unseemly wrinkle marred the space between her thin brows with an expression of bewilderment. "You're exhausting, do you know that?"

"You know," I nodded in faux thought, handing my temper the knife and going in for her exposed jugular. "I do think Dominic mentioned something about that the day they served you your divorce papers. I think he said it during the second or third time we had filthy, *fantastic* sex that night. Or *maybe* it was when I jumped him in your house a couple days later when you were sleeping just down the hall."

Blue flames erupted around her pupils, the heat expanding her nostrils and curling her lip.

"You didn't," she denied like a death threat.

"Does that hurt? Does that *upset* you?" Fury rippled across her porcelain features, telling me I'd hit a raw nerve, so I kept digging at it.

I wanted her pain and her black heart shredded through my fingers, dripping like blood I could smear my name into her skin with so she never *ever* forgot me. "Does that hurt you to know that he was inside of me while you were only thirty feet away? Kissing me, holding me, telling me how much he *loves* me?"

In a flash, the clamp of her fingers were around my jaw, snapping my head back beneath hers as she sneered, "I am so happy I came to watch you *burn*. It'll be a prized memory I cherish for the rest of my life. A life I will spend with *my* husband."

"You don't know him at all if you think he'll ever go back to you." The inside of my cheeks were caught in the slice of my teeth as she crushed

ONE

my face harder, but it didn't alter my volume of resilience projecting up at her. "He's *done* with you. He finally realizes he deserves better and has for a long fucking time."

Scrutiny chiseled her elegant features. "Oh, and you think you deserve him?"

"Fuck no," I exclaimed, scrunching back. "I *know* I don't deserve him."

Her pink painted lips pursed, the lines drawn in her face draining away. "For once, I think you and I agree on something."

She threw my head to the side, discarding me like the trash we both knew I was. My neck whined with a painful crack, and I trapped a wince behind my teeth. A grumble settled in the base of my throat instead as I stretched my jaw out, keeping a watchful eye on the serpent in front of me.

"You're so fucking cliché, you know that, right?" I drawled. "Coming after the woman your husband chose over you is so 2008."

A scoff rode out on a tone of derision, the faint lines bookending her frowning mouth growing more prominent. "You are aware of where you are and *why*, correct? Mouthing off might not be the wisest choice."

"You have me strapped to a chair, kidnapped me from my home, and have hurt *everyone* I love. I can say whatever the *fuck* I want to you."

"And that's where you're wrong." A waft of gardenias perfumed the space right beneath my nose as she planted both hands on either side of the chair. The insanity in her eyes leveled right on me. "*You* did all of that. You put yourself where you didn't belong, so I removed you."

"Careful," I murmured on a breath with her so close. "Your crazy's showing."

She adjusted her angle, blue flames glinting. "You call it crazy. I call it justified repercussions for putting your grabby little hands on something that wasn't yours."

"He's not yours either. You don't *own* him. He can make choices for himself—"

"Wrong," she cut me off, a glimmer of insanity darting across her sapphire stare. "Men need guidance. They need us to tell them what to do or else they stumble dick first into the first slut they meet. Case in point."

The more she spoke, the further her voice detached from sense or logic. Or from fucking reality for that matter. From the quality of her icy tone to the firm grip of certainty in her eyes, this woman completely believed every single batshit syllable she was spewing.

My focus on her narrowed to a squint the harder I stared at the untethered line of reality dangling loose in her blistering eyes.

"You know," I started, cocking my head. "I think I'd actually feel sorry for you if I didn't want to rip your throat out so much. You are *significantly* off your rocker. Like, I'm fucked in the head but you are—"

"We are not comparable, Ms. Sanders." Heather cut me off using a knife dripping in disinterest. *Disgust.* She towed back, adjusting the wedding ring that did *not* belong on her breakable finger. "Not in status, not in standards, not in any way even *remotely* vital do you and I have anything in common."

My head was bobbing in agreement before I registered it, my temper deciding hard and fast that I had another death blow to play since she refused to stop being such a relentless *bitch*.

"You're right. That's probably why Dominic chose me instead."

Sharp eyes flashed up to me, her attention fully at my command. A cruel speck batted to life as she blinked slowly. "An error that will be corrected as soon as you're dead and buried and my shoulder is there for him to lean on as much as he needs until he's over you."

The thought of her hands on a grieving Dominic stopped my breath from coming. The visual of it my brain provided relooped my oxygen through my lungs on a current of fire.

Of *lightning*.

"You are so fucking *demented.*" I bucked my chin up and jerked all my confined limbs in a hopeless attempt. "All you've done since you married him is lie and *hurt* him."

The sleek watch on her wrist garnered her attention, boredom lacing her unfocused tone. "I don't expect you to understand how marriage works."

"Pretty fucking sure it doesn't involve offing the woman he chose over you because you're a psycho *bitch.*"

ONE

Heather wore the perfect oxymoron of an innocent white blouse today, and it rose with her chest as she inhaled and swiveled her snake eyes back to me.

"And that's where you'd be wrong."

She held my eye despite there being nothing of substance in her own to give it gravity. They were empty. Empty and shameless, and my passionately beating heart tripped over the sight.

This *thing* was going back to my home to fit herself inside a picture her own fingers had torn me out of. She was going to slide right in next to Dominic and pretend to care as he grieved the loss of me. She would be by his side as he beat himself up and his broken heart wept for me, never knowing she was the axe that sliced it in two.

His perfect heart would *never* roar with thunder quite the same again, because that's just the kind of love that man's heart created. It was honorable and unapologetic and absolute. He'd dedicated himself to me; his thunder was fate's design of union for my electric soul.

It was a known fact that thunder wasn't as powerful a force without lightning to share the sky with.

It was a lonely noise, crackling and rumbling, waiting in hope for a reply that would never come.

A knot formed in my stomach as I held the devil's gaze. "You're going to ruin him," I breathed.

And not like I did. The ruination I laid on his life was one he claimed to want, assured me he'd never been so happy to be destroyed. What Heather was about to do to him, what she *had* done to him already, was like putting a crack in a glass pane window.

He'd still be breathtaking, but every pair of eyes that fell over him wouldn't have to look twice to see the break in his core or why his outlook was so skewed.

"Do you realize you're not just hurting me in all of this? You're not just killing *me*. You're killing him too. The man you're doing all of this for, you'd be *obliterating* him."

Condescension refocused her eyes and put a nasty curve on her mouth.

"He'll get over it easier than you think."

"You don't actually believe that, or else *why* would we be here?" I chewed up and spit back.

"We are *here*," she enunciated, her face tilting so her razored eyes cut sadistically beneath her sharp browline, "because you're a whore who seduced and fucked *my* husband."

I matched her stare, targeting her dead on.

"A whore your husband loves more than he ever loved you."

The blow landed *hard* on her pretty face, exploding glacier eyes wide and revealing an open wound festering behind them both like sores splashed with acid. *Good.*

When she reared her arm back, I wasn't really surprised.

My head snapped to the side, the burn of her fingerprints stinging along the rise of my cheek. The muscles in my face singed by her blow hooked up on a smirk, my head riding back on an easy swivel to face her.

"Is that how you slapped Dominic that one day? No wonder he was totally fine for our makeout session in the shed right after."

Murder surged like the flames of hell in her eyes, a demon coming from below her pristine surface and possessing her red-tinged palm in a tight fist.

To the tune of a subhuman screech, Heather's knuckles sailed towards the same cheek faster than I saw coming. I didn't *see* anything actually aside from a blur of white fury. Then, a bomb exploded across my face, and anything I saw from that point on was an illusion of pain.

Agony splintered up my skull like shrapnel lodging in my brain, a triggered gasp knocking out of my parted lips. White hot pulses radiated inside my head as I pressed my eyes shut, pretty fucking convinced they were shaking in my skull.

Holy fuck.

A heartbeat had found life in both my temples, my whole head throbbing as I peeled it up from its low hanging recooperation. The taste of metal poured from the left side of my mouth, my tongue exploring the gash left along the inside of my cheek. A sting pricked, pain leaking more blood

ONE

over my probing tongue.

Wadding it up, I painted the ground with an unladylike splatter of rust-colored spit.

Righting myself back up, I blinked out the slow-moving spots of black framing my vision until the near picture-perfect sight of Heather's grinning satisfaction came into focus.

The picture only reached *true* perfection when I cracked a shit-eating grin and watched hers fall.

"That was better," I taunted.

Heather tightened the dainty fist she'd struck me with before shaking it out, and I hoped like hell the imprint of my face bruised her for days to come. My stare clocked the pulse in her neck and how it ticked on and on, climbing faster and harder beneath her skin.

Maybe she was nervous.

Or maybe I'd just *really* pissed her off.

That skyrocketing pulse neared closer to me, sinking below my eye level as devil blue squinted at me. "How is it that you're all tied up and about to *die*, and you're still this goddamn unbearable?"

Blood was already setting up shop beneath my cheekbone as I went to answer her.

"It was fucking *rhetorical*," she sliced me clean off, rage vibrating her eyes. "My *god*, you are a special brand of insufferable. You and your entire family. Or what's left of it. You, and that snot-nosed sister of yours."

Without pause or thought, I spit the blood pooling in my cheek over her face.

A splotch of spit-slick crimson clung to the point of her nose and over her right eye, her mouth falling agape with a gasp.

"Don't ever talk about my sister again."

If I died today, I wasn't going down as the victim Heather tried to make me into.

I was going down with Kat motherfucking Sanders flair.

Everything Heather had thrown at me since putting me here was to break me.

When ripping me from my home and infectious brush with love wasn't enough, she sent Mr. Smith to finish the job. This woman threw every stone she had at my walls, striking me over and over, and yet here I fucking was.

Unbroken.

Sure, I would die. But she'd never forget me.

Every time Heather closed her eyes after I was gone, she'd see me staring back.

She'd never be able to forget my face in the end or the prevailing smile that graced it. Dominic and his enduring love for me would keep my ghost alive to haunt her until she went slowly mad from it. Even *killing* me, she'd never be able to escape me.

My memory would drive her into oblivion where I would be waiting.

Heather retreated with revulsion plunging her neatly plucked eyebrows together, a shriek nipping her lips apart. She wiped her hand across where my spit dripped down her face, scatters of blood and saliva flying off as she shook her hand out.

"That is *it*." Her pin-straight hair slapped the side of her face as she jerked around to scream behind me.

"Tommy, get in here!"

TWO

KAT

My heart froze.

Ice spliced into my bloodstream as the jerk of a rusted door sounded off behind me.

I'd never actually seen Tommy before.

I never thought I'd *have* to see him since Heather turned out to be behind all of this bullshit. I didn't want to see him. Not even half of him. But the pin-prick goosebumps rising on my bare skin told me I wasn't about to get a choice.

Even though Tommy wasn't the mastermind that would cause my heart to stop beating, the sound of his incoming footsteps caused the rhythm of it to go offbeat anyway.

The smell of soured tobacco and aftershave introduced his presence beside me first. The brush of body heat against my shoulder did it next. My nose scrunched at both sensations, a wrinkle of disgust that stayed in place as a body crouched down in front of me, giving a face to the man of my nightmares.

The first thing to catch my eye were teeth.

Dull, yellowed teeth that sat all straight in a row, showcasing themselves in an awe-struck grin just for me.

A slow chuckle seeped out of him first, and it rattled each bridge of my spine the same way it did when it raped my ears during our phone calls.

"Well, ain't it about time, Catnip."

Watching his thin lips form around the voice that'd haunted me from the other end of a phone upended my mask of composure and shook my breath on a heavy rale. *Watching* that voice move behind real teeth and ride out on real breath was goddamn terrifying.

Because it was real.

He was real.

And his very real hand was reaching out to touch my knee.

"Don't fucking *touch* me." Metal scraped the tangible tension in the room as I jerked away from him, the legs of my chair skidding the concrete. Tommy retracted his reach, holding his probing hand up in surrender with that delighted as fuck grin still stuck on his mouth.

He blew out a whistle, giving a slow shake of his dirty head of hair.

"*Whew*, that mouth is always on fire, ain't it? I'm gettin' goosebumps just hearing it in person."

For all I fucking cared, he could rip my mouth off and take it home as a souvenir. So long as he never tried to touch me again.

"You know," Tommy shifted his stance, folding his fingers together as he aimed the off-kilter twinkle in his eyes up at me. "I've gotta tell you, playin' with you these last couple months has been some of the most fun I've had in a while. Riling you and that sweet fire mouth up. Watching Detective Reed lose his head over you being gone." His bottom lip got nabbed up between his terrible teeth, the satisfaction brightening his bleak eyes. "It's been a *real* delicious treat."

"*Fuck you*," I spat. "Keep his name out from between your shit-stained teeth."

Tommy just laughed as I silently spiraled from the images he provided of Dominic lost in his grief and agony of my disappearance. His radiant eyes pictured as raindrops of sadness. His handsomeness sunken in by too much turmoil over me.

"Your mother never quite had that *fire* in her that you have," Tommy said

TWO

suddenly, and my whole world stopped.

Much like it did that first time I found her overdosed on too much heroin. Or the time I found her dead from it.

"She was sad, ya know?" My air stuck in the back of my throat as the man who helped take my mother away from me over the years reminisced about her like they were pals. Like he was *allowed* to talk about her to me. "Always going on about her ex, and money… and *you*."

My face was frozen.

The blood, the muscles, the nerves in it all gone numb. I couldn't breathe. Couldn't blink. Couldn't tell him to shut the fuck up. All I wanted was to rip my hands free and hold them over my ears and scream so I didn't have to hear him talk about her.

But I was frozen in the magnitude of how much this dead-eyed stranger knew about my life.

"You two do look alike though, I'll give her that," he went on because I didn't stop him. *Couldn't.* "She was worse for wear by the end, but I could always tell she used to be a looker."

Tommy took a pause, using it to bounce his stare between my eyes, a sick appreciation speckling the black of his pointed pupils. "She ain't got nothing on those eyes of yours though. I bet they knocked Detective Reed on his ass the first time he saw 'em."

"Tommy." Heather's voice was a razored reminder of her presence from the side of the room. "Speed it up."

"Oh, come on." Realistic disfavor edged along his enamored expression as he gazed up at me. "This is the only time I'll get to spend with her. I wanna make it last."

Tension was cementing the muscles in my neck, stiffening to a headache that radiated up the back of my skull the longer Tommy stared at me. My neck was so stiff in fact, it didn't even know how to move when he brought his hands up and placed them on my cheeks.

Rough fingers caressed my face in greedy sweeps, hardened calluses on his palms scraping against my soft skin that I couldn't move away from.

I simply sat and burned.

From the spaces between my toes to the hair follicles on my head, a fire had taken root.

It'd sprouted so suddenly from the touch I couldn't escape from, birthed from the match of his hands as they dragged their flame across my face that wanted to crack in freedom and scream bloody fucking murder.

I didn't know how it was possible to be frozen in fire, but here I was.

A flame encapsulated in ice that wouldn't melt.

Tommy took liberties with my paralyzed state, caressing a thumb down the edge of my jawline in a slow, almost sweetened motion that made my hollow stomach churn.

"It's a real shame, ya know." Disappointment cradled his graveled voice as he shook his head. "That pretty face going to the grave so soon."

"All the sooner when you stop *flirting* with her," Heather snapped.

All Tommy did in response to her was tweak a small smile. "What can I say? There's just something about this one."

His hand that had been feeling along my jaw took a languid trip down my frozen skin, passing the racing pulse in my neck and giving it a good pat with his thumb. Then his violating fingers swooped down low, scooping the hanging emerald from where it rested against my collarbone.

My heart belted a cry in rejection, hating his hands on something of Dominic's. A glint as bright as the gem itself flashed in his eyes as I felt him turn the necklace in his hand. That gleaming gaze rose to me, sick delight emboldening his stare.

"Might this be a gift from dear ol' Detective Reed?"

The taunt of his voice unlocked—unfroze—my imprisoned lungs so I could begin to breathe again. Except I wasn't breathing oxygen.

I was inhaling *fire*.

It found its way to my lungs, incinerating through muscles and bones to swell its heat up my body. *Knowing* Tommy was putting his smarmy hands on something Dominic so thoughtfully picked out for me with all the love in his perfect heart flamed the fire hotter than ever.

He smacked his lips, digging himself deeper with his shovel of foul arrogance. "I really hope I get to be there when he finds out these pretty

TWO

green eyes won't ever open up again. I'm giddy just thinking about it."

He preened for just a moment, smile lines deepening in his punchable face before Heather snipped him off again.

"Tommy, stop playing and shut her *up*."

"All right, all right."

Reluctance held his voice in surrender as he backed his hands away, taking his focus off of me and landing it on his front pants pocket instead. He fingered around in there for only a moment, the shadows of the room not letting me see exactly what he was doing.

A well-worn sigh left his chest as he pulled something out.

"This was your mom's favorite stuff."

The point of a needle presented itself in the muddy lighting, piercing my heart on sight.

Every breath of fire stopped short, and my eyes went dry and wide. An avalanche of horror swamped my veins and smothered the fire until it was a puff of smoke left for me to choke on. And I did. I coughed and choked and suffocated on the sight of the needle, a wash of poison sitting inside its plastic tube.

No.

"Don't worry." I must have been wearing terror as plainly on the outside as I felt it on the inside for Tommy to offer such a sentiment. He flicked the needle full of death so little spurts of liquid sprayed out. "I'm not giving you the same dose I gave your mom. Just enough to stomp out that fight in you."

I was feeling so many emotions, *thinking* so many zipping thoughts that Tommy's words didn't immediately register.

Once they settled however…

They laid everything else to dust.

Pictures of my mom I'd never be rid of flashed behind my watering eyes that were stuck on Tommy's. Pictures of her slouched over on our couch, spit up crusted down her chin, and her eyes as wide and blank as an empty sky.

A needle sticking out of the bend of her arm.

A needle I blamed her for.

A needle I thought she put there herself.

"You…" The word was a winded accusation, and nothing more followed.

Tommy nodded in my absence of voice, taking the moment to knot a strip of cloth around my upper arm. "She really was trying to get clean. I hadn't heard from her in a few weeks."

Pressurized numbness stretched beneath the tips of my up-turned fingers, blood pressing hard beneath the skin as Tommy cinched the tie extra tight around my arm. I registered the sensation. Not the pain.

Not a single drop of physical pain would ever match the one that speared my heart as Tommy locked eyes with me, cocking his head in condemnation.

"Guess you really messed that up for her, didn't you?"

The back of my throat dried out as my mind pulled blank.

My head was full of smoke that roadblocked any sense from making its way to my brain. All I could do was stare, and I think maybe I was shaking my head. Couldn't be sure.

"I don't…"

And that's all I got out, still not convinced of anything. Not the truth in his claim, not the air drying out my lips, not the life in my lungs. Maybe this was death.

Maybe I had died already and gone straight to hell where I always knew I belonged, and that's why there was so goddamn much *pain* manifesting inside of me right now. It was as if my insides were paper and every inhale I took was a gulp of fire, proving my strength to be so fucking brittle as I went up in flames from the inside out.

"Why?" I pushed from between my teeth, breathing harder as the agony came faster. "It doesn't make sense. *Why?*"

"Because of you."

The reply didn't come from the closed mouth in front of my face, but from the devil herself standing off to the side. My muscles shattered their stiff stance as I snapped my head toward her, watching the words form and drip like venom from her fangs.

TWO

"I never did get to thank you for the heads up you gave me about that meeting Dominic set up. It was a *great* tip to stay ahead of the game."

My rounded stare trapped on her, I scrambled in my head back to the conversation she was talking about.

Horror took a considering second to blossom... before my recollection slammed forward, and dread poured a heavy waterfall through my ice cold chest.

"You told him," I whispered.

Because I told her, she told Tommy.

Before the tides of self-loathing and guilt could take me away, a tidal wave of fucking *wrath* swept in first, crashing hard in my stomach as I finally found my goddamn voice.

"Fuck you!" Tommy jumped back as I thrashed, kicking and screaming and pretending I couldn't feel the hot drip of furious tears splashing my cheeks. "*Fuck you*, Heather! I'll kill you. I'll *fucking* kill you!"

Oh my god. Oh my fucking god.

The room was spinning and so was my head. Everything around me was a twister of blurry grief and a *blinding* need for blood-shed and violence.

Heather didn't even reply to my explosion of sanity or take a moment to mock my tears. In fact, the only thing that stayed in focus in the entire room was the stain of victory on her mouth.

In the whirlwind of fury, there came a tight grip on my forearm.

My reeling world screeched to a stop at the touch of fingertips against the part of my arm where all my veins were protruding the proudest. A needle was coming for them, and all my screams burnt up to ash in my throat.

"If it makes you feel at all better," Tommy lamented, "your mom cried for you the whole time. Kept begging me to stop because of you and your sister. Said she didn't wanna die."

He caught my gaze in a vice, his expression playing sympathetic when we both knew he wasn't capable.

"I think she'd want you to know your name was the last thing she said before she went."

A gong of grief smacked my chest, shaking out a dry sob for the woman I hated for dying.

It wasn't her fault. She *hadn't* left me and Charlotte by the needle of broken promises. The promises she'd made were still intact and buried with her body back home. Tears leaked over as I pictured her and wished I could dig her out just so I could say I was sorry.

I was so fucking sorry and so fucking happy to be wrong about her.

She *didn't* leave me on purpose.

She didn't want to leave me at all.

My sorrow was unstoppable as it ran down my cheeks, soft cries beginning to dribble over my trembling lips as Tommy readied the needle.

"No, no, no, *no*."

I jerked my shoulders as he neared the silver tip to my vein, a feral plea exploding out. "No! No, don't. Please. *Fuck*, please!"

"Better chance of not missing the vein if you stop squirming," Tommy grit through his teeth, clamping his grip down hard, squeezing the bones in my forearm to hold me still. My lungs sucked back a gasp as I watched the tip of the needle touch my skin, scrambling in my head to find a way out of this.

"Stop, stop, stop," I begged, too scared to move and too scared to stay still.

Beneath, my vein seemed to glow in response to the needle's prick, illuminating the path for it in a total betrayal. My veins were made up of my mother's and hers craved the poison inside the needle.

What if mine did as well? What if I was no better than her?

More than a hundred 'what ifs' stormed my brain as the choice of death I'd blamed my mother for punctured my skin and slid nicely into my vein *without* choice, releasing into my bloodstream.

My blood ran iceberg cold, stealing a winter's chill of dread through my entire body.

And then…

It hit.

And it hit *hard*.

TWO

A gasp exploded into the air, shuddering through my parted lips as my head dropped back. Warmth bathed the insides of my skin, riding sunshine along the shallow of my pores. It beamed all the way through my body until it had sprouted up my throat and was shining out of my mouth, pouring golden light around the room.

Tears sprung in awe, watering the blooms of sweet little life unearthing along my flesh to warm themselves in the sunshine. A garden of roses were popping up all over my skin, the soft beauties weighing my limbs down with each sprout.

I didn't care though.

I didn't care about anything, because I didn't *feel* anything.

Not the fear. Not the swallows of grief. Not the pain I'd been born with or the pain I'd adopted along the way. Nothing hurt. Nothing *ached* like a swollen pulsing extremity you couldn't see or touch or lob off.

My fingers were like sparklers and my toes were like jelly. A smile was riding my happy lips without even realizing it'd joined in on the fun. It had slipped up like a reverse thief, dropping off a gift of joy instead of stealing one.

A moan of ecstasy rolled out of me as my neck dropped the weight of my head, giving up on holding it upright.

It was too heavy to fly with, and right now, I was fucking soaring. Above land and sea and neon pastures. Too high up for any of the nasty passengers that lived down below to reach up with their spindly fingers and yank me back down.

None of them could touch me. None of them were *inside* of me anymore, scratching or clawing or electrifying my heart raw. I was free of their pain. I was *safe* with the sunshine and wearing my coat of red roses.

All it took was one hit.

One singular hit…

And I knew why my mom did it.

It was as if someone had ripped the hurt out and replaced it with light. A tiny ball of radiance to keep me forever warm.

Already, I was craving it again before it was even gone.

A soft breeze caressed down the crimson blooms dressing my arms and legs and set them free. By my sides, the wind helped lift me up to even newer heights, rising like my beaming sun until I was standing on my own two feet.

I showed my gift of a smile to the wind at my side, sleepy eyelids falling heavy against my cheeks. The breeze gripped me a little harder, assisting as I put one foot in front of the other as I walked across that proverbial cloud nine.

Somewhere in my head, I wondered if we were really walking on air and somewhere up in the sky. Maybe that would explain the sudden lack of wetness to my tongue the further we walked. I lapped and tried to find moisture in the air that simply didn't exist.

The breeze next to me gave a rasping whisper.

"Let's bring her to the display room."

The words danced around my dissipating mind, slipping their grounding and vanished up into darkness.

A darkness that wasn't there before.

It crept in around the edges of my bright summer sky, chomping up all the light for itself as a greedy little snack. Moaning a cry, my head craned around on a lazy swivel, trying to hold on to the sunshine even if only by my eyes.

But the sun wasn't there anymore.

And neither was its warmth.

Heartbreak cracked my chest in two at the loss, tears bleeding down the split in my body where my heart yearned for the sun. Without it, all that was left was darkness.

And pain.

Blood-curdling, excruciating, blackout... *pain*.

THREE

DOM

The wind was stagnant today at the Walford Plaza Mall.

It was the only thing around that was.

All over the sun-misted back woods were agents, corporal officers, and even S.W.A.T moving about like an army of black ants raiding a dirt mound for takeover. The auction was rumored to begin around 6am. Archie let on that higher ups wanted the event to be in full swing when we charged in guns blazing.

They wanted to catch every single one of these vermin in the act so no technicality on Earth could get them off.

I understood. I did.

But we'd been here for over thirty minutes already, and my fists were thirsty for blood.

"Dude…" Next to me, Ryan fidgeted with the bulletproof vest he and I had both been given as 'consultants' for the raid. "What the hell did we get ourselves into?"

There was a barely tolerable degree of hesitance to his voice as he surveyed the scene around us. This mission was a profound step up from patrol or the cozy-roomed interviews we were used to back home, and the fact that it wasn't exactly by the book or even *on* the books wasn't ideal.

It was the only way I knew how to get my little lightning back, though.

From across the field, Archie Miller trudged over looking agitated and serious. Alert straightened up my spine as he got close enough to earshot.

"Barely even 7am, and I've got the Mayor's office up my ass demanding arrest counts before we've even gone in." He hooked his thumbs through his belt loop right beneath the pocket of his overhanging stomach and sighed. "You boys ready to do some federal rule breaking?"

Ryan grimaced while I kept my face straight.

"Remember, everyone on the team going in thinks you're consultants on Ms. Sanders' case and that you'll be on the sidelines out here the whole time. They cannot *see* you when you go in or we're all screwed. Stay outta their way and their sightline, find your girl, and get out fast."

I gave a stiff nod. "That's the plan."

"And I don't think I have to tell you not to discharge the weapons you've brought with you unless it is *absolutely* necessary, correct?"

Both Ryan and I confirmed aloud, but Archie still pointed his glare my way and reiterated with extra precision. "That is to say that *if* your girl is in there and *if* you find her, no matter the predicament you find her in or who with, you cannot put a bullet between their eyes unless they attempt to put one through yours first, got it?"

Irritation prickled the back of my neck as I chewed up and spit out my affirmation.

"Yes, I've got it."

I didn't want or need a lesson in when or when not to fire my weapon once we got inside. My Glock 22 and an extra round of bullets weighed down my utility belt, but they wouldn't see any action unless of an emergency.

All I wanted was to get going, get moving, and get Kat back.

The walkie on Archie's side gave a crackle, a low-pitched voice coming through in patches that asked if everyone was in position. He grabbed for it, pulling it up to his mouth.

"Affirmative. Everyone ready on my mark."

THREE

He resecured the walkie to his belt, locking eyes with Ryan and I once more. Significance settled around us three like a presence, sitting its heavy weight on my tight shoulders.

"I wanna see you both on the other side of this in one piece, ya hear?"

We both gave a solemn nod before Archie turned his grave focus to just me. "I know how much this means to you and how personal it's been, but I need you just as focused on getting out of there safely as you are on finding your girl. Do you hear me?"

Setting my jaw to the side, I jerked out a nod.

Apparently that wasn't good enough for my old boss.

"Reed, I'm serious. I can see the goddamn blinders your heart has put over your eyes, and I refuse to be the one to go tell that little girl of yours why her daddy's not coming home."

Defense dropped my mouth to fire back, but he cut me a look. "Just think about both of your girls while you're in there. That's all I ask."

Holding his stare, I filled my lungs with his words and let them ruminate. There was an itch in the back of my throat to argue about these 'blinders' I apparently had on that gave me tunnel vision to anything that wasn't finding Kat.

I swallowed past that itch, dampening it down because he was right.

My thoughts about finding and seeing Kat again had become relentless and overpowering. The closer we got to today's mission, the worse they got. I heard her voice in the wind, saw her reflection in windows, and found the shape of her face in the clouds.

My constant thoughts of her were projecting outwards, and even though Maya was the most important thing to me in the world, Archie's reminder was a good one.

Without much more said, my old boss left to get in position and told Ryan and I to hang back for ninety seconds after the rest of the troops flooded in. All of us who were either going in or on standby were stationed behind the swoop of a grainy grass hill at the back of the abandoned mall that gave us enough cover from anyone who might be on lookout.

The rest of the cavalry were in vans and SUVs down the street, waiting for the call to swoop in.

Just before that call came, the rustle of the wind shaking the branches of the white pines circling us came to a hush. For just a few short seconds, everything went silent.

All except the strong beat of my heart between my ears.

Then, the crack of Archie's voice fired off over the walkies of S.W.A.T around us, and it began.

Ryan and I hung back as we were told as line after line of bodies cloaked in black armor pushed forward towards the ominous building. The precision with which they moved was admirable, and not before too long, Ryan and I were following behind in their choreographed footsteps.

The forsaken Walford Plaza Mall was built of two stories and housed an expansive underground parking garage. Blueprints we'd pulled earlier showed over a hundred rooms, and that didn't account for the bathrooms, back offices, or storage closets.

It wasn't a tall structure, but it was wide, and the pockets where the people who took Kat could be hiding her inside were endless.

The crunch of footsteps behind me signaled Ryan trailing close by as we swept down the hill under the cover of dense brush until we spilled out into the open. The building of the mall stood before us, agents on a mission concealed behind its walls. From the information Archie gave us, they were starting their search at the top and working their way down.

Down is where Ryan and I would start.

"There's a loading dock on the side that leads down to the parking garage." Ryan was waiting with concentrated eyes as I turned my head over my shoulder to him. "Ready?"

"Ready isn't exactly the word I'd use, but—" He jerked his head in a quick tilt, a pop relieving tension in his neck as he sent a furtive glance towards our target. "Yeah, let's go."

Moving my stare back out to the mall, I couldn't find myself agreeing with Ryan.

I'd never been ready for anything more in my life.

On silent feet, we made our way to the side of the building. The handle of my Glock grew slick with sweat between my palms despite the early morning chill rolling across the Earth.

Cornering the edge of the mall, I pressed my back to the weather-worn concrete and felt a brush on my right arm that said Ryan did the same.

Behind the wall, there was silence.

Inside my head, I heard her sweet siren voice.

Whispering to destroy the silence she loathed and telling me she was within these quiet walls waiting for me, that she was here and to hurry the fuck up with that classic Kat fire I missed warming my bedside so goddamn much.

Ryan tapped my shoulder and aimed a finger at the loading dock I'd mentioned. It was right where I remembered it, its mustard yellow outside peeling down the sides, not to mention saddled with new coats of neon graffiti.

But it was cracked open.

Just a few feet, but it was more than enough to slip inside without making a sound.

Resecuring my grip around my gun, I pointed my chin to the opening as a signal to move. Ryan's eyes went from me to it, pausing for a significant second before shifting back and nodding.

I didn't love his pause before complying, but there wasn't time to think about it. My feet moved on command from my brain, hugging the side of the building until I swooped beneath the cracked open loading dock door, Ryan following my lead.

The damp stench of mold struck like a wave as soon as we ducked inside, my sense of smell recoiling while my eyes tried to widen to let in whatever light they could. The sun pouring in from beneath the opening in the door washed light where it could reach, but that was only about five or so feet into the downhill slope of the parking garage.

Ryan cursed under his breath at the smell of the place, and I shushed him like I would Maya on a Sunday in church. He held his hands up in dingy, silhouetted surrender and shut up like I needed him to.

Angling my wired focus front, I plucked the palmable flashlight I'd brought along from my utility belt and clicked it on. Ryan did the same. LED lighting paved a coned pathway along the ground, illuminating trails of abandoned filth.

Discarded clothes, stomped on sales tags, and headless mannequins were discarded everywhere, scatters of animal droppings surrounding it all.

Ryan and I plodded through it, careful to not step on anything that might make noise or leave a presence. We were heading downhill into the garage, the outside sunlight vanishing as we trekked further underground.

When the heel of my boots landed on the main floor, an expanse of quiet darkness met us from all sides. No natural drop of light. No fall of footsteps. No whispers for help from a green-eyed goddess.

The lack of activity coiled around the hope I held in my chest, threatening to yank its base right out from under it. Gravel crunched beneath Ryan's shoes as he shifted behind me.

"Maybe their intel on the auction was wrong? The date or location or something."

My jaw set against the sound of defeat he so readily accepted. "We've been here *ten* seconds. We keep moving."

Behind me, he inhaled another fucking pause before letting it out and agreeing with a brusque, "Okay."

Biting back a grumbling sigh in my throat, I tried to push the tone of Ryan's doubts to the back of my mind. He was wrong. I couldn't tell anyone exactly how I knew he was wrong. I just did.

She was here.

I could *feel* it in that sixth sense type of way I felt everything about that woman of mine. Her electricity was in the building, tapping against the back of my neck like a compass trying to lead me back home.

The cone of my flashlight led us further into the parking garage. We'd taken a right once we made it to the main floor, and we were pretty much walking blind and keeping our ears and eyes peeled for any signs of movement.

The ceiling of concrete above us had to have been thick given the lack of noise coming from the forty-something S.W.A.T and officers I knew were

THREE

up there raising hell. The silence was admittedly concerning, gnawing at that pillar of hope trying to stand strong in my chest.

I wasn't the only one feeling off about the persisting quiet either.

"Man, don't you think we would have heard something by now—"

Muffled gunfire from somewhere above cut Ryan and his doubts off at the legs, popping off several rounds. A smile twitched against my cheek.

I could honestly say I'd never been so happy to hear warfare in my whole life.

Locking eyes with him with the help of the flashlight, I cocked my head. "You were saying?"

For the first time since we'd arrived on scene, confidence grew in Ryan's stare. *Determination.* Kat was here just like I knew she was, and now he believed it too.

He and I split to cover more ground in the parking garage now that the enemy knew we were on site and we had to be fast. His flashlight went to the very edge of the garage while I kept checking behind concrete barricades for anyone that might be hiding or signs that my lightning had struck in the area.

I was about to do a final sweep when Ryan spoke louder than he should have.

"*Holy shit.* Over here!"

The staggered quality of his curse struck a cord down my spine, tightening it so hard, I didn't realize I wasn't moving until my heart roared at me to go. My whole body jerked in Ryan's direction, that tight cord in my back stiffening with ice when I saw him kneeling on the ground.

Next to a woman.

An unconscious, unmoving woman.

Waves of dark hair matted over a pale face was all I saw before my world glitched with the petrifying image, and I took off. My heart thundered as I ran, wrestling hard to overtake my logic as my boots slapped the concrete faster and faster.

Logic was pulling on my reins, trying to keep me aware of my surroundings and the potential danger lurking in every infested corner of this place.

My heart didn't care. To it, the only immediate danger was the woman lying in a corner across the garage and if there was a pulse in her veins.

As I got close, my heart won the battle and came pouring out of my mouth in a mangled cry with her name in it.

"*Kat.* Kat!"

My heart was on fire, burning holes through my chest cavity as I skidded to a stop in front of her and Ryan. His fingers were around her lithe wrist, checking for the drumming of life beneath her skin.

I waited only long enough for my patience to completely shatter before dropping to my knees and stealing her wrist into my own hands.

The chill her body held was startling at best. Horrifying at worst.

"Move her hair," I grunted, needing to see her face. "Move her hair!"

Ryan began to gather up the locks of deep brown that were stuck to her face by sweat or God knows what else as I waited to feel a pulse in her wrist. Mine was racing against my sternum, attempting to unsteady my breathing as I skated a glance down her body.

Aside from a pair of black underwear, she was naked.

The bare top of her was mostly hidden by her thin arms, but the littering of ugly bruises up and down her torso were on full display in the shine of my flashlight. Heat swamped my head as I watched the shadow of Ryan's hands sift her hair away, still holding her limp wrist between my fingers.

I need a pulse. I need a fucking pulse.

He removed the final strand that covered her face, and my heart finally succeeded in taking my breath away.

"It's not her."

Ryan twisted his head to look at me even though I couldn't tear my gaze away from the limp woman who wasn't Kat.

"It's not her, man."

No, it wasn't. This woman wasn't mine with her mouth that was too small or nose that was more rounded instead of narrow. She wasn't Kat, and the wave of relief that flooded my stomach was so goddamn powerful, it could have moved mountains.

"Still nothing?" Ryan asked about the woman's pulse, presumed mourning dampening his voice. Finally able to break my stare away from the poor woman's face, I looked to him and shook my head.

Then—

Pulse.

Shock snatched my focus back to her. I blinked, watching the hollow of her throat to see if it would happen again. The sensation was so faint, I easily could have imagined it.

Then, I felt it again.

Pulse.

"Ryan, she's alive." He cursed in astonishment as I prayed to feel the beat in her veins one more time. It came about seven seconds later. "Her pulse is weak, but it's there."

"Okay, okay." Knelt next to me, Ryan began breathing hard, a radiating anxiety overtaking him fast and hard. "What do we do?"

I shifted her limp body up, gathering her in my arms and standing. "Take her outside to the vans. She needs medical attention."

"No way." Loyalty fired hot across my partner's expression as he shook his head. "I'm not leaving you here by yourself."

"You don't have a choice." Without waiting, I shuffled the woman from my arms to his.

He took her because he didn't have much of a choice, but it didn't stop his defiance.

"Dude, I'm your partner. I'm not leaving."

"If you don't go, she dies, Ryan."

His stare challenged mine even though he knew it was true. I appreciated his stubborn display of honor. I really did, but neither the woman he was holding nor the one I'd come here to rescue had the time to wait.

Eventually, he cracked with a frustrated grumble, dropping his head back. He resituated the unconscious woman in his arms and nailed me with a threatening point of his unusually grave stare.

"I better see you on the outside, Reed."

"You will. I promise."

"Don't do anything stupid, okay?"

My lips remained sealed on purpose, unsure if I could make the same assurance.

He started off in the direction we'd come in from, breaking out into a jog until the darkness swallowed him and the woman. Alone now, I shined my flashlight all around to figure out exactly how our mystery girl got to this spot.

I traced the light along the back wall where we'd found her, searching up to the ceiling and back down.

Soon enough, the outline of a door appeared out of the dark.

I stepped into it, surveying for a sign to tell me where it led. On the wall next to it was a little placard with a drawing of stairs on it.

Stairs that went down.

Confusion tweaked my head at the sign, wondering if the drawing was upside down. I didn't think there was anything below the parking garage?

Lifting my hand, I set it on the door knob and gave it a twist.

It opened without resistance.

Curiosity officially upstaged my confusion as I shouldered the door open, ducking my gun in first and shining my light inside to clear it was safe. Checking on my left and right, the narrow space behind the door appeared vacant.

Carefully, I moved inside.

The shower of gunfire was immediately louder in here as I dropped a quick glance to my right and left.

On my left, a hallway stared back at me in the dark.

One that showed a bracket of stairs that led down lower than the blueprints of this mall claimed existed.

Stealing my breath and tightening the grip I had around my gun, I walked towards it, the electric current of my little lightning leading the way.

FOUR

KAT

I remembered back in fourth grade, our teacher, Mrs. Lemons, assigned us a five paragraph essay on what we wanted to be when we grew up and why.

I remembered my hand scribbling down the words with a zealous energy pumping through to my fingertips. I stood up in front of my class that day and stated with pride that I would be a singer on Broadway, belting to the high heavens and bathed in the limelight.

This was before I realized with begrudging acceptance that I maybe didn't have the pipes to cut it.

Mrs. Lemons laughed along with the class in a chorus of giggles as I show-cased for them that same day my *stellar* singing voice. When I finished, she told me my dreams were fantastical, and I remember agreeing with her because I didn't realize what she meant when she used the word 'fantastical'.

My dreams *were* fantastic.

In my fourth grade brain, I was destined to be a star. One of the greats. It was funny the way dreams could be turned on you.

The lights cascading from above were too bright for my sensitive eyes.

My heavy lips pulled back in a wince, tightening my eyelids as I hid my face in my shoulder. Shouts from the audience dismayed with my performance burrowed in my ear canal, gnawing deeper into my head until the inside of my skull felt carved with their grating criticism.

"Spin around!"

"Get on your knees and crawl, baby."

"Do a little dance for us, darlin'."

"Be a good little whore and bend over and show me what's *mine*."

So many orders. So many voices. They all spun around my head like a halo gone bad.

My fourth grade wish had come true. I was a shining star just like I'd wanted to be, plucked from the sky where I belonged and dropped in the spotlight on a stage to perform for my life.

I just never thought my childhood aspirations would become so literal.

A triumphant shout from the back of the crowd pierced the air, silencing the rest of my critics. From the wings of my stage, two strapping dance partners appeared and grabbed me, moving my body this way and that as my limbs followed along in a puppet-like orbit. My head flopped and my neck cracked, the cement filling my bloodstream making standing a goddamn olympic sport.

I tried to stay on my feet, I really did, but the whole of my weight fell into the arms of my dance partners sturdy on either side.

They caught me mid-fall, hoisting me up with sing-songy grunts and helped me perform my masterpiece solo across the floor. My obedient body swayed and glided where they led, falling into rhythm with the music in my veins, each note inspired by the poison put there first.

It was thumping a base in my eardrums as my partners stopped our waltz. The beat was so loud, it deafened the touch of hands my sleepy eyes watched appear out of nowhere and roll down my body.

I blinked and I blinked at the hands, cocking my head as I saw their plump fingers squeeze the sides of my bare waist. I didn't *feel* the wrinkled pair of hands though.

FOUR

They were like ghosts hovering over my body–a haunting presence, but their touch went right through me.

A protest of confusion piled up my throat as I raised my head to confront the phantom hands in front of me. That protest hit the back of my windpipe as I sucked back a scream, locking eyes with ones plucked from the devil himself. Nightmarish and bubbling, those demon eyes burned red hot, searing my cries for help up into ash to fall to the bottom of my lungs.

The devil peeled back his coal-black lips, the forked tongue of a serpent slithering out.

"Bring her to the back rooms."

My back bowed with a winded wail as I was pushed forward, breath escaping my body to flee somewhere safe. Muscles in my legs wobbled and liquified, the trek to wherever I was being taken an effort for all involved.

Eventually, the drug in my veins won out and consumed any strength left, swooping it up and whispering it was okay to take a rest. So I did. The vision of pipes in a ceiling moved over me as I let the weight of my head hang back, the forces on either side of me dragging me along.

Momentary splashes of light faded out as a door clanked open, and the pipe-lined ceiling above disappeared in place of darkness.

Pitch black darkness.

Then, lightning struck inside the darkness.

I gasped at its severe entrance, finding leftover strength in my arms to shield my hands over my burning eyes. I normally loved lightning. I normally *was* the lightning, but all that was left inside of me was rain.

My muscles were water, my bones melted into mud, a pressure beneath my itching skin telling me my electric soul was drowning.

Just then, hands—no, *claws*—encircled my wrists and yanked down.

An explosion of brightness scorched my eyes raw, my misfiring brain jumping between the choice of keeping them closed to save me from the pain or keep them open to watch what was standing right before me.

Or who.

The devil was in here with me, his crimson eyes dripping down the length of me. On either side were his demons that had been disguised as my dance partners earlier, standing sky-high with their pin-prick claws digging into my flesh as they held me up.

For the second time, I went to scream bloody fucking murder.

Only to drop my mouth like a fish and hear nothing come out.

Shock barrelled around my chest, blinking back at the absence of my voice. All the rain inside of me must have drowned it out too, smothering it down, down, down where it was tucked away safe from the man with a sinister grin slicing his gaunt face.

"You're a pretty thing, aren't you?"

Was I? I didn't feel pretty. I felt like sludge. Like over-wrought, helpless *sludge*.

The itch beneath my skin grew sharper nails as the man from Hell drew closer, the point of his teeth glinting in the too-bright light as he curved a wicked smile.

"I like my women real pretty and delicate. Like little butterflies I can capture and admire… then rip apart wing by wing."

A sizzle edged along my jaw as he dragged his fat fingers across it, regarding each tremble beneath my skin with a distorted enjoyment. "Are you gonna be my next little butterfly?"

All the rainwater in my stomach somersaulted and crashed, splashing up my throat to touch my gag reflex. My windpipe spasmed and I choked on air, unable to escape the set of hungry eyes devouring my distress.

I tried to lie to myself that this wasn't happening. Not this. Not now. Not after *everything* I'd survived.

"You know I almost didn't come today?" The scratch at the back of my throat making me choke got pinched to silence as the man wrapped his palm around my neck. My coughing morphed into a garbled gasp as he tightened his fist.

"I had a plane all ready to go when I got a call from my old pal Ray saying he had something special coming to auction today. A fighter with the mouth of a sailor and the face of a goddess. He promised me a sweet deal and said I could even have a taste of her if I came by. A sampling, if you will."

FOUR

My eyes bulged against the pressure in my head as his claws around my neck squeezed tighter. A strangled squeak pushed from between my lips as a voice worse than the heroin scraped down my ear.

"And I… am going to *devour* you, little girl."

His fist slipped away, unlocking my freedom to air that I gulped down fast and greedy. My head fell forward in a snap without his grip to hold me up, the two monsters on either side anchoring my body upright.

"Open up her legs."

Strength I shouldn't have possessed ripped my head back up, keeping it stable just long enough to show the devil in front of me all my horrified shock and for him to show me how tickled he was by it.

"Sweetheart, if I'm going to drop thirty grand on you, I deserve to know what my purchase looks and feels like, inside *and* out. Wouldn't you agree?"

Even if my voice hadn't disappeared, I wouldn't have known what to say.

This is where my lightning would have struck for blood, but it was gone too.

I'd been abandoned by every weapon I'd refined over the years to keep me safe. I was empty. Totally fucking useless. There was nothing but the rain in my body and terror in my heart, both rising higher and threatening to spill out.

Especially when the men at my sides grabbed my bare legs.

Quick breathing worked my tired lungs as my only perceptive note of fear, ringing faster and harder as trespassing hands gripped the underneath of my thighs. Each squeeze of my lungs was a desperate plea for them to stop as the itching beneath my skin became relentless.

It was a full on burn at this point, my flesh set on fire from the inside that even the rain couldn't put out.

I needed to scream. I needed to fucking *wail* as the demons on either side picked me up with devastating ease and peeled my legs apart, splitting me right down the middle. My head dropped back with a soundless cry, eyes crashing closed as I begged the God I wasn't sure I believed in to take it all away.

The water drowning my screams. The man standing between my legs.

My mother's drug polluting my system.

I needed it all gone.

I could survive a lot of shit, but not this. My resilience could sustain hits from my father leaving and my mother turning to drugs. It could even endure my mother's murder to those drugs and falling in love with a man I was certain the universe had handpicked to rewrite my entire theory on the world.

I could slap a bandaid of sarcasm and a coat of snark over those wounds and stay standing.

This…

I *hoped* they killed me after this.

The rainwater inside of me finally reached the backs of my wide eyes, spilling over in teardrops soft as petals down my damp cheeks to water the ground where I was bound to die.

I was like the rose in Blake's poem.

I was like his Abigail.

Petals spread apart, ripped down to my core, withered and wilting into the ground for a permanent dirt nap. She and I would share the same grisly fate that earned her a leading role in that beautiful poem.

Perhaps Blake would write me my own poem one day.

One about the girl of lightning he once knew who burned up into ash and fell from her place in the sky in scatters of defeat. Maybe the next girl to fill my shoes would read my poem as I did Abigail's and wonder if she would join the rose garden at some point too.

The crunch of feet moving across the floor made my heart *scream* because my voice couldn't. The presence of the devil made itself known between my legs, a hot and heavy thing of torture that made me choke on the fluid in my throat. Next came the rough brush of fingers on my inner thigh, skating up and up, coming closer to the barely covered center of me.

The lace underwear they'd put me in would do nothing—*nothing*—to phase his incoming attack.

"I will never tire of how soft a woman's flesh can be," the devil hummed, trailing his blunt nails over my skin. "Especially the young ones. You're so

FOUR

ripe. Fresh and unblemished."

Each word he spoke was like a savored candy on his tongue, rolling around and dripping his indecent delicacies all over me. My own stomach rolled with his voice, chest tightening with every sharp breath I couldn't stop from piercing my lungs. They were coming and going so fast, my panic as tangible and unstoppable as the man running his fire-hot hands up my legs.

Then, the sharpest of pains yet struck between my ribs as those hands cupped the front of my underwear, squeezing my core like he had any fucking right. Pain hardened dead center in my chest as I fought to pry out a scream, a cry, *something* to make him stop.

Everywhere I searched inside my body was a dead-end, no help or defense or fighting energy to be found.

I was *alone*. So fucking alone and so fucking scared.

The muscles in my neck strained as I tried to pull it up, tried to lock eyes with the man putting his filthy hands all over me and tell him to fuck off, but my head went limp from too much effort and dropped to face the ceiling as frantic breathing worked my lungs.

All I could do was pant and cry as the thin shield of fabric over my center got pulled to the side, cold air creeping over my exposed flesh.

The man from hell made a god awful noise of satisfaction in the pit of his throat.

"Perfect, pink, and sweet. Worth every fucking penny."

The pressure in my chest constricted tighter every second he leered at such a private part of me, knotting itself into a thing of pain that I felt press against my breastbone with every violent heave I gave. My mouth dried out while my eyes watered over, dizzying air compacting inside my skull from all the hyperventilating I couldn't get a handle on.

I cried up at the ceiling, stars painting themselves to life in my eyes as if the ceiling was gone and I was staring up at the real night sky.

A perfect *gray* night sky with stars to blind and soothe my panic.

Dominic would be so fucking devastated if he saw his little lightning right now.

All spread apart and numbed into submission.

My tears came hotter and faster as I thought of him, as I pictured his sky gray eyes blanketing over me and screaming like I couldn't for what was happening right beneath him to stop. Agony fisted inside my chest as the tightness there grew unbearable with the thoughts of Dominic, crunching down on bones and organs until something was set to shatter.

I wanted to explode. I wanted to self-destruct into a million pieces so there wasn't a single stable shred of me left to remember what was about to happen. I would rather die in pieces than live with the whole memory of this.

Fingers swept a violation up my center, and I sucked in a huge gasp and held it.

My eyes ran across the ceiling, jumping all over it to try and focus on the design of piping it was made of so I didn't have to think about the fingers probing up and down my core. If I could just think of anything else. Anything at all. I tried, ripping my mind to any distraction that was visible, but none of it could steal attention from what was happening between my opened legs.

The knot in my chest grew fucking claws, tearing apart flesh and bone as the intrusion of the devil's fingers pushed inside of me...

And my sunken voice finally resurfaced with *violent* execution.

The scream that peeled out of me was nothing short of inhuman.

It was like lava pouring up my throat, blasting the walls and roof of the room so the whole fucking thing shook.

"STOP! *Stop!*" Strength I didn't have tried to push my heels away from the violation, my head thrashing weakly as I screeched at the un-fucking-bearable pain.

His fingers were like knives, jagged and sharp-bladed sliding into me, slicing cuts against my soft flesh meant for one man and one man only.

Dark chuckles skipped in glee over my screams, the devil relishing in the proof of my pain. The feral noises that broke out of my chest were embedded with glass shards, ripping up the sides of my throat like the blades cutting back and forth in between my shaking legs.

FOUR

Bleeding. I had to be bleeding.

It had to have been coating the fingers he kept thrusting into me. Everything down there had to have been soaked in my blood at this point as I cried and wailed and begged for him to stop.

It only spurred him on.

My pain was his pleasure. My misery was his enjoyment.

And this was only the beginning.

This man—this *monster*—was going to pay his fee and take me home as his newfangled plaything, and he would repeat this torment over and over and over and over and over.

My voice poured out a symphony of sobs, my whole fucking body quaking as he kept it up, turning over the acid in my stomach as he groaned and stuffed another finger inside of me. Another knife.

I hollered in agony and he cackled in delight, his bestial voice gouging at my eardrums with tales of how tight I was and how much he was looking forward to breaking me in two. Hot bile was rising to the back of my throat, but I tried to keep it down as I screeched around it.

I cried for Dominic. I cried for Blake. I cried for any fucking person to rescue me because I was *not* the hero of my own story. Even as badly as I wanted to be, time and time again, I had been proven to be a bystander in my story at best.

The villain at worst.

When I sucked back another rattling breath, one to keep screaming with until my throat was raw, a sound filled the opportune silence.

The distant pops of gunfire.

The men at my sides holding me apart froze, and so did the blades moving inside of me.

"Boss?"

That inquiry came from one of the demons at my side. More muffled cracks of bullets scattered through the pause their boss gave before answering gruff and flat.

"Bring her."

With his brisk order, the fingers scarring my insides slipped out, and I pictured a massacre of a scene between my empty legs.

There wasn't even relief with his intrusion finally gone.

There was just an abundance of white-hot pain.

Like a ragdoll, I was thrown over someone's back and hung there as the three men shuffled out of the back room. Blood rushed to fill my already heavy head as it bounced against the man's broad back while he picked up to a jog at the devil's impatient command.

Wherever we were going, they were trying to get there fast. Ricochets of gunfire were going off all around us, interspersed with furious shouts from the voices of men, and in my drug-muddled mind, I wondered what they were fighting about.

Men always fought wars over the silliest of things. *Men* couldn't help but shed violence and tears wherever they went. There were only two men in the entire goddamn universe that saved the race from complete damnation, and I was heartbreakingly certain I would never see either of them ever again.

The man holding me over his back turned a corner, and my face lolled across the wide-berth of his back. Cheek squished against a slab of muscle, lazy flutters of my eyelids spliced in the occasional tour of my surroundings.

A dank and narrow hallway, dimly lit and littered with junk on its floors. A moan creaked past my lips as we rounded another corner only to have the devil shout, and the demon holding me screech to a halt. He whipped around in a quick spin, taking my dizzy head with him on a twister that wouldn't stop spinning even as he did.

"Someone's coming."

Huh. Who knew the devil could sound so afraid.

My eyes might have been vibrating in my head, but the haunting face of the man who'd stuffed his fingers of knives inside of me was hard to miss. He was right there, glaring with worry over the shoulder of the man holding me. His other henchman was right by his bosses side, my blurry eyes watching as he eased his hand down towards his belt.

Even in the fucked up state I was in, I could make out the funny shape of

FOUR

a gun.

The wary shine to the devil's stare brightened in the crappy lighting, whatever he was making out in the distance putting him on edge.

I gave a slow blink, trying to wet my dry eyes and refocus my swirling vision. When I dragged my sandpaper eyelids back up, it was just in time to catch my captor's eyes shoot wide enough to fill his face.

"Move!"

He ducked around a corner as he blasted out his order, disappearing at the same time his bodyguard henchman gripped the handle of his gun in his waistband.

A shot rang out before he had time to grab it—and went straight through his forehead.

Shock painted his face as the last emotion he'd ever recognize before his expression faded blank. Lifeless in seconds flat. There wasn't even time to gawk at the bullethole drilled straight through a man's skull before another gunshot chased right after the first.

A loud grunt pierced the air, the man who had me slung over his back stiffening every slab of muscle he had, roaring aloud in agony.

Then, we were falling.

The vice grip over my legs loosened, and the world slipped around me as I slid down his back, arms and head aimed to hit the ground first.

There wasn't even a chance in hell I had to stop or brace my fall. I hit the floor *hard,* arms and elbows crumbling beneath my weight as I smacked head first into the unforgiving ground.

A splitting cry broke my lips in two, eyes finally crushing shut to stabilize not only the spinning from before, but now the pulsing of pain.

The hurt wasn't *so* bad—maybe that was a small blessing from the heroin—but it still felt like I'd gotten a good *thwack* from a baseball bat to the side of the face.

A mangled string of curses sounded off somewhere close by on the ground, the asshole who was holding me before he fell obviously still alive.

Whoever'd shot him hadn't killed him.

They were, however, running straight towards me.

FIVE

KAT

In all the ways I'd imagined death, this had never been it.

Lying face down on a floor that was smushing dirt and who the fuck knows what other kinds of filth into my cheek and filtering it up my nose as I struggled to breathe.

Death was coming for me on quick feet, heavy footfall nearing, and all I could do was close my eyes and pretend I was anywhere else.

Back home with Charlotte, playing card games on the floor or running around the house with makeshift water guns for one of our all-out water battle royales. I saw her sweet round face behind my pinched eyes, willing them not to water as the echoes of death got closer.

I squeezed my eyes tighter, clinging to my baby sister's smiling big brown eyes and toothy grin that were painted so vividly from memory in my mind. I clung to her happiness that I'd brought her while I was alive and tried so fucking hard not to think about the sadness I'd bring to her when I was dead.

The last thing I wanted to remember before death arrived was her.

Her radiance. Her curly blonde hair. Her boundless love that I never came even close to deserving but she gave it to me in *droves* anyway.

Terror rattled in my lungs as I laid there, picturing her, picturing Mom, trying *not* to picture how fucking much it was going to hurt getting a bullet through the brain.

Lonesome footfall slowed until it crunched in the dirt next to my head. My fragile head that was about to be garnished with a metal bullet and crimson blood spilling over the sides.

Material rustled next to me.

A *deafening* final pause held the moment between living and not.

Then, a gentle brush of warmth startled across my cheek.

"Kat, open your eyes."

Recognition delivered the first electric shock to my bloodstream since the poison hit it.

It zapped my eyes right open, shifting over at rapid speed to find a dark-eyed dream in the middle of a nightmare.

My heart gasped between my ribs, breaking the surface of all that rainwater drowning it out and sucking down the sight of him. I traced the curves of his face with my stare, following the hard edge of his jawline to the stubborn point of his chin.

Maybe it was because I was high as fuck or maybe because I was terrified he might disappear, but I retraced my steps back and forth between his hard-lined mouth and those eyes of fire and smoke about twenty times before daring to say his name.

"Blake…"

He jerked out a stiff nod in confirmation before stealing the warmth of his stare away and moving it down my body.

"Are you hurt?"

I filled my lungs to say more, but all that came out was a rasping, "Probably."

The tip of his nose gave an angry twitch, and I nearly burst into spontaneous tears over how happy I was to see that furious tell of his again.

My silly hand, which was feeling extra silly thanks to the evil circulating through my veins, began to lift in want of touching that smooth surface that staged all of his transfixing emotions.

FIVE

"Don't move."

Blake's stiff command gripped my wrist in mid-air, holding it hostage as eyes black as oblivion scouted over every inch of me. I knew what he was doing. Or at least, I think I did. Hunting out any blemish on my skin, any scar, any blood or proof of torture while I was stolen away from him.

The searing between my legs reared its white-hot head in painful remembrance.

My teeth sunk into the flesh of my bottom lip, chewing out a sad little mumble.

"Am I bleeding?"

Boiling eyes jumped straight up to mine. "Where?"

Blake's gaze dropped to sit on my mouth when it opened but came back up to me when no words came out. Instead of words, it was tears. They sprouted like weeds from my eyes and spiraled down my cheeks, stubborn and weaving an unsightly tale that didn't *need* words.

Not if the hellfire surging across Blake's face was any clue.

His full mouth rolled tight and fearsome, and before my muddled brain could register why, he was standing.

Then—

Bang!

Bang!

Bang!

Three quick successions of gunfire bounced off the walls, terror ripping my neck up from the floor. My hand shot out to grab Blake's pants around his ankle, making sure he was still there and still alive and still with me.

Fisting his pants, my slow-working brain moved my eyes up to Blake's outstretched arm where a gun was poised at the very end of it. That gun was angled towards the floor… at the henchman who'd carried me out here.

He was alive when we both hit the floor moments ago.

Now he'd gone silent.

Numbness crept in prickling tendrils across my face, locking my eyes open even though my brain was screaming for them to close. It was like a horrific car accident. Even as badly as I wanted to look away from the holes exploded into the side of his face or the blood-soaked patch of his pants over his knee where Blake must have sent his first bullet, I couldn't.

His head looked like a painting from that famous artist we learned about in school growing up. The one that painted in abstract colors and distorted visions—except I didn't remember any of his pieces to be as horrifying as this.

A warm touch cradled the back of my neck at the same time a wall blocked off my view of the crime scene.

Now, instead of seeing pools of red, I blinked up and saw scorching rings of fire.

Black, roaring, *unapologetic* fire.

Blake had just killed a man right in front of me. Two, in fact. And he did it for me. To save me. To prove he would shed blood on my behalf without me even asking. To show me that sliver of darkness he'd warned me was embedded inside his soul.

Maybe I should have shied away from his touch as he gently lowered my head back to the floor.

Instead, I melted into it.

"I've got you," he promised on a husky breath. The feel of his fingers got lost in my hair, the pad of his thumb curving down my cheek as if he just couldn't help it.

I wasn't any goddamn better honestly, pressing my face into his palm with whatever energy I had left. My eyes fell closed as his large hand cradled my face, the occasional pop of ammunition going off in the distance and Blake and I reunited in the middle of it all.

He was here. He was *here*.

"You weren't there this morning." I smothered the exhaustive words into the center of his palm, burying my face against his skin to hide there and never leave again.

He let me nuzzle my pathetic self into him, curving his hand around to help me remember how exquisite it felt when he dragged his knuckles down my cheek.

FIVE

"When I woke up, you were already gone. Claudia put Heather's men on the job last minute and didn't tell Sergio or I we were off it. I don't think she trusts me anymore."

Rage daggered every syllable of his confession, and I turned my head up in his hold to show him the unending fucking appreciation leaking from my eyes.

"But you still came for me."

Blake caught one of my tears on his thumb, stroking it away and murmuring, "I stole one of our cars when I realized they'd taken you."

"How are you gonna explain that?"

He shook his head, not ever faltering. "I'll figure it out later."

Eyes on him, a flash-flood of warmth cascaded down the length of my entire body the same as it did when the heroin first tiptoed into my system.

Except, I wasn't so sure this flush of heat had anything to do with the drug.

At least, not the chemical kind.

"I need to get you downstairs. This place is a fucking warzone. I assume you can't stand?" Blake watched me for confirmation as he carefully retracted his hand from my face and gripped the sides of his unbuttoned overshirt.

I shook my head just barely, lips drying as I breathed hard.

He looked like he expected that, thick eyebrows stringing straight across in focus as he shrugged off the black short sleeve he had on over one of his white muscle undershirts.

One of his arms slipped between my back and the floor, lifting me up to sitting and holding me stable so I didn't fall back. With his other hand, he worked at slipping his overshirt up my arms that hung like noodles by my sides.

Muscles worked extra hard in my cheeks to try and lift a weak smile onto my face.

I'd almost forgotten the revealing piece of lingerie I'd been stuffed into as Blake tried to cover me up before anything else.

He fussed with the buttons on his shirt he'd put around me to give me some semblance of cover, and I shit you not, a breath of laughter walked up and out of my mouth. His handsome face was all squished to the side in concentration as he tried to button me up.

"Don't you think…" I paused, inhaling a shallow breath. "We can do that later?"

Blake paused, gaze falling to the buttons in his grasp.

His expression rescribbled a dawn of realization over itself, and in this hellhole of misery and torture, there it was.

A little drop of light.

Blake brought with him a little bit of moonlight. Just like he always did when the world was darkest around me.

My heart hammered an off-tune beat in my chest as Blake dropped the shirt and nodded almost bashfully.

"Yeah. Yeah, probably."

The task of buttons abandoned, he slipped one arm behind my back and the other beneath my legs, scooping me up off the floor. My tired lungs held onto a gasp as he stood fast, the tornado spinning in my head from earlier making a drastic reprise.

My eyes slammed shut, fingers fisting the lined material of Blake's undershirt in some poor attempt to stabilize the dizziness. A whine as pathetic as they came peeled out of me, and I buried my face against his chest.

I let go of the gasp I'd been holding onto, breathing him in instead.

Cigarettes' aroma flowered inside my lungs, blooming its bitter scent all over until my insides were bogged down by plumes of smoke. And I *loved* it.

Right now, I needed it.

Blake didn't fit the cookie-cutter mold of a knight in shining armor that all the storybooks I'd read growing up told me to expect to save me.

He wasn't a saint. He wasn't a golden boy.

He was darkness.

And I was magnetically bound to every raw bit of it.

"There's a garage underneath this whole place that's off the map. It's

FIVE

where everyone enters and exits for these things so they're not caught in case there's a bust." I gave a feeble nod so Blake would know I was listening. "That's where I parked. I'm going to get you there, okay?"

I tried to shift closer to the rumble of his baritone voice in his chest, nuzzling there. "I don't care where you take me." The lines in the material of his undershirt rubbed across my forehead as I lifted my head up just enough to rest my cheek on his shoulder and look him in the eye.

"Just get me out of here."

Intensity smoldered Blake's eyes as they stayed locked on me, a flashstorm of his electric emotions crackling across his strict features. There was determination and wrath and a tailwind of something else my sleepy brain wasn't quick enough to catch.

He secured me even tighter in his arms and nodded.

We took off in the direction Blake came from, but that was as much as I watched before allowing my eyes to shut.

I didn't know the location we were going to after the garage, but I didn't have enough energy to care either.

So long as Blake was leading me there, I was fine with wherever we landed.

SIX

DOM

The narrow hallway I'd been following spit out in what appeared to be a dead end.

Disappointment threatened to sink my hope as I moved through the underground. The space eventually opened up into something bigger—more cavernous like the parking garage just above it. Empty too.

There were wide stone pillars evenly spaced throughout to keep the secret structure from collapsing, and I used each one as a barricade to hide behind as I made my way through.

Precise movements ushered me across the floor by the guide of my flashlight, unwilling to let go of my optimism that she might be down here. It was a *hidden* underground section of the mall, for fucksake.

That had to mean something.

Creaks in old pipes and plops of what had to be sewer water stirred in the air as I patrolled the grounds. My boots crushed dirt and dust beneath each step, my awareness was so heightened that every pace I made sounded like an explosion to my perked ears.

In fact, it was *so* distracting, I almost didn't hear the answer to my prayers coming from the back far corner.

SIX

An echo of masculine voices shouting.

A rush of promise swirled inside my chest, a prickling sensation that made my heart race faster. The voices could be from other officers working the raid.

Or…

They could be from the kind of men who knew *exactly* where my feisty brunette was.

Sweat beaded at the back of my neck, tension tying through my jaw as I picked my foot up and followed the noise. The furious voices guided like a light in the dark closer to the back of the extensive space. I resecured my grip around my gun the nearer I got and the louder the tempers of each man rose.

The more distance I cut between me and the shouting, the more I was able to make out some of what they were saying.

"…fucking pepper sprayed me!" One of the voices exclaimed in a childlike whine despite the half statement coming from a mouth that sounded objectively male and adult.

"Can you both shut the fuck up and go get in your van?" Another voice tangled into the souring mix, much more grounded and low-pitched than the first. "I don't know if you hear the *bullets* flying around upstairs, but we should probably keep moving away from them."

"Oh, and we're just supposed to *leave* you with her?"

Goddammit, a *third* voice.

"She was *my* responsibility in the first place." That was the second man again, and he sounded only a few moments away from blowing a fuse.

"Yeah, then you screwed up and now the bitch is ours," taunted the first man.

The chill of the nearest barricade to the shouting men welcomed my back as I pressed against it, listening for any more information about who they were or who this *'her'* was they were arguing out.

However, what came next from the other side of the cement wall wasn't intel.

It was the sound of fighting.

A strictly masculine grunt—almost a *growl*—reached my ears just before the wail of pain that followed behind it. The hair on the back of my neck prickled as one of the men shouted and cursed, and then another joined in on the yelling.

Bitter curiosity gnawed at my gut to put faces to the criminal voices.

Fishing out the small mirror I'd brought along from my belt, I held it up so it faced me and angled the reflection over my shoulder and around the barricade.

A blurring glimpse of someone shot up from the ground, and I quickly jerked the mirror to follow where they went. Which wasn't far.

They froze the second they got to their feet, giving me a perfect shot of their round face and balding head. I immediately recorded their image to memory. There was a trail of blood leading down from his nose and a splash of shock that held up his expression as well as his hands.

He was standing in surrender, and I moved the mirror to find out what he was surrendering to.

The reflection of another man slid into the picture on my mirror.

That one holding a gun aimed in ready at the other man's head.

"I'll put a bullet in the hollow space between your eyes without blinking. I'm here to do a job, and you two fucked up that job. Now let me clean up your mess."

That threat came from the low-pitched voice of the second man. I took a moment to watch him, to see his nostrils flare as he held the gun with inscrutable ease to another man's forehead. This second guy was younger than the first, but his stance and aura said he'd been around long enough that he wouldn't second guess pulling that trigger.

Finally, the owner of the third voice spoke up, attempting to calm the situation now that a firearm was involved. I skated the mirror over to find him dressed just like the first guy who still had his hands up in surrender, but bigger in stature by at least a foot.

It was probably safe to assume that if the second guy was this trigger-happy, they all likely had ammunition on their person and weren't shy about using it. I knew I couldn't take all three men on by myself.

SIX

I was alone. I had no backup. No radio. Confronting the men on the other side of this barricade would be the most single-handedly moronic thing I'd done in my thirty-one years. Archie's voice was in my head ordering me to go back where I came from and not to do anything incredibly stupid.

I was half a second away from abiding by the lashing he was giving me in my head.

Then, I angled the reflection of my mirror back towards the second guy. And everything changed.

He wasn't where he was before with a loaded gun ready to play target practice with a man's skull. He'd moved over a few feet, and I found him next to a blacked-out SUV. At the trunk end of it, actually.

And he wasn't alone.

A woman was there with him, hunched over with her hands on her knees like she was about to be sick. Puzzlement narrowed my stare on her reflection, noting her mass of dark hair that curtained in front of her face and how her feet were bare.

What was even stranger than her presence was this second man and how he reacted to her.

He watched her *acutely*, rubbing a hand over her back like he was comforting her.

As if he cared for her.

Apparently she said something to make him laugh because a small smile broke up his strict features and confirmed that yes, he was definitely younger than his partners. A person's smile tended to reveal them, and his helped me put him anywhere between the ages of twenty-three to twenty-six.

His focus went back to the woman, his hand on her back moving up to sweep beneath her hair and cup her chin. There was a short-lived attempt to lift her head, but before I could see her face, she crumbled during the effort and pressed her head against the man's chest and reached up for his hand.

He grabbed hers without pause and held it.

There was something very, *very* peculiar about these two.

At a first glance, I'd have pegged the woman as a victim of trafficking brought here against her will. Except what victim sought comfort in their captor, and what captor gave it so readily?

The man tried again to help the woman stand, steadying her waist with one hand and guiding her lolling head up with his other.

Watching in my mirror as he helped her head up slowly, a bizarre tingling sensation began to crawl up the slats in my spine. If I hadn't been hiding, I would have shifted against the weird feeling.

To add to the tingling, an inexplicable and sudden warmth seeped through my ribs, the heat speeding up my heart like it was being chased with a lit match.

A ringing—like a fire alarm—started between my ears as I scrutinized the woman closer as the man brought his hand across her face.

Something in my chest *squeezed* before I ever even saw her.

And when he finally pushed the raven-colored hair crowding her face away, I knew exactly what it was.

It was my heart... *bellowing* that it'd found its other half.

For the narrowest of seconds, everything in the whole fucking universe felt like it stilled.

The wind outside. The waves in the ocean. The orbit of the Earth.

Everything stopped.

My eyes devoured her reflection with a pounding heart after having nothing but memories of how she looked to hold me over for the last miserable month.

She was perfect. My *god*, she was still so perfect.

And alive. She was *alive*.

And she was unquestionably not okay.

Kat's tear-stained cheeks punched through my stomach and left a fistful of fire. Distress contorted her gorgeous face, and in all the ways I knew this perfect woman inside and out, I knew that pained look of hers.

She was about to pass out.

Determination snapped my mirror closed and shoved it back in my belt

SIX

so I could wrap both hands around my gun.

My little lightning was fading fast.

Sense and stealth be damned, I was going after her.

Now.

SEVEN

KAT

By the time we reached wherever Blake intended to take me, I'd all but fallen asleep.

"Hey." The gentle nudge of Blake's voice went along with his hand trying to stir me awake by squeezing my knee where he held me. "I know you're tired, but I need you to stay awake just a little longer."

I whined into the crook of his neck in return, burrowing deeper into the smoke-infused pores of his skin in full-on rebellion.

"Come on," he encouraged, hot breath sticking to skin as he spoke soft and sweet right in my ear. "We're here."

A groan protested from the back of my throat as I felt him begin to lower me, touching my bare feet to the cold ground. He didn't let me go right away—thank fuck. The world was still a barren black around me with my eyes shut.

They did *not* have any plans of opening soon.

I was so fucking sleepy, but Blake kept swatting my hand off the snooze button.

His big hands steadied their warmth on the dips of my waist as I tried to take my own body weight back, even though all I wanted to do was throw my arms around his neck and bury myself in him again.

SEVEN

I didn't give a flying fuck how weak it made me to want that either.

I *wanted* Blake's comfort, and I think I goddamn well deserved it too.

The second Blake's touch vanished from my waist, I wobbled back on my heels and tried to curl my toes into the ground to keep standing. Except… the muscles in my toes and legs weren't really anything more than jelly still, and in one shaking breath, I was folding back down.

An arm swooped around my waist, catching me mid-fall and securing me against a chest of warmth and muscle.

"I've got you."

And I believed him every bit when he said it.

I managed to hike my limp-noodle arms up to rest on his forearms so I could try to stabilize myself some. Blake ushered me back in small shuffles, helping me find a seat on what felt like the lip of a car.

When I peeked an eye open, it confirmed that I *was* sitting on the back of a car.

"Where the fuck did a car come from…?" My muddled words made it out in lazy succession, a slur of sleepiness dripping from each letter.

"We're in what's basically a hidden bunker." Blake kept a protective hold beneath my forearms while he stood in front of me so I didn't fall or slump. "There's an underground road connected to it not on the maps, and this is sort of the garage for it."

A muffled waterfall of gunshots poured through the walls around us, and I arched a curious brow up at Blake who was already watching me.

"I assume a deal went sour." Black eyes drifted down my face and back up again. "Now the whole thing's gone up in flames."

Funny he'd used the word *flames* considering that's exactly what he was.

A living, breathing, lethal flame.

And he kept me so fucking warm when the rest of the world was a blistering disappointment.

Blake shifted on his feet in front of me, severity carving his features as he looked between my eyes.

"I have this car, and I have the keys. Can you drive?"

Frustration crushed his coal-black eyes to rubble and rolled his mouth extra thin as I shook my head. I could barely stand. Putting me behind the wheel of a car wasn't exactly genius.

My fading focus was on his face as thoughts rolled across it. Shallow breaths barely touched my starving lungs as I watched him, but they were all I could muster down.

It was as I sat there with my eyes on him, breathing just barely, that a panicked burn started dead center in my chest.

And not because of the lack of oxygen.

The searing ache spidered out inside my ribcage as the realization expanded through my body.

He wasn't planning to come with me.

That was the only reason he'd ask if I could drive. Because he wasn't planning on it.

"You can," I breathed, desperation winding me faster than the heroin ever could. "Drive away with me."

The second the proposal was out there, the ache scoring inside my chest transferred its blade to Blake, cutting the same pain across his eyes.

"They'll come after us. If it's just you that doesn't come back, they'll think a buyer took you or you were killed in crossfire, and they won't look for you."

"But can't they think that for you too? That you came here and..." I paused to struggle for breath, Blake scrutinizing my effort with radiating concern. "And you got killed like me? Then we could both escape."

That made sense, right? I knew I was still high as hell, but that *sounded* like a sensible plan.

"Kat," he sighed my name on an uncertain lament.

"What?" My fingertips dented determination into his forearms where I held him for stability and so he wouldn't fucking leave me. "I don't see any way this doesn't work. You're just scared that it will."

The weak muscles in my neck gave up as he towered closer to me, dropping my head to rest against the car as he hung his above mine.

"The only thing I'm scared of is you not getting out of here because you're just that fucking stubborn."

SEVEN

"You're right," I huffed, switching my eyes between his. "I am, so you're just gonna have to get in the goddamn car, okay? This plan *works*."

The flame of a man standing so close I could taste the hesitation on his hot breath absorbed the plan like a slow infusion, the smolder of his jagged black diamond eyes flickering with indecision.

With possibilities he'd only dared dream of.

He was realizing he didn't *have* to live out a life sentence as a flame in the darkness if he came with me. His potential to be more was boundless if we were to escape now. He didn't belong at that brothel, and we both knew it. He belonged out in the world where his flame could dance in the wind or light a girl's heart on fire.

He was a goddamn forest fire of passion, and some lucky flower deserved to be consumed by him. It was such an *easy* surrender to have Blake devour you with just one look.

One electric look.

Like the one he was giving me right now.

My head went light as air in seconds; I was already too breathless as it was to sustain one of his oxygen-stealing looks, and he should have known better than to look at me like that right now. Though, somewhere in the back of my foggy mind, I knew it wasn't really his fault.

It was our energy—that volatile thing moving back and forth between us that had been there since day one that I could acknowledge but didn't have the guts to name.

A simmer tracked down my face as Blake moved his stare across it, pondering what to do. *Considering*. Emotion tangled a knot in my throat as he really truly thought about running away with me.

Then, a complication with a grating voice manifested out of thin air.

"I fucking *told* you this was one of our cars, Becks." My muscles were too spent to lift my head to see where the condemning voice was coming from, but Blake's attention ripped from me to up and over my shoulder to give me an answer.

Murder hardened his expression to granite in seconds flat.

"*Blake*." The same voice slapped the air with accusation. "What the hell, man? What are you doing here?"

Midnight eyes slid back over to mine, a bitter edge to his voice as he lied. "I got word saying shit went sour, so I drove out here to save your ass."

"I call bullshit," the guy behind us spat. "Or else why is *she* back?"

Blake's fire-breathing attention flashed behind me as he snapped his teeth and snarled.

"Do you want to go back to Ray without the money *or* the product?" Silence met his nauseating cover-up of a threat. "Didn't fucking think so."

Speaking of nausea…

A vicious bout of it cramped up my stomach, my face pinching and a groan resonating. I made a grab for my aching stomach with one hand, not considering the balance I'd lose if I let go of Blake's forearm until I was already folding face-first into his chest.

My nose squished against his sternum as I slumped, his rumbling voice tickling it all the way up my sinuses as he encouraged me to stay awake and keep my eyes open.

The pathetic whine that I buried into his shirt sounded more like a sob, and the weight of Blake's hand rested on the back of my neck to soothe down my misery. His fingers were just beginning to tangle in my mass of hair when the asshole who showed up last minute piped up again.

"Are you sure you're here for us and not because you missed fucking her? Everyone on the circuit has been talking about how you've gone all puppy-eyed for the new whore Heather brought in."

With a noncommittal grumble, Blake kept brushing his soft touch up and down the back of my neck. "Everyone on the circuit needs to get a fucking life so they can stop caring about mine."

"What do you expect?" The voice stepped closer. "You walk around like you're better than all of us every single day of the year and then decide to stick it in the lowest common denominator bitch Ray has to offer?"

Surprise jolted my drowsy brain when a second man's voice joined the outrage. "Plus, she fucking pepper sprayed me!"

I did?

"Can you both shut the fuck up and go get in your van?" Blake snapped, his fingers tensing against my scalp. "I don't know if you hear the *bullets* flying around upstairs, but we should probably keep moving away from them."

"Oh, and we're just supposed to *leave* you with her?"

The first fucker's voice cracked like a whip across the empty garage and froze Blake's hand in my hair. Slowly, the warmth of his fingers retracted all together, and I peeked one eye open just in time to see that same hand lock into a fist.

"She was *my* responsibility in the first place."

Darkness slithered beneath the vibration of Blake's deep voice, a foreboding alert that curled the hair on my arms. The second sorry man who'd interrupted us clearly didn't hear it.

"Yeah, then you screwed up and now the bitch is *ours*."

The breath I had left tightened in my throat as I felt it. As I *felt* Blake's bad overshadow his good, smothering out his light to a lonely scream in the darkness.

He folded both my hands over the lip of the car so I wouldn't fall off, and then he was gone, leaving a trail of fire blazing behind him. My heavy head wouldn't even cooperate to watch where he went as a feral noise emerged from the deepest pit of his wickedness.

Then, the sound of skin hitting skin bounced off the walls.

A pained shout ripped a bolt of terror through my chest, and spontaneous strength from the fucking gods twisted my neck over to see who it came from.

Some burly guy in all black was keeled over to the side, hand on his face and cursing up a storm. There was another guy in all black behind him, bigger than his friend and the kind of familiar that stirred nerves in my cramping stomach.

And then there was Blake.

Standing tall and grounded, his bare shoulders strung taut in the small break of light over our heads. His back was to me, but the grip his emotions had over his muscles was tell enough of what was likely one of his poisonous glowers hardened on his face.

The man he'd punched righted himself, and the murder burning a ring around his dark eyes was also an uneasy kind of familiar.

A noise of battle parted his teeth, but Blake won the war with one quick flash of his hands.

And the gun he withdrew from his waistband.

The weapon was only aimed at one person, but everyone in the garage froze like they were also being held at gunpoint.

"I'll put a bullet in the hollow space between your eyes without blinking," he threatened with a fascinating calm. "I'm here to do a job, and you two fucked up that job. Now let me clean up your mess."

From some dark depth within me, electricity crackled awake.

A strain of lightning *purring*.

The rebirth sizzled around my heart, making a slow circle around the organ going haywire. It was bouncing around my ribcage, smashing itself against walls like it was trying to *avoid* the returning lightning.

Because it knew.

It *knew* why the lightning had chosen this exact moment to resurface.

My heart wanted to stay gullible. Its goal was to deny, deny, deny as long as possible until I was out of here and miles away from the truth. The truth *hurt*. The truth was *gutting*.

The truth was that I wasn't the only lightning bolt in this garage.

Blake was lightning, and he'd been striking me with his mutual fire since the moment we met.

It was his fire that reached out and reignited my spark at the brutal proof of all that made him wicked. His moral gray was smeared *sinful* black as he aimed his gun at another man's head, a magnetic darkness haloing his lean frame.

He'd flick his finger and end a man's life to save mine, and the worst parts of me *loved* knowing that. They *craved* it. My broken pieces had been screaming for his from the top of their lungs, trying to convince me that our lightning could fuse them together to create a masterpiece like none other.

All these weeks, I'd been covering my ears and trying to drown them out.

SEVEN

I'd been chanting my love for Dominic over and over again in my head so I wouldn't hear the truth about Blake coming from my soul.

But now, it wasn't any use.

The truth was fucking deafening, and I couldn't bother pretending I didn't hear it anymore.

The two men backed up and backed down, freeing Blake to come back to me. Thank fuck too, because the guilt of acknowledgement had made me even more sick to my stomach. I hunched over, resting my hands on my knees as the mouth sweats began rolling down the inside of my cheeks.

The weight of a hand settled on my back, tingles running up and down the whole thing as Blake began rubbing small circles over it.

"I'm either going to pass out or vomit," I told him.

"Well, let's hope you do one before the other."

The corner of my mouth ticked up, and I breathed hard through the nausea. "You want me to throw up and then pass out in it? Sick fuck."

The melody of his rare laughter knocked around my chest as he let it go free, digging the guilt deeper as just the sound of it warmed every single inch of me.

"How are you still this smart-mouthed right now?"

I did my best to shrug. "It's a gift."

His hand kept smoothing circles over my back, his touch so gentle for a man who'd almost killed another minutes ago. It felt so fucking good that I wanted to weep, wanted to break down into sobs right there in the garage for how good it felt to have his tender touch all to myself.

His fingers were like mercy drifting over damnation as he glided them up to sweetly cup my chin, trying to lift my head.

"Kat..."

"Oh, *God*." My head sank into his chest as a ruthless wave of sickness crashed over me, pouring down my body until every fiber of my skin *hurt* with the overwhelming need to vomit.

Without thinking, my hand was in the air, reaching out in search of something by its own accord. Yet, when his fingers found mine and folded around my hand, it was another truth I couldn't deny that I knew what I was reaching for all along.

"I can't drive like this," I huffed. "You *have* to come with me."

Pressure squeezed my hand in his as I listened in on the drumming of his steady heart. His chest rose in a deep breath beneath my forehead, and between that and his heartbeat, Blake could have lulled me to sleep with his inner melody.

Exhaustion pulled down on my eyelids while Blake pushed up on my head, his fingers a gentle encouragement beneath my chin. My muscles whined the whole ride up, the rolling tide of nausea waning and rising as I was forced to move.

It was a clusterfuck of feelings up in my head, my skull compact from edge to edge with blitzed-out mania. The only thing keeping me from falling over and exploding my colorstorm of crazy all over the ground was the heated hand cradling the side of my face.

Blake led my head upright, tender fingers sweeping my waves of matted hair from my forehead to clear a path from me to him.

And there he was.

On the other end of calamity was him. Two eyes of darkness and a soul of poetry.

I was all loose limbs and loose heartstrings in Blake's arms, a malleable thing of dirty acceptance for what had always been breathing between us. It wasn't *just* a connection.

It wasn't *just* chemistry.

It was another dose of fate.

And I was eternally damned for it.

Blake curved a knuckle down the edge of my face, watching his skin ride mine with tongue-tying intensity. My heart throbbed an unfamiliar beat between my ribs as that severe stare rested on mine.

The mark of conclusion had been stamped in his pupils.

"Don't watch what I'm about to do," he murmured darkly.

My shallow breath caught in my chest. Oxygen stopped flowing altogether as I looked between his decided eyes, the resolution in them setting free a swarm of fireflies in my stomach.

SEVEN

They buzzed and warmed my insides. They filled me up with flutters of something *stupid*. Something I'd sworn off completely.

Something that felt a little like hope.

Sensations popped and sparked beneath my skin as Blake reached back to where he kept his gun in his waistband. His eyes never left mine.

He's coming with me, my mind whispered. It also whispered he was about to kill off the two men behind us who could rat us out, but I didn't listen to that part. I just honed in on the goddamn *orchestra* of buzzing that was igniting between us, shaking the atmosphere, dancing over my skin.

All I heard was *us*.

Our lightning brewing. Our symphony singing. Our fates clashing.

And then...

I heard a boom of thunder.

"KAT!"

The loud shout shocked me back, bristling in confusion. For a delusional second, I thought the boom had come from Blake, but when his eyes blew wide with alert and his head twisted to the side, I knew the thunder had come from somewhere else.

Some*one* else.

I traced the line of sight Blake had followed.

There was a silhouette of a man.

A man with towering height and broad shoulders whose arms had to have equaled the wingspan of a humongous bird. Like an eagle. He was running at us with the same grace and power in his body as an eagle too, his focus fixed on me and no one else.

We stared at each other across the distance as he ran out of the shadows, the wash of light on my end of the garage revealing him in one earth-shattering second.

Air swept my lungs in a jerking gasp.

Shock rounded my eyes.

My whole world tilted and fell at his feet, all of me ready to follow suit and obliterate for him in fireworks of awe and joy and stupid fucking love.

Our stupid fucking love.

Dominic, my brain acknowledged because my mouth wouldn't. It was too stunned. Too overwrought. Too busy trembling as the happy burn of salt blistered the backs of my eyes. My throat constricted, my heart burning a fire set by the match of disbelief.

He *found* me.

How the fuck had he managed to find a rotting daisy in a field of weeds?

Silver-ringed eyes thundered for me as he ran my way, every single cell beneath my coat of skin singing his name as he called mine out again.

My heart *slammed* forward, trying to break through my shell of shock and run to him, throw myself in his arms and bury our stupid love inside of his wide chest so no one could ever take it away from us again.

Our unfailing love charged through every crevice in my body, filling me up and lifting my foot to take off and run towards him. A smile twisted up my cheeks.

Electricity shook in my veins.

Before I finished that first step, a shot rang out.

And then a shit load more came right after.

Horror flushed out the love in my blood and turned it pin-prick cold as bullets whizzed past my ears and ate up the distance to Dominic. He skidded fast and threw himself behind a massive pole or barricade or what-the-fuck-ever, disappearing from the two men next to me who'd aimed their guns at him.

"Stop," I tried, only to find dread had stolen away my voice. *Panic*.

"Get her in the fucking van!"

The bigger of the two men shouted orders over his shoulder while popping off bullets in Dominic's direction. Metal bounced off concrete walls around us, the terrible sound punching my gut as I searched for my voice to make this stop.

I needed to make *all* of this stop.

I needed to get to him. I just needed to—

"Kat, let's *go*." Urgency gripped Blake's voice as he wrapped a hand around my arm, pulling me up off the back of the car.

No, I wanted to cry as he dragged me behind him, but my mouth wouldn't

SEVEN

work. All I got out was a mangled whimper as I tried my fucking best to put all of my strength into my heels so Blake could *feel* my resistance.

It was useless, and I stumbled in his trail until my knees gave out and I came inches from feeling the scrap of concrete against my bare skin. Blake's forearms anchored beneath my armpits in a last second save, his mouth coming right against my ear.

"Come on, Kitten. Stay awake a little longer for me."

A sob split my heart in half as his endearment hit it, tearing the broken pieces apart for all my grief to pour out of. Blake thought he was doing something good. He thought he was saving me like all the times I needed him to in the past.

He had no idea a future I thought was lost for good had come to rescue me this time. Salvation was just on the other side of that barricade, throwing his striking baritone orders my way.

"Kat, get down!"

His voice that I missed so fucking much dove under my skin and tried to puppet my muscles to do exactly as he'd said, but the drugs had cemented them too tightly.

I struggled to move their weight, but neither they nor Blake would let me go. He kept trying to get me inside the car he drove here like we planned, and I kept trying to force the words out that he needed to let me go.

And then, he did.

It all happened in a halved second.

His hands were steady beneath my arms one moment, and I was falling through the air the very next to the tune of Blake swearing out in pain.

Cement slapped my face as I hit the ground, pressure palming my cheek where the ache of impact would normally be. My brain rattled around my skull as I tried to fix my vision enough to find Blake.

He was a dizzy blur above me, clutching his shoulder with a pained grit across his mouth.

The heart inside of me *squeezed* to death to see him in pain, trying to hurt me as much as he was hurting in an instinctive act to mirror our afflictions.

Both the men in my life yelled out to me for different reasons, and my heart fucking *wailed* at the sound of them both needing me. It felt like the organ was trying to tear itself in two directions, one half reaching out to Blake while the other half cried to be with Dominic.

The screech of tires interrupted the shouting from Blake and Dominic, rubber burning against the concrete right in front of my face where I was sprawled out. Boots hit the ground next, shouts from the two other men digging into my ears.

"Blake, grab her and get the fuck in!"

"I *can't*," he grunted.

The sound of a heavy door sliding open pushed through the air in place of gunfire, and I watched through a blur of tears from beneath the van as a pair of strong legs came out from behind the stone barricade and started running towards me.

A cry poured to the ground as someone hoisted me up off of it, dirt embedding beneath my fingernails as I tried to cling to rock. The whole ocean was in my head as I got thrown over a broad shoulder, sloshing around and burning saltwater behind my eyes.

My hands started grabbing at air feebly and blindly, hoping to find resistance at the end of my fingertips. It was useless; *I* was fucking useless as I got dropped into the van, hard metal meeting my back, and a curse from Blake immediately following.

"*Fuck*, Becks! Careful with her!"

"She's about to pass out anyway. Calm your tits and get in!"

Becks was right. I was about to drift away as the ocean in my head dragged me down deeper and deeper, my hopes of being enveloped by a thunderous gray sky bleeding darker and blacker.

The vehicle swayed as more weight added to it.

"Drive!"

The van quaked beneath my body as the driver followed Blake's order so fast, the door to the van hadn't even shut yet. A chorus of shouts exploded inside the van as bullets dented the front of it and probably the tires.

Pride swelled my cheeks with a grateful smile as Dominic smartly tried to blow out the tires so these men couldn't take me away from him *again*.

SEVEN

He was such a goddamn hero, and I was so painfully in love with every single piece of him.

"This fucker definitely hit the tires," someone said. "We've got about twenty miles until they're flat. Let's *go!*"

"No…" My head shook against the van's floor, heart throbbing inside my chest. "*No.*"

The return of my voice might have been small, but the conviction behind it was *roaring.* It rushed through my bloodstream and fused inside my haggard muscles, fueling them with strength to roll to my side and make a swipe for the edge of the open door.

"Kat, no!"

Fingers tangled with mine that were reaching for leverage and pulled them back, fisting them against my chest.

"*Yes,*" I grit between clenched teeth, shaking my shoulders against the body that I knew was Blake's by the burnt aroma that clouded my head. I struggled against him, huffing wildly. "Let me g—"

The van spun in a quick turn, slicing off my voice in a gasp as we jerked around, and Blake's arm locked me in tighter against his chest. My hands vice-gripped his forearm as the world spun, the van turning so its open door faced in the opposite direction.

The direction that my own brand of heaven was in, coming for me with love firing in his gunmetal eyes.

Love… and terror.

The distance between us was getting bigger and scarier, no matter how hard he pushed his body to get to me before it devoured our future.

I reached for him with my free hand and wailed, gunning for one last touch. I refused to blink away my streaming tears and have one less millisecond of our eyes on each other. I'd need a million more seconds of looking at him to get me through a lifetime without it.

Heartbreak tethered across our connection, the agony scoring Dominic's eyes the same vicious kind ripping a blade up my chest.

This was the last time I'd ever lay eyes on Dominic Reed.

This was the last time he'd ever lay eyes on me.

My heart was tearing itself apart inside my chest, shredding itself to pieces to litter the bottom of the dying organ. Falling in love with Dominic had given it new life.

Losing him was killing it all over again.

His face, anguished and desperate, would be the last picture of him I'd take to my grave, and I hated it. I fucking loathed his pain because he didn't deserve it. He was so much *better* than to be hurt by someone like me.

He was so much better than the people who he surrounded his life with, and if it was the last thing I ever fucking did, he deserved to know it.

Right before the door to the van closed and I lost him forever, I sucked back one final gust to warn him with. To save his life with my dying breath.

I used that breath to scream out one word.

One name.

"Heather!"

Her name soared from my lungs just before the van door slammed shut.

The hard metal inside of the van took Dominic's place, and a tangle of screams and sobs poured from the hole in my chest where he'd been ripped from. The pain of his loss splintered so deep and was so *immediately* agonizing, I ran my palm down my front to check if I'd been shot.

I cried and rocked back and forth against the momentum of the van as we drove away, a hand brushing away the rivers running down my cheeks. The ocean in my head finally took over after a while and drowned me into a black-out sleep.

And I seriously hoped I never woke up.

EIGHT

KAT

As it always went with disappointments, they were reliable sons a bitches.

I woke up the next day, despite not wanting to.

I was alive, despite not wanting to be.

It wasn't an easy or deep sleep I'd been in either. It was some fresh hell in the middle where I was *aware* in my sleep. It was like I was floating inside my own head, trying to convince myself I should be sleeping, but my brain wouldn't get with the program and make it happen.

It was a horrible day of sleep, and I was somewhere between delirious and devastated when I eventually woke up later that night.

I was *beyond* exhausted, and maybe if I were a touch more naïve, I could've blamed the lack of sleep on why I did what I did later that day.

Unfortunately for me, I wasn't a naïve woman.

Just a bad one.

When I broke out of my prison slumber, it was with a dried coat of tears crusted on my cheeks. Either they were from earlier, or I'd been crying in my sleep. I rolled over on the bed, discovering in the same swooping second that I was even *on* a bed.

My bed?

No.

My fingertips felt along the fabric of the single sheet, knowing the truth embedded in the rough feel of linen the same as I knew the knot of dread that tied together in my chest.

...I was back.

Back in the house.

Back in the house of horrors in my room with no windows, no way out, and no godforsaken hope.

The swell of panic built in my chest as fast as a dam giving way. It spilled quick-acting hysteria between every rib and bone as I laid there on that stiff bed, my head too crowded to find the words to tell my body to move.

My eyes wouldn't even open.

They didn't want to see. Being blind in denial was better than accepting being basically dead, right?

In another life, I was a denial *wiz*. If it had been a class offered in school, it would have been the only one I aced without cheating from my textbook or off my desk partner. In my past life, I was a goddamn expert at reforming the truth to what fit better into my fractured view of the world.

Then I came *here*, and that skill died.

It was a slow death that started with what would happen to me while I was here and ended with Blake.

Blake.

His invading name stung like a prick of poison behind my forehead and convinced my body to finally move. My hand slapped over my necklace sitting against my heart, squeezing it like it *was* my heart, and the tighter I gripped it, the closer it would come to exploding.

And then maybe the pain would stop.

Then maybe the pain will stop...

The mattress bent beneath my fingers as I attempted to fist it in my other hand, lightning creeping through my blood and needing *something* to dive into. It slithered through my veins like a wraith, sneaking its electric tendrils beneath my sweat-damp skin and *zapping* each nerve ending.

EIGHT

Smoothed edges of the emerald grew biting as my grip around it turned vicious, shaking harder and harder as I squeezed my eyes shut just as tight to keep a hold on my denial.

I needed this one. *Fuck*, I really needed it. More than I ever needed a shield of denial in all my twenty-one years.

The memories on the other side of its door were monstrous, reaching in ear-splitting shrieks over the barrier to get to me. I was crouched on the other side of denial's door, hands over ears and singing myself a melody of distraction from the high-pitched wails shattering the hinges on the wall between us.

It was slipping, the nightmares piling on top of each other to use their crowded weight to break the door down.

With a tiny cry splitting my lips, that denial finally gave way, and the mountain of memories I'd rather have forgotten came crashing in all at once.

Heather. Tommy. The confession over my mother. The heroin. The hypocrite I was to the heroin. The auction. The men. The devil's knives inside of me.

Blake.

Dominic.

A dry sob tumbled off of my quivering bottom lip as I remembered—as I remembered seeing him and crying for him and losing him all fucking over again.

There was a searing ache in my chest that I attempted to rub out with the heel of my palm as I wretched my eyes open and forced myself to sit up.

The room I'd left no more than a day ago hadn't changed one fucking bit.

The walls of the brothel seemed to sulk for me as I batted my dry eyes all around it, the water stain on the far wall rearranging into a frown while the popcorn ceiling appeared to elongate its tiny white protrusions from above as if to contribute its own tears.

There was nothing more useless than tears.

Except hope, but we all knew that one already.

I turned my head and ignored the stiffness in my neck as I spotted something on the nightstand next to me.

Something cold that made my blood run *hot*.

The heat helped push me up from the bed and wander on tingling feet towards the nightstand. The foggy weight in my skull slid to one side as I cocked my head at the glass of water and wondered how long it'd been sitting there given the wet ring of condensation collected at its base.

Maybe minutes.

Maybe hours.

I didn't know.

What I *did* know was the feeling of lightning curling around my bones as I stared at that single fucking lousy gesture and figured whose guilt I was *positive* it came from.

The glass was a welcomed cool against my fire-hot skin as I grabbed it and poured it down my throat that felt as dry as if I'd swallowed sawdust. My insides felt just as raw, but water wouldn't help heal that ache.

Nope, *fire* was my only satisfaction.

A goddamn explosion, to be more exact.

I pulled the glass from my lips, water dripping down my chin, and I *swore* it steamed right the fuck off my boiling skin. My fumbling fingers found the glass's way back to the nightstand, blindly pushing it back in place with my gaze stuck on the door across the room.

My bare feet tempted one step closer to it.

Then another.

My strides grew longer as my pacing moved faster until my toes were at the frame of the door, my hand coming up to hover over the handle. The metal was lukewarm at best as I formed my fingers around it, giving a small tug.

The handle didn't budge, which wasn't surprising.

The next little tug I gave wasn't really so little.

Wood rattled against its framing as I jerked back on the door once, then twice, then six more times.

EIGHT

The lock kept up its job, jamming in place as I yanked and pulled until I was just fucking shaking the thing. My lips curled up over my teeth, baring at the door like an animal giving warning that it was about to pounce.

My claws were priming, bloodlust diluting my senses until all I saw was blurry red and all I scented was the bittersweet smell of hatred.

A feral huff broke between my gritted teeth as I gave up ripping the handle off, my shoulders rising and collapsing fast as I geared a glare up across the white wooden door. My lip twitched, arm rising back to—

"Hey!"

A sting swallowed my hand whole as I slapped my open palm against the door, pausing and waiting for a response from the other side.

Nothing.

"I said fucking *hey*!" More stinging and more slapping that eventually turned to pounding with both fists. "Heather, Claudia, Sergio, fucking *anyone*! Open this goddamn door!"

My lips touched to shout *his* name too, but the betrayal was too heavy to sustain on my tongue. It fell away in place of more yelling and more banging my fists and knees and feet against the door. The thing shook in terror beneath my beating, begging with each violent rattle for me to stop, but I didn't. I *couldn't*.

Not until someone answered that I could bleed all my terminal pain into.

Time was a blur as I struck that bedroom door over and over, but it couldn't have been that long until someone answered. I still had *loads* of fire-hot energy running rampant when the sound of the lock unclicked.

It wasn't until the person who answered came through that it all froze over.

He took one dominating step into the room, covering the whole goddamn thing in a smoke cloud of darkness in seconds.

"You're up."

His mouth barely moved.

The two monotone words that came out of it wrestled between his stiff lips just to be heard.

They struck me in a whiplash, those two words. They ripped me back in time to a month ago when he and I first met, standing in almost these exact same positions, him uttering those same two words to me as he did just now.

This last month with him was like a year worth of seasons. We'd met in a bitter Winter, frozen hearts icing each other out. We'd come to an understanding in a fresh breath of Spring that quickly melted to a sweltering mirage of something between us in the heat of Summer. In our final week, we'd fallen like leaves in Autumn at the feet of one another, admitting without words how much we were going to miss colliding when the wind swept us apart.

Now, all of that time—all of *us*—had gone up in flames.

My bare heel squished into the carpet as I took a slow step away from him. Blake watched me retreat with a strict expression, the flames of our wreckage burning around his jagged pupils.

"Get out," I said on a breath. A singular, shaking breath.

Blake let out a controlled sigh of his own through his nose, his temper pulsing in the backs of his jaw. Then, instead of leaving, he closed the bedroom door behind him.

"Are you fucking deaf?" My legs drew me back further. "I said *get out*."

I actually got to *watch* the decision to ignore me trigger across his hard-edged features.

"I know you're ma—"

"*Don't*." My warning was as pointed as my finger aimed at him, holding him in place across the room. "You don't get to *speak*. You don't get to try and *explain*. All you get to do is *leave*."

His shoulders rolled back, his posture annoyingly straight. "Kat—"

"What the f—I said *leave!*"

A strike of lightning blinded my next move, peeling white hot venom through my bloodstream and across my vision as I spun a 180 and landed my hand on my empty glass. With a screech, I lobbed my arm back and felt the smooth glass leave my fingertips, but I couldn't see for shit where it was going.

Shattering glass splintered the thick air, echoes of its destruction

EIGHT

reverberating inside my ear drums and sounding *so* fucking sweet.

I fluttered my lashes to blink away the lightning, breathing like I'd thrown an entire china cabinet rather than one little glass. Blake was standing adjacent to the door, black eyes on me as he breathed equally as hard.

"You have bare fucking feet, Kat. You're gonna hurt yourself now."

I blustered back, hand coming flat against my chest. "Am I supposed to think you... *care* about my wellbeing? Is that why you brought me back here? Because you *care?*"

His nostrils broadened, my retort rippling guilt across his face. This was one instance where Blake's inability to dull his vibrant emotions might have been to his disadvantage since it gave me even more ammo when I already had a freaking arsenal.

"That wasn't the plan." His eyelids sunk low and dragged his voice down just as heavy as he pinched the bridge of his nose. "None of this was the plan..."

"You *think?*" The accusation ringing in my voice shot across to Blake, his head hung low. "The plan was to get me as far away from here as possible, and instead you brought me back. You took me, kicking and crying, away from someone who was there to *save* me."

"I—"

"That was Dominic! Did it ever occur to you that the man running at me, *screaming* my name, just might know me?"

Blake's eyes were sharp as razors as they sliced from the floor to me. "I didn't realize it was him until we were already driving away."

The point of his glare nearly punctured my bloated temper, but I kept a loose leash on my wrath and my teeth clenched tight.

"That's the shittiest excuse for ruining someone's life I've ever heard."

Blake cast his stare off to the side. It wasn't until the lousy bedroom lighting hit that particular angle of his face that I noticed the bloodshot quality to his eyes, like he'd been digging his thumbs into them for hours and hadn't slept in probably a day.

Good.

Apparently the glass I'd thrown had hit way past the door since that's where the glass clinked as Blake kicked a few pieces to the side.

"I fucked up." He knocked his boot against more broken glass to clear it. "I know I did."

I almost—*almost*—gave a hog-worthy snort.

"Biggest fucking understatement of the year."

His thick lashes drew up as he slid an electric glare my way. "I'll fix it."

"How?" I exploded, hands flailing at my sides. "I doubt there are any more auctions coming up, and even if there were, Claudia didn't trust you enough the first time to take me! How in the hell do you expect to pull anything off now?!"

"Claudia may not trust me, but Ray makes the final calls."

"And I'm just supposed to trust *you*?"

Blake seemed to bite back what he really wanted to say, instead chewing out a fib.

"I don't care if you trust me or not."

"Why would I ever trust someone that fucking *lied* right to my face?" I erased a step between us, and not on purpose. My body was traveling all on its own, lightning conducting my movements, my temper, my *everything*.

Contempt narrowed his stare to a slit, his body looming closer.

"When did I ever lie to you?"

Another thoughtless step aimed his way. "Every single time you pretended to care if I lived or died was a goddamn *lie*."

Blake didn't continue our tango of tempers, holding his ground only a few feet away from me. I bet if I looked down, I'd have found his big hands curled into fists.

But I wasn't breaking this tension-taut eye contact, and neither was he. "Is that what you really believe?"

"Yes," I seethed, jabbing my chin up at him.

His mouth, the same mouth I might have described as perfect a day ago, slowly rearranged into a sneer. His jaw clicked, black flames flickering on me as pure malice dripped between the lips of that once perfect mouth.

"Well, then that makes you pretty fucking ungrateful, doesn't it?"

Shock smacked my eyes wide, the not-so-friendly fire beneath my skin

EIGHT

snapping and popping.

"*Excuse me?*"

Whereas other men might have backed down at this tipping point, Blake fucking prodded at my hellfire. "I don't need to repeat myself," he barely got out between gnashed teeth. "You heard me."

"*Ungrateful?*" My eyes switched fast between his. "What the fuck is wrong with you? You just signed my death certificate, and you're calling me *ungrateful?*"

Jaded eyes made a fast bee-line above my head as Blake poorly tethered his control in each chopped word.

"I'll get you out."

"No, you fucking won't!"

Before I knew it, I was charging forward with raised hands and a killshot in sight. My palms pushed against his hard chest, shoving him back with as much strength as my wrath provided. Which was a hell of a lot more than was normally hanging out in my noodle arms.

Even with the added strength, Blake only stumbled back a little, pissing me the hell off even *more.* He righted himself back tall and sturdy as anger burned a dangerous pathway across his face.

"*Don't* do that."

The rebel in me threw its head back and cackled, reveling in defiance as it brought me and my angry hands right back to his chest where I shoved again. *Hard.*

He teetered a few inches and nothing more, flexing his hands at his sides. Something resembling a warning rumbled in his chest that I promptly fucking ignored as I lunged back in for a third push.

That time, he'd had enough.

The growl in my throat sharped to a gasp as Blake caught my wrists and slung my arms behind me, bowing my back as he covered my chest with his. He sealed us together, molten body heat bathing every inch of my skin I just now remembered was still mostly bare.

All I had was the red lingerie and his unbuttoned shirt.

If I hadn't been so fucking pissed, I might have actually been embarrassed.

I struggled against him for all of three seconds before his grip around my wrists turned punishing. A snarl snapped my head forward to curse him out face to face, but I froze before I could as I realized why the scent of cigarettes was so suddenly overwhelming.

He was right there, close enough to singe my tongue with the taste of smoke.

"I told you… not to do that."

Of all the things that could or should have been going through my head at that second, all I could wonder was why the fuck humans need to *breathe* to survive.

I'd have fared just fine in that moment if I didn't have to inhale his exhales or feel the wires in my brain shorting out just because he was near. It was a shitty reason to lose all your sensibilities, and my pride *knew* it, but my lightning was betraying me.

It was trying to get closer to his, trying to make me wonder what happened when lightning struck lightning.

I was a curious motherfucker, but I was a stubborn one more.

"*Let me go.*"

I chopped each word up between my teeth, having nowhere to look but right up at him.

I'd gazed up at this particular night sky hundreds of times over this last month. I sought out its stars that were few and far between and prided myself that I could *see* them against so much darkness.

Blake said it made us special that I could see them.

Lies were always prettier when spun by the tongue of the wicked.

It didn't make us special. It made me fucking *stupid*. I'd been so caught up in the fact that I could see his rare stars that I never connected their dots to make out the full constellation of our story. If I had done that, I'd have seen clear as day the neon message I was seeing now.

Blake was my cancer, and Dominic was my cure.

I'd spent so much energy focusing on the *speck* of light in Blake when there was a fucking sunbeam in Dominic. He was all good—he was *too* good—and he found the good in me and loved it back to some semblance of health.

Blake weaved poetic words about our darkness and made me *glad* for the pain that'd brought me here. To him. I'd gotten so good at ignoring his darkness because he made me comfortable with my own, *proud* of it even.

Love was terminal, but what did it matter if you were already dead inside?

Dominic spent *so* much of his time reviving my half-beating heart, and I'd be damned if Blake strangled it back to the blackened thing it used to be.

Eventually, Blake untangled us and let me move away from him. I went as far back into the corner of the room as possible where I could finally breathe clean air rather than smoke-coated danger.

My hand lifted to split into my hair and push it off my forehead while the other tugged the button-up closed across my tits. My head was pounding all of a sudden, whether from the lack of sleep or the excess of emotions was anyone's guess.

"God, this is a mess." I slipped my head into my palm, squeezing it with all five fingers. "Such a fucking mess."

Blake's reply was stiff from across the room. "I know."

My hand dropped to smack my leg, ringing my incredulity through the air. "Great input. Great, just—" My pinched fingers came up to my lips and released in a flair of dramatics. "Chef's kiss."

Maybe I should have taken my foot off the pedal when the tip of his nose twitched how it did right before he lost it, but I didn't feel like slowing down. Actually, I felt like driving right off the edge and taking casualties with me.

Dark eyes peeked beneath a strict and furious browline. "I *said* I'm sorry."

"Actually," I held a correcting finger up. "I don't think you did. And what good would an apology be anyway? I'm still *stuck* here. You still took me away from the man who was there to *save* me."

Blake inhaled my fury like it was fire, burning his restraint down to a thin crisp. White teeth peeked beneath rigid lips as he repeated, "I didn't know it was him."

"Bullshit," I spat. "I don't believe that for a fucking second. You *knew* it was."

"Well, maybe you'll excuse me for being confused after your little boyfriend *shot* me."

Now that'd been a slap to the heart I wasn't ready for.

All on their own accord, my eyes ripped down to his shoulder and the bandage wrapped tightly around it. A tinge of red pressed from beneath on one side of the white bandage, and suddenly, breathing was a hell of a lot harder.

I vaguely remembered that moment in the garage—a shot going off and Blake swearing out. I hadn't put two and two together that it was Dominic who'd given Blake that bullet wound.

Staring at the bandage, I tried like *hell* to feel proud of Dominic for putting a bullet in the guy who took me away from him. I tried to force the feelings, prying them to the surface… but they wouldn't stick.

Frustration more than anything rallied around my chest that I didn't feel happy that Blake got hurt. I should've laughed at his pain, cheered that my boyfriend put a hole through his arm like he deserved.

Instead, every single inch of me was screaming to close the distance and hold him close because I could have lost him.

What if Dominic's aim had been better...

What if the bullet was just a few inches over...

I slammed my eyes shut, squeezing them tight to keep thoughts about him out. They didn't belong there. Only *Dominic* belonged there. Him and his perfect love and light.

Not the darkness. *I* didn't belong with the darkness.

Blake was already watching me in that intense way of his as I wrenched my eyes open, electric fury buzzing beneath my vengeful tongue.

"I hope it hurt like a motherfucker," I snapped, teeth bared.

The darkest shade of torment fanned up his face, tearing up his eyes and looking more painful than the bullet that tore through his flesh. His upper lip flinched like it was afraid of whatever was boiling beneath.

"I think you'd be surprised at the level of pain I can withstand."

"Well, that's good to know since all I can think about right now is how

EIGHT

badly I want to come over there and fucking *throttle* you through the door!"

"Would that make you happy?" He pinned me beneath a look so fire-hot, my skin actually began to sweat. "Would taking a shot at me finally make Kat fucking Sanders *happy*?"

"What would make me happy is if you didn't blow our one shot at getting away! Dominic was right there!"

"Well excuse me, but I didn't know that I was supposed to let him have you!"

I bristled back, eyeing the man across the room who'd spoken those strange choice of words like he was a stranger himself. My chin pointed at the floor while my stare stayed tacked on his, speaking each word pointedly so there was no mistake to be made.

"I am *his* to *have*."

Blake's stare flashed with pain, the brightest flare of it I'd seen yet, sweeping my heart by surprise and making me wish for a weak second that I hadn't said those words to him.

Even though they were true.

Malice contorted his face. "Fuck this."

He turned over his shoulder and took two long strides towards the door before spinning back around just as fast and coming over to me with conviction searing his irises.

"You know I went there for you, right? I risked my life to get to *you*. And I don't think I've heard one single fucking thank you out of that loud mouth of yours."

I blanched openly, jaw nearly touching the floor. "You want a thank you? Is that it?"

Regret diluted the confidence coloring his stare as a humorless chuckle tipped over my lips. "Oh, excuse me, but *thank you* for bringing me back to this hellhole. *Thank you* for ripping me away from the man who'd come all this way to save me."

I closed the gap between us in stalking steps with every false thank you I handed to him, each one hardening his expression.

"And thank you *so* much for basically signing my death certificate all over again!"

"Kat—"

"What were you thinking?!" I exploded, eyes drilling into him. "What the *fuck* were you thinking, Blake?"

In a snap, he was toe to toe with me, proving us as equals in our rage. "I was thinking that I'd already lost you once, and I wasn't going to lose you again."

My next words stumbled on my lips, falling into a wasteland of confusion.

"But… but that was the point. The whole point of our plan *was* to lose me. To get me anywhere but here!"

"Yeah, well maybe I didn't want to lose you!" He all but shouted in my face, towering over me and bathing me in his concentrated breathing.

"That's not your decision to make! If you're lonely here, *leave*."

I touched my fingertips to his sternum again to push him, but warmth enveloped my hand before I could, Blake holding my palm to his chest.

"I'm not lonely," he spoke, staring right through to my fucking *soul*.

I snatched my hand free, balling them both up at my sides. "Then *what* are you?"

"I've already told you." Black flames danced across my face, flickering dangerously. "I'm hopeless. Fucking *hopeless*."

"Do you want my *pity*?"

"*No*."

"Then what do you want from me!?"

Suddenly, Blake dropped his face really low, digging his answer beneath my skin.

"*Everything*," he rumbled, hot breath nipping my lips. "I want *everything*."

My brain suddenly misfired and shorted out, shutting down all thoughts except for one.

Everything.

Everything could mean so many things, so many easy or simple things. Maybe if I was the same person I was a month ago, I could have lied to myself about what Blake meant when he said he wanted everything.

Unfortunately I wasn't that same girl, and my denial was already falling

EIGHT

short.

"You want everything," I breathed just to taste the truth, tangling our air and watching it stir flames in his eyes.

Sparks of *lightning*.

My heart spasmed an outcry, wailing at me to close my eyes and pretend I didn't see the proof in front of me. It was trying to pretend it didn't see it or feel it either, but that was the catch-22 about feelings.

They were as non-consensual as they were brutally honest.

I didn't *want* this.

I didn't want the chemistry or the connection or the fucking heart attack that came whenever we were close enough to touch.

I didn't want him to want me.

If I could fall to my knees and beg him to hate me, I think I'd prefer that instead.

He hadn't said a word or moved a muscle since professing what he wanted. *Everything*. His partial confession had ripped all the rage from my bones and left a hollow space for something even more hazardous than my rage to trickle through.

My curiosity.

There were incorrigible sensations winding up my throat that planned to ask for answers to questions I shouldn't want to know. I should have tried to swallow them down, should have tried to scream instead of lending my voice to these dangerous questions, but I didn't.

I tracked my eyes between his, feeling the tables between us slant to something *truly* uneven for the first time.

"What does that mean exactly? You want *everything*?"

A buzzing crescendoed in the air, lifting every hair on my arms with not-so-subtle anticipation. His Adam's apple moved beneath his skin as he swallowed thickly.

His eyes, not for one second, ever left mine.

"You know exactly what it means."

I was shaking my head before he even finished speaking. "I can assume, but I don't *know*."

"*Yes*, you do."

"Everything could mean a lot of things, Blake." He slammed his eyes shut and started retreating as I kept arguing, leaving me no other choice than to chase him down. "Just tell me exactly what you mean!"

"You don't want me to do that," he threw over his shoulder, blazing away from me over to the door. Terror squeezed my heart as he laid his hand on the handle, and my strides broke out into a sprint until I laid my fingers around his arm and pulled him back.

"I'm asking, so I clearly *do* want you to tell me."

Blake faced me like it was *painful*. Like his muscles were blades and each move towards me was gutting.

"Why?" His baritone voice was haggard, utterly fucking spent. "*Why* are you asking?"

"Because I wanna know!" I yelled like it was fucking obvious.

"*Why?*"

"Because I *deserve* to know."

He reached behind him to cup the door handle, eyeing me sharply. "I should go."

"Don't you fucking *dare*."

The metal handle whined under his grip as he squeezed the thing, warning bells going off in my head as smoke clouds rolled in from all sides of his glare, swallowing any speck of light left. He was *all* darkness and *all* threatening, and I fucking swore even the walls shook in fear of what was building between us.

"*Goddammit*, Kat," he cursed, voice a grated strain. "Don't do this."

"Don't do *what?*"

"Don't *push* me."

"I wouldn't have to push you if you would just tell me!" The more I pressed, the louder the voice in the back of my head screamed for me to stop.

The door handle rattled loudly in relief as Blake abandoned it, every bit of his potent darkness focused on me. "You are so fucking *stubborn*."

"Yes," I nodded, my heartbeat pounding in my ears. "I am. So just *tell me*."

EIGHT

Almost as if he was begging, he croaked, "Not this."

"*Why* not?"

His eyes snapped shut, my name coming out a sharp warning. "*Kat.*"

"*Blake.*"

With what looked like cinder-blocks holding down his eyelashes, he ripped his eyes open and fixed them on me. Self-restraint made a black sand timer out of his stare, showing me as each last drop dwindled down until it was gone, and all that was left was a man decided.

Burning eyes fell to my mouth as a curse fell from his.

"*Fuck.*"

My feet were rooted to the floor in suspense as Blake ate up the space between us, coming in hot until his hands grabbed my face—

And his mouth covered mine.

Shock zapped life back into my bloodstream as another pair of lips touched mine, basic instincts kicking in fast. My hands came up and shoved his chest, pushing him away so he stumbled back and my feet made a quick retreat on their own.

Blake caught himself and found his footing, both of us not moving or saying a goddamn word.

Holy shit.

He kissed me.

Blake… *kissed* me.

We stared each other down in silence, nothing but our labored breathing to fill the quiet. My hand rose through the air to touch the tingle of where his lips met mine. My whole mouth felt like it'd been brushed by a match, the simmer undeniable and my mouth watering for more heat.

And I did feel a sting of it coming on.

But not on my lips, and not the kind I wanted.

Heat pricked the backs of my eyes, hot tears swelling like the sun itself was watering their growth. Blake switched his eyes between mine that were fastly watering, a hot sting of rejection filling his own.

My heart jerked painfully, petals of tears running over so fast, I didn't even bother catching them. They traced cold lines down my cheeks, and

Blake watched them fall with a jagged break widening in his stare.

His lip curled up in a quiver of resentment just before he spun for the door.

I honestly had no idea what I was doing anymore as my foot lifted to follow, my crumbling heart taking hold of the reins.

"*Why* would you do that?" My palms flattened against his back, pushing and hitting as he kept on walking away. "*Why?!*"

Angry tears poured down my cheeks as I followed and shoved him, slapping his back and crying because I didn't know what else to do or how to stop it. I pressed him, and he kissed me. I pressed him, and *he kissed me.*

"Why would you do that?!" I shouted, pushing him again as he reached the door.

In a flash, Blake whirled around, locking his grip around my upper arms and spinning me until my back hit the door. I gasped—I think. My brain was a scrambling madhouse as Blake closed in, my head knocking back against the door as he trapped me.

"Tell me not to do it again," he breathed like a *threat*.

Like a warning he knew I wouldn't follow.

My lips parted fast to deliver the words… but all that came out was a whimper.

Blake's eyes were blacker than I'd ever seen them as he held me, like the ocean at the dead stroke of midnight during a storm. Waves were tumbling and crashing, but you couldn't *see* the danger unless you were already drowning in it.

I'd tried so fucking hard not to drown in Blake.

In the beginning, I didn't understand this *thing* always moving between us, and then once I understood it, I got pretty fucking good at ignoring it. I brushed it off, I renamed it to try and trick myself, I avoided it until it hunted me down and *demanded* to be recognized.

Blake didn't break our eye contact as more waterworks spilled over, spelling out my weakness for him on my cheeks so he could read it and I could weep. I was a wreck inside, heart thrashing and crying and beating itself senseless because it was just so confused.

EIGHT

It knew I had a love with Dominic that was so pure and good and *powerful*, but it couldn't deny that with Blake, there was something uniquely intrinsic about us. Something *rooted* in our souls and raw and apocalyptic to any willpower I had left to say no to him.

Fate was such a vindictive bitch to steal me away from a perfect man and put me with a man that was perfect for *me*.

Staring at Blake through the burn of saltwater, I felt my heart collapse and wave its white flag, wanting to touch and explore and *burn* with him.

Blake and I were fated to explode into oblivion, and I *wanted* it.

I wanted our spectacular fucking ending now more than ever.

The energy between us was absolutely *screaming* at this point as I bounced my eyes between his, his challenge burning in my veins.

Tell me not to do it again.

I lost more tears as I thought about how easy it should be to say. *Don't kiss me. Don't kiss me. Don't you dare fucking kiss me again or I'll hate you forever.*

Consequently, the only person I'd end up hating after this was myself.

"I can't," I admitted, voice breaking.

My horrible, dirty, filthy confession left my lips and reached out to Blake, the loose grip he had on his emotions showing me the *exact* moment it hit him.

I didn't know that a million colors existed on the spectrum until I saw them all tornado through his eyes. Black, blue, silver, gold—fuck, *every* color was a feeling of his, a messy, chaotic, *beautiful* feeling.

Somehow, he was shocked and not at all surprised. Pained and relieved. Ecstatic and miserable. Anticipating and dreading.

He wanted me, and I wanted him, and we were both fucked for it.

My breathing turned to panting as his smokey eyes charred over with *need*, a strangled curse escaping his lips and evaporating the last of my ability to put a stop to this.

The buzzing in the air hit its climactic chorus.

Rough palms cupped beneath my jaw.

Soft lips struck down on mine, and Blake and I did what we were destined to do… and we sank.

Our passing ships finally collided, exploding in the darkness we both were made of.

White hot energy *burst* beneath my skin as Blake claimed my mouth, a whimper edging in my throat. Sensations of ecstasy went zipping from the tip of my head to my curling toes as he kissed me like he'd been dying every second up until now. He stole my air without regret to fill his starving lungs, moved his lips over mine to restart his blackened heart with the friction.

He was a thief I'd invited in to ransack and destroy me because it was really only fair. I'd been sneaking away pieces of his heart all along, and it was his criminal right to ruin me for it.

I wholeheartedly believed Blake wanted the imprint of his mouth on mine, to bruise the memory of this kiss into the fabric of my swelling lips so that I never forgot the harmony between us. However dark, however malignant it was, he wanted me to remember it.

I had to reach up and anchor both my hands around his forearms just to survive the intensity of it. My tears were still slipping fast because my heart was *still* breaking, but he and I both ignored them.

They were like rainfall during a hurricane.

White noise against the wreckage of lightning tearing apart the world outside.

Blake brushed his thumbs against my tears as his only acknowledgment, cleaning my guilt away so we could both keep pretending it didn't exist. Or at least I thought.

My grip around his forearms broke away as his hands that cupped my face slipped in opposite directions, one binding around my bare waist and the other breaching into my hair at the nape of my neck.

Suddenly, my head was being yanked back, and my lips were the loneliest kind of cold.

Blake was breathing hard when I flashed my eyes open.

"Tell me to stop," he demanded.

Panting just as hard, my brows lugged together. "What?"

EIGHT

"Tell me to stop." As if he couldn't help himself, Blake dropped his forehead to mine, voice exhausted of all restraint. "You're crying, so you should tell me to stop or else I won't be able to. I'm not strong enough to stop myself anymore unless you tell me to, so just…" A sigh that tasted like anguish washed my parted lips. "Just do it."

If he meant to say that in hopes it would stop the flow of my tears, boy was he fucking wrong. They only came on stronger, Blake brushing them away one by one with a look of torture grooved along his face.

As much as I should have wanted to oblige him and tell him to go away, I knew with sweeping certainly I couldn't. Not now. Not after I'd had a taste of the apple before the poison took hold.

Blake truly was my cancer, and right now, I would willingly die from his affliction.

I shook my head weakly, rolling my tender lips together. "I'm not crying because I want you to stop," I whispered, all of me trembling in the harsh spotlight of ugly truth. "I'm crying because I don't."

I watched the stars align in his midnight eyes as he understood me—*our stars.*

We were constellations written out of our reach, meant to meet, meant to fall, and meant to crash. Our destiny was destruction and implosion, and all we could do was brace ourselves.

Needing no more proof that I was powerless just like him, Blake closed the gap and pressed his lips back to mine where they didn't belong, but we were both too fucked to care.

We kissed each other the exact same way—too fucked up to care how desperate our roaming hands were, how greedy our lips were, how wrong every single touch of it was.

I couldn't even say that it didn't feel wrong, because it did. It felt like when the heroin first hit my bloodstream, and I was craving it again before it was over.

Kissing Blake felt like the kind of wrong that felt too good to be right.

My addictive personality wanted a *deeper* hit of him, to suck him into my soul where he'd live forever as my permanent personal high. So I did the thing all bad people did and I pushed us further, sliding my tongue along the seam of his lips until he *groaned*.

Until he gave me the same pleasure back and pushed his tongue inside my mouth.

More stars. More fireworks. More hell on earth that tasted a fuck of a lot like heaven.

Blake sighed into my mouth, a thoroughly satisfied noise, stroking my tongue with his and tasting like dwindling smoke and all things wicked. That was right around the time my feet left the ground, Blake lifting me with his good arm that he had squeezed around my waist, his other tangled in my hair to deepen our kiss.

We both made a noise at the same time that bordered the line of agony and pleasure as we kissed so deeply, I could *taste* lightning on my tongue. A delicacy too potent to survive, but here we both were, handing ourselves over to it like fools.

I was shameless just like he was about wanting to be closer, wrapping my arms around his neck and memorizing the texture of his hair between my fingers. I wanted to memorize everything about him, how his heart hammered when I fisted his hair, how hot his hands were as they roved my body, how wet and plump and perfect his lips felt after being ravished by mine.

I wanted to record all of it to memory before we had to stop.

And we'd have to stop soon. Blake knew it too, and maybe that's why he set me back on my feet but didn't dare let me go. No, he spun us around away from the door, walking us back until the plush of the bed hit my legs.

He didn't push me down on it, and I didn't offer to climb back. Neither of us were fools enough to think anything of this kiss was about sex.

It was all about us and finally fucking admitting how brightly we would burn together.

"This is what I mean by everything," he said between stroking lips and heavy breathing. "I want your kisses, your smiles, your tears, your soft fucking snoring in my ears every day when I wake up."

I let out something between a sob and a laugh, and he kissed me harder

EIGHT

because of it.

"I want everything there is to have about you, Kat. Every goddamn piece of you."

Fuck, his tone was so certain and his kisses were too addicting. If things were different, I would have stayed in that room kissing Blake until my lungs gave out. My heart knew that if Dominic wasn't in the picture, there would be nothing to stop me from being with Blake in every way two people could come together.

I'd give myself over to him with zero reservations.

But not only was Dominic in the picture, but he was the *center* of my picture. My heart would always revolve around him like he was my sun, and Blake and I would never be what we both knew we could.

So I gave us one last good kiss—*no*, not just good.

Epic.

I gave us a kiss to last an eternity just like we would.

Blake and I, what we felt, what we were—the stuff of stars and lightning and destruction—would last forever. Even after we left each other, even after this kiss ended, we'd always be parts of each other that would last.

Blake and I were infinite, a sequence that would never end.

With greater difficulty than I'd ever done anything in my whole life, I pulled back from our kiss, trying not to cry.

It wasn't fucking working, the broken shards of my heart stabbing up my throat as Blake pressed his forehead to mine. Our breathing steamed up the space between us, blurring away the longing that was already stretching between our mouths.

I couldn't look up at him. I didn't have the guts. All my guts were sloshing around in my stomach and screaming at me about what a coward I was.

They were right, but I couldn't break down with him here.

He'd comfort me and hold me, and I didn't deserve any of it.

I tried to steady my breathing, but it still came out a shaking mess. "I need you to leave…"

He actually stopped breathing, the push and pull of burnt spearmint over my face pausing entirely. "Kat—"

"*Please*," I cut him off to beg. "*Go.*"

Reluctance consumed him, nothing subtle about how badly he didn't want to leave. There wasn't going to be anything subtle about my breakdown either, my bones already quaking with the impending category five disaster.

The first thing Blake took back to himself were his hands, slowly removing them from my waist. Next, he picked his head up off of mine, leaving my forehead feeling feverish in that way that was both cold and scorching.

The last piece of him to go was his chest that'd been so fixedly pressed to mine. He stepped away, allowing dead air to fill back into the hollow space around my body where his had warmed and kept my heart company.

Now, that same heart was bleeding. Just bleeding all over the place. For him. For Dominic. For all of us.

It kept pouring out agony as the floor creaked with each step Blake retreated back to the door. I still couldn't look at him, keeping my watering eyes pinched shut as I pictured each stride he took away from me. I even imagined his painfully handsome face turning over his shoulder to give me one last wanton look before I heard the door open and close.

And silence took over.

Brutal, *mocking* silence.

I crumbled faster than a building imploding under the pressure of the silence, tears rolling out fast as my knees hit the floor. The first sob broke out of me and crashed the quiet to pieces, exploding in tiny truth bombs all over the walls.

My shame, my selfishness, my betrayal splattered like guilty blood on the walls as I cried myself fucking senseless from the agony.

But the pain, *god* the pain was one I'd worked hard for, wasn't it? I'd *earned* this pain all on my own with my stupid fucking actions and my stupid fucking heart.

And there wasn't a person alive who could lie to me with a smile and say I

EIGHT

didn't.

NINE

DOM

"What part of 'you're off the case' didn't make it through your brain, Reed?"

For the last ten minutes, I'd been standing with my back against a squad car while Chief Thomas chewed my ass out. He'd even driven all the way down here to Atlanta to do it in person.

Things blew up, including mine and Ryan's cover story for being here, as soon as he raced out of the mall with that girl we'd found passed out.

Chief Thomas had been going on about how insubordinate I'd been, how reckless, and how I embarrassed him and our entire department, but I was barely registering any of it.

My mind was still with Kat.

I'd seen her.

I saw her perfect face. I heard her perfect voice.

And then I lost her.

All goddamn over again.

"Dammit, Reed!" His fist pounded on the trunk of the squad car, jarring me from my thoughts long enough to spare him a cursory glance.

He was pissed.

"You better damn well give me your *full* and *undivided* attention when

NINE

I'm speaking to you considering the bull you and this hero stunt are gonna put me through."

I rolled my mouth together to keep the disrespect biting behind my lips restrained, replying with the only thing that mattered.

"She was here."

"I don't give a rat's ass if *she* was here. *You* shouldn't be."

This time, it was my hands that rolled together to keep the fists that were forming at their ends from swinging.

"You had orders, Reed. You directly disobeyed those orders, and you dragged Detective Locklin into it."

"All Ryan did was drive me up here." The lie came out as stiff and stale as the air had turned outside at the Walford Mall. There were still a few straggler news crews and corporals putzing around. Archie and the rest had already left. "I guess he tried to follow me once I went against orders, but I never saw him inside the building."

"That's because he was busy saving a young girl's life." The Chief tossed that fact at me like it was holy water and I was the deranged and misguided. "Thank the Lord for that silver lining in what's otherwise a mountain of horse shit because of you."

"Sir, Kat was *here*. I saw her—"

"Well, that's interesting because no one else did, so all's we have to go on is your word, and I'm not sure how much I trust that nowadays."

The lack of waver to his voice and the strict point of his stare made my jaw clench so hard, I heard bone crack. I could have done or said a lot of things to move the conversation in a conducive direction—apologized, pleaded for forgiveness, promised him my tail was tucked back between my legs where he liked it.

Instead, I met him with the same rigid disappointment he was giving me.

"I'm sorry to hear that."

His mustache was even more paled by sunlight as it moved over his hidden upper lip.

"I'm sorry to mean it."

The chief and I stood with our arms crossed in a parallel to each other, and I realized the stance was two-fold.

On his side was everything I saw myself becoming if I stayed the course. A man of the law who'd served his time on the job and did his due diligence to stay in his lane and rise through the rankings. There was a version of me that had pictured with pride myself standing in the Chief's shoes twenty years down the line.

That picture still existed, but pride no longer framed the vision.

More like unease.

All I'd ever wanted was to do good. I wanted to be a good father and husband, a good man, a good officer of the law who protected the innocent and people he loved. For a long time, that's exactly what I did. I was happy chasing the bad guys I was told to chase and content in the image I'd created for myself.

Model employee, model citizen, model father and husband.

Four out of four had been compromised in the last few months alone. I'd become the poster child for insubordinate and reckless, I was distracted whenever I was with Maya, and in just a few weeks, I wouldn't even be a husband anymore.

I wouldn't recognize myself if I met the man I was today six months ago. In fact, the two men probably wouldn't even get along. The old me would regard the new me with judgment and contempt. He'd probably be a little bit of a dick, too.

Because in all truth, he would have been envious.

Today, I was a man in love. A man no longer living on the sidelines of his own life.

The Chief sighed, his distended belly falling and rising as he held my stare. "I'm really disappointed in you, Dominic." It took the spontaneous strength of ten men to keep my eyes from rolling. "You have so much *promise*. Before all of this nonsense, you were everything a subordinate should be. Respectful, dutiful, a real *yes* man."

"I was compliant and passive in every way that mattered," I shot back.

It was a soul-crushing thing to realize you were a passive passenger in your own life, but that was where Kat came in. She shifted my gears from

NINE

neutral to drive and stomped her foot on the gas.

I'd thank her every day for it once I got her back.

And I *would* get her back.

"And when did being compliant ever become a bad thing, Reed?" Chief's eyes narrowed, his crows feet deepening. "Is that something your mistress put in your head? Because I happened to like you just fine before all of this."

The word *mistress* spewed into the air, and I nearly lost that flimsy grip I had holding back my fists. That cheap and filthy label didn't belong anywhere near Kat.

She wasn't my mistress.

Against all odds stacked against us, she was the great love of my life.

I bypassed his question, knowing I'd end up cursing him rather than answering.

"Sir, are we done yet?"

"Dominic," Chief shifted his stance and heaved another sigh, and I assumed that no, we weren't done just yet. "I'm going to ask you a question, and I want an honest answer."

I nodded him on, despite that nagging itch in my sternum saying I probably didn't want to hear whatever he was about to ask.

Of course, the itch was correct.

"It's not a secret that you've changed since you started seeing that girl, but your *life*... it's a disaster, is it not?" *Rhetorical*, my brain answered so I didn't. The chief was far from done. "Your marriage has fallen apart, you've risked your life and now your job for that girl when you've known her for, what, six months? That girl has turned your life upside down and—"

"Sir." I held up a hand to stop him. "Are you asking me if she's worth it?"

With the utmost serious look about him, he nodded.

"Yes. Yes I am."

I stood there for a moment, the breeze outside playing with my hair, and stared long and hard at the chief. This was a man I respected the hell out of who clearly didn't hold any for me. Or else he'd have kept that insulting fucking question to himself.

From the moment I told him about my indiscretion, I lost any good standing I had with him, and I would have to make peace with that. I couldn't change how he saw me if he chose a limited view.

However, how he chose to speak about Kat…

I'd rearrange all his teeth in his mouth to help correct how he spoke about her.

"You're right that I've changed, and you're right that my life has been turned upside down," I began, voice steady as a boulder. "But you're wrong about her."

Chief Thomas didn't blink away his disappointment that I'd chosen to defend my love for Kat quickly enough. I saw it skitter through, and it only added more steam to the wildfire in my heart.

"*That girl* absolutely flipped my world upside down, and I am grateful every day that she did. I'd been barely living before *that girl* came into my life and revived it. She is smart and wildly funny, and she'd probably tell you that no, she's not worth it because that's the kind of selfless, hardheaded woman she is. She loves fiercely and proudly and has given me more happiness and laughter than I've ever had before. *That girl* has given me a second chance and a kick in the ass that I didn't know I needed, but my *God*, did I need it."

Surprise with a side of fear serviced the chief's stare as I stepped into him, bringing my conviction up close so he wouldn't mistake it for anything less.

"And *that girl*, her name is Katerina Sanders… and she's worth it all."

He breathed deep and audibly, digesting my impassioned response.

From somewhere off in the distance, an engine revved to start and a bird squawked in the sky. The world kept moving as he held the silence, nothing discernible to his expression.

"I guess it's a good thing you feel that way then." Chief paused for a beat, and regret flickered in his tired stare. "Because you're hereby suspended from the force pending an investigation."

He ducked his gaze to the ground as he laid out the verdict, too much of a

NINE

coward to look me in the eye as I absorbed it. Maybe it was a good thing he wasn't looking though, because I definitely forgot to hide the momentary impact of shock.

I rocked back on my heels, skirting my gaze up to the blazing sun, and breathed deep.

When I heard Chief Thomas was driving up here, I prepared myself to be suspended or even fired. I broke his rules, and I knew there'd be repercussions. I'd accepted that my actions had consequences, and I didn't regret coming here one single bit.

Didn't mean his ruling didn't still leave a sting on my pride.

Chief laid his hand palm up out to me. "Hand over your badge, son."

I removed it quick so the sting wouldn't linger.

Laying my badge in his hand, I stomped down the feeling that I was handing over a part of myself. The day I'd received that shiny bronze badge had been the happiest day of my life until the day Maya was born. I cherished that chunk of metal for years.

Now it was gone.

"Hopefully this'll be a wake up call for you, Reed." He pocketed my badge, giving me a cursory glance. "Get your head back on straight."

Smartly, I shoved my own hands in my pockets to keep them from fulfilling any promises to my temper.

"With all due respect, Chief, I don't need a wake up call." I caught his curious eye as I straightened my spine, using my height to stare him down. "All I need is her."

Flashes of my beautiful girl's face, tear-stained and screaming, ran behind my eyes, and my jaw cemented down with a stiff exhale.

She was out there. She *needed* me.

Now my chains were loose, and as if she was standing right behind me, whispering her siren voice into my ear, I heard her tell me to run with it.

Run without a rule book and see how freedom felt against my skin.

My boots crunched against asphalt as I turned and walked away from the chief without being dismissed, deciding exactly where I'd start on this off-beaten path to find my girl. Determination roiled hot in my veins.

I needed answers.

Which meant I needed to have a chat with a certain soon-to-be ex-wife.

TEN

DOM

I'd been back at the house for hours before Heather finally walked through the front door.

The sun had begun to set behind the home I used to call mine, basking a softer light in the living room than the conversation that was about to commence inside of it deserved.

If a meteor shower of fire and brimstone were happening outside instead, that'd be a hell of a lot more fitting.

My parents had moved their things over to my place after I got back, eager to be anywhere else but here when Heather arrived. Maya had gone with them despite her pouting.

She'd been without me for less than forty-eight hours, but according to her, it'd felt like a year.

Truth be told, it felt like that to me too.

Watching Kat disappear inside that van had taken an easy couple years off my life.

The fight I was about to have with Heather was sure to knock off a few more.

Condensation sliding down my glass of bourbon wet the pads of my fingers as the front door opened and echoed closed. I watched the droplets roll down the smooth glass, remembering the night Kat made me a drink much better than this when she first watched Maya.

She'd intrigued me that night and simply never stopped.

Intrigue had turned to love and love had turned to loss.

I was a man at the end of my rope to get her back by my side, back in my bed, and back in my arms. It was also true that I'd rather take that same rope and tie it around my neck before I had to have this conversation with Heather.

She was going to be pissed.

Royally, fantastically, murderously *pissed*.

But I had to ask.

The rhythm of her heels clicked against the tile like they always did whenever she went anywhere with hard flooring. It was like her own anthem or entrance music. Even if we went somewhere with carpet, she'd bevel her feet to bring attention to whatever pair of designer shoes she was wearing.

During our marriage, if we left an event without a wife making an envious comment about her shoes or a husband grimacing at the price tag, Heather would be in a huff the whole ride home.

As she poured out of the hallway and into the living room, she was anything but in a huff as she found me sitting in my red chair, an easy smile on her slender face.

"Home empty-handed, I see."

My glass of bourbon took the brunt of my reaction as I quietly strangled it in my palm.

I should have known that's why she floated in here on cloud nine.

Tossing back a mouthful of alcohol, the bitter poison corroded away the nasty reply charging up my throat. Instead, I bypassed her comment altogether.

"How was your weekend?"

She seemed surprised that I asked, cocking a manicured brow up at me while setting down her purse. "You suddenly care?"

A weathered sigh rolled through my chest as I shifted in the chair,

TEN

exchanging my drink to the other hand to wipe my wet palm on my slacks.

"I was just making polite conversation, Heather."

She bought it, or at least pretended to, sauntering over to where I sat with a prized smirk on her mouth. "And I'm supposed to assume we're being polite now?"

I gave a noncommittal grunt. "Better late than never."

My neck was forced to crane back as she stopped next to the chair, and I quickly wished I'd chosen a different starting position for this battle. Her baby blues focused on my drink in hand, a curious ring running around them both.

I didn't like that look of hers. I never really had.

"Are we drinking to commemorate the nanny's memory?" Her long legs took her back towards the kitchen. "Because I'll drink to that."

I swiped my hand fast over my mouth, physically blocking anything from escaping it. Steam expanded within my ribs, filling my lungs full of hot air I couldn't let out.

Not just yet.

I scratched my fingers along my growing scruff as Heather snatched a bottle of chardonnay from the refrigerator to pour herself a glass. She watched the white wine splash around the glass with that tiny smile still spackled to her face, my blood pressure escalating every second it stayed put.

It was one thing not to cry over Kat's absence.

It was another cold-hearted thing to relish in it.

My conversation with Ryan on our drive back from Atlanta wormed into my brain as I watched her cheers to Kat's misfortune. My stomach turned the same sick way it did then, and the bourbon wasn't helping anything.

There could have been lots of reasons Kat screamed Heather's name right before she disappeared inside that van. Ryan and I came up with a short list of top contenders on the drive back.

Kat was plainly in bad shape when I saw her, so it was possible she was hallucinating that Heather was there when she cried out her name. She could have been referring to another Heather entirely, and my ex-wife had nothing to do with it. Ryan had even pitched the idea that Kat was trying to tell me it was okay to move on and go back with Heather as her final selfless act.

I hadn't had a genuinely good laugh in weeks, but that last one did it.

The Kat Sanders I knew would burn in hell before setting me up with Heather, and I'd happily join her.

Of course, when we'd exhausted all the sensible reasons, only the insane ones were left.

The ones that brought me to sit in this chair and nurse this ridiculously expensive alcohol.

All I needed to know was where she was this weekend.

Then I could move on. Then I could turn my focus back to reasons that made sense and leave this insanity in my rearview mirror on the road to finding Kat.

But I wouldn't be able to stop agonizing about it until I asked her point blank. The question was like a bad meal I couldn't stomach anymore, and I just had to get it out so I could feel better.

"Did you work this weekend?" I tipped my glass back, filling my mouth with the pleasant sting of good liquor as Heather readied for her first sip of chardonnay.

She met my stare across the room.

"I did."

"Were they out of town listings?"

"No, actually. A few new homes popped up in the charming little neighborhood across from the church on 5th."

Specifics were good. Specifics were harder to lie about.

"My parents said they didn't see you at all," I kept going for good measure. "You must have enjoyed the hotel you were staying at."

"It was a Ritz. Of course I enjoyed it."

"The one in downtown or the one on Fairbanks Ave?"

"Downtown. They have the indoor pool I like."

I nodded slowly, digesting her story and finishing off my drink. "Did you see anyone while you were there?"

TEN

She eyed me over the top of her glass, arcing a taunting brow.

"Like a lover?"

Unamused, my jaw set. "Don't play coy."

"I'm not." She took a polite sip of her wine. "Would my husband care if I spent the weekend with another man?"

I thought about it honestly and then answered the same way.

"No. I would be happy for you." *And send a prayer up for the poor schmuck.*

Heather wrote me off with a dramatic eye roll. "That's just your guilt talking."

Irritation tickled the back of my throat, an eye roll of my own barely refrained. We couldn't run off the tracks already. If we started screaming about my affair, we'd never get to screaming about anything else.

And I still needed answers.

"So no one saw you this weekend?" I pressed.

In a blink, diamond blue eyes hardened over the lip of her wine glass. Suspicion cut in from all sides. My gut fisted tight.

"Dominic, are you *interrogating* me?"

Instead of lying, I set my empty glass on the floor and bit the bullet.

"Is there a reason I should be interrogating you, Heather?"

As expected, she didn't take well to that.

Hot blue flames erupted in her eyes, her glass of wine abandoned as she came barreling around the kitchen counter.

"What kind of question is *that*?"

The heat of her anger brushed against mine as she skidded to a stop in front of me. Holding her glare, I laid my palms flat on the arms of the chair and pushed my weight up until I dominated the height difference between us. Even with her heels on, I had a good advantage over her as the air thickened with contempt between us.

"The kind I need you to answer now," I rumbled explicitly.

She openly gawked, her mouth falling apart while a rue little twist occurred at both ends.

"Oh, that's rich. So you think you're allowed to ask *me* where I was this weekend, but all I get to know about your weekend is that you went 'out of state', probably searching for Little Miss Bitch?"

Heather's glare cut back to watch me, knowing I'd physically struggle not to explode as she slandered Kat right to my face. My already cramping stomach rolled over as I realized just how much Heather enjoyed using Kat to hurt me.

But she wouldn't go that far, my logic butt in. *She isn't capable nor does she have the resources to go that far.*

The nerves in my stomach settled as my logic set in.

And not a moment too soon.

"You could have asked me," I stated, keeping my tone neutral. "As Maya's mother, you have that right."

As if my offer was daft, she scoffed. "Why bother when I know you went down to Florida?"

I pulled back, watching my ex-wife curiously.

"Why would I go to Florida?"

She brought her hand up in the air, gesturing flippantly. "Because that's where they found that one girl you were looking for all summer."

My head cocked at her, wondering in silence if I'd told her that information or if the news stations had shared it. Must have been the news because Heather and I were barely speaking when Jessica Serrano was found.

"I was in Georgia, actually," I offered, stepping around her.

Or at least, I tried.

Biting fingers caught around my bicep, jerking me back to see her eyebrows meet her hairline.

"Georgia?" Jaded blue eyes switched fast between mine, like she was expecting me to be joking. "What would make you go there?"

"A tip."

"From who?"

Maybe a few years back, I'd have told her, but we didn't have that kind of relationship today, nor did I trust her with any information about Kat.

"That's classified."

The urge to fight me blazed across her stare, pink-painted lips pursing

TEN

and the grate of her teeth almost audible. She fought it back though, smothering it down and sealing her temper tight. The clamp of her nails retracted from my arm as she took a step back, but kept the point of her gaze daggered on me.

"Well, did you find anything there?"

She'd schooled her voice back to a tone uninterrupted by emotion, but being with the woman for nearly thirteen years provided me with a dictionary of her expressions.

This one, tight eyes and mouth, meant she was upset but didn't want to tell me why for some reason that would likely come back to bite me in the near future.

If that expression ever came up during one of our countless fights, it always made me nervous.

That feeling of concern was worse now.

So I lied.

"Like you said, I'm home empty-handed."

Neither of us relinquished our terse stare-off for quite some time, her inhaling deeply and pretending to accept that was all there was to it and me trying to dissect what her intrigue in Georgia meant.

Probably nothing more than surprised that I'd briefly gone back to our home state.

Probably nothing more, my logic reassured.

With that out of the way, Heather was surprisingly the one to refocus the conversation. Her browline jumped just barely, ticking in a dangerous kind of way.

"What, so am I a *suspect* now?"

Hearing it said aloud dropped a particularly heavy load of bullshit on my shoulders.

It made no fucking sense.

The notion now out in the wild, it brought my hand up to pinch the bridge of my nose, a dull headache digging at my temples. "Look, I'm aware it's complete lunacy—"

"*Good,*" she cut me off, tone clipped and furious. "Not only is it lunacy, but it's completely insulting. You're up in arms about where I was this weekend when you left your family to go gallivanting around looking for your *mistress*."

"That's not—"

"And how do you think your daughter felt being put second to Ms. Sanders *again*, Dominic?"

My attention ripped up, sharp as a fucking ax.

"My daughter is second to no one."

"Oh please, babe." Heather shouldered past me, heading back towards her abandoned wine. "That's more of your guilt lying for you."

I planted my feet firmly in her direction. "And just how am I lying?"

She found her place behind the kitchen counter again, a shard of incredulity nailed through her eyes. "Can you honestly tell yourself that you've been the prize of fatherhood since that *tramp* came into our lives?"

Her insult slammed against my chest, ruminating around in the hot air of my lungs, testing me—*pushing* me—to be as hateful as her.

"I'd say until the last month or so, Maya was happier with Kat around than she'd ever been," I replied, resistance lodged in my throat.

"And what about this last month? Has she been happy then, or do you not even know because you're so focused on the nanny's case that you haven't had time for your own daughter?"

"She was at my place six days last week, Heather. *Six*. Your leg to stand on is toothpick thin, don't you think?"

Her hands went palm up in surrender. "I'm just telling you what Maya told me."

The hot steam boiling up to my head suddenly quieted, draining out to leave a cold dew of unease in its place.

My chest got a little tighter as I asked, "What did she tell you exactly?"

A flash of annoyance whirled around her eyes as she swallowed the gulp of wine in her mouth, pulling the glass away. "You're all she talks about when she's here. Lately, it's all about how you're not around or working at home so you can't play her ridiculous games." She pointed her glass in my direction, a look of pre-confirmed suspicion aimed at me. "I presume

TEN

your mom's been picking up a lot of the load?"

My heart felt blindsided, an ache blossoming out of the unexpected turn our conversation had taken. I rubbed the heel of my palm over my chest, but not even that smoothed out the pain.

"When she's here, she's an incredible help, yes," I answered almost unwillingly.

Like she'd pulled an ace straight out of the deck, Heather tilted her head. "And when she's not, do things like quality time and bedtime stories go by the wayside?"

I tried to hold Heather's stare. I really did, but a well-worn feeling of shame weighed my gaze down and dropped it off to the side. My shoulders slumped, the fight taken right out of them.

"Occasionally," I mumbled, admittance never tasting so bitter.

Not every night she was with me, but enough to make me feel like shit, I'd passed the duties of bedtime kisses and stories off to my mother. I basically lived in the rabbit hole of Kat's case, digging myself deeper every day to find her.

Maya and I still spent the mornings together where I made breakfast and she'd talk my ear off with every thought she had. Was it a tad more difficult to concentrate on all she was saying when my night before was spent working and worrying if the woman I loved was even alive?

Yes, sure.

But I didn't realize I'd gotten so distracted that Maya would talk to her mother about it.

She didn't go to Heather for anything these days, really.

If she'd felt strong enough in her little heart to talk to Heather, then I'd really dropped the ball.

The anthem of Heather's walk clicked around the tile in the kitchen, coming out to where I stood in a pool of guilt. She tipped her chin up at me, forcing me to catch her eye.

She blazed with victory, her glass of chardonnay clutched in one palm like celebratory champagne. The scent of gardenias was suddenly overwhelming as she took her victory lap a step closer to where I stood, brushing her arm against mine.

"This is just a suggestion, but how about you stop worrying about nonsense like my whereabouts and start worrying about how much you're willing to slack off as a parent for a side piece?"

She didn't stick around this time to watch her insult ripple across my face. Honestly, I didn't feel much of a reaction in my muscles anyway. My entire body was still drowning in that pool of guilt, too heavy to react to Heather's slur when it was too focused on how right the rest of what she said was.

Suddenly, I craved a second glass of bourbon.

Maybe even a third.

I trudged back to the glass I'd set on the floor and scooped it up, tearing apart my head trying to figure out how to fix things with Maya while I kept looking for Kat.

My daughter still came first, and *god forbid* it was her life in danger, I'd focus on her and pray to fucking God the police could find Kat. That wasn't the situation however, and battling the balance of being a good father to my daughter while trying to save the woman who made both our lives better would be tricky.

I walked over to the kitchen counter where I'd left the bottle of bourbon uncorked. Sighing, I rested my empty tumbler on the counter, my elbows sinking down on the granite next.

I needed a nap. I needed a thousand fucking naps.

But all I had was $400 worth of bourbon, so bottoms up.

As the first sip hit my tongue, I decided I'd just have the one and then head back home. My dreary eyes lazed across the counter, noticing Heather forgot her purse down here.

I picked my heavy arm up and slid the thing over—*another* piece of designer shit that cost way more than should be legally allowed. My lips wet as I tipped back another swig, getting ready to call up to Heather and tell her she'd left her purse.

The breath I was getting ready to shout with caught in my throat as something inside the purse snagged my eye.

TEN

A folded piece of paper.

The glass and a half of bourbon in my gut suddenly curdled.

It was a receipt for gas, the date, timestamp, and location the gas was purchased at facing up at me. A spontaneous heat swamped my body as I blinked down at that folded piece of paper again and again.

The receipt glared at me, my palms beginning to sweat as I read it.

Date and timestamp: Yesterday at 6:13 am.

Location:

Atlanta, GA.

ELEVEN

KAT

The next morning, I woke up with a splitting headache and to the alarm of a loud *bang*.

I jolted up on the bed, headache bashing around my skull and punishing me for moving or even waking up at all. The headache was a dear gift from last night and all the tears I'd cried out until I was a dehydrated husk of shame.

The loud bang, well that'd be from the asshole who just busted into my room.

"Get up. Boss wants you."

It was Sergio's voice that scraped across the room, and before I'd even stepped foot into this new day, I hated it.

Blake hadn't let anyone else deal with me, let alone come into my room, since we became close. The fact that he wasn't here now was a devastation. I felt his absence with every part of me that could feel, and it felt like all the blood in my body had been ripped clean out.

I was flesh and bones but nothing warm underneath.

And I had no one to blame but myself.

I cradled my throbbing head as I got off of the bed and let Sergio grab my arm and pull me into the hallway. There wasn't much use in fighting him now, was there?

I was a dead woman walking.

My bare feet could hardly keep up as Sergio yanked me down the stairwell, muttering about picking up the pace. We reached the first floor, and I remembered as a sweeping of gazes came my way that, yeah, I was still *only* in Blake's shirt.

During all my crying last night, I took off every bit of the lingerie but the underwear and buttoned up Blake's shirt so it could hug me during the night and I could pretend it was him.

Theresa was in the kitchen as we passed it, as were a few other girls including Zoey. Theresa kept her gaze down while Zoey caught my sight, a curious worry knit between her eyes that followed me back until a wall cut us off.

He led me down the same hallway I'd been down when I first arrived at the brothel, and I wondered which of Heather's parents I was about to face.

After being drugged, assaulted, and crying all fucking night long, I was in no shape to deal with *anyone*. But I assumed I kind of didn't have a choice, which summed up my life pretty exactly.

We reached the same thickly wooded door from a month ago, and Sergio rasped his knuckles on it. Not even a second went by before—

"Come in."

The voice inside was just as dry and hollow as the first time I heard it.

Looks like it's Daddy Dearest for me today.

Sergio opened the door and, just like the first time we did this song and dance, shoved me in so I toppled and almost ate it on the really expensive rug inside. Except this time, I didn't have the same energy to snap around and give Sergio the evil eye.

I didn't have *any* energy left.

Must have cried it all out.

The door shut behind me and locked me in as I pushed my shoulders back and pretended I had any strength left to hold them back with. My dry eyes went first to the large desk in the same place it was a month ago with the same devil sitting behind it like he was then too.

Ray and his massive desk and the ugly brown furniture hadn't changed since the first time this horror scene played out.

There was, however, one *key* out-of-place difference.

And it began and ended with the other man inside the room, his hands behind his back like a soldier at command and his attention straight ahead.

Blake didn't turn to look at me as I entered.

He didn't even flinch.

The hollow winter sitting in my veins grew colder, *biting*.

"That's quite the peculiar attire choice, Ms. Sanders." My wide-eyed focus ripped from the back of Blake's head to Ray, the point of his stare fixed on my bare legs. "Don't feel bothered to dress up on our account."

My knees knocked together, fingers pulling the hem of Blake's shirt down as far as it could go. Maybe it was working in such a degrading business for so long, but Ray had mastered a way of talking that was both objectifying and condescending.

That skill wasn't just a language he'd mastered on his tongue, but in the way he looked at you.

I felt like a prized meat that he knew was rotting on the inside.

"Blake here has been filling me in on what happened at the auction yesterday." Ray steepled his fat fingers together on top of his desk, deadened eyes latched on me while I tried my fucking damnedest to not look at Blake. "It seems you'll be staying with us longer than originally scheduled."

Seems that way.

"I've already contacted the buyer I had picked out for you to see if he was still interested in a purchase, but unfortunately he's looking to stay low on the radar after the FBI's raid." I didn't even have time to drop to my knees and belt my thank you's to whoever in the universe deserved them for that small miracle before Ray kept going. "This entire mess is a headache I didn't need." He pressed closed his aging eyes, his wrinkles digging deeper at the sides. "But we'll make due with what we have."

He peeled his eyelids back up, finding me at the receiving end of his satisfied cruelty.

ELEVEN

"And we still have you, Ms. Sanders." The sinister spark in his eyes brightened. "I am going to make a small fortune off of you yet."

There was something so strange about standing in this same spot I was a month ago, being read the same story all over again where the ending hadn't changed one bit. I tried to rewrite a new ending—Blake and I both had—but the villains in this story were still victorious and the damsel in distress would still die.

Nothing had changed.

At the same time, everything was different.

I was different, my insides rearranged to make room for these new feelings that I couldn't explain or defy. They were a part of me that I didn't think I'd ever understand, but I wasn't sure I was meant to either.

Fate. Love. Serendipity. They were supposed to be confusing.

Those words were made up of nonsense, and that's why my head was so full of it lately.

Blake's was probably full of it too. His nonsense was just prettier than mine. A poetic mess.

Mine was a total clusterfuck.

"Our options are limited for how to proceed now that the auction fell apart and your buyer is no longer interested." My nonsensical brain found a way to focus on each and every terrible word coming out of Ray's mouth, even when it was trying *everything* to reach out and see if my connection with Blake was telepathic too.

"What started as a favor to my daughter has quickly reached the point of inconvenience, and I think we can all three agree it's in everyone's best interest if you were gone sooner rather than later, Ms. Sanders."

He slid a heavy-lidded look up to Blake, a smug glint to his peeking smirk. "I'm sure no one's more ready to get rid of her than you."

Blake chuckled—a dark, hollow noise—and it rattled around my bones like a scream in an empty house. He tipped his sculpted chin towards the floor, a lop-sided smile showing on his profile.

"Got that right."

Some three words were built to warm your heart.

Those three words were built to destroy mine.

It crumbled fast, every falling piece made of sharp glass that cut and maimed my insides raw; even breathing felt like a gust of icy wind blowing against a festering wound.

So much for all of those scars I'd gathered throughout the years that were supposed to harden my heart to a steel trap. As it turned out, none of that mattered.

Every single one of us was walking around with glass hearts in our chests and hammers in our hands. Some of us destroyed others before they could take a swing at us. Some of us were simply blindsided, waking up one day with a hole between our ribs and a shattered mess left inside.

I was one of the blindsided idiots.

Maybe Blake was just saying what Ray wanted to hear. Maybe he really wanted me gone now that I'd hurt him.

That was the heartbreaking part.

I couldn't tell.

I couldn't *feel* him.

Ray delighted in Blake's consensus, leaning back in his chair so it rocked with his weight. "That's good to hear. My wife's been up in arms about you and this one back here." He gestured a lazy finger my way. "She's convinced herself something's going on between the two of you. Tried to get me to fire you for it."

The muscle around my spine twisted too tight, refusing me to move or breathe.

Because being *fired* around here didn't mean what it meant at any other job.

Blake didn't seem phased. Didn't even drop a hint that he was worried I nearly got him killed. He kept his gaze forward and his voice flat.

"I can assure you that's not the case. Ms. Sanders is part of my job, and that's as far as our relationship extends."

It was all I could do not to let my hurt show as it tangled up the muscles in my neck, chipping away at the stiff expression I held over my face. If he and I were alone, I would have let it run free like dripping paint, not afraid

ELEVEN

to show him just how vivid my hurt was because of the words he'd chosen.

Because when it all boiled down, he wasn't entirely wrong.

Ray gave an acknowledging grunt, pulling open a drawer to his desk and producing a fat cigar. "I tried to reason with Claudia, but she wasn't interested in hearing sense. I asked her what man would bring the woman he's in love with back here rather than just let her run free, but—" Unlit cigar captured between his fingers, Ray dragged a pointedly amused look up to me.

"Women are willful creatures, aren't they, Ms. Sanders?"

I hadn't been expecting to be addressed, so all I gave was a jerking nod.

Satisfied, Heather's father brought his attention to fishing out a lighter and shifted gears back to business. "Without any future auctions coming up in the area, I've given Blake one week to find you a personal buyer. The process is more intimate, more paperwork on our end, but the payout will be double what we would've gotten at the auction."

Instead of a lighter, Ray placed a box of matches on his desk. Old school matches.

"If he can't find you anyone for our asking price or higher, we'll move you to one of our out-of-state facilities." The rip of sparking fire tore into the air as he struck a match across its cardboard box. Orange flames erupted on the tiny stick trapped between his fingertips, stretching tall and fat before dwindling down. "For your sake, hope Blake finds you that buyer. You might not find our other facilities as... *charming* as here."

My eyes were on the lit match as it drew towards the end of the cigar Ray stuffed between his teeth. No one spoke as he took his time, flexing his power to hold the conversation—my fate—in suspense until he finished puffing his cigar.

Which was fine. I couldn't say anything anyway.

Nope, pretty sure my throat had closed right up when he mentioned 'other facilities', and the hand of fear hadn't let my windpipe go yet. In fact, I was pretty light-headed by the time he finished priming his cigar and blanketed the room in a cloud of dizzy white smoke.

Ray's attention wasn't even on me when he resumed talking, but on the fat tobacco stick he was savoring.

"I'll set Blake up with a camera to take the photos that get sent around to potential buyers looking for a female with your specificities. If you choose to *not* participate in the photoshoot, the alternative is a permanent stay at our other facilities. As I already stated, you might not find our other stays as accommodating as you would a buyer."

He made his mouth into an O around the end of his cigar, puffing and filling his office with cursive trails of smoke.

"It's either one man who gets to play with you whenever he wants or hundreds," he regaled, voice thickened by the smoke he talked around. "The choice is yours, but I imagine by the look on your face, I won't be hearing of any issues in regards to the photos."

My face.

What the fuck must my face have looked like right now?

A deer in headlights, leg caught in a trap with wolves descending on all sides?

Yeah, that probably about summed it up.

"I never like when business gets *messy*, but I'm a man who made a fortune out of nothing…" Ray tapped his index fingers against the burning cigar, embers dusting into the air. "And I'll make a fortune out of you, Ms. Sanders."

He turned his cold stare up to Blake.

"Run her buyer across my desk whenever you get one."

Blake nodded an affirmative, "Yes, sir."

"And don't accept anything less than 100k for her."

"Will do."

"Good man." And just like that, Ray waved us off. "You're both dismissed."

Those words were like a rope loosened around my neck, oxygen flooding back in and immediately tasting so fucking sour. My whole face wrinkled and repelled the cigar smoke slathered all across my tongue.

The flavor was horrible, and I found myself wishing it was Blake's smoke in my mouth instead.

My head got all foggy with this kind of tangy smoke as I pivoted on my

ELEVEN

heel towards the door to leave. I wasn't really thinking as I reached out and grabbed the door handle all on my own. Not until a swarm of body heat attacked me from behind as another arm shot out and grabbed the handle first.

"Let me do it."

Both my hand and heart froze as Blake's voice rode over my shoulder and nestled inside my ear, a gruff and detached thing.

He got the door, probably not to be a gentleman or any dumb shit like that, but because I probably shouldn't be going around opening doors willynilly on my own around here.

Much less in front of the boss.

Blake let me duck out first and followed next, shutting the office door behind us. The hallway was empty, Sergio nowhere to be seen.

Blake and I were alone.

His presence was at my back, but I didn't offer to turn around. Truth be told, I was scared shitless to look him in the eye. Those eyes of his were fucking graphic, and I didn't have the ovaries enough to read what they wrote about me after what I did to him yesterday.

My guess was that he didn't want to see me either since he didn't look my way once in the office, and even now on the other side of it, he just brushed around me and jutted his chin forward.

"Come on."

He didn't even grab my arm to pull me along.

Blake just moved away from me, his long legs taking him farther and farther and expecting me to follow. Albeit hesitant, I scurried to catch up and realized fast that we were heading back to his bedroom.

At just the idea, my stomach scrambled like a bowl full of eggs, cracked shells and all.

I'd practically *lived* in his room for a month, and now, as we reached the threshold of it and he opened the door, my feet suddenly grew roots and refused to budge.

Blake moved inside, making it halfway in before realizing I wasn't behind him. His chin led the turn over his shoulder to pivot back to me, and in one second that was either really thoughtless or entirely against either of our control, our eyes found each other across the distance.

And I was *breathless*.

Breathless in less than a *second*? I didn't even know it was possible to lose all of your air that fast, but Blake's fire didn't follow the rules of physics or biology or really anything for that matter.

His fire was lawless, and I was a chronic victim to it.

As expected, his eyes were fucking shouting at me. Things I didn't want to hear. Things I already knew and hated. I actually had the thought to cover my ears *and* my eyes as turbulent emotion zig-zagged across an onyx black canvas.

It was so much. It was *too* much.

And all my fault.

"I don't think you really wanna be caught standing outside my room right now."

My lips parted in a dry pop, words surrendering on my tongue.

He had a point.

So I nodded and uprooted the soles of my feet, stepping to the other side of Blake's door and shutting it softly behind me. The corner of his floor suddenly looked *hella* interesting as it gained my full attention, my back pressing against the door and my bare toes digging into the carpet.

I even caught myself wringing my fingers together like a scolded and scared little kid.

That's kind of exactly how I felt. Like I'd shrunk down three sizes and shouldn't be allowed to do anything without *real* adult supervision ever again.

"Can you not stand so fucking far away?" Blake snapped suddenly, shattering the quiet. "I'm not gonna kiss you again if that's what you're afraid of."

Oh shit.

I nearly fell over trying to catch that elephant in the room he'd just lobbed my way.

"I'm not—" I cut myself off, pissed to hell that he'd managed to fluster me in such a short amount of time. "I'm just *digesting*, okay? Everything that went down in the office just now was… a lot."

The weight of the world dragged his eyelids closed, a somber breath rolling out.

"None of it's gonna happen."

My heart skipped several beats. "Really?"

"Yeah."

Skepticism slanted the angle of my head. "Seemed pretty cemented in place back there."

Contempt flickered a lightning strike across his shaded stare. "Had to make the show look good for the boss."

Understanding quieted my distrusting brain as I gave a slow nod, barely able to hold his gaze.

"So…" I eased one very small step closer. "You're not finding me a buyer?"

"I don't know what I'm doing." He dropped his head into his hands, pressing the heel of his palms against his eyes. "I just said that to buy us more time."

"You think there's a point to trying at all?" I asked, not because I was cynical, but because I was realistic.

Blake ripped his head up from his hands, black flames glinting with dangerous spite.

"I *said* I'm getting you out of here."

"Okay." I nodded fast in surrender and backed off the subject. It might have been the first time I backed off of any argument *ever*, but Blake deserved a win.

Plus, I wasn't in any position to fight him.

If he wanted to keep trying to find me a way out, I wouldn't stop him.

I just wouldn't blame him either if he came up empty-handed.

Blake's mouth flattened to a grim line almost immediately, probably realizing why I gave in so easily. My eyes fell to his thinned lips, remembering against my will how contrastly plush and full they felt moving against mine.

My mouth tingled, like static electricity looking for a charge.

I rolled my bottom lip between my teeth, biting down on it hard enough to make it whine and put a stop to the sensation. That electric tingling feeling had meant danger before last night.

Now, it was the definition of consequence.

Instead of looking at Blake's mouth, I looked around his room. His pack of cigarettes on his nightstand caught my wandering eye first, his ashtray catching it next.

"Holy shit." I was moving before I realized it, cutting the distance between Blake and I in half. "How much did you smoke last night? There's gotta be a fucking pack's worth here *alone*."

My eyes were on his tray of overflowing cigarette butts when he palmed the whole thing in his hand and crossed to the bathroom, throwing back at me, "My smoking habits are none of your business."

I traced his steps, placing my feet in the flames he'd left behind. "It is when I know why you do it," I called after him.

The sound of him emptying out the ashtray against the trash can in there echoed in hard knocks. I waited for him to finish with my hands fit to my waist and standing on the line where his bedroom carpet met his bathroom tile.

His dark head of hair came around the corner, eyes searing me in a drive-by glare.

"And why's that?"

I whipped around to watch him set the ashtray down, tossing my threat right at his back.

"Do you really want me to say it?"

Every muscle I could see beneath his black shirt froze, tension tightening the air. He couldn't really be all that surprised that I'd figured out his die-quick scheme, could he?

I'd pegged that masochistic addiction of his within my first week here.

As I expected, he didn't make me say it. Just hovered a few fingers over a brand new box of Marlboros, tempting that death we both knew he was racing towards.

I still couldn't believe he smoked close to an *entire* pack of those last night.

His lungs must have been blacker and sicker than they'd ever been.

And all because of a kiss.

A diseased kiss, at that.

Our souls were already sick with grief, sick with death, sick with love when we met. We were walking and moving and living because our bodies worked and our brains functioned like they should, but there was a virus lying dormant in us both.

When we met, it stirred. When we touched, it popped an eye open to keep watch.

When we kissed each other last night, the virus finally erupted to life like the opportunistic bitch it was and began its takeover. It spliced itself into the molecules Blake and I were individually made up of and fused them together.

It fused *us* together.

Our souls that were already so sick and so broken finally found a cure in one another, a warmth to the cold, a relief to the pain, the eye of the hurricane we'd been just barely surviving.

But it was a double-edged discovery.

You see, the cure in and of itself *was* the disease.

Wanting each other were the symptoms. *Taking* each other was the cure.

Knowing we could never have each other was the interminable disease.

I kicked my toe against the carpet, sheepish and miserable. "See? I told you that you wouldn't ever want to be anything other than enemies with me."

Our night back in the kitchen with the cupcake and stories of dates and darkness felt so far away now. Even though it was only two nights ago.

Blake was already watching me when I peeked up, the scorch to his stare saying he knew exactly what I was referring to.

"I'm all fucked in the head." A pathetic huff of a laugh poured between my lips as I gestured a flimsy hand up to my head, my front teeth nabbing the corner of my lips and chewing my voice out in a mumble. "I fuck everything up."

My stare was having trouble staying still on his, my chest feeling all bruised and sore. Blake wasn't having the same problem, gripping my gaze like a death wish.

"I like that you're fucked up, so your method of rejection is flawed."

I shook my head fast, the words coming out like they couldn't be stopped. "I'm not rejecting you."

Black eyes narrowed on me, and even I had to wonder what the hell I meant by that.

"Then what are you doing?"

I inhaled deeply, eyes bouncing all over his room wishing the answer was written somewhere in it. "Trying to accept responsibility? I don't know, *apologize?*"

Whenever I thought his eyes couldn't get any darker, any *hotter*, he proved me wrong.

"I don't want to hear that you're *sorry* for kissing me."

"I'm not sorry for that," I said, again without thinking and without being able to stop the words. They sounded confident too, and in the same second I said them, I realized I actually meant them. "And I don't regret it either."

Also true.

The kiss was wrong. There was no questioning that. There was also no questioning how much I fucking sucked for letting it happen. No, *pushing* for it to happen like the storybook villain I was.

But I didn't regret it.

Blake deserved better than for me to regret it. He deserved a lot better than me in general. He shouldn't be stuck with feelings for someone who shoves him to the edge of something he doesn't want to fall off of because he knows how much the impact at the end of the fall is going to hurt.

But I didn't stop. I kept pushing him and pushing him because I was greedy and I wanted to *know*. Maybe I was a bit of a masochist too, because I just so *badly* needed to confirm everything I already assumed about us.

Blake and I *were* special. Our diseased souls meshed like broken glass fitting back together. It was painful, and there was no escaping without scars, but the end result was something breath-stealing that reflected rainbow shards of light straight through our darkness.

He and I filled in the empty wounds and holes that life inflicted on both of us and made something fractured but still *whole*.

Dominic was already so whole when we met that he and I together were like fitting the entire night sky around the sliver of a crescent moon.

He consumed me and protected me.

Blake balanced me and all my crazy.

There was a softening to his strict expression so subtle, if he was any other person, I would have missed it. He even seemed to breathe a little easier hearing that I didn't regret our kiss.

I made a mental note to loathe myself harder for the pain he'd been in thinking I would.

"Then what are you trying to apologize for?" he asked, shifting slightly. This deep rumble of his was the sweetest sounding as of yet, but his glare was still bitter.

"Pushing you when you told me to stop."

"I did tell you to stop."

"You begged me to," I corrected, helping him and hating me.

He nodded. "And you didn't listen."

"I never do." I shook my head, breath wobbling as my weakness flowed over. "I'm... *dumb* that way. I'm stubborn and I'm selfish and I'm stupid and I'm sorry. I'm *so* sorry."

I forced him to know what it would feel like to have me all to himself, and then I took it away.

If I ever did manage to get out of here, and I got to tell Dominic what happened, I almost hoped he left me instead of forgave me. I wasn't sure I could handle being forgiven for something that hurt the two men in my life that gave a shit about me.

Blake and I stared at each other long and hard, his thickly shaped brows outlining a story of suffering while I could feel the guilt shaping out mine. A quiet exhale sunk his gaze to the floor, and he ended up walking right past me.

I stayed where I was until I heard the overhead fan of the bathroom turn on, but not the door close. On hesitant feet, I turned to see light spilling out of the wide open bathroom door.

Blake was standing inside, head hanging low with his good arm on the counter, his hand splayed out to hold up his weight.

I followed and fucking prayed I was reading the invitation of the open door right. I took it as a good sign when he didn't throw me back out when I came up next to him inside the bathroom.

I took it as a better sign when he let me touch him.

We stood side by side in the mirror, his bandaged shoulder sitting a good six inches higher than my perfectly uninjured one. His body had been broken to save me while I got away with nothing but scars on the inside that you couldn't see.

Daringly, I let my hand float up towards him, grazing my fingertips across his arm just beneath his bandage, not realizing until my skin touched his just how cold my hand was. I dragged my touch up the smooth skin of his bicep, feeling his warmth, his strength and fragility tied between his muscles, realizing all at once it wasn't just my hand that was cold.

All of me was freezing without Blake.

Him and his familiar fire.

"I never meant to hurt you," I whispered, tracing his coarse dressing.

Saltwater pushed at the backs of my eyes as he let me touch him, a lump strangling my throat that I tried to ignore. The hair on the top of my head tickled as a heavy exhale blew down on it. My heart, the bruised and confused thing that it was, cried for me to grab his arms and throw them around me so I could bury myself against him to stamp out this pain in my chest.

Several softly buzzing seconds went by before I heard him swallow thickly, murmuring deeply.

"I know."

Air rushed into my lungs, grateful for the sound of his voice. I even got a little stupid in my thankfulness, kissing my forehead to his arm and dropping my hand to his wrist to hold him tighter.

ELEVEN

"If you want to kick me out of your room—"

"Shut up," he clipped, exasperated.

"Okay." I nodded against his arm, all breathy and willing to do whatever he said. "Shutting up."

We stayed like that for a few moments, me gripping his arm for dear life and drinking down mouthfuls of relief and Blake not moving a muscle. That was until he pulled away the arm I'd been clinging to and made my eyes go wide asking why.

"You're holding onto my fucked up arm," he mumbled, slowly tracking his stare around mine.

"Oh," I breathed. I fucking *knew* that. "Sorry."

Now, there was about a ruler's width of space between my chest and his, and the ball was entirely in his court. I was helpless from here on out, gazing up at him and waiting to see what he'd do.

"I suppose I should be relieved that you feel it." He caught me watching his lips move, understanding brimming in his smokey stare. "Wasn't so sure after you read the poem."

It took a second before I realized he meant *his* poem. The one about the rose.

The one I thought was about his Abigail.

Dots connected in my head, chest clenching. *Aching*.

"I'm the rose?" I asked, afraid of the answer that was already in his burning eyes.

"And I'm the moon," he confirmed.

And Dominic was the sun.

God, how fucking heartbreaking was that? But also so goddamn beautiful. Was that considered poetic irony?

Fuck if I knew. It didn't matter.

I was the rose, and I belonged to the sun while the moon stood in the dark and watched the whole thing. The fact that Blake so *profoundly* knew it made me want to breakdown all over again, but he stopped any of that embarrassing nonsense from coming.

And all he had to do was reach up and touch me.

A feathered graze of his knuckle across my cheek, gently brushing away a strand of disarray hair behind my ear, and that ache in my chest went right out.

Like water pouring over a campfire, it steamed out fast and left *such* a pleasant sizzle.

"Do you hate me?" I whispered, shamelessly chasing his soft touch by pressing my face against his hand. His knuckles curved around sweetly, his big palm cupping my cheek as he studied every inch of my face.

He shook his head, but his mouth remained set and unmoving. Again, he didn't need to say any words. How he felt was already expressed in his eyes.

He didn't hate me.

But he might have felt something just as dangerous.

"I really am sorry."

As I said it, his stare fell down to my mouth. He studied the lips he'd kissed senseless, and I let him. Rolls of memories played across his eyes, some tender, some heated, some heartbreaking. He replayed our kiss and thumbed my bottom lip as if he could touch the torrid memory of it.

I stayed silent and still as he took one moment for himself.

To savor. To memorize. To be selfish.

At the end of it, a ghost of a smile hovered his lips as his stare came back to mine.

"It was worth it."

TWELVE

DOM

First thing the next morning, I hit the road and got Ryan on the phone.

"Dude," Ryan's slang hit my ear, burning my patience down to the brittle bone. *Dude* was not the first word I wanted to hear this morning. "I just heard what Chief did to you. I feel like *shit*. You should have said something—"

"It's fine," I cut him off, turning the steering wheel with one hand. "It was my idea to go down there. I was prepared for the consequences."

"Still, you shouldn't have taken *all* the heat."

The backs of my teeth knocked together, tightening my jaw in frustration. I didn't call to talk about being suspended. It wasn't exactly my favorite subject.

"Ryan, I need a favor." My car rocked as I pulled into the gas station on the corner by my new place. Ryan was all too quick to agree to help.

"Yeah, man. Whatever you need."

I wasn't sure he'd be so keen once he heard the favor.

"I need you to track Heather's phone." Pulling up next to a pump, I jammed the gear into park. I sat back in the driver's seat, listening impatiently to the silence on the other end.

Getting antsy, I asked, "Did you hear me?"

"Yeah, yeah I heard you." His voice had gone up an easy two octaves. More silence stretched over the phone line, and I could practically hear him overthinking.

"*Ryan*," I stressed, popping my driver's side door open and turning off the car. "I need you to do this for me. You're at the station. I'm not."

"Okay, but *why*?" His voice morphed to a hush on the other end like he was crouched at his desk trying to make sure no one heard our conversation. "Does this have to do with Kat saying Heather's name?"

"That, and she lied right to my face when I asked her where she was this weekend."

"She did?"

I hummed an acknowledgement, sliding my debit card into the pump, and paid for the gas. "She told me she was at the Ritz here in town, but I found a receipt for gas in her purse that said she was in Georgia."

A sharp exhale went between the line. "Holy *shit*. That's weird."

"What's even more weird is that I called the Ritz, and they did have a Heather Reed on file for this past weekend, but no one showed up."

I started pumping gas into my Explorer as Ryan digested.

"Dude, that's so confusing."

Trust me. I know. "Which is why I need you to track her."

A pause lingered between us, and I could smell his hesitance flaring up again.

"Do you plan to follow her?"

"That is sort of the point of tracking someone, isn't it?"

"Sure, but—" He broke off, jitters crawling underneath his voice and upending his previous confidence. "Do you know how sketchy that looks to track your ex-wife? Or how much trouble we could get into?"

"Ryan, I'm already suspended. Worst they can do is officially fire me, and I'm not all that sure I'd care at this point."

The lie tasted as bitter coming out as I thought it might.

I'd care. I'd care a fucking lot if I lost my job because of all of this. My job—by definition—was to serve the people, and isn't that exactly what I

TWELVE

was doing trying to rescue Kat? If I saved a life, it shouldn't matter that I had to work slightly outside of the restrictions of the job which were downright fucking debilitating.

If they fired me for this, the bruise it would leave on my ego wouldn't fade for years.

But the bruised ego would be worth it if I got Kat back. A job was just a job, but someone like her was once in a lifetime.

Ryan groaned into the receiver, his resistance collapsing.

"When did *you* become the bad influence on *me*?"

My gas tank hit its limit and I pulled the nozzle out, giving Ryan the credit he deserved in my head for how correct he actually was. I *had* turned into the rebel between us.

Talk about a plot twist.

Another sigh into the phone and then his voice got quiet.

"Give me ten minutes."

He hung up, and I went inside to grab a bottle of water and a protein bar. I didn't know how long I'd be on the road or where exactly I was following Heather to. Could be close. Could be hours away.

By the time I got back to my car, Ryan had called me back with a location on Heather's phone.

"She's at the *docks*?"

"That's what it says here," Ryan confirmed, puzzled like I was. I thanked him and hung up, wondering what the hell my prissy ex-wife was doing all the way down there.

The docks weren't exactly a high-end part of town. We had a small port that went out of there that handled a tiny portion of the state's largemouth bass and catfish game. The docks were mostly that—a half mile of docks loaded up with fishing boats and your occasional small-town, seafood eatery.

It wasn't any place Heather had stepped her Prada-wearing foot before.

And I'd know. When we first moved down here, I used to ask Heather if we could bring Maya down there so I could teach her how to fish. My dad taught me when I was around her age, and I wanted to create those same memories with my own kid, but she put her foot down.

She said the docks were dangerous and dirty and no place for a little girl.

But maybe they were a place for grown women and their dirty little secrets.

I made the forty-five minute drive down that way, a headache creeping up the muscles in my neck that'd been strung as taut as steel ever since last night.

Actually, ever since Atlanta.

Scratch that again.

I'd had a permanent fucking headache since the moment someone took my girl away from me.

It was blazing against my temples as I pulled into the cluster of parking spots sitting facing the water in front of the marina. There were only three other cars in the lot, all of them empty with their owners likely out fishing and enjoying the partly sunny day.

Not sitting in their cars stalking their ex-wife.

This was, admittedly, not one of my finer moments.

Still, I shifted my car in park and killed the engine, doing a quick sweep through my front window for any passing brunettes with a slim figure and a purse full of secrets.

There wasn't a sign of her anywhere, and I threw back a swish of water to cool down my body temperature that was escalating per second I sat there waiting and dreading. I didn't want to see my ex-wife. Almost ex-wife.

Whatever.

In fact, I'd never *not* wanted to see her more.

She'd be so out of place here amongst the running groups of kids and fishermen with their cut-off sleeves and overhanging guts. She'd clash like a glitter bomb exploding all over a place like this. After I sat there a few minutes, I began to convince myself that if I hadn't seen her by now, she probably wasn't here at all, because how could you miss a twelve carat diamond rolling around in the mud?

The answer?

You couldn't.

TWELVE

No matter how much you might have prayed to death you could.

Out of the corner of my eye, walking in her classic anthem heels, I saw her.

And I was right. She was a sore thumb strutting down the worn wooden docks in her designer heels like it was a Paris runway.

My heartbeat thumped up into my throat as I sat up, pushing my sunglasses up into my hair so there wasn't anything obstructing or warping my view of her.

Even as I watched her move down the line of boats, I still couldn't believe it was her. My logic tried to say the sun casting a reflection against the water was playing tricks on my eyes.

But the longer I watched her move in a way both delicate and predatory, I knew there was only one woman on Earth who could execute such a contradictory walk.

"What the hell are you doing here?" I mumbled to myself, shifting forward in my seat to get a closer view of Heather as she passed six or seven average sized fishing boats before stopping in front of one.

I squinted, watching her mouth move in the distance as she said something to no one. She cast her gaze around the area, tapping her foot, visibly impatient.

And mad. Why was she mad?

Heather huffed dramatically, lifting her hand to shade above her eyes. Movement caught my attention coming from the boat she perched herself in front of, someone emerging from inside.

Every muscle in my body tensed.

I blinked and I blinked at him, positive now that something in the air was making me see shit that wasn't really there.

He *couldn't* really be there.

He offered his hand to help her get on board, and she swatted him away and climbed right on his boat all by herself. He cracked one of his smarmy grins and said something to make her browline furrow.

I couldn't move or take in oxygen as I watched them interact, an alarm blaring in my head that this wasn't right. It was screaming that I needed to move and get to her and rescue someone dainty like her from someone violent like him.

But she didn't appear to need rescuing.

Heather moved right past him and dipped inside a part of the boat that was covered and hidden like she'd done it a hundred times before, and he followed her inside.

They both disappeared and left me to spiral and wonder…

How the *fuck* did Heather know Tommy Lynch?

* * *

It was just under a half an hour before Heather reemerged.

My stomach ached the entire time she was in there, and it'd taken every resistant cell in my body working overtime to not bust inside his boat while she was on it and demand to know what the hell was going on.

One thing was crystal clear: this had *not* been their first interaction.

Heather was too at ease as she left down the dock, sliding her sunglasses on and walking like she always did—as if she had the entire world and everyone on it hanging by her fingertips.

My steering wheel got a good strangling as she stepped onto the sidewalk and walked out of view.

I couldn't run after her and shake her down for answers yet. Cornering Heather without knowing *exactly* what for was asking for an attack I wasn't prepared for.

She wasn't the one I was sticking around for anyway.

Tommy peeled out from inside his boat not too long after Heather departed. The sun bounced off of his face, and I imagined my fists doing just that whenever I got close enough.

This goddamn parasite had been beneath every stone I'd turned over

TWELVE

searching for Kat, and now I find him with Heather?

No level of filth he'd sink to should have surprised me anymore, but using my ex-wife to get to me wasn't one I'd anticipated, and I cracked all ten of my fingers as I stepped out of my car. Every bad thing that happened to Kat started with this motherfucker, and I was about to make damn sure it ended with me.

Tommy moved off of the docks, sauntering towards the line of restaurants on the water's edge. He passed the Seafood Shack: the place he'd used as an alibi on the day Kat went missing.

Luck must have been on my side because he was coming my way. Car keys flashed in his palm as he twirled them around his fingers, looking off at something and not at all aware of my presence. My head twisted to the side as a Jeep beeped and unlocked only a few spots down from where I'd parked.

He was angling himself right for it, and I decided now was a time as good as any.

Hand on my car door, I slammed it hard enough to startle the wafting sea-salt air and Tommy too.

His head jerked in my direction, eyes falling on me as I folded my arms over my chest.

"You making it a habit now to fuck with the women in my life?"

The air was actually pretty nippy outside, but the anger boiling beneath my skin was doing a good job at keeping me warm. That, and the smug smile that curled up across Tommy's face once he saw me.

That eyesore cranked the furnace up tenfold.

He slanted in my direction, stuffing his hands inside his jean pockets.

"You following me, Reed?"

I gave a composed shake of my head. "Just felt like going fishing. See if I could reel in a big catch."

A glint of teeth showed as he flashed a shit-eating grin. "Aw, is that how you think of me? Hate to break it to you, but I'm just not that sweet on you."

"Are you sweet on my wife?" I squared my shoulders back, planting my feet firm against the asphalt. "That why you're meeting with her inside your dinky boat?"

"Ain't she 'bout to be your ex?"

Tension sewed together my jaw and cemented my teeth in silence. Amusement widened across Tommy's face, and the blood in my fingers tingled.

"Is that the reason for your sudden interest in her?" I asked.

"Who said anything about sudden?" He drifted another step my way, cruel enjoyment speckled in his shark eyes. "Who says we haven't been shacking up for months since you got yourself that pretty young thing to play around with? The one that went missing. Oh shoot, what's her name?" He snapped his fingers, pretending to search in his head. "Katherine something?"

I sawed my jaw from side to side, focusing on my breathing so I couldn't focus on how easy it would be to snap him in half like a fucking twig right now.

My hands were shaking for it, *begging* for it, and he would have deserved it too.

Instead of giving into bloodlust, I played it cool and leaned back against my car, crossing my feet at the ankle.

"Unfortunately for you, Tommy, I'd know if you were sleeping with Heather."

His intrigue piqued as he closed in another step.

"Oh yeah? How's that?"

"Because I saw her coming off your boat just now, and I know what that woman looks like when she's spent and satisfied. The only thing she looked coming out of there was bored and irritated."

Tommy cast his stare off, hollow laughter knocking around his chest. When he brought his eyes back to me, it was with a noticeable notch carved out of his towering ego.

"Nah, *bitch's* not really my type."

"So then why were you with her?" I pressed.

"Why don't you ask her that? Seems silly that two married folk can't find

TWELVE

a way to talk to each other."

Tommy was only a few feet from me when I began to re-strategize in my head how to get the answers I needed from him. He wasn't going to play along like this.

I flickered a quick survey of our surroundings, noting only one gentleman about thirty feet away who had headphones stuffed inside his ears.

"Communication was never one of Heather's strong suits," I replied, forming a plan.

"She was communicatin' *fine* with me just now."

"And what exactly was she communicating?"

His face was so fucking punchable. "It's too fun how badly you wanna know. You're a riot, Reed. You know that?"

"And you're getting on my last nerve," I spoke through dwindling patience, willing him to just move *one* step closer.

"Oh really?" He cocked a wily grin, eyes narrowing on me. "What're you gonna do if I hit it? Smash around a table and a couple chairs like you did when you were asking me about that missing girl of yours?"

Tommy was having the time of his miserable life as he got up nice and close, crossing the finish line right up to me.

"What's a good ol' boy like you gonna do to me?"

I held his taunting stare over the bridge of my nose for only another half a second before acting. My hands came up, pushing down on his shoulders as my knee went soaring up. I nailed him right in the stomach, a winded rush of pain coming out of him as he keeled over to grab around his waist.

But I wasn't done and sent another quick jab of my knee right to his groin, thinking of my little spitfire when Tommy went down like a ton of bricks.

My wingtips scuffed right next to his head as I shifted to watch him properly squirm around like a wounded animal.

"That about answer your question?" I mused.

Him being relatively immobile and groaning in pain made it easy enough to shuffle his dead weight into the backseat of my car. I nabbed my spare pair of cuffs from my back pocket and secured them around his wrists, slamming the back door closed.

I gave a cursory sweep of the area to confirm no one was watching before jumping in my front seat and starting up the car.

"Where the fuck'r you takin' me, Reed?" Tommy whined from the back.

I shifted into reverse and backed out of the parking lot, ignoring his question.

Because truthfully?

I hadn't a goddamn idea.

THIRTEEN

DOM

Thirty-five minutes down highways I didn't recognize and passing tiny towns I'd never been to, I pulled off into a thick throng of forest on the side of a winding dirt road.

There hadn't been any passing cars for a few miles, so it felt like a safe enough time and place to disappear behind the wall of trees and leaves all surrendering their vibrant green to the greedy chill of winter.

My Explorer swayed as I drove us over uneven terrain, the inside of the car oddly quiet.

Tommy hadn't said a word since we left the docks, and I hadn't offered any. I'd spent most of the drive asking myself what the fuck I was doing or how I planned to pull it off.

I didn't have to ask myself if it was the right thing to do.

I knew it wasn't.

The non-stop cramps squeezing my gut knew it wasn't.

But I'd been doing the right thing my whole life up until recently, and it'd landed me here—driving to the backwoods with Tommy Lynch handcuffed in my backseat because he knew things about my wife I didn't and more about Kat's disappearance than he was letting on.

And I'd do as many wrong things as I needed to get her back.

Pulling into a dense section of tall-reaching trees, I parked the car and turned off the ignition. Silence stretched the length of the car, making the air inside heavier and breathing through the thought of what I was going to do more difficult.

Tommy was already watching me as I lifted my gaze to the rearview mirror.

His eyes were dead even now. Hollow. Any genuine human emotion had been carved out of him a long time ago. When he and I first met almost a year back, I walked out of that interrogation with the creeps clinging to my skin.

Now, that had all slid off and what was left beneath was an itch.

An itch from a pest I'd been swatting at and trying to trap for a year. I finally had that pest right under my boot where I wanted him, ready to squash him out so he'd leave me and my family the fuck alone.

I popped open my car door, exchanging the keys in my hand for the revolver tucked in the back of my pants. When I woke up today, I didn't know I'd be needing a gun. I only put this one in my glovebox in case of an emergency, but I wouldn't call this so much an emergency as I would a plan B.

Or C. Or I for insane.

My meticulous, structure-reliant brain kept yelling at me about how asinine this all was, and I agreed. It was off-the-walls nonsense.

But no one ever wrote songs or poems about how love was sane.

Yanking the handle on the back door, it swung open and revealed Tommy slouching inside. I stood to the side, gesturing with my gun.

"Get out."

Eyes half amused, half egocentric slid my way. "You gonna rough me up again if I don't?"

I swallowed an impatient breath of fresh air, flicking my stare out to the forest.

"Thinking about it."

With a groan, Tommy got out of the backseat, making a show of rolling his neck and shoulders and hissing about his cuffed wrists. "I like this new style on you, Reed, but you're kidding yourself if you think you can do this."

Biting the side of my cheek, I jerked my head forward. "Start walking."

Tommy dropped his head backwards with a sigh. "You're not a killer."

"Who said I was going to kill you?"

"Well, that gun you're holding does a pretty *bang up* job at telling the story. No pun intended."

He cracked a small laugh at his own dumb joke, and I nearly pistol whipped him across his cheek right there. Angry sweat beaded over my forehead, my skin ripe with loathing.

"Walk. That way." He didn't budge. *"Now."*

With an overdone sigh, his legs finally started moving, and I followed close behind as we ventured further into the brush.

The whole trek back through the trees and buzzing sounds of nature, I thought about a camping trip my father took me on when I was eight.

I complained the whole first day about how loud the woods were—the birds, the bugs, the wind, everything around us. I told my dad I felt like the forest was yelling at me, and he said it probably was because it knew I didn't have any appreciation.

He lectured me about all the things nature provided for us from oxygen to shelter to food, and that if I never learned to appreciate all that nature did for me, the loudness would never go away.

So I tried my best to do as he said for the rest of that trip.

Eventually, the rustling died down, the chirping simmered to soft morning melodies, and everything went still.

The rest of the camping trip went by in a haze of fishing, climbing, and too many s'mores. At the end when my dad and I were packing up our tent, he turned to me and asked, *"Do you hear that?"* Perplexed, I shook my head. He nodded with a relaxed smile and said, *"Exactly. When you're at peace in the woods, the woods are at peace with you."*

If what my dad said back then was true, then the woods were *incredibly* intune to my lack of peace right now. The trees were rustling and yelling all around us as we walked, shaking in fury even though there was no wind to be felt. Birds flying overhead chirped in protest, accosting me for what I was about to do in their home.

Nature was judging the crap out of me right now, and it honestly had every right.

"Stop here," I ordered, deciding fast on a flat surface of mostly rocks and twigs.

"You sure you don't wanna go any further?" Tommy swiveled to face me, loaded up with a wink. "I can be a bit of a screamer."

Don't shoot him. Don't shoot him. Don't shoot him.

I swapped my revolver briefly to my other hand, swiping the sweat off my palm that'd built despite the lack of heat in the air. Tommy blew out a slow whistle between his teeth, not even bothering to pay the man with a gun any attention.

"Is this where you ask me if we're gonna do this the easy way or the hard way, Reed?"

Holding a sigh in my chest, I shook my head.

"No, Tommy. We're long past the easy way."

Hoping my nerves weren't showing on my face, I opened the cylinder of my revolver and, one by one, shook the bullets out.

All except for one.

"Have you ever been shot?" I asked him.

He rocked his head from side to side, an unworried gleam to his stare. "Nope."

"Have you heard of Roulette?"

He sunk a lazy glance towards the gun, smirk twitching. "I assume you mean the Russian kind?"

"Good guess." I slammed the cylinder closed and spun it around until the ticking stopped and the bullet locked into place. "You get five chances to tell me what I want to know and one chance to get a bullet to your kneecap."

A lazy, lopsided smirk tugged up his face, the glint to his eyes purely deranged.

"Heard those hurt like a bitch."

"I've heard a bullet to the head hurts worse, so I'd play along."

"Okay, okay." He kicked a foot behind him, steadying it on a tree trunk. "Just one condition."

My jaw clicked, biting out a, *"What?"*

"I get to ask you questions too."

I felt my eyes go heavy holding his stare, already spent on his bullshit before it began.

"Fine."

Tommy beamed like sun rays were splitting between his teeth, and all it did was remind me how badly he needed them all rearranged by the courtesy of my fist. I brought my thumb down on each of my fingers not holding the gun, popping them to relieve their need for violence.

"All right. First question." I cranked back the trigger of my revolver and aimed it at his knee. "Where is Katerina Sanders right now?"

Tommy's patronizing chuckle intertwined with the noises of the forest, composing an unsettling mix. "Wow, going straight in with no warm-up questions or nothing? Just balls deep, *no* lube."

"Tommy," I all but fucking growled like a grizzly.

"I told you already, Reed." He flattened his smug mouth, shaking his head. "I don't know your girl. Never met her."

Without hesitation, I pulled the trigger.

An empty click went off, hollow of impact. No bullet.

"That's one," I threatened.

Tommy let out a stiff bark of laughter that echoed through the negative space between the trees, haunting and making the bushes around us shiver.

"That ain't fair. I answered your question."

"You *lied*."

"You know, it hurts that you don't trust me, Detective."

Red dots spotted my vision, and my finger lost its temper and pulled on the trigger again. I knew the shot would be empty, but the shock in Tommy's eyes sure wasn't.

"You didn't even ask a question," he exasperated.

"No," I agreed. "You just really piss me off."

Tommy sunk back against the tree, a look of startled awe blowing his eyes wide.

"Oh, oh, *oh*, what has this girl done to the good-natured Detective Reed I know and love?"

I tipped my chin up. "Is that your question?"

He thought it over, taking his sweet time before deciding, "No. No, I've got one already in mind."

With my gun, I gestured to go on and get it over with. He flooded his chest with cedar-scented air, laser-locked on me in a way that made my jaw tense.

"What's it feel like?" he finally asked.

"What does *what* feel like?"

"The feeling that you never really knew the woman sleeping next to you." My windpipe closed up, crimson tinting my sightline. "The woman who fucked you, who carried your kid, said I do at the altar. How does it feel to know so *little* about your own wife?"

My feet were crunching leaves and snapping twigs before my brain caught up to the fact that I was moving. Blood red smeared across my world as I hooked an arm back, a snarl pulling back my lips as I swung for his face.

It was an unforgiving impact, my fist smacking across his face so hard, the wind gasped in shock. Tommy cried out and fell to the ground sloppily, grunting and rolling over roots while I stood over him and watched.

Shaking my hand out, I huffed, "It feels a little bit like that."

Tommy had caught the ground face first, so I wasn't surprised to see clots of soil printed on the side of his forehead as he rolled over onto his back.

I was a little shocked to see blood.

It was smudged across his upper lip, a strike of red going halfway up his cheek. Blood meant he was human, flesh and blood just like me.

That was the shocking part.

"You got a nice right hook there." He spit to the side, expelling a glob of wine red saliva. Breathing heavily, he cranked his attention back up to me.

"How long you been wantin' to do that?"

"About a year." I sniffed, backing up a few steps. "That also eats up your next question."

Tommy cursed under his breath, and I reset my position with my gun aimed for his knee.

"How do you know Heather?"

His mouth drew thin as he shook his head against the dirt.

"Nah, now you're just asking me to shit where I eat."

Confusion settled between my knitted brows. "You work with her?"

"Do you want to use that as your next question?" He cocked his head that'd caught dead leaves in his salt and pepper hair.

"*Yes.*"

"Then no. I don't work with her. I work *for* her. Lots of people work for your little miss." He fucking *smirked*. "She's a busy bee."

My confusion deepened, dipping behind my forehead and hurting my brain.

"She's a *realtor*," I reasoned, watching the lines of his face closely for a lurking lie.

"She's a fucking evil *genius* is what she is." He hawked another line of spit to the side, touching his tongue to the slice in his fattening lip. "Playing all sides while her husband plays detective, even though he's as blind as a fucking bat."

My teeth crunched. "*Meaning?*"

"It means you're a goddamn joke, Reed. Your wife sets the stage for the joke, and you're the punchline. You have been for *years*."

Every word out of his mouth knocked around my brain but didn't hit any buttons that made sense. He was being just vague enough to screw with my head, and I hated to admit it was working. The feeling of spinning out was getting to me, my cheeks burning hot, blood pressure rising, heart jackhammering under my sternum.

Nothing he said about Heather made any sense. I'd known that woman for thirteen years, and even on her worst days where she made me want to punch a hole through every wall in our overcompensating house, she was no more vindictive than any other suburban wife and mother.

But then why did she lie about last weekend?

My head drooped into my free hand, squeezing at the temples as I tried to focus.

Okay, question. I needed a question.

I forced my eyes open, zeroing in on Tommy laying on the dirt floor and hating that spark to his stare as he watched me lose my mind.

"When was the first time you met my wife?"

Apparently, I'd chosen the right question.

That delighted spark in Tommy's eyes went supernova. "Couple months after you hired yourself that nanny. She woulda found anyone for the job but picked me since I already had an in with the Sanders ladies."

Great. More answers that didn't make any sense. Frustration licked up my spine, each vertebra turning molten as I grit my teeth.

"And what *exactly* was the job you two did together?"

"Oh, it was real easy." Tommy paused, allowing a vile grin to climb up his cheeks. "Get the attention on me so no one looked at her."

"God fucking *dammit*." Earth shuddered with every step I charged over to where he was on the ground, lifting my leg up and sitting the bottom of my shoe on Tommy's chest. I dug the heel of my foot between his ribs, catching and relishing in the twinge across his face.

"No more bullshit obscure answers," I snarled, timbre digging deep and lethal.

Tommy sucked in a sharp gasp, pain contorting his face as I pressed my foot down on his chest, the gift of a crack imminent.

"Reed, what the fuck?" Finally, fear had found a home in Tommy Lynch's voice. I put some more pressure behind my leg, wanting to see it blossom in his eyes too. He squirmed beneath me, fighting like the vermin he was.

"I answered your questions, I—*shit*."

"Your answers weren't enough." More pressing from me. More hissing from him. "You know more than you're letting on, and that's breaking the rules of the game."

Through shallow panting, Tommy fixed his eyes up to me.

THIRTEEN

"I've told you *everything* you need to know. You're just too fucking trusting to see what's been standing in front of you for years in her Jimmy-fucking-Choos."

I didn't like where he was going, but I needed him to continue.

"Keep talking."

He tried to kick his head back into the dirt, gasping for relief from the pressure of my heel knifing between his breakable bones. "*God*, Reed, don't you ever wonder why so many of your cases go cold or your leads just up and disappear? You leave your work just lying around in your office thinkin' it's safe there."

"And you're saying that Heather messes with my cases just to fuck with me? There's no rhyme or reason for her to do that."

"Jesus. H. Christ." He winced, trying to cave his body into the earth and away from my foot. "You really have no idea what family you married into. It's a whole other level of fucked up you couldn't even *dream* of in your worst nightmares, and you got your green-eyed girl all tied up in it."

Familiarity rode the gritty syllables of his voice as he mentioned Kat, and the blood moving through my veins chilled.

"I thought you said you didn't know Kat Sanders?"

He raised his goddamn eyebrows at me and cocked a weak grin.

"Guess I lied."

Motherfucker.

"You know, you really were asking for it fucking around with someone like that behind your wife's back. Gorgeous, young, and a goddamn *firecracker*. Haven't you ever heard the phrase, 'there's nothin' more dangerous than a woman scorned'?"

Deriding laughter tried to shake his body beneath my foot until he choked in pain, but the deviant smile never left his face nor did the crazed fire burning in his eyes.

"That girl of yours *really* is something special. I'd break a hell of a lot more than my marriage vows for a taste of fire like hers." Around us, nature began to scream as Tommy spoke of things he shouldn't. Branches shook, wind screeched, leaves flapped as if trying to fly from the turmoil filling me. He kept going, and so did the screaming. "I think it's my turn to ask a question, and ever since I met her, I've been itching to know how my little Catnip is in the sack. Someone that fiery oughta be a ride of a—gah!"

The sound we'd both been waiting for finally serenaded the lands as I crushed my foot into the base of his ribcage, feeling the crack of two ribs give way beneath my shoe.

Tommy howled in pain as I moved my foot around in different angles to see which one made him suffer more.

"Sta-stop!" His eyes rolled back white when I finally lifted off the pressure, a perfect contrast against his beet-red face. He took in a few shaking breaths while beads of sweat sprouted and dripped down his forehead.

"You broke," he struggled for air, clinging to wisps of oxygen, "my ribs."

"Yeah." Tension wiring my jaw shut, I passed a glance down his broken chest. "I did."

I searched for the feeling of remorse for a few seconds, but it just wasn't where it should have been. Instead, all I found was more heat. More rage so fiery hot it was actually cold.

My body didn't know whether to shiver or sweat as I watched a man I hated twitch and writhe in the dirt with the bugs he so rightfully resembled. He let out a grateful gasp as I lifted my foot off of his chest and paced a few steps away. His shallow huffs filled the eerie silence the forest had cast between us.

Moments ago, it was rioting. Now, nothing but peace.

Maybe that's why I didn't feel bad as I reached inside my pocket and fumbled around until the hard brush of metal grazed my fingertips. Casting my stare out over the dense miles of greenery, I plunked those bullets back into the pockets they belonged.

"Do you want to know something?"

My tone was as calm and smooth as the breeze that slithered through the trees.

Still panting in pain, he agreed. "Yeah, what?"

Thoughtfully, I closed the cylinder of my revolver back in place with a poignant click.

"I'm tired. Exhausted, in fact." Taking a deep inhale, I said, "I'm tired of being lied to. I'm tired of not having the woman I love back home and safe."

The peace of the moment was interrupted only by dead leaves disintegrating beneath my shoes as I stalked Tommy's way, resecuring my fingers around the handle of my gun.

"And I am so *goddamn* tired of you screwing with my life."

Tommy lifted his head up, gaze widening as he found himself at the wrong end of a barrel. His face drained of blood, eyes jumping up to me.

"You said you wouldn't shoot me if I answered your stupid fucking questions!"

One of my eyebrows arched up.

"Guess I lied."

A singular gunshot muffled Tommy's shout as they both echoed through the woods.

He rolled around on the forest floor, thick veins protruding beneath his reddening neck as his throat stretched with a violent scream. Tears even leaked over from his eyes, watering the earth below as he cried out in pain.

"My knee! Oh my-*fuck*, you fucker!"

Stashing the gun in between the waistband of my jeans, I watched his agony bleed out of his blown-out kneecap with satisfaction running through my bones.

"The highway's about a half mile that way." I pointed in the direction we came even though he wasn't paying any attention between all the crying and splintered bones. "I'm sure someone will find you before nightfall."

Tommy stopped groaning only to shout. "You can't leave me here! I'll tell everyone what you fucking did when I get back!"

"I don't think you will." I fished my phone out of my front pocket and showed him the front screen. "I've been recording since we got out of the car, and you've incriminated yourself in at least three felonies in that short amount of time."

"But you shot me! You're guilty on there too!"

I tapped my thumb to end the recording, pocketing my phone.

"Then I guess if we're both smart, we'll keep our mouths shut."

Tommy kept yelling at my back as I turned away from him and started back towards the car. His voice faded out as I emerged from the trees, climbing back inside my car and starting up the engine.

Sitting in my car, I wasn't the same man who left it.

My skin felt different around my bones and muscles, stretched tighter and thinner somehow. The man who walked out of this car less than an hour ago had never shot anyone. That man hadn't broken another man's ribs because he didn't like how he spoke about the woman he loved.

Throwing my arm over the passenger seat, I backed out and got onto the road to go home, leaving the righteous man I used to be behind in the woods.

That man lived a life of lies.

He lived blind.

Now, whether I liked it or not, my eyes were *wide* open.

FOURTEEN

KAT

The night of my apology, Blake and I warred with where I'd sleep. I didn't want it to be awkward, and he didn't want to make a big deal about it. After two cigarettes and one high-tempered fight, Blake tried to leave his room and I ran after him and clung to his back, begging him not to go.

He didn't but made me agree to stop making things weird. I did but I made him agree that I could still hog most of the bed.

Win, win, amiright?

The next night wasn't so tense as we remolded ourselves back into a routine. We read. We bickered. We snuck out to the kitchen for a late night treat when my growling stomach interrupted our watch of To Have and Have Not.

That brought us to today.

It was Blake's lunch break, and he'd come back to be with me. He pocketed a candy bar he'd gotten when he was out on an errand earlier that morning and threw it my way when he got in. I devoured the chocolate *after* being reprimanded by Blake for eating it while reading one of his books.

Apparently chocolate fingerprints on classic poetry was a big no-no?

Candy gone, I told him to toss me another book, any poet of his choosing. He chose Lord Byron.

Blake plucked it from his shelf and flipped through a few pages, handing it over to me before turning his focus back to his bookcase in search of something for himself.

The pages of this book in particular were extra soft as I ran them through my fingers—the kind of soft that came from overuse and dissolving strength in the strings of the paper.

I feathered a touch over the delicate letters on the page of a poem titled, *She Walks in Beauty.* My eyes scanned the first few lines of the poem, and all breathable air escaped my body.

She walks in beauty, like the night
  Of cloudless climes and starry skies;
  And all that's best of dark and bright
  Meet in her aspect and in her eyes

Jaw gaping and heart stuttering, I looked up to blame the man who'd handed me *this* book on *this* poem on purpose. He wasn't watching me, his attention intent on his rows of books which made his awareness of what he'd done even more shameless.

This darkness and light shit was really getting to me lately, and Blake being so blunt about how attracted he was to it wasn't helping.

Fighting not to pout and throw the book at his beautiful head, I huffed loud enough to be dramatic but kept my lips sealed as I gave my focus back to the book of poems.

I'd heard of Lord Byron in an English class in high school before dropping out. From what I remembered, he was a pretty big deal to the poet's society. I only really remembered him because his most famous work, *Don Juan,* was all about some dude fucking a bunch of women and it made a class of twenty seventeen-year-olds hoop and holler because *sex.*

I got comfortable with my back against his headboard as Blake found a book of his own and came over to the bed, sitting down next to me.

FOURTEEN

The mattress rocked as his shoulder brushed mine, leaving a mark of heat on my bare skin. We both turned our heads as he settled in next to me, locking each other in with a look of challenge almost playful and intimacy almost dangerous.

Neither of us said a word, but his spirited eyes fell to the poem I'd decided to stop on and *boy*, did they say a whole fucking lot.

"What?" I nipped, jerking the book close to my heart.

"Nothing." He shook his head, and I smelled bullshit. "Just an interesting poem to choose."

I glanced down and read the title back to myself. *The Dream by Lord Byron.*

I snapped my attention back to Blake who was mooning silently down at his own book. Deciding I wouldn't get any reading done with this one judging over my shoulder, I scooted to the wall adjacent to the headboard, my back going against the wall and my legs bridging over Blake's.

The room fell to a quiet buzz as we read to ourselves, but that only lasted maybe two minutes. Because by the time I reached a quarter of the way down *The Dream*, my heart was practically screaming.

Harrowing, blood-gurgling, guilty screams.

The poem was all about a boy who loved a woman who didn't love him back—fucking *ouch*. The boy kept loving the woman even after she married someone else, and one line in particular jumped off the page and bit a chunk right out of my heart.

She knew she was by him beloved—she knew
  For quickly comes such knowledge,
  That his heart was darken'd with her shadow.

Tears—honest to fuck *tears*—misted my eyes as I read those words over and over and over.

Was I a shadow? Was I something that hid in darkness and ate up the light?

Yeah. Yeah I fucking was.

It got even worse as the poem went on because the woman wasn't even happy like she thought she would be with the man she married, and both she and the boy died miserable.

Was Lord Byron trying to tell me something? Or were my brain and heart just so completely fucked by this point that I'd find deeper meaning in a hot pocket wrapper?

I'd become half frozen, half on fire as I sat on his bed holding his book in between my sweating palms. Now I got why Blake made a face when he saw this poem. He recognized the significance of it before I'd even grazed the first line.

I was a shadow of affection. I was a tumor of love.

I was the kiss of death.

I'd smeared my death all over Blake's lips when I kissed him back, signing his last will and testament with our tongues that vowed he would give me his heart even if he didn't want to. He'd have to live without his heart, all the while knowing he could never have mine in exchange.

Not now.

When I looked up to see if Blake had used his ticket to get a front row seat to watch me silently implode, I didn't find him staring at me like I thought.

Not my face, at least.

His intense burn was on my bare legs perched over his. He was watching them like he'd never seen a pair of women's legs before and didn't know whether to push them off or hold them closer. He hadn't noticed I was staring at him when he lifted a hand to hover over one of my knees, slowly placing it down.

Skin to skin, I barely concealed the hitch in my breath as his big hand wrapped around my whole knee, drenching my bare legs in flames.

The fact that my shorts hadn't combusted yet was a sheer miracle.

My lips parched as I waited and watched him, Blake scrutinizing how our bodies felt when they collided with an innocent touch. In the quiet, he dragged his thumb down my thigh, painting the sensation of his rough padded finger into my snow-white skin.

FOURTEEN

He did it again, corrupting an innocent touch with a brush of fire.

"Why're you doing that?"

It was a wonder the words came out since I was holding my breath.

Eyeing his thumb riding my skin, he rumbled, "Because I shouldn't be able to."

It took a few moments for his words to click, but once they did, the click was volcanic. Icy hot guilt erupted from my heart, pouring down my insides and freezing my blood like early morning dew transformed into frost by Winter's cold bite.

Even a splash of embarrassment poisoned my petrified bloodstream.

I hadn't even thought about it when I put my legs over his. I'd just done it like it wasn't even second nature, but first. Touching Blake, being close and intimate with him, wasn't something I thought about or had learned to get used to.

It was an instinct built into the fabric of who we were when we were together, like breathing. Touching him in any small or big way wasn't something I had to think about doing. It just happened, and like with breathing, I didn't even notice it until it became problematic.

And being the fucking careless idiot who draped herself all over a man who wanted her but couldn't have her was definitely problematic.

The muscles in my legs shattered the ice constricting them and jerked to move.

Blake's fingers clamped hard around my knee.

"Don't."

His face was a hard-lined thing of beautiful pain as he requested I not take away the thing he wasn't allowed to have. I imagined the boy from Byron's poem imploring for something as simple as a touch from the woman he loved and couldn't help but wonder if they would have died happy instead if she'd given it to him.

I stayed where I was and relaxed my muscles so he could relax his. Blake went back to reading *A Tale of Two Cities* and left his hand on my knee, feeding me his warmth and feeding our parasitic addiction to each other.

My head was too unfocused now to go back to reading. Plus, I had a biting feeling all Lord Byron had in store for me were more mind- and heart-fucks.

No thank you, kindly.

So I closed my book and placed it to the side, letting my stare wander around his room. On the nightstand next to the bed, something new caught my eye.

"Is that the camera you're supposed to use to take pictures of me?"

Blake twisted his head to follow where my gaze was, slowly shutting his book. He exchanged it out for the camera, which was a clunky old-school polaroid.

"Yeah." The wide rounded lens stared back at him, a frown marring his face while he glared down at it as if he could see every degrading photo Ray had requested be taken with it. Acid corroded the lining of my stomach as I remembered what happened to Abigail and realized Blake might be holding the camera that helped kill her.

"I'm obviously not going to take photos of you." The polaroid camera went back on the nightstand, Blake pushing the offense to the very edge.

Deciding the essence to the air tasted too heavy, like spoiled cream, I leaned forward so my chest hugged my knees and smirked like a brat.

"What? You don't think I photograph well?"

His jet black stare cut up to me. "You're not funny."

I scoffed and rolled my eyes, mock singing, "Lies, lies, pretty little lies."

Dark eyes dropped to my mouth, his inspired mind probably picturing music notes hanging off my lips as I spun the silly tune. God, what I wouldn't give to crack his head open and have a peek inside. I bet I could get lost for days in his world where the skies were made of poetry and the seas were made of pain.

There was a captivating mixture of both expressed in his intimate eyes as he studied my mouth, a sonnet of longing written in exquisite black ink.

"Do you *want* me to take photos of you?" he challenged like a threat, gravel roughing up his voice.

"Not those kinds of photos. Everyone knows those kinds of photos belong on phones where you can crop your face out."

FOURTEEN

I smiled a cheeky smile, and Blake let his signature eye roll go free.

Now *this* felt like familiar territory. It felt like us, and I wanted to commemorate it.

Crawling to my knees and reaching across Blake, I snagged the polaroid and decided we'd make a good memory out of a shit ton of bad ones. I sat my ass back on the bed but scooched so I was next to Blake against the headboard again.

"Let's take a picture."

"I don't like pictures."

"Well too fucking bad."

I positioned the camera my way, trying to remember if I'd ever used one of these before. Just hold the red button down and point, right?

"I'm not getting in any photo." Blake crossed his arms beside me, the sear of his gaze warming the side of my face. Writing off the old school camera as figured out, I turned my focus to him and rested my head his way.

"All you have to do is smile," I said.

"I don't smile."

"Liar. You smile with me all the time."

He settled his head my way against the headboard, mirroring me. "Only because you're being fucking ridiculous all the time."

"I think you mean *charming* and *adorable*."

And then the thing he claimed didn't exist wriggled into view. I gasped like I was seeing a comet, even pointing up at his smile.

"See? Now you have no excuse not to take a picture with me. Just hold onto it!"

He groaned but never lost his lopsided grin. "Kat—"

"Just keep smiling!" I fumbled with the camera, turning it around in my hands to face us. "Think of puppies or rainbows or orgasms, and *keep smiling*."

"Orgasms?" he chuckled as I squished in closer to his side.

"Yeah, things that make you happy." My right arm whined as I held the clunky camera up with it, not realizing it would be so awkward or heavy to hold. The front of the polaroid was smiling at us, and I put my pointer finger on the red button.

"Just find your happiness and say cheese!"

A flash that could have re-blinded the blind ripped across my vision, the smile I was holding nearly falling into a gasp.

"Holy *shit*," I cursed as soon as it was over, pinching my assaulted eyes closed. A square of bright white light pulsed behind my closed eyes, me being pretty fucking sure that flash was now a permanent structure of my vision.

Blake lifted the camera from my hands at the same time I heard the click of our picture spit out from it.

"Oh god." No amount of batting my eyes was helping drain that bright sucker away. All I got were color-faded splotches of what was in front of me as I tried to focus on Blake and our picture which I *think* he was holding. "Aren't you supposed to start shaking it or something?"

He shook his head, turning the photo face down on his nightstand. "No, that's a myth."

Oh. "Are you sure?"

"Yes."

"Maybe you should shake it like twice, just in case?"

"Jesus *fuck*, you're stubborn."

"And you took a picture." I poked his good shoulder, careful not to touch him for too long. "It wasn't that hard, was it?"

He didn't answer, but the heavy-lidded glare he gave me was riddled with amusement he'd totally deny if I asked him to admit to it. His eyes were *alive* right now, breathing with life instead of fire.

I'd done that. Put that second wind of light there, and as a certified shadow, I was glad to have done something outside my nature.

A stupid grin wouldn't fall off my cheeks as I sat on my feet, getting comfortable on the bed again. "And now you have it forever," I told him.

The spirited gleam to his stare didn't exactly fade, but it sharpened. Like a fine-toothed lightning bolt aimed at me.

"You want me to keep it?"

"Don't you want something to remember me by?" *You know, when I'm*

FOURTEEN

not just gone from here but gone for good.

Blake said he'd figure something out for another escape, but... I wasn't sold. There was something inside of me, almost like a separate entity that had hollowed out a place for acceptance in my chest. Would I keep kicking and hoping for a miracle?

Absolutely.

There was just a small part of me making sure death wasn't a total disappointment.

Blake held my stare, thinking of a time not so far from now when his bed would be empty without my shadow to fill it. The loneliness was already striking a fresh fire to his eyes, a single flame looking for a heart to warm.

He slid his attention back to our photo sitting face down on the nightstand. The curious part of me wanted to know what we looked like together in a carefree snapshot, but the picture was his and if I saw it, I might want to steal it.

Slowly, he picked the photo up and slid it between the pages of his notebook, closing and keeping it.

My shit-eating grin deepened. "Sap."

He shot me a glare that broke my smile into a permanent feature on my face, soft laughter trilling out as I grabbed my bottom lip to try and chew it back. Blake watched me with the softest eyes I'd seen on him yet, and it was that look that kept the easy words flowing.

"You pretend like you're a take-no-shit badass, but you're really a big softie. You're like these caramels my grandma used to eat."

Still dashed with humor, his eyes narrowed in question. "You're comparing me to an old woman's hard candy?"

"Yeah!" I slapped my fingertips to his thigh in excitement. "They were hard as rock on the outside. I almost broke a tooth on one of them once, but if you sucked on them long enough, you'd get to the soft gooey stuff in the middle. That's you."

The side of his mouth trembled, delicious mirth sparking in his eyes.

"I can't decide if you're perverted enough to have said that on purpose or you're totally unaware."

My forehead scrunched, zipping back through my mind for what I'd said.

Caramels. Hard. Soft. Sucking—

"Oh my god, I totally missed it." I blinked at Blake, dumbfounded. "My pervert skills are waning."

Blake chuckled while I reeled.

"This is *unacceptable*," I protested, my eyes wide on his. "It's probably because all I've been reading lately is your fancy poetry! Quick, make a dick joke."

"Don't blame poetry."

"I *have* to blame poetry. That's all I've been reading!"

"Do you exclusively read porno magazines at home?"

I scoffed like he was absurd and looked at him the same way. "No one reads *porno* magazines anymore. Get your dick outta the 80's."

Blake rolled his eyes to the side, a soft twitch at the corner of his perfect mouth. "I think your pervert prowess is nicely intact."

For another five days, was on the tip of my tongue, but I swallowed it back because I didn't want a fight. I knew it was weighing on him what would happen if he didn't get me out of here. A few times, I tried to ask him what the plan was, but he always shut down on me and it just wasn't worth it.

I'd rather talk with him than fight with him if it was all pointless anyway.

"I don't think I've heard you make a single dirty joke in all the time I've known you," I said to keep the conversation light. It was working too, Blake's sharp features remaining soft and relaxed.

"I don't have an interest in them."

"*All* men have an interest in *all* things dirty, jokes included."

He gave a shrug so suave and smooth, it should have been outlawed in the confines of his small bedroom. "Then I guess I'm an exception."

I *felt* those words with my soul, knowing intimately and with every square inch of me that they were true. I breathed the words in, trying to force a response out fast so the easiness of our conversation wasn't lost, but I failed so *so* epically.

"I guess you are," I murmured, even my voice failing the effort to stay

FOURTEEN

cool and collected. *Fuck.*

It was just so *true*. Both he and Dominic were enigmas to the male species.

All my life, men had been such unfailing disappointments. My father, my boyfriends, men on the street, men at the store, men *everywhere* were only concerned with themselves and their dicks.

Then there was Dominic who shattered the pattern of disappointment, and it honest to fuck scared me. Maybe that's why falling in love with him was so exhausting and overwhelming. I was having to unlearn everything I knew about what to expect from a man in order to make sense of why I was allowed to fall for one.

Then Blake came along and basically ripped my heart a new one.

I mean, who expects to find a guardian angel in Hell?

Even his face was sort of angelic looking, all strict lines and high cheekbones and eyelashes as full as wings. He wasn't an ordinary angel though. His halo was made of fire and his soul of damnation and scars. He was gorgeous ruin searching for salvation.

And he honest to God took my breath away.

"You shouldn't look at me like that," Blake said after letting me brazenly stare at him for long enough.

"Like what?"

A muscle in his cheek jumped, his voice toiling out like thick smoke.

"Like I'm not the villain."

My eyes darted back and forth between his, heavy, achy emotions souring my gut.

"You really think you're the villain?" Disbelief thinned my voice out to a shocked whisper.

The tip of his nose twitched, midnight eyes storming.

"Well, I know I'm not the hero."

My eyebrows were a furrowing giveaway as I sat there and stared at him. I twisted my neck to the side, trying to repuzzle his statement in my head to make sense of it and failed. My focus swung back to him, a beast of defense slamming its fists against my ribcage.

"Okay, I don't wanna get all sappy and shit, but you *do* realize how many times you've saved my life, right?" I cocked an indignant brow, jutting my chin forward.

He wasn't having it.

"And you're sitting here, right back in a prison because of me."

Eyeroll.

"That was a *mistake*."

All oxygen in the room seemed to contract, poking an odd pressure at my chest as Blake produced the fire vicious enough to snuff it out. It was flickering in his dangerous obsidian eyes as he said, "My whole fucking life is a mistake."

Defensive lightning shot me to my knees on the mattress, shoving my hands against his chest. "Don't *say* that."

I was a head taller than him now, hovering over him as he pointed his sculpted chin up at me, jabbing it and letting me watch the charcoal of his eyes smolder and crack.

"Do you know how many lives I could have saved and didn't? Or how many lives I've taken with my own hands because I was told to or just fucking wanted to?"

"You mean like those men who hurt me?" I threw back, chasing his lightning with mine.

"They were still *men*."

I shook my head, my hair falling around us. "They were monsters."

Our tempers were draped inside my waves of dark chocolate hair, steaming up our faces and feeding off of each other. My temper loved the taste of his, rich and smokey and *raw*.

"Maybe I'm a monster," he confessed, believing every single insane syllable of it.

My heart was going wild in my chest, hating every second of him thinking something so terrible about himself. I had to make him see what I saw in him, make him see the angel of scars I was so addicted to.

"Except, I'm not scared of you."

To prove it, I sank back down to sitting to even our leverage and then

FOURTEEN

gave him all of it by closing the distance between us. Our chests hit, breath tangling as I made myself an easy target. "I can put myself right in front of you, and I know you won't hurt me. Someone bad would. They'd take advantage of me, but you won't."

His nostrils broadened, an inferno framed beneath his thick, dark brows. He was practically vibrating against me.

"I could slit my wrists and know you'd put pressure on the wounds," I rasped, watching him as closely as he was watching me. "You wouldn't let anything bad happen to me."

His heart was slapping against mine between our pressed chests, *brutal* whacks that made me think it was trying to break out and escape over to me. It wanted me to take it and hide it inside my chest of broken glass, risking fresh scars and permanent damage just so long as we could be bleeding hearts together.

And his heart already bled so much. *God*, did it bleed all down his sleeves and prove with every single vibrant drop how he could never be anything even close to evil.

"Just because you've done bad things doesn't make you a bad person." I slipped my hand between us, flattening my palm over his hard sternum that thrummed from beneath. "Just because your heart is broken doesn't mean it doesn't beat with the right intentions."

A flurry of fierce emotion blasted inside his eyes, and in the very next second, we were falling back. Hands with the potential to crush locked around my upper arms, pushing me back with Blake coming down on top of me.

My back bounced against the mattress only as much as he allowed, holding me down tight and boxing my legs between his thighs. My eyes flashed up to his as he pinned me down, drenching me in his unfiltered, gritty power.

"What about now?" Darkness eclipsed his deep voice above me. "Do I scare you now, Kitten?"

Staring up at him with my pulse racing, I could see how badly he needed me to say yes. Not a want, but a *need* to be recognized as the bad guy. He'd cast himself in the role for so long, and it would probably make hating himself harder if he thought he could be anything more.

But he *was* more. He was more than more.

"Do it," I challenged, soft and unshaken. A wrinkle formed a V between Blake's eyebrows as I stared him dead in his fire-breathing eyes. "Hurt me. Put your hand on my cheek and make it welt."

Pressure squeezed into my frail upper arms as his grip tightened, his whole body practically shaking in tremors that begged to be bad. He wanted so fucking badly to be something he could keep on hating, and if I wasn't so strung out on proving him wrong, I might have been crying.

Beneath him, I pressed my head back into the bed, sheathing my thin neck for him.

"Put your hand around my throat and take away my air." A bath of trembling hot air drenched my unguarded neck, his fingers around my arms twisting. "Do it if you're so bad," I taunted in a wisp.

We spent so many seconds like that.

Me, spread back as willing prey, baiting the lion with the promise of an easy meal.

Him, dominating a potential kill and trying to convince himself to take it.

You could actually hear our heartbeats in the air, throbbing and ticking and waiting to explode.

A war waged a losing battle across his feral gaze, the dark vices he was hoping to convince himself he possessed waning by the second. He was cracking slowly, his goodness splintering from beneath that hard facade, fracturing his expression into a masterpiece of agony. Uneven, jerking breaths petered between his parted lips, dripping his torment down on my tongue to catch like snowflakes in the bitterest winter.

I tried to move my arm, and he let me, loosening his hold so his fingers were a soft graze over my skin as I pulled my hand up to touch his face.

I cupped his cheek like he'd done to me so many times, thumbing the shadow of bristles roughing up his smooth jawline. I couldn't tell you how many times I'd wanted to do this, to give into the addiction to touch him

FOURTEEN

like this and savor the feel of his sharp jaw cutting along my soft palm.

His breathing stumbled as I curved my thumb down the side of his face, pretending this was all for him, that I wasn't getting as much of a high off of this as he was.

"Just because something's a little broken doesn't mean it's not perfect," I whispered gently, watching his eyelids collapse and squeeze shut.

Then his head came down too, our foreheads kissing and noses brushing and my breath nearly slicing open my throat. He released an exhale that ate away at my lips like a drug with teeth, nipping and chewing my heart into a pile of stupid mush.

Yeah, I was stupid, *stupid* mush.

He stayed just like that for a while against me, breathing and resting. His irises sparkled when he revealed them again, almost like a weight in them had been washed clean.

My stupid heart made my stupid hand caress his stupid face all stupid over again.

A tiny curve touched the corner of his mouth.

"When'd you start saying shit like that?"

The same curve twisted up my helpless lips.

"Now can I blame the poetry?"

FIFTEEN

DOM

"Do you have the transcripts from where Heather got her realty license?"

Reaching across the coffee table, I grabbed the manilla folder with the word 'career' scribbled in green marker across the front and handed it to Ryan.

"Her license is legitimate and so is the course she took to get it." Ryan flipped through the papers I'd handed him as he listened. "Did you ever hear back from the people who run the licensing classes?"

"Not yet. I left a voicemail early this morning, so we should hear back any minute."

I nodded, ignoring the brick in my stomach as we sat around my living room and rifled through the last thirteen years of my life with a woman I was supposed to know inside and out. Apparently, I hadn't even scratched the surface.

"So neither of you went to college?"

Impatiently, I flicked my eyes up to Layla, staring at her beneath a strict and heavy browline. "No, I went straight to the Police Academy and she went into real estate."

"Or so we think," she corrected, probably not meaning to scorch my

FIFTEEN

nerves.

Drawing my focus back down, I murmured, "Or so we think."

Ever since Ryan told her I saw Kat last weekend, Layla had been in rare form. Gone was the withered woman of tears and fear I last saw at the station. The woman sitting criss-cross on my living room floor now was determined as hell and snappy.

Maybe too snappy, but that could also just be that my nerves were long past shot to hell.

Ryan was elated to have Layla back to her old self, and I would be too soon.

Once we had Kat back, then I'd be as elated as a man could be.

Files, pictures, and stacks of sticky notes cluttered the top of my coffee table that we all three sat around, sifting through Heather's past. I shared most of what Tommy said during our confrontation in the woods with Ryan, leaving out that small part where I shot him in the knee.

The only person I'd tell about that misdeed was Kat.

"Hey, hey." Both Layla and I looked at Ryan as he picked up his work phone, the screen lighting his face. "Just got an email back from the Better Business Bureau about Heather's real estate company."

I didn't mean to, but I held my breath just before he answered. I remembered the day Heather told me she wanted to open up her own real estate company after we were married and name it after us.

Reed Real Estate had been one of the shiniest moments from the early part of our marriage. We toasted to her and to us when she got the email decorating her as a full-fledged business owner, and then we made love on our worn leather couch we bought together for our first place.

Heather sold that couch the very next month.

"What does the email say?" The dread in my voice wasn't even halfway concealed, my grip on a copy of our marriage license frozen.

Ryan glanced up at me, his eyes falling immediately back down to his phone screen.

"You're not gonna like it." Unstoppable pity lined his voice, and I dropped the marriage license like it'd grown teeth and bit me. "Reed Real Estate was never a registered business with the Better Business Bureau. Technically, the company never existed."

Frustration surged through me, loud and pissed off.

"How?" I pinched the bridge of my nose where the oncoming, now daily headache was beginning to bloom. "That doesn't add up. She had *money*. She had a *lot* of money and went on work trips and to open houses all the time."

Dropping my hand to my lap, I took a deep breath and tried to convince my cramping gut to settle down. In the middle of trying not to throw up, two pairs of little feet came stomping down the stairs.

"Daddy! Can Charlotte and I use the scissors?"

Sliding my hands down my face, I twisted my head around to where Maya was standing at the bottom of the stairs gripping the railing with Charlotte just behind her trying to climb over it.

"Where are your safety scissors?" I asked with rocks in my voice.

Pushing a wild strand of hair behind her ear, her big blue eyes shifted away from me. "I don't know…"

"I've used, um, adult scissors before, and I never cut myself, so I could do it."

My gaze jumped back to Charlotte as she climbed down from over the railing, holding my stare like she wasn't just five.

The longer I stared at her, the more I thanked God that she didn't have Kat's eyes. In every other way, Charlotte resembled her older sister, and it was beginning to kill me more and more.

I saw Kat in the way Charlotte would crinkle her nose or in her mischievous smirk. I saw her in her mannerisms or in the confident way she'd walk and talk. She even had sprinkles of Kat's humor, hold the crude and perverted jokes.

Tearing my eyes away from her, I looked to my daughter. "I think there's an extra pair of your safety scissors in a drawer in the kitchen. I'll go look in a bit."

"But our fortune tellers need to be made now, Daddy. Please?"

Out of the corner of my vision, Layla stood. "How about I go help you

FIFTEEN

look in the kitchen and we let your dad stay here, yeah?"

I shared a grateful glance with her as she walked over the mountain of papers we had strewn everywhere and helped lead Maya off into the kitchen.

Instead of going on the hunt for scissors, Charlotte performed a big leap off of the bottom stair and came running towards Ryan and I. She stopped next to me, her mouth pursed to the side as she examined the papers on the table.

"Are these maps to help find Katty?"

Reminding myself she wasn't a kid who liked bullshit answers, I told her honestly, "They're more like clues."

Charlotte scrutinized the files closer, touching and turning the papers closest to her as if she understood what any of it meant. I hadn't told her I'd seen her sister last weekend yet. I didn't want to get her hopes up before I could deliver Kat back to her as good as when she left.

"Do you know where she is?"

She looked up at me like I had all the answers, and my chest about goddamn exploded.

"Sort of," I managed with a nod.

"Good, 'cause I miss her a lot. 'Specially with Mommy in Heaven."

Okay, *now* my heart exploded.

"Charlotte! We found the scissors! I got em!" Maya came barrelling back through the living room with tiny pink scissors clutched in her hand and Layla trying to catch up behind her.

"Hey, kid! Haven't you ever heard not to run with scissors? That's like kid safety 101."

Maya's stare cut to mine, her lips already stirring in a pout.

"No, ma'am." Her pout intensified as I shook my head and donned my dad voice. "Ms. Layla's right. Plus, we walk in this house. We don't run."

"Katty and I used to have races in our house all the time!" Charlotte chimed in, beaming as proud as could be.

My mouth parted, a responsible reply waiting to fall over.

Instead, I almost smiled. "That doesn't really surprise me at all."

Nostalgia for a memory that wasn't even real clobbered my heart as I imagined Kat running around this very house, her melodic laughter floating behind her as Charlotte chased her. Maya would join in, and I'd catch all three of them, bringing them down to the floor where we'd all sprawl out, smiling and the perfect picture of happiness.

Layla waved a hand through my fantasy and sent both of the girls back up the stairs to Maya's room. "Go finish your fortune cookies or whatever."

"Fortune tellers!" Maya corrected, disappearing up the stairs with Charlotte in tow.

"Speaking of fortune cookies." Ryan sighed and sat back against the couch. "We should probably order some takeout. This could be a long night."

Layla nodded. "I'm down."

"I don't care."

"Come on, man." Ryan pulled Layla down on his lap as she walked back over, and I steered my gaze away from them. "When's the last time you had a decent meal?"

"I've got a bit more on my mind than keeping up with three balanced meals a day."

"I know. I just—"

A ding from his work phone cut him off, another email pinging through. All three pairs of eyes in the room cut down to it, the air charging with anticipation.

That, and a heavy dose of dread.

Slowly, he reached for his phone and opened the email. His eyes scanned it over in silence before giving any sort of reaction, but my heart slammed around in my chest like it already knew it was a death sentence. It had to be a reply from the people who ran the real estate program back in Roswell that Heather attended.

Or claimed she did.

Remorseful blue eyes rolled up to me, Ryan's expression giving it away. "Dude—"

"She never went to any real estate school, did she?" I didn't want to hear

FIFTEEN

him say the whole thing, so I beat him to it. As if owning my own wife's lies out loud made up for the fact that I'd missed them all.

Ryan gave a somber shake of his head, and I lowered mine to rest on the back of my fist and shut my eyes.

Tired.

So fucking tired.

"So…" Layla's voice drifted off on an awkward current. "If she isn't a real estate agent, then what does she do?"

"Tommy said they worked together, right?"

Sighing, I lifted my eyes that felt too heavy in my own head back up to Ryan.

"He said he worked *for* her." Casting a glance over the mess of papers on my coffee table, I mumbled, "Which makes even less sense."

None of this made any sense.

"Why doesn't it make sense?" Layla asked.

"You mean aside from the fact that he's a drug dealer and she's a suburban housewife?" Ryan flinched at my unforgiving tone, but Layla was unphased.

In fact, she was just as bitter in return.

"*Yeah*. She lied about her job, she lied about where she was this weekend, she wasn't exactly subtle about how much she hated Kat." She rose off of Ryan's lap, passion pitching her voice higher. "It doesn't take a genius to jump to the idea that she might have hired Tommy to mess with Kat."

Ryan tried to diffuse. "Babe—"

"Normally, I would agree with you," I jumped in, defense vibrating inside my chest. "But this isn't as simple as messing with her. Kat was kidnapped. She was taken to another state. She was at an auction to be *trafficked*."

"Yeah, and Heather was in that same state and *lied* about it."

"Yes, I'm aware. Thank you." I worked my hands in and out of fists over my knees, trying to itch the scratch to put them both through walls. "Heather may be vindictive, and she may be a liar, but she is not a criminal. Whoever has Kat is well-connected to the black market, and that's not Heather."

"Didn't Tommy say something about Heather's family?" Ryan broke the stare down between Layla and I, bringing our attention to him. "What do you know about them?"

"Not much." Brushing a hand back through my hair, I thought out loud. "It's just her parents, and they were never too fond of me. I haven't seen her dad, Ray, since Maya was born. Her mom makes a trip down for Maya's birthday each year and that's about it."

"Where do they live?"

"Back in Roswell where Heather and I grew up."

Ryan blinked at me, tilting his head. "That's just outside of Atlanta, right?"

I nodded, not liking the anticipatory hold on his expression.

Ryan blustered back, slapping his hands on his knees. "Dude, don't you find that at least a *little* weird? You find Kat in Atlanta where Heather and her parents both *also* happen to be?"

Frustration looped through my jaw, stringing it tight. "And your point is?"

"My *point*? My point is that Tommy said you have no idea what kind of twisted family you married into. One thing we can't figure out is how Heather would pull any of this off by herself, but what if she's not working with just Tommy? What if her parents are in on it?"

My headache pulsed with his theory, and I lowered my voice from any small ears listening. "Do you realize how fucking insane you sound right now?"

"Yeah, I do. But what else makes sense?"

"None of this," I bit back too fast. "None of this makes *any* sense."

Before I knew it, I was on my feet, pacing around the living room like I could run away from the desperation bubbling up inside of me. "I've known Heather since high school. We've grown up together, we've lived together, we've had a kid together. There shouldn't be anything I don't know about her."

Ryan's lips thinned as Layla's stare fell to her lap. I threw my arm out her way to get her attention and prayed like hell what I was about to say would save my sanity.

"Don't you think if Heather had anything to do with Kat's disappearance

FIFTEEN

that you of all people would know?"

Ryan shot me a look for bringing it up, but what other choice did I have? Layla was the only one of us who'd been around the same people who took Kat, even if she didn't remember much.

She pursed her mouth and set it to the side. "Actually," she began, and my head screamed and told me to run out of the room before I heard whatever was about to come next. "Ever since you told Ryan that Kat said Heather's name, there's been something just *eating* away at my brain. It's been the weirdest thing. Like… like when you have something on the tip of your tongue and just can't remember what it is?"

She focused her wide gaze on me. "I kept thinking about when you interviewed me again at the station and I had that panic attack."

My jaw sawed back and forth. I remembered.

"I couldn't figure out why I was triggered out of freaking nowhere like that," she kept going, her eyes and hand gestures getting bigger. "I was *clearly* far from okay, but there was just something I couldn't put my finger on that set me off."

My tongue moved like it'd been replaced by a boulder, not wanting to ask but needing to know.

"Did you remember what it was?"

Sincerity was bright in her eyes as she nodded. "I did. You said Heather had just left when Ryan and I got there, and do you remember what I asked you? The *first* thing out of my mouth?"

The boulder in my mouth moved to my chest, sticking there and sawing against bones every time I breathed. I thought back to that day at the PD, pain springing beneath every pore of my skin as I remembered exactly what she was getting at.

"You asked me what the smell was in the air," I replied, mouth full of cotton.

"Because I *remembered* it." She came closer with all of her enthusiasm, not realizing or just not caring how much it burned me. "Even if I didn't know I remembered her perfume, my brain remembered smelling citrus—*gardenias*—the day Kat switched places with me."

"Which would mean Heather was there when Kat was taken," Ryan hollowly filled in the blank that I wished he hadn't.

The room was silent for several seconds as I thought.

The desperate bubbles in my stomach from earlier were brewing stronger and sizzling louder. They built up in my chest, popping and bouncing off organs as they traveled up.

It doesn't make sense. It doesn't make sense. It doesn't make sense.

"You were heavily drugged that day," I heard myself saying. "There's no way you could accurately—"

"*Dominic*," she exasperated.

"*What?*" I lashed back at Layla, shouting loud enough to break the promise I made to Kat to save the children from hearing me yell. "Do you realize what you're asking me to believe? That the woman I've spent the last thirteen years of my life with has been *lying* to me every single second of it? And not just lying, but screwing with my job behind my back and plotting to off our nanny?"

"Dom—"

"Do you know how much of a fool that would make me? A detective who couldn't even see that his own wife was feeding him bullshit every single day of their lives together?"

"That wouldn't be your fault," Ryan argued. "You trusted her and she knew it."

Yes, I did.

I trusted her blindly, and everything they were trying to get me to believe would mean she used my blind spot against me to hit me where it hurt most.

My head spun as I lost my footing in all the lies, falling through the complete madness of it all. Heather pretended she had a job she didn't. She pretended she didn't know Tommy. She pretended she wasn't in Atlanta last weekend and lied right to my face about it all.

So many lies. So goddamn tired.

"Dom, just *think* about it objectively." Ryan's voice chased me around the living room as I kept pacing. "If you didn't know her, she'd have been a

FIFTEEN

suspect from the beginning. She has motive and opportunity, and did you even *see* her the day Kat was taken?"

"Before she went to work, *yes*."

"But she doesn't work!" The truth slapped me across the face, blood rushing in my head to drown out my denial. It tried to stay afloat, tried to keep kicking, but all of the puzzle pieces were falling together on top of it, making too many connections to ignore. "If she wasn't going to work on the day Kat was taken, then where was she going?"

I squeezed my eyes shut, heat lapping at my skin beneath my clothes. I wanted to strip naked, go upstairs, and break the goddamn shower until it spit out ice instead of water. Anything to escape the heat and these questions that made me want to smash everything in sight.

The day Kat was taken was over a month ago, and I thought about it so often. Finding her note, finding Layla's car, finding nothing of Kat but a bag empty of anything but pepper spray and her phone.

From the back of my mind, a memory *stabbed*.

A knife.

The knife.

"Kat said she brought a knife," I remembered aloud. "In her note—"

"We never found a knife on scene," Ryan cut in.

It was that same second that an epiphany opened up beneath me, a gaping hole that I dropped through with nothing to grab onto. The contents of my stomach rose up my throat, my body quickly draining of all heat, blood, bones, muscles, everything until I was empty of everything but the truth.

"That's because I found it back in our kitchen a week later."

The sound of my own voice was detached, a hollow sound filling a silent room.

I wrote the knife off. When I found it back in our kitchen, I assumed I was wrong about it being missing the day Kat was taken.

Because it didn't make sense. Because it *shouldn't* make any sense.

The living room was spinning now, the furniture and pictures on the walls dragging across my vision like smeared paints. I pinched my eyes shut to make it stop, but all there was in the darkness was her. Heather's deceptive smile stretched across my mind, making me want to rip my fingers down her porcelain face to shred the lies in it.

"She was there when they took Kat…" I murmured, half out of breath, half choking on the words. "She's known this whole time."

I stood in the middle of my living room, arms hanging heavy at my sides and completely frozen. Something cold stung the flesh of my palm, and my eyes fell down to see a glass of water being placed in it.

"You should drink." Ryan's voice was foggy, a distant order I didn't follow.

I couldn't think about basic functions like drinking at the moment.

Not when I couldn't even swallow down what was right in front of me.

There was just too much to get down, too much to focus on, and all of it making my stomach sick and head dazed. Just how much of this was Heather? Just the set up, or did she have a heavier hand in trying to murder the woman I chose over her?

No amount of rationalizing her secrets did any good. Not when I had this hideous feeling that this was merely the tip of the iceberg of Heather's deception.

"I need air," I muttered half-dazed to myself. "I need air."

Breathing in a burdensome gulp of oxygen, I handed Ryan back the cup of water and wiped my palm with condensation against my pants. Just as I turned to leave out the door and bathe my hot skin in the chilly night, my phone vibrated in my back pocket.

Pulling it out with a labored sigh, I glanced at the screen—

And froze.

"Who is it?" Ryan moved closer to see the unknown number flashing across my screen. "I don't recognize the area code."

"I do," I replied, stiff and on edge. "It's from Atlanta."

SIXTEEN

KAT

I woke up the next morning alone.

The battering of rain coming down outside ended up being what stirred the sleep from my brain enough to roll over in Blake's bed and realize he was gone.

Which wasn't abnormal. He was usually gone when I woke up.

But I also usually heard him leave and watched him go.

I wasn't a light sleeper back home between sharing a room with Charlotte and watching over Mom on the nights she'd tweak up. Here, deep sleep was a dream I couldn't even remember anymore. I woke up every couple hours during the night, thinking about Charlotte or Dominic or death.

Maybe that's why I was so especially tired last night, passing out on Blake's chest just a few minutes into him reading me a chapter from *A Tale of Two Cities.*

When I opened my dry eyes only a few hours later, Blake hadn't moved either of us. My head was still on his chest, and the book was off to the side, abandoned so he could wrap an arm around my waist.

I should have moved. I *knew* I should have moved.

Instead, I made a vow in my head that if I found my way back to Dominic, I'd make myself forget how comfortable it felt to sleep in another man's arms. I made that vow and then I closed my eyes, falling back asleep on a chest filled with smoke.

Blake had four days left to find me a buyer.

I'd asked again yesterday about a plan, and he didn't say much. Last night, when I woke up for the second time, I cried about it.

My tears were silent and my sobs were soft as I thought about death and everyone I'd hurt by dying. Picturing everyone's face when they found out was what brought on the waterworks last night. Layla, Mrs. Sharon, Maya, *Dominic...*

Charlotte made me cry the worst.

Eventually, the giant puddle of tears I'd wet Blake's shirt with woke him up. I froze when I felt his breathing change and held my sobs back between sealed lips, crossing my fingers that he would go back to sleep. Instead, in the dark of his room, his strong arms circled around me and hugged me tight, neither of us saying a word as I broke down to pieces.

Blake never needed to ask me what was wrong and never asked me to talk about it.

As big a fan of expressing emotions as he was, he knew I just wasn't.

I also sucked at it, so there was that.

Sighing, I laid in his bed and rolled around in the sheets, stuffing my face against his pillow and sucking down his fresh scent of aftershave and cigarettes. Longing coiled tight inside my chest, missing the man that belonged to the smokey clean aroma.

Should I have considered unpacking how attached I'd gotten to Blake in just over a month?

Probably.

Instead, I kicked my legs from out beneath his sheets and found a nice way to distract myself instead. And I mean *nice*. Like a good deed.

I, Kat Sanders, was going to do a good deed for another person.

Standing up and sweeping a glance around his room, the momentum to follow through on this whole good deed business sort of hit an early snag.

As a detainee, I was sort of working with... limited resources.

I couldn't get him flowers, and given how those things sort of tended to die, I wanted to steer clear of anything morbid. 'Cause, you know. My impending doom and all.

I couldn't bake, I couldn't get him a gift, I couldn't even make him something stupid like a card.

I had nothing to give in return to the guy who gave me safe shelter, food, and saved my life like a bajillion times. Oh, except for heartache.

I was good for loads of that.

God, I fucking sucked.

In the end, my 'good deed' amounted to cleaning his room for him. I ignored the fact that I *probably* should have been helping tidy up all along and started with the bathroom.

Once I finished in there, I made the bed, picked up any clothes on the floor, and organized his nightstand and bookshelf.

As I was smoothing out the wrinkles on his comforter, the bedroom door opened behind me. Springing up, I did a quick spin to find Blake standing in the doorway, a white bag fisted in his hand and a perplexed look sitting on his face.

My gut did a flip-flop as he studied his room.

"Did you clean up in here?"

For whatever bizarre reason, a rush of embarrassment flooded my bloodstream, boiling my skin and making me shift in place. Curling my fingers into my palm, I shrugged.

"A little."

Still not moving from where he was, he shot me a look of sincere confusion. "Why?"

Cool, now I felt like a dumbass.

"I don't know…" More shrugging and awkward eye placement as I looked anywhere but at him. "I just wanted to… do something for you, but like, I can't *do* much since I can't *go* anywhere, so I cleaned. Which is dumb." Sighing, I dropped to hide my heating face inside my hands. "This was really dumb."

"It's not dumb." Blake was fast to defend my stupid gesture, and I wanted to crawl inside my skin and die because of it.

"It's totally dumb," I grumbled, ignoring a voice in my head telling me to shut up. "You don't have to make me feel better about it, really."

Was I making this a bigger deal than it was? Should I stop talking about it? Why can't I stop talking about it?

Dear god, I had word vomit.

"I'll throw shit on the floor again to make it how it was." Cue fake, forced laughter.

Blake exhaled a sharp sigh.

"Look," he kicked his bedroom door closed behind him, "you're really cute when you're flustered, so could you shut up and just accept that I appreciate you cleaning?"

My jaw shot open, mouth going dry in seconds flat.

It took me a few moments to recuperate, struggling to make my lips close and form words again. "You have *got* to be the most blunt person I know."

He raised an eyebrow to me. "Then you haven't met yourself, Kitten."

My whole body tightened for a split second before releasing.

That *fucking* nickname.

At this point, I couldn't tell whether I loved it or hated it when he used the name. *Yes*, Dominic had used it first but he'd also only used it once. Blake had at least five 'kitten's under his belt with no sign of stopping. I responded every time he used it, and so did my heart, giving a little spasm that I couldn't tell whether it was a good or bad sign.

"What's that?" I asked, referring to the bag in his hand.

Holding the bag up, he drew a cheeky grin.

"Breakfast."

"*What?*" I felt my eyes go wider than they were seconds ago. "That's not fair! You can't try to one-up my nice gesture."

A gentle laugh tumbled from his lips. "What?"

"Well, I can't exactly go out and get you—what's in the bag?"

"Egg and cheese croissant sandwich."

"*Fuck*, that sounds delicious."

"Well, then stop complaining and eat it."

SIXTEEN

The bag soared across the room as Blake tossed it my way. My stomach turned over with hunger as I caught it and felt the warmth of the sandwich inside steam up my palms, the smell of grease wafting through the air.

"Is this why you were gone when I woke up?" Sinking my teeth into the croissant, an unruly moan ripped through my chest the second the buttery crust melted on my tongue.

I caught Blake watching me with sprinkled amusement.

"I take it you like the sandwich?"

"It's heaven." Shoving a bite that was too big for my mouth down my throat, I asked through chewing, "Did you get one for yourself?"

He shook his head with a soft smile, watching me. "No, I ate before I left."

The sandwich was half gone already, my empty stomach filling with grease and cheesy eggs. Fuck, it was so good.

"You went out for more than this, right?"

Blake shirked my eyeline, swinging his focus elsewhere. "Yeah, I had a few errands to run."

"God, what's freedom like?" I mused around another big bite. Swallowing, I asked, "Let me live vicariously through you. What kind of errands we talkin' about?"

Blake dropped some spare change on the nightstand I *just* cleaned.

"Boring ones."

"Like what?" Crinkling paper filled the beat as I crushed the empty sandwich wrapper with both hands. "Come on, paint me a picture with all those pretty words in your brain."

The cords of his neck tightened, a tick pulsing in his jaw.

"There's nothing to paint."

My head dropped back with a scoff. "Come on—"

"Did you get enough to eat?" he cut me off, pitching his voice louder than mine. My lips popped open, thankful I'd already finished the sandwich so half-chewed egg didn't come spilling out.

What the fuck is up his ass?

"Are you avoiding the question?" A question about *errands*, of all things.

"I'm not *avoiding* anything." Except his nostrils flared like he was. "There's nothing to say. They were errands. Now they're done."

Worry clenched around the bones in my chest as I drifted a step closer to him. I was about to ask him if something had happened while he was out when he shrugged his long-sleeve overshirt off, leaving him in only a white undershirt.

He turned to toss the overshirt in his hamper when I saw it—the same blood-stained bandage he was wearing yesterday and the day before wrapped around his bicep.

"When's the last time you changed your bandage?"

He gave a cursory glance at his upper arm. "Couple days."

My head jerked forward with shock. "Are you kidding me?"

"It's not a big deal. I'll be fine."

"No, you won't. Those things can get infected if you don't clean them properly."

Blake arced a high brow at my tone—all responsible and shit—and it had me moving across the room to him, snagging a few of his long fingers in mine and towing him behind me into the bathroom.

"Did you clean up in here too?" he asked as I flicked the light on.

"Yes. Now, stand still."

He did as I said as I knelt to the floor to the cabinets below the sink and started rummaging through the limited items he had stored down there. A few loose bandages, peroxide, Q-tips, shaving gel, a spare bottle of his body wash, and a half-used roll of gauze.

"Kat, you don't have to do this."

Reluctance consumed every deep syllable of his voice as I set the bottle of peroxide and roll of gauze up on the bathroom counter. With a sigh, I stood and faced him.

"I'm pretty much responsible for you getting shot so yeah. Yeah, I do."

It was the *least* I could do, right? Between this and cleaning his room, I was about .5% closer to making up for all the bad shit I'd done to him.

Only 99.5% left to go.

"I barely even feel it," he tried to argue.

SIXTEEN

"*Hey.*" I pinned his gaze with mine, all business and no bullshit. "I'm changing your nasty ass bandage. Suck it up."

I went back to getting things ready on the sink, knowing without seeing it that he was rolling his eyes. Blake was *always* rolling his eyes. I hiked myself up on the bathroom counter for better vantage, getting comfortable on the cold granite as I beckoned him to come in closer.

Blake stayed exactly where he was, not moving a damn inch.

Unamused, I shot him a look that told him to stop fucking messing around. In return, he jumped his thick eyebrows up at me and sent the same look back. This went on for some time—longer than it should have. We talked through mimicked expressions and pointed glances, an unyielding stubbornness tethered between us.

He wasn't budging and I wasn't having it.

"Oh, for fucks sake." Fed up, I stretched my legs out and latched my feet behind his waist, dragging him in closer.

This was another one of those *glorious* moments I didn't think completely through.

Blake stumbled into me, catching himself between my legs and against the counter. Surprise rippled through my lungs as his chest crashed into mine, my legs fumbling to lock behind his back as I lost my balance.

My hands shot to his shoulders on instinct, and his went straight to my bare thighs in what I think was instinct of his own. He grabbed onto me and I grabbed onto him, the two of us becoming an unintended tangle of limbs trying to stabilize each other.

The real problem with what I'd done didn't become clear until about two seconds later when we both looked up at the same time. Our gazes clashed, inescapable tension pulsing sharply between us.

And our mouths.

Which were consequently only a few inches apart.

Whoops. Shit. Fuck.

"Sorry," I breathed, almost screaming as Blake let the weight of his gaze fall victim to us and drop to my lips. He studied them, his eyes looking as though they'd been dipped in a mixture of bright embers and charred ash.

Fuck, they were beautiful and so was he.

Even when he was doing something he shouldn't.

In fact, it sort of made him even more beautiful.

Silence strung out between us, but I didn't try to end it. In the past, I'd had a targeted hatred with silence in any capacity, but with Blake, the quiet moments didn't seem quiet.

In our shared silence, we had some of our loudest conversations.

Like now. The dialogue was screaming from our closed lips, speaking of cravings and consequences and tortured hearts. Slowly, his hands on my thighs indented their grip, squeezing until I was sure all ten fingerprints of his were branded into my skin.

Then, he released.

His touch left my body as he retreated like he'd escaped a brush with death. His hands balled to fists at his sides, and I wondered in my fucked up head if he was trying to hold onto the feeling of me or crush it.

"Let's get this over with," he mumbled, his resonance low-pitched and guarded.

Fuck.

I'd done that to him. I'd done that same goddamn hurtful thing to him *again*.

Self-loathing carved through my chest and took away my breath because I didn't deserve it. My lungs starved and my brain said *good*.

Someone bad like me deserved to starve.

The wicked didn't deserve to *get*, they deserved to have *taken*. The problem was Blake could empty me out from head to toe and take it all: my blood, my bones, my oxygen, my soul.

But he still wouldn't find the thing he was looking for.

I got to work on his bandage, carefully removing the old one that'd become stiff over the days. Neither of us spoke as I peeled away the cloth of dried and dirty blood, revealing the wound beneath where Dominic's bullet split through his flesh.

A hiss sucked through my teeth, heart cracking as I took in the evidence of Dominic's wrath.

SIXTEEN

"It's inflamed." The wound was a furious red, almost like a kid had taken a bright red crayon and drawn a messy outline where the bullet passed through his arm. Spots of pus seeped from the core of where it hit him, the whole area swollen and angry. "And maybe infected," I added.

"I'll survive."

I grabbed the bottle of peroxide and tipped the open top over onto a piece of toilet paper that I'd wadded up. "This might sting a little, so—"

"I'm not a child, Kat." He spared me a furtive glance. "You don't need to lie to me."

"Well, in my defense, I'm normally doing this *to* a child, so that lie comes with the whole spiel."

A frown split down his face, head turning to catch my stare. "Your sister?"

Having his eyes on me and Charlotte's presence in the air, I smiled without thinking.

"Yeah, she's kind of a clutz." Always falling out of trees or taking spills around the house during one of her many make-believe adventures. She'd never had any big injuries, thank fuck, but that girl definitely earned her scabs and scars.

Setting the peroxide down, I pressed the wad of alcohol-soaked toilet paper to Blake's festering wound and waited. At the *most*, he flexed his jaw, but that was his only reaction.

So I kept talking and kept cleaning. "She'd scream bloody murder any time I had to fix up her cuts with more than a bandaid. One time, she even hid a bloody knee from me for *hours* after she fell outside until I noticed red stains on our couch."

A puff of laughter came through his nose. "She sounds stubborn."

"Oh my god, you have no idea."

Roguish eyes slid my way, glowing gently. "I think I do."

I ran my teeth over my bottom lip, biting down to keep a grin from cracking my face. It ached the insides of my cheeks regardless of being captured, and I all but gave up.

At least things were getting back to easy flowing again.

"*Anyway*," I said pointedly, trying to keep myself and my ditzy smiling in check. "All of this to say, she'd turn into a fucking banshee anytime I had to use peroxide."

Now that got a chuckle. Small and deep, rich and smooth.

"Spoken with true love."

"Well, *duh*." I finished cleaning his arm, grabbing the roll of gauze. "I love that girl more than life. She was the only thing that kept me going when things were really bad with our mom."

Yeah, Blake knew about my mom. All about her. The dirty details, the sweet details, the heartbreaking ones I'd cried to him about after I learned how she really died.

"That's admirable." Blake watched my fingers circle his bicep as I ran a brand new bandage around it. "I just ran away to the nearby beach whenever things got bad at home. Didn't have anyone to stick around for."

Yeah, and I knew about Blake's trauma too.

His mom's addictive vice was alcohol, and his dad was just as shitty as mine, but at least when mine left, he stayed gone. Blake's dad came back every few months just to fuck the wife he left, eat all their food, and throw them both around a bit before disappearing again.

Rinse, recycle, repeat.

"Maybe if you'd had someone to take care of, you'd be better about letting others care of you instead of being a stubborn ass about it." Blake's signature eye roll entered the conversation as I playfully nudged his shoulder. His *good* shoulder.

"And maybe you're the pot calling the kettle black," he mused in return.

A spark to argue fiercely and thoughtlessly triggered in my brain, but something reached up and pinched it out. I wasn't sure what it was, maturity or whatever, but it tied around my tongue and changed its direction.

"I used to be really bad about it." The first time Dominic and I kissed, it was because he told me my weakness was wanting to be submissive enough to let someone take care of me, but I was too afraid to let it happen. His weakness, the romantic bastard, was me. "I fought people tooth and nail who were trying to help me, but…"

SIXTEEN

I trailed off, consumed by thoughts of the last month of my life.

"But what?"

My lips popped open at the sound of Blake's voice, my eyes switching between his.

"I let you help me."

The revelation tasted light and sweet on the tip of my tongue, but it only bittered Blake's stare.

"You don't have much of a choice."

My eyebrows bounced up on my forehead in consideration. "True."

If he didn't help me, I didn't eat, didn't sleep safely, didn't live past my expiration date.

"But I think it's more than that," I continued, discovering the words thoughtfully. "It just feels… easier with you. I'm not worried about how I sound or if I'm vulnerable or weak. I'm just all sorts of messy."

I finished with a wooden laugh, crossing my dangling toes that I didn't just make things awkward.

When I finally mustered the guts to risk a look at him, I found Blake with warmer eyes than anticipated. I almost forgot the color of them wasn't purely pitch black, but this full-bodied brown that made me crave a bite of melted, sweet dark chocolate.

That way I could drink it down and finally feel like I'd had my fill of him.

Blake watched me as if he knew my sweet tooth was throbbing just looking at him.

"Messy understands messy," he murmured.

My heart set off beat as we held each other's stare, acknowledging with closed mouths the downright beautiful mess we were.

My lightning fucking *purred* in my veins, and I kicked back a sharp breath, dropping my eyes back to something safe like a bullet wound.

"Speaking of messes. My sister—"

"Smooth segue."

"Thank you." A quick clearing of my throat unclogged the tension stuffing up our breathing space. I'd almost finished rewrapping his arm. "Charlotte would fly off the handle *so* hard whenever I had to use peroxide,

I ended up having to make up a game to get her through it."

"What was the game?"

I waved him off. "Oh, it's dumb."

"What if I want to play?"

"You don't. Trust me." Pleased with how the bandage looked, I pinched the strip of gauze between my fingers and ripped off a finishing end. "Do you have tape?"

"Only if you tell me what the game is."

My shoulders slumped, a huffed laugh pouring out with his name in it. He mocked me back, sliding my name along the same melody I'd drawn his out with, pinning me with a pointed look that said he wasn't letting this go.

Groaning and fighting down a grin itching at my cheeks, I gave in—a very *un*-Kat-Sanders thing to do. Honestly though, I was happy to eat up any opportunity to talk about Bugs.

"So," I hardly missed the wink of victory smirking in his eyes. "Charlotte was going to scream regardless when I came anywhere near her cuts with peroxide, and trust me, that girl has pipes that could shatter glass."

Blake let a quiet chuckle shake his shoulders, and I had the super insane crazy person thought to hug him tight enough that I could feel his laughter roll through my body.

God, I was losing it.

"So I told her she was allowed to scream, but only once, and that we would do it together. She would pick the silliest word or phrase she could think of, and we'd yell it out together whenever I put the peroxide on her scrape."

"And that worked?"

"Like a charm. She'd always be laughing instead of crying or screaming by the end of it."

The complex man of pain and lightning softened right before my eyes.

"You sound like a pretty great older sister."

Me, the complex girl of pain and lightning, hardened right down to her very core.

SIXTEEN

"Yeah…"

Maybe at one point during the last five years, I'd glimpsed the line of greatness with Charlotte. Not now. If I was so great now, I would have found a way to beat the devil and make it back to her. I would have clawed at the walls of this place until my nails broke and fingers bled and I made it out.

No, I was the kind of awful sister who left on a broken promise. I didn't know it was broken at the time, but that didn't matter for shit. If I died, *none* of this mattered.

I'd been quietly hating myself and wallowing for long enough that the air had gone stiff. Blake hadn't moved the heavy burden of his gaze off of my face. He was waiting to see if I wanted to talk about why my voice had been sucked away for the last thirty seconds inside the giant break in my heart.

I didn't.

"Anyway." Another smooth as fuck segue. "What would your word be?"

One of the things I loved most about Blake was how he didn't push. If I didn't want to talk about something, then he let me hide inside whatever distraction I picked out.

Softly, he shook his head at my diverting question. "I don't know."

"Oh, come on. It could be anything!" I pushed my shoulders back and sat straighter, rolling my head around my neck before leveling my concentrated stare on his. "The first thing that comes to your mind. No second guessing. No changing your answer. Just look straight at me and choose a word."

His chest rose slowly as he breathed deep, the flames of his eyes particularly focused.

"Only one word?"

I nodded once. "Only one word."

It wasn't like I was asking him something hard or for an essay in response. Just one word. One easy, simple, silly word.

Except there was nothing easy, simple, or silly about the way Blake was staring at me.

No, no—*through* me. He cut right through me with his eyes of bladed beauty and locked in on my soul, baring it like it belonged to him. Like he knew every intimate detail of it inside and out better than I did.

Honestly, he might have.

My breath had gone up in the flames of Blake's eyes as he looked at me like no one had ever managed to before.

Again, my lungs were starving and again, my brain chanted *good*.

"Do we have to scream it?" he finally whispered.

My eyelashes fluttered in weakness, wanting to end the game. "Blake—"

"Star-crossed."

My eyes snapped wide open. I froze. "What?"

He'd never looked more certain of anything in his life as he repeated on a low caress, "Star-crossed." He dragged his softly glowing gaze across my face. "That's the first word that comes to my mind when I look at you."

I tried to not have a visible reaction but knew I failed when I heard my sorrow catch in my throat.

"Really?" I whispered right back.

He nodded, the portrait of stunningly heartbroken. "I told you I was hopeless."

A hopeless romantic, I wanted to correct, but I couldn't find my voice again.

It'd fallen inside the growing break in my heart from every time Blake reminded me it could be us. His heart *ached* for it to be, and I wanted to shove my hands against his chest and scream at him for dragging us down into the ocean when we could have been so safe in the pool.

It wasn't his fault that we couldn't hate each other.

But it was my fault we couldn't love each other.

Water gathered on my eyelashes as I blinked, lowering my focus to Blake's lips so I could watch his magic words form as I pleaded, "Tell me the meaning of star-crossed."

I knew what it meant. I just wanted to hear it from him.

I watched his bottom lip part from his top and remembered when my lips were fit in between those two.

SIXTEEN

"It's two stars made out of the same fire who have the misery of meeting."

My chest *squeezed* in pain and pleasure. I was right. They were words of magic.

"Why is it a misery?" I breathed.

"Because that's all they'll have. They're meant to be an epic constellation written in to the sky forever, but all they do is meet. They go on existing and never see each other again, but they always know. The universe created someone explicitly for them they'll never be able to have, and isn't that a misery?"

Oh god.

My heart had turned into a fist, punching from beneath so hard, I lost my breath in the pain.

"I hate that," I whispered, heartbreak narrowing my airway.

He cracked the saddest smile. "I'm not too fond of it either."

Sitting there on that sink, all I could think was about how badly I wanted to scream.

Not just one word. All the words. I wanted to scream *all* the words for letting this happen. It'd only been just over a month, and that shouldn't be enough time for this to happen. *This...* intensity and attachment and insane depth.

That should be reserved for people who've known each other almost five years. Not almost five weeks.

It didn't make sense. Blake and I didn't make *sense* to my fucked up brain.

How could I literally feel like my heart was beating outside my body because of him and those pretty fucking words he'd just spun around my head?

And how could I feel like stabbing myself just because I put that sadness in his eyes that he worked so hard to pretend wasn't there? I wanted to wash it away, scrub his soul until it was clean of me. I wanted to do whatever I could to take his pain away.

To let him know he wasn't alone.

To let him know I felt the same way.

We *were* star-crossed lovers in this universe, and I knew it. I could *feel* it in my sick soul. In another timeline, in another life after this one, Blake and I would get to find out what loving each other without consequences was like. Perhaps, in another life, we've loved each other already and that's why not being able to love each other now was so devastating.

Tears slid down my cheeks as proof of the devastation. Blake reacted fast, wiping them away like he was grateful for the chance to touch me.

Sniffling, I swallowed back a small sob. "I cry so much around you."

He nodded gently and without judgment, collecting every falling petal of saltwater on his rough thumbs.

"Yeah, but you're beautiful when you do it."

A fresh wave of tears rolled out for him to catch, and I wondered if he'd said something so unguarded and romantic just to watch them fall. I wound my fingers around his forearms, clinging to him as he cupped my face and cleaned my misery away.

Small hiccups shook my chest as we anchored ourselves together through my tears.

Any excuse to hold each other, right?

My face burned hot as Blake thumbed the corner of my eye, wetting his skin with my sorrow.

"Have I ever told you how much I love your eyes?"

I shook my head, sure before he spoke that I didn't want to know how much he loved them.

"They're a shade of green I've never seen before, and when you cry, they glint like emeralds." His mouth barely moved as his deep voice rumbled through it, mesmerized by the thing from my father that I hated so much. "I could write a thousand poems about them."

Holy fuck, my *heart*.

My heart was being squeezed to death with every tender word he shouldn't have said but was too far gone to stop himself. He wanted me, and he couldn't have me. All of his cards were on the table, his heart bleeding for me all over it, not even knowing how I felt in return.

He'd always done all the talking and confessing between us. All I'd done was kiss him and throw him out. He didn't know he wasn't alone in this madness strung out between us. He didn't know how fucking lovable he was or how *easy* it would be to fall for him.

All he knew was rejection and pain, and I'd never wanted to soothe anyone more in my life.

"I—" The words I wanted were on my tongue, sitting there with *such* potential to heal, but I was overthinking it. *How do I put it?* In my pause, Blake fixed his damning eyes on mine and all thought in my head dried right up, leaving only my heart to step forward and speak its truth.

"I don't know if this makes it any easier, but I want you to know that—" I swallowed thickly. "If it wasn't Dominic… it would be you. I would love you."

Blake shut his eyes before the last word escaped my lips. His hands left my face and turned to fists against the bathroom counter on either side of my legs. He breathed deeply, standing statuesque for several moments. My eyes were all over his hardened face, searching for signs that what I'd said had made any of this better.

Worry gnawed with sharp teeth at my insides as a focused exhale released through his nose as he stood so painfully still.

Then, like a lightning flash, he wasn't still anymore.

Blake ripped his eyes open, a gasp hitting the back of my throat as he pinned their blaze on me, showing me a depth of agony I wasn't ready for.

"It *doesn't* help actually." The words barely made it out, sliced between his gnashed teeth. "It just makes it that much harder."

A dry sob climbed out of my chest, crashing into my hands as I buried my face in them. My shoulders caved as I panted untamed, hating every single inch of myself and how I couldn't just say *one* thing right.

All I did was hurt. All I was good for was pain. What the *fuck* was wrong with me?

"I'm sorry. I thought—"

"I know," Blake cut me off, pain festering in his voice.

Why the fuck couldn't I do anything right? And not even just now, but *always*.

Fucking up was my thing, wasn't it? Some people's thing was golf or arts and crafts or always being the one with snacks.

My thing was corrupting everything around me.

There wasn't a single person in my life who I hadn't ruined with my poisoned touch. Maybe it's good that I was put here. Maybe Heather wasn't wrong.

Maybe I did deserve to die.

"You should hate me," I mumbled into my palms.

Blake's sigh was audible. "We both know I can't do that."

Because he wanted to love me. Because he had feelings for me. Because I'd poisoned him with a kiss.

"But I deserve it." My fingertips bent as I pressed them into my skull, gripping tighter and tighter, wanting the sensation of blood beneath my nails. "For every bad thing I've done, I *deserve* to be hated. You should hate me. My sister should hate me. Dominic should *definitely* hate me for all the terrible shit I've done."

"What about the good things?"

My head snapped up, released from my fingers' pressure-hold to stare him dead in the eye. "I haven't done anything *good*."

In fact, I was insulted he gave me the credit of being capable of goodness.

"I left my baby sister thinking I was saving her, but now I've just *abandoned* her. I somehow tricked a man who is so goddamn perfect into loving me, and I just *know* he's in hell trying to find me. And while he's tearing himself apart looking for me, I'm here with *you*. I'm laughing with you and feeling things for you and *hurting* you, because I'm selfish and my wires are all fucked up. My heart isn't even inside my chest anymore because Dominic has it, but I still couldn't stop whatever this," I threw a quick gesture between our chests, "is from happening! It-it's like you were inside of me before I ever met you. You're just so… *familiar*. I don't get it. I don't *get* it."

I finished my long-winded self-deprivation on a soft sob, folding into myself and just fucking weeping. Dirty guilt drenched my insides, coaxing out and inspiring my pathetic sobs. My insides were bogged down by the shame, heaviness like I'd never felt weighing on my muscles and tiring out

SIXTEEN

my lungs.

The world was still blacked out behind my closed eyes when body heat tickled my skin and the heady scent of him burned my lungs. Warm hands covered the dips of my waist, squeezing gently.

"You can't take the blame for us. Neither of us got much of a choice."

Fresh salt breached beneath my closed eyes, my fingers tangling in his shirt as emotion choked my voice.

"Because we're star-crossed?"

A weathered sigh was the only warning I got before Blake rested his forehead against mine. My heart spasmed for the millionth time, and I pressed myself against him, chasing his comfort even though I shouldn't.

His breath warmed my lips, minty and burnt, and I wondered just how close he was to kissing me.

I wondered if I'd stop him.

He nodded our heads together as one.

"Because we're star-crossed, Kitten."

SEVENTEEN

KAT

Three days before I was supposed to be sold, Blake took me down for breakfast.

He said the crowd had been so big for the Line Up that only one girl was left, and she wouldn't bother us if we popped in for a quick bite to eat. Ray was out on business, and it wouldn't matter if Claudia saw us since Ray didn't believe her when she was right on the money about something going on between us.

It sucked big balls being a woman in a man's world, huh?

That one leftover girl was helping herself to breakfast when Blake and I got down there, and Blake was right. She ignored me like I was the goddamn bubonic plague coming around on a second wind.

Whatever. It was still nice to be out.

Scooping a fresh chunk of fluffy eggs out of the metal tin with my spoon, I turned to Blake over my shoulder. "What's your last name?"

His brows scrunched as he plucked a piece of bacon from my plate. "Dawson. Why?"

"Just realized I didn't know it." My fingers pinched around a glazed donut, plopping it on my plate before sucking the sugar off my fingers. "Does it mean anything special?"

SEVENTEEN

"No. It's biblical."

"What about Blake? What does that mean?"

He broke off a bite of bacon between his teeth, following close behind me. "Black, but also bright."

"Well, if that's not a metaphor just waiting to be written by some closet poet."

A smirk was already wriggling up my lips before I peeked up at him. He was waiting for me with flattened amusement on his face, and a dopey grin broke out on my mouth.

He sent his eyes back in a roll, nudging me by the small of my back to go find a seat at the counter. I chose the barstool at the end, its legs scrapping the silence as I pulled it out and sat my ass on its cushion.

Blake stood to my left and my legs swung that way into his gravitational pull without thinking. I was just a girl happy to have a donut, ripping off a wad of it between my teeth that was too big to chew like a lady.

Blake's eyes were on me, dancing over my face as I mauled a pastry.

After a moment, he asked, "Does Sanders mean anything?"

"Fuck if I know."

"Is Kat your entire first name?"

"No." Shaking my head, I swallowed. "It's Katerina."

Appreciation blossomed around his eyes, brightening their shine on me. "That's pretty," he rumbled.

"My mom thought so too. It means pure." To add to my unladylike chewing, I hawked a real debutante laugh. "Guess I really missed the mark on that one."

Agreement sizzled in his stare, warming his focus on me a touch hotter than was safe for our combustible chemistry. He shook his head of dark hair just once, eyes on me.

"You're as pure as sin, Katerina Sanders."

I nearly fucking choked on my donut.

Those words and the smooth cadence he used to deliver them slid right underneath my skin, smoothing their wicked velvet touch down between my legs. All of my nerves down there clenched in a way that made my brain go *oh shit*, and I immediately started shaking my head.

"Mm, nope. You can't say shit like that to me."

I was still shaking my head in denial when Blake donned a look as if I were nuts.

"Why?"

"Because it's hot!" I exclaimed like it was obvious to the whole world.

The whole world excluding Blake apparently.

"How is what I just said *hot*?"

Motherfucker. Even the word 'hot' on his tongue made me wanna suck on his.

"You put 'sin' and my name back to back and said it in that whole tortured artist kind of way that basically speaks directly to my ovaries."

Amusement rose his dark brows up his forehead, his eyes bouncing between mine to confirm I was really serious. The corner of his mouth inched up, eyelids drooping just enough to turn his spirited gaze into a hooded sliver of trouble.

"So you're turned on right now?" He pointed his rugged chin to my hand. "Eating a donut?"

I did my best to breathe and shrug. "The donut honestly makes it all hotter."

Soft laughter cast his head to the side, showing me his strong profile before he swung his full attention back to me, a damning grin tugging at his cheeks and my heart.

"You're so fucking weird, Kitten."

I didn't have time for a retort before a new voice erupted into the kitchen.

"And you two are so fucking *cute*."

Both Blake and I snapped our heads towards the noise, my pulse skyrocketing and crashing in almost the same second.

"Zoey," I sighed, swallowing down my panic.

She nodded and did a little wave. "Yeah, hi. I had to come get more lube from the closet but was stopped by the freaking hormones flying in here, *jeez*."

An exaggerated chuckle jiggled her cleavage that was one good shake

SEVENTEEN

away from being nips out. Her platinum blonde hair had grown dark roots since I'd last seen her. She pinned her mossy green stare on Blake.

"Blake, I've never seen you laugh." She snorted. "Or flirt."

Defense dropped a film over his eyes. "I'm not flirting."

"You're flirting," Zoey and I condemned at the same time.

A wrinkle scrunched between his heavy-set brows, a flush of crimson tinting the rise of his cheeks. I leaned in and grabbed his simmering stare, smiling through a whisper.

"And now you're blushing."

A steamed exhale pushed through his nose, admonishing black flames igniting.

Then, Zoey threw a bucket of ice on us both.

"Are you two fucking?"

Blake rolled and slammed his eyes shut, his full mouth thinning. Her question put a freeze around my heart, icing the stagnant organ with a frostbite that ached a lot like guilt.

Dragging a glance her way, I muttered, "No."

Zoey tilted her head, pouting with her lips that were painted ruby red today. "Well, you should. I'm betting it would be stellar. I'm choking on the chemistry here."

Tsking and not knowing what the fuck else to say, I lazily saluted her. Yeah, *saluted*.

"Thanks for your input."

She batted an audacious wink my way and then left to go choke on some dicks instead of mine and Blake's chemistry. Which, speaking of, was now bristling.

Crackling in the air like burning firewood.

The sensation was in my lower stomach too, fizzling uncomfortably at the mention of Blake and sex in the same sentence. My ankles scratched together as I tried to distract myself from the feeling, but all I ended up doing was scratching another itch entirely as I rubbed my legs together.

Blake clocked my shifting, taking it in with dilating pupils that were now blacker than black. It was right around then that I started regretting not throwing on a bra before we came down here.

I didn't think it would *matter* if I went braless.

It was just supposed to be a quick breakfast.

But now my nipples were twin peaks for all to see as Blake untied his burning focus from my bare legs and dragged it up. Slowly. So fucking slowly, like he was dragging an unlit match up my skin, gathering friction, gathering heat to spark a fire.

When he finally met my stare, I lost all words in my brain. Every single one of them scattered and fled, terrified of that fevered look in his eyes.

"Are you thinking about it?" His baritone voice dripped like honey, thick and sticky, sliding down my throat as I drank him up.

Hot air dried out my lips. "What?"

My messy breath must have touched his lips and ate up his sanity because he lowered his face over mine, drawing in close enough to kiss me.

"Given how flushed you are, I'd say you know exactly what."

God-fucking-*dammit*. My core contracted around nothing, and I silently begged the universe to take away whatever it was that emboldened Blake to be so bluntly seductive today.

Yes, I knew what he meant and *no*, I wasn't thinking about how nirvanic it would be.

But now I knew Blake was.

He was thinking about sliding himself inside of me and swallowing my moans. He was thinking about how I'd feel around his cock, what positions he'd take me in, and how my skin looked naked and glistened with our impassioned sweat. He was thinking about how we'd fuck the same way we communicated: deep and raw and feverish.

Blake had thought about it all, and he was challenging me to deny that I hadn't.

For once in my life, I chose the safe route.

"You're flirting again."

The confidence bulleted in his eyes didn't shrink one goddamn inch. "I'm aware this time."

Oh, this was bad. This was as bad as the sticky excitement pooling

SEVENTEEN

between my legs as I stared up at a man who was not Dominic. I loved Dominic. I loved fucking Dominic. I loved how he taught me how it felt when you made love instead of just stuck one body part inside another.

I loved him, I loved him, I loved him.

The chill of guilt remained inside my veins despite my chanting, honing in on the molten heat still fresh inside my core. The clashing temperatures confused my body into a delirium, dizzying my head and begging me to go lie down anywhere that wasn't here.

Alone.

Before I could make my legs of jelly dash away to somewhere safer, a danger worse than infidelity waltzed into the kitchen.

"Ms. Sanders."

Her voice had claws that raked down my spine, stiffening my shoulders up to my ears. Blake went still too, but only for a forgetful second before curving in her direction, slinging his hands behind his back to stand at attention.

Claudia ignored him, every bit of her beady focus stamped on me.

"Enjoying breakfast?"

Unsticking my voice from the back of my throat, I nodded. "Yeah." I palmed my fork, stabbing it in my food. "You should try the waffles."

And stick a knife in them before eating it.

I hadn't said that last little part out loud, but Claudia's snippy blue eyes narrowed as if she read my subtext loud and clear. She upturned her nose at Blake.

"Do you want to bother coming up with a lie for why you have her down here?"

"She needs food." His response was swift and professional. "We can't sell her to a buyer if she's emaciated."

"A buyer you've yet to find, correct?" Her thin brow curved up like a hook, ready to drag us both down. Behind his back where only I could see, Blake's knuckles bleached of color he squeezed them so tight.

"I'm working on it."

She pursed her wrinkle-ringed mouth at him, heels clacked as she moved closer.

"Go up to Ms. Sanders room and check the camera outside her door, would you? Apparently, no one on staff has seen her come or go from there in a few days, and as Head of Security, I thought you might like to check on that."

All the food I'd consumed cramped up inside my gut, threatening to make a dramatic reappearance. Victory sparkled like broken glass in Claudia's bulleted stare, a check-fucking-mate neither Blake or I had been expecting.

She was checking up on me, on *us*.

Mouth sweats drenched inside my cheeks as a swamp of heat suddenly rained sweat down the back of my neck. Blake's fists were shaking now, and every stupid bone in my body wanted to tie our hands together so we had something to hold on to as our worlds rattled.

"Don't worry." Claudia side-stepped Blake, creating an exit path for him. "She'll be right here waiting when you get back."

His broad shoulders rose with a stiff inhale while I screamed at him in my head to *move*. Lightning was sewing the muscles together in his back, curling them tight beneath his shirt, and I knew better than anyone what happened when that lightning snapped.

He wasn't dumb enough to kill Claudia right now in cold blood.

But he might have been pissed off enough to do it.

Thankfully, only a couple *obvious* seconds stretched between them before Blake moved, retreating upstairs to the room I hadn't stepped foot in since I got back from the auction.

Both Claudia and I watched him go, a little voice in my head praising him for not turning back to steal one last look at me. I wanted him to. *Fuck*, did I want him to so I could steal my own dose of comfort from his eyes, but he and I were both in deep shit as it was.

With Blake gone, Claudia sauntered over to where I sat, taking his place. The smell of her pungent perfume choked the burnt air Blake had left behind, every shallow breath I took from that point on stinging with her presence.

Still with her head turned to watch where Blake had left, she said, "I cannot wait until you're gone and his head can unclog of you."

For as undisguised as her hateful comment was, I'd never felt a stronger sweep of relief.

If she was talking about Blake in future-tense, then she didn't plan to kill him.

Just me.

Just me was fine.

I clicked my tongue, nodding down at my food that would now go uneaten. "Three more days."

"Actually," She whipped around, jolting me back in my seat. "That's why I wanted to find you." The unusual chipper quality to her tone curled a shiver down my spine. So did the way she looked at me as if confetti cannons were shooting off behind my back.

"There's been an update to your proceedings, and I wanted to see the look on your face when I told you."

My eyes rounded in my head, and I knew I'd just given her some type of upper hand by showing fear, but I didn't fucking care. Not if she knew something I didn't.

"It seems we've beat the deadline by a full day, Ms. Sanders." Pride bloated her tone while dread packed mine, my voice getting smothered down to a wisp beneath it.

"Meaning?"

She paused, deliberately holding the suspense around my throat like a noose before cinching the knot. "You've been sold, Ms. Sanders. Ray's signing your paperwork at Reeves as we speak."

As if someone had put their fists around my lungs, they stopped moving.

In the suffocation, I searched between her eyes for a lie. I didn't find one. My bottom lip searched for my top to form some words, but it didn't find that either.

Feeling in my mouth, my face, my fingertips went numb, so I guessed my blood had vanished too. Everything was just… cold.

Even the air I used to speak with was stale and frozen. "But Blake didn't—"

"Find your buyer?" She barely angled her head at me, but even that small gesture reached levels of condescension I was honestly jealous of. "Yes, call it a *hunch*, but I wasn't quite sure he ever would, so Ray put out some feelers to the community. This morning, we got a bite."

A smirk slithered across her lips that reminded me so much of her daughter's. "It seems you made quite the impression at the auction, and in less than two days, you'll be someone else's problem."

She closed her eyes, floral pink eyeshadow globbed on her lids as she breathed deep, contentment radiating out of her perfume congested pores. When she exhaled, her rosy eyelids snapped open, venomous blue waiting beneath.

"I just couldn't wait to tell you the good news."

She reached over to my plate, prizing herself a grape from the handful I'd grabbed to eat. Her too-long-nails thieved the piece of fruit, bringing it towards her painted lips.

"I'd say it's been a pleasure but," the side of her mouth twitched in delight, "I hate lying."

She plopped the grape in her mouth and turned her back to me, walking away with the stride of a winner.

And I... lost.

I lost.

EIGHTEEN

KAT

Time.

Time wasn't something I'd given much thought to before I came here. I took it for granted like I did most things in life, always expecting more and wasting what I did have.

In the end, I think time is one of the fattest lies we're fed as people. We eat it down as if the buffet is endless but never stop to think for one realistic moment that it could be taken away at any second.

Humans are gluttonous creatures, but we're the worst with time.

We expect all of it and throw our hands up and call it unfair when the seemingly infinite supply is cut short. When it happens to those around us, we clutch our chests and thank whoever we pray to that it wasn't us. *God forbid* it ever be us.

But what about when it is? What do you say to the eighty-year-old diagnosed with cancer? What do you say to the little girl no more than ten who will be hit by a car one morning walking to school?

What do you say to the twenty-one-year-old woman who has to do the death-delivering herself?

After Claudia told me Ray found me a buyer, and I had no less than forty-eight hours until my time here was up, I realized what I'd have to do. It probably should have scared me how easily I came to the conclusion, but it didn't rock me in the moment.

Not when Blake found me and took me back to his room either. I wasn't really thinking about being scared as he tried to get me to tell him what Claudia had said. I lied, obviously. Told him she was threatening to put me back in the Line Up if I stepped out of line or was seen around the other girls again.

I didn't feel scared when we went to sleep last night either. Blake read to me again, and because I knew what I knew, I let myself lay on his chest with zero guilt and zero reservations. He held me and stroked my arm as he read sweet sonnets from John Keats.

I think he was secretly his favorite.

From Blake's lips, he read of immortal love and gut-wrenching separation. And of death. He gave a romantic voice to John Keats lyrics, both of us clutching each other harder as he read from a letter the poet wrote to his love.

My love has made me selfish. I cannot exist without you-
I am forgetful of every thing but seeing you again
My life seems to stop there- I see no further
You have absorb'd me.

We went to sleep, and strange as it was, it was the first time I slept through the night since I got to the brothel. I wasn't scared to sleep. I wasn't scared of what would happen to me when I woke up because I *knew*.

I was in control. The last thing I'd ever do in this place was control my own body and my own fate.

And I could rest easy knowing that.

That didn't mean that come morning, I didn't wake up with tears already blurring my last first glimpse at a brand new day. I rolled over in Blake's bed and reached out to where I knew he wouldn't be.

His warmth still stuck to the sheets though, so I knew he hadn't been up long. I laid in his spot in the bed and breathed him in, the cigarettes he smoked each morning and each night burrowing in my lungs with the pleasant sting of death.

Soon, that sting will be everywhere.

The shower kicked on in the bathroom, and I used the twenty or so minutes I knew I had to get my affairs in order. Isn't that what people who were about to die called it? Getting their *affairs* in order?

The last six months of my life had been one giant affair with love and grief.

They'd also been the greatest of my short life.

While Blake showered, I stole pages from his notebook and wrote letters to each person I loved about how great it all was. Layla got one, Charlotte got one, and Dominic got pages worth.

Blake's I laid on top of them all. Since he'd be the one to find me.

My wrist ached from so much writing when I finally heard the shower turn off. I hid the letters beneath my pillow and quickly made the bed so Blake wouldn't do it and find them before he left for the day.

The bathroom door creaked open, thick clouds of steam rolling out, fusing the bedroom with heated drops of condensation that clung to my bare legs. Blake emerged, a white towel wrapped around his hips and his hair painted black by the water to match his palette black eyes.

Those drops of midnight fell on me, recoloring with surprise.

"You're awake early."

Sucking back a big breath, I nodded and cast my gaze around. "Yeah, just one of those mornings where I couldn't fall back asleep."

My focus wasn't aimed at him, but I assumed he bought it since he went about his morning routine as usual. No, I wasn't usually up and at 'em for his morning routine, but sometimes I'd lie awake and listen to it.

There was something soothing about listening to him go about his life, brushing his teeth and shaving his face and getting dressed. Sometimes I'd roll over and watch him leave, and sometimes he caught me looking.

He'd gift me a small smile, and I'd give him a sleepy one back.

This morning, there were no smiles since I was already up and moving, and I cursed myself for not staying in bed long enough to get one last little gift. Instead of watching him leave, I watched him get ready. I guessed he'd already had his smoke for the morning, because he was brushing his teeth.

Then came shaving his face, carefully dragging the razor down his sharp jawline as he watched himself carefully in the mirror.

I wondered if he'd still use that razor tomorrow after it helped me die.

There wasn't any telling how long I spent staring at him, getting lost in the tan grooves of his stomach muscles contracting as he moved around in the bathroom, losing myself in hazy thoughts of blood and pain, pouring and pouring and pouring until they both ran out.

Apparently, I'd been staring long enough to catch Blake's attention.

"What's on your mind?"

I jerked at his unexpected question, blinking myself out of a daze. "What?"

"You've been staring, so I asked what's on your mind."

Blood.

"Oh," *Fuck.* "Just staring to stare. I'm a certified degenerate, and there's a half-naked hot guy walking around the room. What else do you expect from me?"

It was a solid save, because he laughed right away, making up for the morning smile of his I'd missed out on. His laughter was charity to my damaged soul, wrapping it in warmth it didn't deserve.

When it died down, longing carved a plea inside my chest for it to come back. Blake wrapped a fist around the front of the towel hanging over his hips, a lazy smirk tugging up his mouth.

"Perv."

Then he shut the bathroom door between us in an effortless act, slicing off our gazes that held on till the last moment.

"You like it!" I called through the wooden door, nailing the charade in place before dropping my head back to the ceiling. My hand made a necklace around my throat, squeezing where the tears were fighting to break free.

Not yet.

Once he left for his morning shift, I could break down all I wanted, and

EIGHTEEN

I would.

Blake didn't know I'd been sold, and I wasn't going to tell him. He and I were mirrors of each other, thinking and feeling as if we were one fucked up brain and one sick heart. I wouldn't put it past our unique tether for him to figure out what I planned to do if he knew I'd been sold.

When the bathroom door opened up again, Blake was dressed. Dark jeans and a black V-neck. Water droplets clung for dear life to the column of his neck just before he brushed them away, dismissing them of their right to touch him.

It was in that same sweeping second that I realized this was the last time I'd see him.

Tears I'd warded off gathered behind my eyes, trying to blow my cover and corrupt my last visual of him. *Pesky motherfuckers.*

My hand was still wrapped around my neck, fingers digging beneath my collarbone as I ducked my head, willing the tears to hold off for just another few minutes.

I didn't look up again until I was *sure* I was safe.

Except even with dry eyes, Blake picked up on my weirdness.

"Are you okay?"

My mouth went bone dry and my tongue stuck to the roof of my mouth when I went to answer him. So I just nodded and mumbled, "Yeah, yeah."

He didn't look totally convinced, but if he had any accusations lined up behind his lips, he didn't let them out. He just kept scrutinizing me with his eyes plucked from Heaven and dipped in the fires of Hell.

The floor creaked, and I felt the sound move inside my chest as Blake started my way. Slow strides and concentrated eye contact carried him over to me, each step he took shaking my heart off its hinges. I was trembling, *visibly* trembling, when he reached the bed where I still sat. My head craned back to keep his stare, my breath all jerky and uneven as I stared up at him.

He was quiet over me, tracing his shadowed stare up and down my face. "You're bleeding."

Astonished, I breathed, "What?"

Could he predict my future now on top of everything else?

My breath was suspended, my plan hanging in the balance as Blake lifted a hand towards my face. The slightly salty touch of his thumb rested on my lips, guiding the bottom one out from between my teeth. A sting raced beneath the sensitive skin as he thumbed it softly.

"You chewed your lip open."

Shock filled my chest. Relief settled in next.

"Oh, th-that's nothing." I hadn't even realized I'd been gnawing on it.

His fingers wound around my chin, gripping it so I couldn't look away from him.

I didn't want to.

"Stop biting your lips."

He said it like a threat to keep me safe and unharmed, and it had both sides of my cheeks rising into a grin beneath his hand.

"Sir, yes, sir."

Cooling embers made up his brilliant eyes, the corners of them both upturning as he fought off amusement of his own. My chin and every other inch of me went cold as he dropped his hand and moved towards the door to go.

"How about I bring you an extra chocolate donut today?"

I watched him go, losing all the air in my chest.

I managed to spit out a "Sure" and "Thank you" and that seemed fitting.

I wouldn't say another word to him ever again, and those two words seemed like a good way to say goodbye. They encompassed so much I wanted to tell him.

Thank you for helping me when you barely even knew me. Thank you for being different from every monster here. Thank you for trying so hard to save me. Thank you for not judging me when I was weak. Thank you for keeping me sane when I wanted to scream. Thank you for letting me scream when I couldn't be sane anymore. Thank you for your darkness and making mine not feel so alone.

Thank you for loving me without telling me.

Blake placed his hand on the doorknob and turned to me, and I was honest to fuck struck by just how stunning he was. If I could have closed my eyes with his face as the last picture my brain ever registered and died the very next second, I would. If somehow I could will my heart to stop beating so he was the last thing I ever saw, there wouldn't be anything that could stop me.

His beauty was an otherworldly send off which I was undeserving of for what I was about to do.

Blake lingered in the doorway a few seconds longer, which was fine by me. A few seconds more for me to soak up all of him I could. My lightning was snapping inside my veins, trying to force me over to him for one last touch before my fingers went numb for good, but I couldn't risk it. He already looked like he didn't want to leave me.

He always had that look about him lately.

I caught him staring at me a lot over the last week, always with that look that longed for more time, more of me, more of us.

"I'll be back," he told me from the door.

Not soon enough.

But I nodded like I'd see him again and tried to smile the same way. Blake idled longer than necessary, and the terrifying thought struck that maybe he could see the outline of my heart pounding beneath my skin. Maybe he knew.

Fuck, there was no way he'd know?

Curiosity nailed between his dark eyes and straight through my chest bone. It was breaking. *I* was breaking right in half thinking he'd maybe found me out, thinking about how this was the last time we'd ever get to look at each other like we'd happily go up in flames for the other.

My heart rocketed up my throat as he finally opened the door to go. We held on for one last moment, and then he turned over his shoulder and left.

The door closed between us.

Tears flooded over the very next second.

They splashed my cheeks and I let go, folding over and choking on a sob.

I didn't want to say goodbye to him. I didn't want to leave him. I didn't want to *die*.

But I wouldn't be sold. I'd let a lot of bad shit happen to me over the last twenty-one years, but I drew the line at being reduced to a product that some man could own and rape and ruin.

My body was my body. My life was my life.

I decided what happened to both, and *fuck* anyone for trying to take that away from me.

Rage heated my tears from beneath as they sliced down my cheeks fast and unstoppable as I got up from the bed and grabbed the letters I'd written. I walked into the bathroom on legs I honestly couldn't feel, finding my shaking fingers on the light switch.

The room flickered to life slowly, fluorescent lighting casting its odd shade of brightness against the pristine white surface. Momentarily, I paused to wonder how my bleeding corpse would look in the poor lighting.

Carefully, I placed all four notes on the bathroom counter, making sure Blake's was on top. My wet eyes moved to the shower pressed up against the side of the bathroom and the black thing laying innocently on the edge of the tub.

Sniffling, I walked across to it and lifted it between my fingers, struck by how lightweight something so potentially deadly was.

Small deaths were everywhere, weren't they?

Blake would find me when he came back to bring me food later. I'd be lying on this white tile floor, lovely crimson blood rushing out of the long gashes in both wrists. It would pool around me, sticking to my pale skin and clotting in my outspread hair. Stupidly, I worried about it ruining the carpet that met that bathroom tile. It would be stained red for weeks as a reminder.

Of what I did. Of what I left him to find.

I knew he wouldn't believe it at first. He would drop to his knees and shake me, cover my swollen wrists to try and stop the bleeding. I could picture him leaning over my limp body and moving my hair back from my face, talking to me and then screaming at me, begging me to open my dead eyes.

Blake was so much like the razor I held in my palm.

On the outside, dark and hardened, one wrong move away from making you bleed. On the inside however, much like the razor, he was fragile. Sharp-edged defenses that crumbled with a singular blow from me, the shell of the razor breaking apart beneath my fist just as Blake would do beneath my death.

In the end, I had three thin blades in the palm of my hand.

And that was when I finally felt the fear.

It bubbled beneath my forearms, tingling hardest in the place it knew I was about to rip through. Breathing hard through my mouth, I turned my left wrist over—the one I'd slice first—and watched my pulse thump beneath the transparent skin. The veins I'd aim for glowed blue with flowing blood that in minutes would splash out red against the blank canvas of my skin.

Maybe there was art in death.

Or maybe Blake and I just read too much poetry about death last night.

My mouth dried like sandpaper had been scrubbed all along the inside. I couldn't stop moving my fingers, watching my thick veins protrude and flex with strength I was about to lose. Would it hurt? Fuck, would I scream?

Oh god.

I tipped my head back to the ceiling, trails of cool tears sliding down the sides of my face to wet my ears and the baby hairs around them.

How the hell had it come to this? *Why* did it have to come to this?

I wanted to scream at the sky for how unfair this was like every person who knew they were dying before they wanted to. I wanted my tirade, my final tantrum, so I could whip my middle fingers out and flip off any god or higher being that had a ticket to watch my final show.

Fuck them and *fuck* this.

I didn't want to die.

I just wanted to go *home*. I wanted to hug my baby sister one more time. I wanted to lay in her bed and read her stories until she fell asleep on my chest. I wanted her small breaths tickling the curve of my neck as she passed out cold.

I wanted to walk inside our house when our mom was still alive, and I wanted to see her smile.

When she was well, she had the *best* smile. It was like hot chocolate on a cold day, warming me up and filling my stomach with nostalgia. I wanted her smile and her hugs and our family back together, sans my father because *fuck* him too.

Snot tickled my nose and I wiped it away with the back of my hand, weeping harder as I thought about Mom.

Would she be there when the lights faded? Would I see her face in the darkness and feel her arms around me, whispering in my ear that she was so happy to see me?

Soft sobs padded the small room from corner to corner, quaking my chest that was filling with some of its last breaths. My knees wobbled like they wanted to give out, but I anchored myself to the counter so I wouldn't fall down.

If I was dying, it wasn't on my hands and knees, *god-fucking-dammit*. I would stand until there wasn't enough blood left to fill my legs.

Only then would I fall. Only then would I rest.

"Holy—" A harsh hiccup cut me off, slicing my voice in half. "Sh-shit."

Weightless air fogged my head as I lost control of my breathing, hyperventilating to the white noise of the bathroom fan as it sang along to my last few moments.

A whimper squeezed my eyes shut, fat teardrops falling out and salting my quivering lips.

"Okay," I whispered, covering my eyes with one hand. "Okay…"

I pinched one of the blades between my two fingers, sliding my skin across the smooth edges as I wept and wept and fucking wept. And I kept nodding—nodding for no one to see me in some silent encouragement to keep going.

Keep going and going until the blade hit.

Sucking back a wet sigh, I forced my heavy lids open so I could give myself one last look before it happened. Bad move. I was pathetic, a splotchy faced mess of snot and streaking tears, dark hair an unkempt frame around my face, and puffy red bags sitting beneath my eyes.

Blake was right about one thing.

My eyes did look like emeralds when they were drowning in sorrow.

Blood flushed my cheeks all the way up to my forehead and down my thin neck as if it was rising to the surface, knowing its big number was coming up.

Was there a Heaven after this? Was there anything after this?

Was there a place up in the sky for wicked people like me to still look in on the ones they loved and left? I think I could be okay with dying if I got to watch the people I loved live their lives. Mom and I could watch Charlotte grow up together, go on her first date, get into college, walk down the aisle of her wedding.

And I could check in on Dominic from time to time to make sure that he was happy.

Even if I couldn't be happy with him.

Even if I couldn't be the one to warm his bed or make him smile or be by his side till death do us part, I still wanted him to have it all. Dominic Reed deserved *all* the love in the world.

He'd given me all of it when I didn't think I was capable of any of it.

He made a bouquet of roses out of the thorns and weeds I gave him, turning a mess into magic. Our love was *magic*, and magic never died, right? That's what all the storybooks said.

I thought of his sky gray eyes and how much I loved them as I tapered the edge of the blade down my first layer of flesh, teasing the skin and prolonging the inevitable. Irritation blossomed a pinkish red along my forearm as I scraped the razor's edge up and down, filling my head with romantic memories of the first time Dominic kissed me in his garage.

As I nestled the blade with unsteady hands over the thickest vein in my wrist, his ocean deep voice was in my ears telling me he loved me for the first time right before we made love.

Dominic was everywhere inside my head, his thunder and perfect love swelling as I pressed the cool blade against my skin, splitting the flesh… and welcoming in death.

Blood hadn't even welled to the surface yet when the bathroom door slammed open.

My head snapped in its direction, gasping loud as Blake stormed inside, eyes ablaze with fury that sunk to my wrist and the blade trying to split its way inside of it. His nostrils flared, angry nose twitching as he charged my way, slapping the blade out of my fingers.

"No!" I cried as the slice of silver went flying.

My reflexes were working before my brain was, my will to die lashing my hands out to grab for the next one.

Metal pinched between the tips of my fingers as I picked it up, making a sloppy swipe towards my left wrist. A cry tore my lips apart when strong fingers locked around my hand with the blade, yanking it away from my body. I struggled, flailing as Blake swung his other arm around my waist, drawing me against his chest as we stumbled back.

We hit the wall behind him hard, jarring my body through his.

His thumping heart beat against my back as we wrestled, his grip around my right wrist tightening.

Harsh, hot breathing tickled right above my ear as he growled, "Drop it. *Now.*"

"No!" I tried to squirm against him, but he was just too damn strong. His hand around my wrist constricted with obscene pressure, moans of frustration and pain pulling up my throat. The poor bones in my wrist were whining and begging, and I finally surrendered, dropping the blade to let it clatter to the tile floor.

Blake swept his leg out fast and kicked it to the other side of the bathroom. It slid all the way across, he and I breathing heavily with his arms locked around me.

"Let me go!" I thrashed and bucked my body against his. "You have to let me do this!"

"Like hell I do." The more I fought, the harder he held me. His warm lips and sharp teeth moved against my ear. "That was so fucking *stupid.*"

"Yeah, but it's *my* life to be stupid with."

"It may be your life, but it's mine to protect." He sighed. "No matter how fucking hard you make it."

EIGHTEEN

"You can't protect me anymore, Blake! You *can't*."

"Tough shit," he seethed in my ear, his threat winded but absolute. "I can and I will until the goddamn end."

Motherfucker. He didn't get it. He didn't know the end for me was a done deal as of yesterday. He didn't know why that razor blade across the room was my only option.

And I couldn't tell him.

I couldn't tell him we *failed*. He'd find out soon, but not from me. I'd given him enough heartbreak as it was. I wouldn't be responsible for that blow too.

Not when I was already planning it out in my head how I'd do this all again tomorrow.

And this time, I'd lock the fucking door.

"Fine," I huffed, rolling my eyes closed. "Fine."

All resistance depleted from my sore muscles as I accepted the deal of living one more day. Tomorrow before the buyer came, I would do it. Today, I guess I'd fucking live.

My neck loosened to loll back against Blake's shoulder, both of us heaving a sigh together as I gave up.

Slowly, Blake slid his back down the wall and took me with him. We sunk together until we sat on the cold-biting tile, his arms still imprisoned around me because it'd be dumb to let me go just yet.

We sat and we breathed, Blake stretching out his legs around mine that were scrunched up to my chest. The open bathroom door faced us, my eyes occasionally drifting to the blade feet away on the ground.

"So how'd you know?" I asked.

My head moved against him as he inhaled a deep sigh. "You pick at your lips when you're nervous. This time, you bit right through them. You didn't feel right when I left. I don't know that I can really describe it."

"Wow," I murmured. "I've never rendered a poet speechless before."

Blake ignored me, his breathing in my ear trying to find a controlled rhythm again. Eventually he gave up and let his face drop to hang in the crook of my neck, the tip of his nose ghosting along the curve of it. His arm around my waist loosened, finding its place on my left arm to hold it like he was holding my right.

Together, he lifted both of my hands in front of us, the inside of my wrists facing in.

"I barely cut myself," I observed.

Blake slid his hands over the back of mine, rolling my fingers closed beneath his. His fists curled warmth and strength around mine, my hands dwarfed beneath his that I couldn't help but note were a couple shades tanner.

Perks of being allowed out in the sun, I supposed.

Heavy silence sealed us together, both he and I staring at our hands. The small but jagged cut I'd made on my left wrist bored back at us, an unearthing of blood barely visible beneath. Blake took a thumb and brushed it across my pathetic excuse for a gash, my speck of red smearing to a soft pink beneath his touch.

The weight of his chin rested on my shoulder.

"Barely is too much," he whispered.

Weakness rattled in my lungs, heartbreak splintering deeper than ever before as I laid in his arms. To be loved by him was an experience of masochism I never knew I'd crave. I sunk further into him, nestling against him and wishing I could burrow beneath his skin and spend the rest of my time breathing there.

We spent a few moments like that before his head picked up from my shoulder, his jaw grazing my cheek as he looked up.

"Is that a note?"

The accusation in his lethal tone vibrated the air, tying up my muscles around my bones.

"Four, actually."

I felt his heartbeat *clunk* extra hard against my back. "You wrote *four* suicide notes?"

"One for everyone I wanted to say goodbye to."

He didn't ask, but given how blaring his curiosity was, he didn't have to. I pointed my chin up at the letters on the counter.

EIGHTEEN

"The one on top is for you."

He filled his chest with the information, running his thumbs along the tops of my knuckles. He waited a good long while before asking what I knew he would.

"Can I read it?"

It was my turn to take a big breath now, trying to hit all the nerves bubbling up in my stomach as I thought about what I'd written and him reading it. I thought I'd be lying in a pool of my blood or in a body bag when he finally read it. Being here for the humiliation was *not* part of the grand plan.

Groaning, I scrambled around to face the other way until my knees were on either side of Blake's hips and I could properly bury my face in his neck to hide from the embarrassment.

Mumbling against his shoulder, I said, "I can't watch if you read it."

Something almost like a serrated laugh of astonishment pushed out of his chest. The heat of his big hand found the back of my head, tingles sprouting along my neck as he traced a few fingers down it.

"Are you embarrassed?" he rumbled against me.

I nodded.

"Is it sappy?"

Groaning, I gave another nod inside the slope of his neck.

His smile was vivid in his voice as he dragged another tender touch over the top of my spine. "I'm sure it's not so bad."

Then he was reaching for it and I was whining, squeezing my eyes shut against his skin as his body shifted beneath me to grab it off the counter. He settled back against the wall, and I knew he had it in his hands. My heart plundered against my ribcage as it remembered just how much of itself I'd handwritten into the fibers of that letter.

My sick little heart was all over that flimsy piece of paper, and now Blake had it.

"All right." He nudged his nose against me. "You ready?"

I promptly fucking shook my head *no*.

He started reading anyway.

"Blake," He stopped immediately, his tongue clicking and his rough voice finding my ear. "You got my name right."

A chuckle shook his body as I jabbed my shoulder forward to nail him in the chest. An easiness drifted into the air as his laughter settled, the tips of his fingers weaving into my loose hair and playing with it.

His deep voice picked up my words again as he started reciting my letter aloud.

"If you're the moon and I'm the rose, then everything they taught me about photosynthesis in school is utter bullshit..."

The first sentence of the letter dropped off on a dazed note, and my pulse thwacked harder beneath the thin skin of my throat. I waited for him to continue in semi-mild agony, and it took a while, but eventually he cleared his throat and kept going.

"The sun is what feeds the flowers, but you're what feeds me. And I don't mean that just literally. God, I hope you laughed."

And he did, and it was mercy for my wayward soul just like every other time he laughed for me before. I needed to see it. I needed to *see* his laughter, so I pushed myself out of hiding in his neck and scoured my eyes over his face until I saw it.

Until I saw his proof of laughter dimpling both sides of his cheeks.

I didn't even realize I'd reached up and touched his smile until the corner of his mouth closed around the tip of my thumb in a move that might be described as a kiss if we were lovers.

For he and I, I didn't know what to call it other than heavenly.

With my palm to his cheek, he kept reading out loud. "Maybe it's parasitic. Maybe it's unhealthy, but what you and I have is what breathes life into me each and every day that I've been here."

Eyes that I was thoroughly addicted to cut to me, alight as he searched my face as if to ask me if my words were real—as if to ask me if *I* was real. The best I could do for him was to not look away, answering him with our brand of silence that composed louder words than I'd ever spoken.

"You said that we're both made of darkness, and that's why we see the little bit of light in each other, but what if it's not light, but diamonds?

EIGHTEEN

What if we aren't seeing the light that's lasted but the indestructible beauty that built inside us both?"

An awe-struck shine scribbled across his stare, his breath coming harder as he kept reading.

"Diamonds are formed after unbelievable pressure, and so were we. I like to think that we're both hiding diamonds in our souls, and you can see mine and I can see yours because our broken pieces reflect off of each other. Maybe that's why I feel you like you're a part of me. Maybe that's why we're star-crossed."

A wash of messy breathing tangled between us as Blake lost some battle he was fighting with himself and brought my forehead to his, squeezing the back of my neck. He rubbed our heads together, not daring to take his gaze away from my written words.

"But the thing about being star-crossed is that we have infinite galaxies to get it right, don't we? We're the stuff of forever, Blake Dawson." His voice collapsed into a whisper as he said his name. "You and I are forever."

His eyes slammed shut, not even bothering to read the rest where I thanked him for all he'd done and asked him to deliver the other three notes. He just held me tight and looked like a man who'd forgotten how to breathe. A little wrinkle marred the middle of his forehead too.

I wanted to erase it myself, but Blake looked as if he'd shatter if I touched him more than I was. Even when he opened his lips to talk, it was with serrated glass infused in his vocal cords.

"I think you have a touch of poet in you, Kitten."

A fresh layer of torture blanketed his handsome face as I breathed a soft laugh for him, not thinking about our proximity and how he'd taste my laughter on his lips. His next exhale was barely controlled, choppy with heartache cutting it to bits.

"I want to kiss you so badly, it hurts," he rasped with strain. "It physically *hurts*."

The space between my ribs filled with a slow-rise of fluttering lightning at his brutal honesty.

Maybe I should have been surprised he said that, but I wasn't. Maybe I should have felt shame for sitting over his lap like I was, but I didn't. Maybe I should have moved back.

Maybe. Maybe. Maybe. I hated maybes.

Which was why my reply was so resolute. "Okay."

"Okay, what?"

I said it before I could chicken out. "Kiss me."

His eyes snapped open, hesitation streaking through. With our foreheads still pressed together, he shook his head.

"That's not smart. This isn't our galaxy. Remember?"

Sitting myself taller on his lap, I nuzzled his nose with mine. "Then pretend it's our goodbye."

Blake was right. This wasn't our storyline to live happily-ever-after. Our hearts weren't built to make it in this universe. Mine was built for Dominic and his was built for some lucky lady that I envied so much it *burned*, even though neither of us knew who she was.

But she wasn't here, and now I knew for a fact that I'd never see Dominic again in this lifetime. Our last kiss was in the rain, and if it had to be the last one he and I ever had, it was a *damn* good one.

Probably the best kiss we ever created together.

Blake deserved something like that, didn't he? For all he'd done and for all of his not-so-secret affection, he deserved a kiss better than our first.

That one was rotted with guilt from the moment it began. I wanted to give him something pure, something he could hold on to when he needed to remember me after I was dead.

As if unable to stop himself, Blake blew out an audible sigh so I could taste the ache of his feelings for me. "What kind of fucked up person would I be if I kissed you after you tried to off yourself?"

He attempted a chuckle, but I could see in his eyes that he meant it. I could also see his restraint waning thin and the darkness closing around his pupils as they kept traveling down to my lips.

"The same kind of fucked up I would be for telling you to kiss me after trying to off myself."

A terribly strained moan creaked from between his parted lips. He shook his head as if to say no at the same time his hand on the back of my head slid forward to cup my face. Beside us, he flattened his hand with my letter to the tile, leaving it there so he could grab my waist instead.

His dark-eyed focus was on me as he slipped his fingers beneath the barrier of my shirt, searing my bare skin with his unadulterated touch as he palmed the small of my back. Skin to skin. Darkness to darkness.

Diamonds to diamonds.

Slowly, he tilted the brush of his nose to the side of mine, angling his mouth just over mine. Our breathing had slowed to concentrated pushes and pulls, feeding off of each other like we'd been doing from day one. The subtle graze of his mouth whispered over mine, like burning embers brushing sweet fire across my lips.

Blake tested how we felt together, nudging his bottom lip across mine once, twice, three times.

Then he captured them all at once with his, kissing me for the last time.

It wasn't a question of if we melted into this kiss. It was a question of how we were possibly going to pull ourselves out of it as we left behind our skin and bones and entangled together as fragmented souls.

His lips were softer than clouds as I moved mine against them, becoming nothing but a hum of happy lightning. Our mouths dragged together slowly, taking our time, appreciating the feel of each other, the taste of *us*.

Through his body, I could feel his heart pounding the longer we kissed and part of me never wanted to stop knowing I could make his heart race like that. The brush of his tongue was a gentle question at the seam of my lips, and I opened up to answer it, kissing him deeper and sweeter as our heartbeats rammed.

His hold on me was somehow both tender and firm, holding my face like I was petals of a rose while anchoring around my bare waist like I would disappear any second.

Not until tomorrow, I wanted to whisper.

I wasn't sure how long we stayed like that, kissing sweetly, kissing deeply, kissing to say goodbye, but eventually we pulled apart, both of us breathless and lost in the other.

"Tell me a story," I murmured, fidgeting with the edge of his collar. "One that has a happy ending."

Blake did exactly that, no questions asked.

We got comfortable in each other's arms on the bathroom floor as Blake started a story he promised would be happy. He told another one after he finished the first, and we stayed like that for hours.

Blake weaved tales of happiness and triumphant adventures, bravery and true love. He told me as many happy lies as he thought I needed to hear to make up for the ending my story was given.

It was a sad one. Anticlimactic if I was being honest.

And it was coming tomorrow.

NINETEEN

KAT

There are some days you'll always remember.

No matter how old you get, what diseases pick apart your mind in old age, some days of your life just *stick* with you. Sometimes those days are good. Sometimes those days are bad.

It's always one or the other.

It's rarely ever both.

My last morning didn't start like most mornings at the brothel had, and not just because I was about to die and all. When sleep stirred from my head on that final day, and I went to roll over to find Blake's empty spot—it wasn't empty.

And I didn't have to roll anywhere to find him.

My right arm was suctioned across his bare chest by the heat of our skin and just where I'd left it last night when I couldn't keep my eyes open anymore. Blake slept beneath me, our legs tangled and the sheets at our feet. Blake ran hot. Like really really hot. We almost never slept with the sheets on or else I think we'd actually melt.

Laying on his chest and counting his even breaths, I wondered how long I could steal this time before I had to wake him up. I was like… 97% sure he was late for work. Being late for work here probably wasn't like being late at other jobs.

A slap on the wrist there might translate to a bullet in a kneecap here.

It was selfish to keep him, and I was a self-admitted selfish asshole but not so selfish to get him shot. Again.

In my head, I was counting down from ten to the dreaded one before I'd wake him up.

Around eight, his heartbeat skipped a few pulses.

Around six, his breathing changed.

Around three, his hand twitched overtop of mine.

At one, he jerked himself awake with a startled gasp.

My stare flew up, finding him with eyes wide open and panicked. Clipped breathing wrestled inside his chest as I pressed my palm right over his slapping heart.

"Hey, you're okay," I soothed. "You're okay."

As soon as my voice touched him, the arm he had cradled around my waist tightened and his eyes collapsed shut. He clenched his jaw extra hard, tension pulsing at the backs of it and his nostrils flaring as he breathed through them.

In and out, each measured breath calmed his heart beat by beat.

I stroked my thumb across his sternum, watching him closely as he came down from the panic.

Gradually, his long eyelashes fluttered open, fixing his stare on the ceiling. His breathing had finally evened out, but I kept my chin resting on his pecs and my gaze on his face just in case that changed.

His Adam's apple slid up and down as he swallowed, blinking up at the ceiling.

"I had a dream," he said simply.

"Seems more like a nightmare."

He paused, breathing deeply.

"It was."

A tingling at the back of my brain told me I wouldn't like the answer, but I asked anyway. "What was it about?"

"You and I were at a lake. One I remember from when I was a kid. We were on this old dock, and everything was peaceful. Then you said you wanted to go swimming in the lake. I told you I didn't think it was safe, but you didn't listen."

"Naturally."

"You jumped in and went completely under. The lake swallowed you up, and I started calling for you. I was panicking and reaching under the water for your hand, but I couldn't find you. You were just gone."

Dread swelled inside my windpipe, freezing all the air inside my chest like dry ice.

My nose squished against his chest as I dragged my face down so I couldn't see, pressing my forehead to his sternum instead.

"I'm sorry..."

Sorry that he had such a horrible nightmare. Sorry that it was about me. Sorry that I probably caused it by trying to off myself yesterday. Sorry that I was going to do the same thing today.

Blake left silence between us where all he did was rub his thumb in circles on the back of my hand still on his chest. The feeling was encouraging a heaviness back over my eyes, and if I didn't stop him, I'd be asleep in no time.

There wasn't any time left for sleep today.

There wasn't any time left at all.

Reluctantly, I pulled my head up enough to fit my chin back against his sternum, flashing my eyelids open. "Don't you have to get up for work?"

"Not today."

Surprise tweaked my eyebrows together. "Why not today?"

Shit, was he staying to watch over me? Did I spook him too much yesterday? I needed him gone if I was going to get my hands back on that razor.

For the first time since he'd woken from his nightmare, Blake curved a look down at me. He stared at me down the bridge of his nose, not saying a word. A shadow of longing slipped over his face, darkening every sharp and elegant angle and making my heart twist around my ribs.

I *loathed* myself for that look. I loathed myself for being the shadow.

My hand experienced a cold front as Blake's warmth left it, making a home down the side of my face instead. It started by clearing a strand of wavy hair that'd fallen over my forehead, and once he pushed it away, the tips of his fingers lingered on my face as if magnets were buried beneath our skin.

He stroked the rise of my cheek, looking every bit like a man who could have stayed in bed all day long touching me. He was entranced and I was putty, wanting him to do whatever made him happy before I died and made him so fucking sad.

It was a shame he had to go and break that trance.

"I know you know about the buyer."

Shock rippled beneath my face, contorting my features and rounding my eyes.

"Wait—" I sprang up to my knees on the bed. *"You* know about the buyer?"

Blake sighed and closed his eyes, sitting up at the waist and rubbing his palms into his eyes. He was taking way too fucking long to reply, so I lashed my hands around his and dragged them down from his face, holding them hostage as I hit him with another question.

"How long have you known?"

My widening eyes bounced between his that were shockingly steady on me.

"Since the day it happened."

My head jerked forward, something that felt a hell of a lot like betrayal sinking my stomach. I sank with the heavy feeling, sitting back on my heels with my heart squeezing up my throat.

"Why didn't you tell me?"

Despite the daggered betrayal I must have been nailing him with, Blake didn't seem punctured by it. He traced his simmering eyes across my face like he'd done a thousand times before climbing off of his bed.

I wasn't surprised when the press of his fingers appeared on the back of my neck, his thumb digging into the space under my chin and guiding my head up. It forced our eyes together; mine were dangerously close to watering.

NINETEEN

"Do you trust me?"

My lips parted, unintentionally inhaling the significance of that question. Memories of the first night I spent in his room blinked across my mind—the night we'd made a *deal* not to trust each other. It was so easy to agree. Why would I *ever* trust a man like him?

Now, all I could think was how could I not?

Staring up at those eyes of pure moonlight, I couldn't think of a time he gave me a reason not to trust him. He came through again and again, and maybe that's why he kept my buyer a secret? It was the one time he couldn't come through, so he hid from the truth as long as he could. Maybe he didn't want to scare me. Or maybe he was still hoping for a miracle until we woke up just now and realized we were fresh out of those.

Whatever the reason, I decided that I didn't care.

I spent so much of my life being *mad* for dumb shit or even justified shit. I didn't want to die mad too.

So I nodded. Even attempted a small smile.

Blake didn't miss the opportunity to touch the corner of it, and I was glad he didn't. I kind of liked when he did that. I was going to miss it.

"When I get the call," he started, absentmindedly tracing his thumb up and down my jaw. "I'll have to take you back to your room."

I'd gotten so used to the invasion of blistering terror in my veins, I didn't even react to it.

"Just like that?" I softly asked. There was both a pink disposable razor and broken glass in that room. It was good to have options.

His head moved in a nod like the muscles in his neck had rusted over. A deep V chiseled between his thickly shaped eyebrows, a muscle jumping in his cheek.

"Just like that."

* * *

Blake got the call not even two hours later. I was coming back from the bathroom when it happened. Blake was sitting on the edge of his bed when I got out, wiping my hands on my shirt when I spotted him.

His head was in his hands, phone facing up and sitting next to him.

I froze.

His suffering was tangible, thickening the air with dewy dread that stuck to my skin like slime. Somehow, on frozen toes, I made it over to where he sat.

His low-hanging head rose when my bare feet entered his sightline, our eyes falling together. A fucking *bomb* went off inside my chest, saw-toothed shrapnel piercing my heart that stopped it cold. Agony *shredded* his stare as if the emotion had real talons, tearing up his black sky eyes, the raw break of our Armageddon bleeding through.

My throat went so dry, I almost choked trying to swallow enough spit to talk.

"It's time?"

The soft backs of his jaw constricted, his voice a foreboding baritone note.

"It's time."

The walk back up to my room was quiet on the surface.

Beneath each step Blake and I took, however, was an ache loud enough to shake the house to its bones. We arrived at the plain white door, both of us slowing to a stop. Blake reached to unlock it, and my breathing stumbled as I saw his hand.

He was shaking.

Like the dance we'd done almost a week ago, I stepped into the room but spun back to face him as soon as I was inside. We were only a few inches away this time compared to last when I still didn't understand what was between us and he still fought it.

Neither of us were confused or fighting anymore.

We were just us. Blake and Kat. And we were speechless.

It was stupid to think there were any perfect set of words that could sum

NINETEEN

up everything I wanted to say to him now that I didn't have the cop-out of a letter to hide behind. Words were too simple for all I felt. The only way I could think to describe it would be to take his hand and plunge it inside my heart so that he could *feel* what I was feeling right now.

Hell, for all Blake and I were, he was probably feeling it too.

No, not probably. *Unquestionably.*

The ungodly ache in my soul was scribbled all over his features in messy, jagged lines. The lightning screaming in my blood was the same brand riding up the ropes of his neck, protruding the thick straps of veins as he struggled not to burst beneath the feeling.

That's exactly what this horrible moment was: both of us trying not to burst into shouts and tears under the weight of this goodbye.

I honest to fuck didn't think I'd ever been so sad in my life.

Like a plug had been undone behind my eyes, water started pooling in them no matter how fast I blinked them away. Blake watched the tears pile higher on the brim of my eyes, distress writhing in his because he couldn't stop them.

He couldn't stop any of this.

"I expect you to publish that rose poem about me." Pain split into my bottom lip as I chewed the thickest part of it over, trying not to fucking lose it. "Someone needs to keep my legacy going."

I tried to laugh because that seemed like the right thing to do, but it collapsed into a dry sob halfway through execution. Blake's chest caved in like my sob knocked the wind out of him, and when I looked back up, red-rims were circling his glass black eyes.

The sight of his own tears swarming knocked the wind out of me right back, my palms immediately reaching for him and flattening against the side of his face.

"Please don't worry about me," I pleaded in a watery voice.

He rolled his lips together, sniffling.

"Kind of hard not to."

"If you cry then I'm going to cry, and you know I *hate* crying."

With sadness holding steady in his waterline, he gently swept his thumb beneath my eye. "You're already crying, Kitten."

Feeling the wetness staining my cheeks, my lips quivered uncontrollably as my throat pinched. "I know," I wept, throwing my arms around his neck.

Blake swept me up in his arms, sealing me against his chest as I buried my face inside his neck and drenched the whole thing. The burnt aroma of him choked me harder than my sobs as I realized I'd never breathe that smokey scent again.

I was gripping him so hard, I would have been scared I was overdoing it if he wasn't clinging to me just as bruisingly.

"I already miss you so much," I cried, digging my fingers into his shoulders as I held on tighter. A broken sigh rattled his chest, and he did us both a disservice by slipping his hands up the back of my shirt to lose any barrier between us, reminding us both how inimitable a sensation it was when we were skin to skin.

"You shouldn't miss me, Kitten." He scratched calming lines up and down my spine. "I'm not worth missing."

"*Stop* that." I pushed myself back to lock our gazes. "You're worth it. You're worth everything. *Everything.*"

It was an affliction worse than death to watch a surge of saltwater gather on his eyelashes because of me, because I *believed* he was worth gold when he believed he was worth pennies.

A strangled breath pulled my heart closer to his, knocking our chests and bridging our heads together. The flavor of desperation was ripe in the steamed air, my fingers locking around his neck because I knew our time was running out.

"Promise you'll think of me," I whispered.

"Every single fucking day."

"Promise me you'll send my letters."

A sharp sigh warmed my face. "Kat, you're not *dying*—"

"*Promise me.*"

He held his tongue for just a moment, eventually nodding against my forehead. Sniffling and satisfied, I pulled back just enough to look at him properly one last time. My tears were trying to sabotage me by blurring up the vision of him, but Blake wiped each one away as fast as they ran over.

He stroked away each tear I cried as if they were made of holy water, and he'd been dying for redemption.

"Have I ever told you I don't like the phrase 'I love you'?" My stomach buckled even hearing those three words on his unguarded voice. "I've never said it to anyone before. I always thought if I was going to say it to someone, it would be something unique to us instead of a phrase everyone used."

"Blake…"

"From the day you got here, I knew you'd undo me. I wasn't sure how, but I knew I was done for." He studied his fingers as they traced tear-damp lines above my eyebrows, sliding down the side of my face. "You're my rose, Kitten."

A fist of tears clogged my throat as Blake gently guided my head forward, ghosting his lips over my forehead. Steady breath washed my skin as he hovered there, every sound in the world suspended so all I heard was his pointed whisper.

"You're my rose."

My heart *thunked*, hearing the words he didn't say.

Before I could even think about forming a response, Blake pressed a kiss to my forehead and ripped the door closed between us.

And he was gone.

Just like that.

The sizzle of his kiss lingered on my forehead, the impression of his final words branded on my heart.

You're my rose.

Those three words spun my head around, circling and dizzying my world as I turned from the door, thinking everything and nothing at once.

I love you.

He said it. He fucking *said* it without saying it. A violent sob tried its damndest to rip me to the floor, drop me on my hands and knees to cry so hard that I threw up Blake's admission of love. It was too rich sitting on my stomach. Too fucking powerful for someone weak like me.

It was a miracle I stayed standing on my wobbling legs, an even bigger one that I didn't puke all my anxiety up. My hand clenched over my rolling gut, waves of sorrow clashing with my desperation because I *still* had to kill myself. Blake's love wasn't enough to keep me breathing.

It was just another sin I had to take to my grave of things I'd stolen when I had no fucking right.

In my dazed hysteria, I happened to glance in the corner of the room. The corner where the glass I'd thrown at Blake a week ago should have been left shattered. My neck jerked in a double-take, widening stare searching for the broken glass. Even a shard of it.

But it was gone.

A subtle panic thrummed beneath my pulse. Ticking. *Ticking.*

Someone had been in here to clean it up? Blake? Maybe Theresa? It was *broken glass.* It would make sense that someone would clean it up, right?

I kept telling myself that as I made a beeline for the bathroom. The same shitty fluorescent lighting slapped on, flickering awake and revealing the bathroom.

The very clean bathroom. Spotless, in fact.

"No, no, no, no." Desperation shot me forward to rip back the curtain of the shower, eyes scouring for a flash of light pink death.

Nothing.

My knees hit the tile in front of the cabinets below the sink, tearing open the doors.

Nothing.

The entire bathroom was empty. No broken glass. No pink razor. Not even a fucking bottle of shampoo to poison myself to a slow death with.

"*Fuck.*" My hands shot up into my hair, strangling strands that pulled against my scalp. Blake. This must have been fucking *Blake*, stealing my second chance at an escape. He thought he was saving me, but he was *killing* me, didn't he see that?

"Fuck, fuck, fuck!"

I shot to my feet, slamming my fists against the sink. Angry panting swelled my chest up and down, up and down, *think, think, think.*

NINETEEN

From just outside the bathroom, a noise pierced my labored breathing. The bedroom door unlocking.

My buyer.

He was here.

Terror ignited in my veins, springing my whole body forward to slam the bathroom door shut. It closed with a bang, and I pressed my back up against it, propelling every ounce of strength I had behind my legs to keep that door shut.

On the other side, the distinct sound of the bedroom door opened and closed.

If I hadn't thrown up out there, it was sure as shit about to happen in here.

Blood and nerves shook in my hands that I couldn't keep still. I balled them into fists and pressed them against my eyes, blacking out the world.

"Please be a dream. Please be a dream. Please be a dream." I whispered this plea on repeat, wishing as hard as I could that I would wake up in bed. My bed, Blake's bed, any fucking bed would do.

I needed this to be some kind of fucked up dream and not really happening.

This isn't happening, isn't happening, isn't happening.

"Kat?"

A muffled voice came through the door.

All my shaking stopped.

"Are you in there?"

My world started to tilt.

"Kat, open the door."

The voice resonated through the wood, and still I was falling. My whole world was sliding to the side, tumbling off its axis so I was left dangling. In suspense. Holding onto the door handle behind me for dear fucking life.

No way...

The pulse in my neck quickened as my flat feet found their way around to face the door. I stared at the white wood between me and the person on the other side, not blinking, not moving, not thinking.

Because my thoughts would have been fucking asinine if I'd let them speak out.

There was no way they were right. There was *no way* my crazy brain wasn't just making up whatever shit I wanted to hear right before I died.

Still, I placed my cold-tipped fingers on the brass handle and turned it. Breath stuck to the back of my throat as I watched the door swing wide open...

Revealing who stood just on the other side.

TWENTY

DOM

The sun was shining today.

For the first time in five weeks, that felt right.

The golden ball in the sky decided that today was a day that deserved some light, and I couldn't have agreed more. I was back in Atlanta, Georgia. I had a S.W.A.T team thirty men deep behind me.

I was getting my girl back.

She was here. Looking up at the white-painted plaster of the house I was hiding against, waiting in the shadows where I was told, I wondered if her back was against the same wall and if we were almost touching.

Kat had been in this house for five long weeks.

It was a miracle I hadn't punched through the wall yet to pull her out.

Casting a glance around the corner of the house, I marked the set of painter's vans parked on either side approximately a hundred feet or so down the road. Each one had ten highly trained men waiting inside for the signal.

Archie was smart to deploy vans and set up trucks up and down the lane disguised as laborer vehicles. They fit in well with the clean-pressed suburban outfit this neighborhood wore.

Beneath, it was fucking filthy.

For the tenth time since I'd been on scene, I tapped my anxious thumb against my phone to light it up.

Nothing yet.

Feeling nerves run up and down my arms, I shoved my phone back in my pants pocket and gave a cursory glance around. Maybe I could squeeze in a few push ups to work off some of the anxiety before this guy showed up.

A lock unlatched on the fence that fell in line with the side of the house, and there was my answer.

My spine straightened and shoulders rolled back, relaxing my face just enough so that it didn't read, *'I want to put my fist through your skull.'* He'd been the one to call me, which gave me the ability to call Archie and set this whole thing up. I supposed that meant I had to be nice enough not to give him double black eyes.

A man with dark hair ducked out of the gate in the white laminate fence, notching his foot between the gap so it wouldn't close. I started his way at the same second he fixed his stare on me.

Damn. Guess he already has two black eyes.

They weren't black due to the privilege of anyone's fists, unfortunately. This guy just had the darkest fucking eyes I'd ever seen on another person. The hate in them emboldened their rancid color even more.

"Are you Blake?" His nostrils broadened, and my ego stirred that the sound of my voice visibly bothered him.

He didn't nod or confirm or do anything helpful except ask, "Are your people in place?"

Satisfaction that was entirely barbaric fizzled in my chest as I noted my voice was a pitch deeper than his.

"They are." I stepped close enough to get a good look at him. "How's Kat doing?"

His cheeks that were a little sharper than mine and his jaw that was a little more rounded and clean-shaved clenched as I said her name. His nose that had been broken at least once before crinkled, his eyes shading as he averted them out.

TWENTY

"She's ready."

That didn't really answer my question, now did it?

"Is she okay?" I pressed, nearing without meaning to or thinking about it. The implication running hot beneath my tone wasn't subtle either. He came a step closer as well, hitting just an inch or two below me.

Another infantile but pride-warming triumph.

"You think I'd call you to come get her and then *hurt* her?" This guy smelled like he'd been rolling around in cigarettes and aftershave as he looked at me like I'd grown a second head. "Now I see how Heather got away with as much shit as she did."

He clicked his tongue, jabbing his chin up. "Nice catch by the way, Detective."

Heat flared up the back of my neck despite the chill of Fall in the wind. "You've got a lot of attitude for someone I could arrest right now for harboring a kidnap victim."

"Yeah, and I'm also the only reason you're getting her back," he snapped back twice as hard. "How about you think about that before you start a game of whose dick is bigger."

Trying to get back on track so this didn't end with my hands around his neck, I forced out, "You were supposed to text me when the sale started."

His eyes flickered to the back of his head quick enough that I almost missed it, pinning me with a glare.

"I forgot. Think you can forgive me?"

This fucking guy.

Before I could respond, he was heading back inside the gate and grumbling at me to follow along. I focused on the back of his head as I followed him behind the fence, trying not to enjoy the fantasy of a bullet blowing out the back of it.

This fucker was smeared all over this case. First, when we got his name off of the phone call Kat made to 911. Second, when Layla helped a sketch artist come up with a portrait of the guy who brought her food once while she was taken, and it looked a hell of a lot like the one walking in front of me.

Then the auction where I watched him with Kat right before he rode away with her.

He was a felon any way you spun it. Despite him helping us take down this entire operation, it didn't change my stance on wanting him behind bars. It was where men like him belonged.

"I looped the camera feed on the outer perimeter of the house and on her room so you can get her in and out cleanly," he threw over his shoulder as we walked through a backyard that was nothing but garden green grass. He stopped at the side of an outside door attached to the back of the house. "The only higher up here today is Claudia, and she's with your buyer, so you should have enough cover to get in and get out."

Heather's mother's name hit like fresh acid in an already open wound. I was still struggling to wrap my head around the whole thing.

"I shouldn't need more than five minutes," I told him.

"*Two.*" My jaw ticked as this guy found the balls to correct me. "There's no reason it should take you more than two minutes to get up to her room, get her, and get out."

I knew I shouldn't have pushed it.

My brain was even screaming at me to keep tight-lipped and move on and go get Kat.

Somehow, I heard myself talking anyway.

"I never did ask why you decided to blow the lid on this operation." I folded my arms across my chest, narrowing my stare. "You'll lose your income, your housing, and probably put a big fat target on your back. So why'd you decide to call me?"

He kicked his head to the side, a muscle in his cheek jumping. "You know for a guy who hasn't seen his girlfriend in five weeks, you do an awful lot of talking instead of running to go see her."

His attention swung back to me, unapologetically writing out with the black ink of his eyes how much he couldn't stand me. It'd been evident when he called me a few days ago with this plan, and it was evident now. This man loathed me before we'd ever spoken a word.

And I bet I knew why.

TWENTY

Reaching back to palm my weapon, I nodded him on. "Let's move."

"No weapons."

My reach for my glock slacked. "You're not serious."

The jut of his chin said he was.

"God-for-fucking-bid someone sees me bringing you through the house, you need to look like a customer of the brothel. Not some jackass ready to blow the place up." I could all but *hear* this twenty-something-year-old man rolling his eyes at me as he turned for the door that led inside the house. "Stash the gun and let's go."

Against every better judgment, I moved my hand away from my gun right before following a felon into a house with a bunch of other felons.

Dammit, love really did make a man stupid.

We moved inside, my hands careful to close the door without noise behind me. Once indoors, the first thing to hit me about this house built of sex and crimes was the smell.

Like warm sugar.

It threw me more than I'd like to admit, digging notes of home and comfort inside my brain instead of disgust. It smelled like someone had been baking something with vanilla and cinnamon, maybe french toast or pancakes.

But who would be making a home cooked breakfast in a house filled with degenerates?

Moving past the conflicting smell, he led me down a dim-lit hallway before instructing me to hang back. I kept my back sealed to the edge of the hallway wall as he disappeared to presumably make sure our path was clear.

When he came back, I was scrutinizing a rustic painting on a far wall that looked an awful lot like one Heather had decorated our home with. A snap got my attention, and he jabbed a finger at me to follow.

Behind him, I murmured, "I still can't believe a brothel is running out of a neighborhood like this."

His focus stayed ahead, unphased. "What rich suburbanites get away with would shock you."

We passed a gourmet style kitchen with not a soul in it and spit out into a foyer that fit the gaudy characteristics and size of a small ballroom. Coming up to a curving staircase, he took each landing two at a time, so I did too, following him up to a second story of the house.

My heart drummed faster beats the more we traveled, pushing out thoughts of Heather and the crimes she committed in this house that was honestly so over-the-top extravagant, it fit her taste precisely.

My only thought was Kat and getting my mouth back on hers.

We strode alongside a white-wood railing that was an extension of the staircase, passing two, three, four closed doors before Blake stopped in front of one.

"This is where she's been staying?"

I watched him fish out a pair of brass keys, not meeting my stare as he replied.

"This is her room."

My gut shifted around his second dealing of an answer that didn't exactly clear up my question. Before I could examine it, a loud sound from inside her room jarred the stiff air.

Alarm cut my eyes to him. "What was that?"

"Sounded like a door slamming."

He didn't seem particularly worried, glaring down at the doorknob as he inserted the key and unlocked the door. My heartbeat had climbed up my throat as I watched him push it open. I shouldered past him, busting my way into the room with my expectations sky-high.

They plummeted when I didn't immediately find a woman of wild brown hair and vixen green eyes. Emptiness clouded my bones as I scoured a bedroom that was equally empty.

A bed, a bookcase, a nightstand and no Kat.

"Kat?"

A creak in the floorboards whipped my head back as Blake entered, giving a soft nod behind me. Madness sloshed around my limbs as I snapped forward where he'd pointed, noticing a closed door to the side.

My feet raced for it. "Are you in there?" I called.

TWENTY

I wasn't sure I'd ever heard louder silence than when no one replied.

Out of my peripherals, Blake came forward. I flashed my hand out, palm facing his way to hold him in place.

My shoes flushed in slow steps with the floor, coming to stand against the barrier between us. I steadied my hands on the frame, bringing my forehead to the door as if it was her, speaking as if I was right in her ear. I hoped I was.

"Kat," I rumbled, rolling her name around my mouth like sweet sin. Even I felt the vibrations of my voice in the white-painted wood; I was sure she did too. "I need you to open the door."

Several seconds went by with nothing.

Then, the wood creaked as if someone took their weight off of it.

I bolted back a few strides to give her some room as the brass handle twisted and turned. After five weeks of hundreds of miles between us, all that was left was a door.

A door that was cracking open.

A door that was swinging wide.

A door that was gone in the next second.

TWENTY-ONE

KAT

Maybe I was dreaming.

Maybe I'd already taken a razor to my veins and let out all the blood and this was Heaven.

The only thing I knew for certain was this couldn't be real.

Dominic wasn't here. He couldn't be. It made less sense for him to be here than for his wife to be the one that put me here in the first place. No, this was either some sadistic dream of my own subconscious or the best *'Welcome to Heaven!'* mirage the angels could have given me.

Dominic wasn't standing right in front of me.

Those weren't his eyes. Not his *real* eyes. Though, they were just as brilliant. Maybe more so. The gray had grown more stunning since the last time I remembered seeing him.

One thing was for certain about this dream Dominic.

He was still fucking *smoking*.

Was it sinful to want to fuck in Heaven? Could I even fuck a mirage? I'd have to find someone to get me a manual of dos and don'ts for this whole Heaven thing.

Dream/mirage Dominic cracked one of those crooked grins of his that showcased his dimples the best, and my knees went weak.

TWENTY-ONE

"I don't get a hi?"

Was it possible to die if you were already dead? Because I was pretty sure the fireworks going off in my chest were going to cause an electrocution, and I was about to bite the big one all over again.

Death by voice of a God. *Check.*

Maybe God-like men such as Dominic had special permissions in dream Heaven, and that's why he was here. I didn't know how this shit worked. All I knew were the curves of his dimples as he smiled warmly and only for me.

That, and that none of this could be true.

"You're not real," I whispered to myself, because well, who else would I talk to?

Sure, mirage/dream Dominic had proven he could talk, but his words weren't real. They were comforts that my brain provided from memory and nostalgia, but nothing real.

Dominic's brooding browline that I *so* missed furrowed only slightly.

"What?"

"You're not real." I spoke a little louder this time, clearer, meeting his intense stare. He obviously needed help coming to terms with his existence—or lack thereof.

The sharp cut of his jaw sliced the air, his head ticking to the side.

He dolled out the smallest and surest of nods. "I'm real."

I matched his nod with an equally as doubtless shake of my head. "No."

My focus drifted down his front, admiring how refined and detailed this version of him was. From the gasping stretch of material over his large biceps and the breadth of his shoulders to the masculine spidering of veins in his forearms, he was perfect.

He looked just like my Dominic.

Only he wasn't.

"No..."

"Kat," the dream spoke.

God, the letters of my name had never been more crisp than when executed by his tongue. I felt his voice ride down my spine, curling like a dominant finger along each vertebra and pushing them all straighter. My shoulders righted, back arching at attention as if he had pulled a string taut inside my chest.

The familiar reaction widened my eyes on his, wondering how he'd done that when all of this was imagined.

My throat got a little scratchy, a little dry, as I tried to swallow.

"You're not real."

This time, he took a step forward. Slow. Deliberate. Eyes never leaving mine.

"Yes I am." He was resolute, face carved with determination as he ate up our distance with calculated steps.

"You're not." My voice squeezed, tears fisting my throat that made my certainty wobble.

Could you cry in Heaven? Could you feel the wetness on your cheeks in a dream? The pads of my fingers swiped at slipping tears, rolling the coldness around the tips as my breathing started to shake.

"You're not real." But he was still coming at me.

He paralyzed me from the neck down so all I did was hyperventilate and soak my cheeks as he reached me, nudging my toes with the tips of his shoes. I wondered if they were wingtips.

"You're not real," I repeated, crying, breathing harder.

Hands so big they could have taken over my face cupped both of my tear-stained cheeks, warmth proving its existence in his body as it transferred to mine. More tears spilled over, my heart constricting so tight, I thought I might pass out.

"You *can't* be real," I whimpered one last denial before a pair of lips kissed it gone.

It was fast, chaste, sending a shock wave throughout my entire system.

"I'm real." He spoke the promise over my lips, giving me time to catch up. "I'm here." A tender ghosting of his mouth over mine. "I've got you." He kissed the corner of my mouth, whispering deeply against it, "I promise I've got you."

A gasping sob climbed out of my chest, washing both our mouths with

TWENTY-ONE

disbelief. With lightning fast hands, I pushed him back just enough to see him. To *really* see him. My wet eyes flashed between his, collecting every fleck of silver and counting every monochrome shade to make sure they were all there.

Not *only* were they all there, but so was something else. Something only Dominic possessed.

It rolled through his gaze, rumbling tremors inside my heart as the thunder found its little lightning.

"Oh my god," I half cried, half gasped.

My denial shattered into a thousand tiny fragments, all of which I passed through as my galloping heart dragged me forward to throw myself in his arms. Dominic caught me like he *always* did, hoisting me up so my legs were around his waist, his hands were in my hair, and our lips were falling together.

And I was home.

Lightning ricocheted around my chest, striking my heart to revive it over and over again as my mouth pressed to his. We didn't even move our lips or dive our tongues into the other's mouth even though we could have.

We just *held on*.

We just clung to each other, those pieces of ourselves re-linking, our mouths re-memorizing, our hearts getting reacquainted. I smashed my lips to his as if I thought I could actually fuse our flesh, squeezing his strands of thick silken hair between my fingers.

It was that pressure on the back of his head that brought Dominic back to life, pulling my bottom lip between his teeth and chewing it over like he hadn't eaten in five whole weeks. His tongue flicked inside my mouth, taking me—just fucking *taking* me—like a man took a woman and made her his.

I realized crying and moaning were basically the same thing as the noise I let out against his mouth sounded like both. This was it. This *was* my heaven with the taste of sweet mint on my tongue, the smell of a crisp early morning in my nose, and thunder twining in my veins. I drank all of him in, matching every greedy swipe of his tongue, biting back on his lips when he nibbled mine, getting drunk as a person could get on the taste of pure love.

Oh my god, I loved him. I *loved* him.

It was maybe the only thing in the entire universe that could have made me stop kissing him at that moment, but the thought popped a gasp from my lips and pulled me back.

"I love you," I said in a breathy rush.

His lust-drunk eyes fluttered open, dilated pupils overtaking their color. Which, *fuck*, he was so sexy when he looked like he wanted to eat me. That primal elixir dousing his eyes was slowly upstaged by the light rising within them as he registered my words.

In seconds, they were *glowing*, his kiss-plumped lips blooming into a smile.

"I did it." I searched between his eyes for the pride I knew would be there. "I said it. I said it, and I'm not having a panic attack. *Look*, no tears."

Well, except for the ones he was sweetly wiping off my face. But those were *happy*. Not panicky like they were when I first tried to say those words.

Holding me tighter, he bumped his nose with mine.

"Quite the progress, Ms. Sanders."

"*Yeah*. It is." Those three little words were already lined up on the back of my tongue to say again, but other words tumbled out first. "You're here." A kiss. "You're *here*." Another kiss. "How the *fuck* are you here?"

Instead of telling me with warm summer eyes how in the hell he managed to find me, bitter winter chomped up all his warmth as he snapped his head to the side.

"You didn't tell her I was coming?"

From the side of the room I hadn't paid any attention to came a fierce voice.

"I wasn't taking any chances on you not showing up."

My stomach plummeted in time with my heart.

A crack actually popped off in my neck I jerked my head towards him so fast. I barely registered the pain as I found Blake leaned up against the door,

TWENTY-ONE

arms folded over his chest with his fire-hot eyes burning holes through Dominic.

Oh my god.

I scurried out of Dominic's arms and tried not to think about Blake watching all of that. The reunion, the kiss, the 'I love you' I gave Dominic minutes after Blake gave me one of his own.

The pain of his pain was inescapable, intensifying every inch closer to him I got. He refused to glance my way, still trying to make Dominic go up in flames with just a feral look. Despite him not looking at me, my eyes were all over him.

"You did this?" I asked on an astonished breath when I stopped less than a foot from him.

Blake's nostrils flared, throat working as he barely moved his lips to say, "Yeah."

"How?"

He shrugged, moving his hole burning to the floor instead of Dominic. "Found his number and called him on a payphone a few days ago. Here we are."

"There's a whole team of S.W.A.T and F.B.I agents set up around the perimeter waiting for Ryan to give the signal from inside."

Scrunching my forehead, I whipped back to where Dominic had spoken. "Ryan's here?"

He nodded just once, a ghost of pride curving his mouth. "Ryan's the buyer."

I bustled back. "Holy shit."

This was a lot to take in.

Turning back to Blake, I studied his face with amazement filling every other beat of my heart. This was huge. This was *monumental.*

"I can't believe you—you're ending this? *All* of this?" I gestured around the room.

The brothels. The trafficking. The drugs. The auctions. The life-ruining.

Blake sniffed aloud, head low and still sulking. "Figured it was about time I did one thing right."

One thing? I wanted to shake him, hug him, slap him for that slight at himself, but worry took over first. "Does that put you in danger? To turn in an entire *assembly line* of criminals who know exactly who you are? Or will they all be in prison? Does Ray have connections—"

Oh my god. How have I not—

I snapped back to Dominic, jaw dropping. "Heather's the one tha—"

"I know."

Heavier words had never existed until now. They were a punch straight to the gut, to hear him know something so awful, to see him struggle under the weight of it, to feel the burden of this awful thing settle on our relationship.

I felt like I could literally see him picking up the responsibility of what happened to me and resting it on his shoulders. Add that to his trust being skewered to the bone by Heather and the bags of trauma I'd added to my truck load during all of this, and Dominic and I were a couples therapist's *jackpot*.

We'd deal with all of that… later. Maybe never. Maybe it was time to start up a new game of *'how long I can avoid my issues'* and see if I could beat my best score.

On a trembling breath, I turned back to Blake. He was digging the toe of his shoe into the floor, his mouth pressed into a thin line. I eased one step closer to him, willing him to look up at me.

"You need to stop risking your life to save mine," I breathed.

As if the words were acid to his ears, he flinched. "You need to stop thinking I'm a hero."

"You *are*." Determination in my feet erased our gap, my hand palming his cheek and forcing his head up so he *had* to look at me. "Do you realize how many girls' lives you just saved?"

Smoking black eyes bored into me, unapologetic and dazzling.

"I really only care about one," he murmured just for me.

There he went again. Stealing all my air. It left my lungs in a painful squeeze, fanning over his face on the way out and probably making his affections way worse. How I was holding his face couldn't be any help

TWENTY-ONE

either, so I slid my hand down to land on a more appropriate place on his chest, right over his heart.

His heartbeat ran wild underneath my fingertips.

My thumb ran softly over his sternum. "Why didn't you tell me about any of this?"

Reluctance remolded his features, a sharp exhale teeming through his nose. "I wasn't going to tell you and get your hopes up in case he decided not to show. I had a back-up plan in place if he didn't."

"Of *course* I would show." Dominic's voice sounded closer than it was before. "She's my girlfriend."

In his slashing delivery, I couldn't decide whether the word 'my' or 'girlfriend' sounded more deliberate. Both hit Blake with the same brutal impact, his expression contouring as he snapped his teeth at Dominic.

"I wasn't taking any chances."

"*Hey.*" I sliced them both a look that said to save the pissing contest for later. Dominic's jaw worked to the side, but he nodded, keeping his unfriendly stare locked on Blake.

Sighing, I steadied my focus back on the man in front of me who was again looking anywhere but at me. I couldn't even *begin* to imagine how shitty this was for him.

Or how he'd been the one to do it to himself. For me.

Bringing Dominic here was essentially pouring boiling water on his 3rd degree burn.

Emotion tacked to the backs of my eyes, pushing tears forward that sat on the brim. Whether by accident or that enigmatic tether between us, Blake looked up the moment my eyes filled.

Anguish pinched the middle of his forehead together, full lips parting. "It was selfish to not tell you, and I'm a bastard for doing it." *What?* "But I wasn't taking the chance of you being disappointed or that things would be different after you knew."

Slowly, understanding parted my lips.

He thought I was crying because he didn't tell me the plan, not because I was so moved by it. And because he misunderstood my tears, I now understood why he *really* didn't tell me.

He was afraid if I knew Dominic was coming, it would have changed the last few days between us. And he was probably right.

I'd spent the last forty-eight hours thinking I was dying and thinking I'd never see Dominic again. I was resigned to both facts, and they influenced my reckless behavior by a *lot*.

Like trying to kill myself, for starters.

Or kissing Blake again.

I wouldn't have done any of that had I known I was being rescued. I probably wouldn't have slept in the same bed as him either or been there for him this morning when he had his nightmare or stayed on the bathroom floor with him yesterday sharing stories or read more John Keats with him last night.

We wouldn't have been us—this unique, intimate, inexplicable *us*—and that's why he didn't tell me.

Vulnerability was sewn along his face as he gazed down at me, willing me not to hate him for keeping it a secret.

Honestly, maybe I should have. Maybe I should have been furious.

But I wasn't even close to it.

This was probably just another example of ways Blake and I were equally fucked, but I understood why he did it. In a way, I was glad for it.

"I probably would have done the same thing." My whispered admission softened the edges of Blake's face, his dark chocolate eyes melting just a little.

Dominic was a staggering presence standing on the other side of the room that I knew was watching us. I already knew he'd have questions, and my stomach twisted in knots knowing I'd have to answer them, but that didn't matter right now.

All that mattered was that he was here. They were *both* here.

"I can't believe this is happening," I breathed, adrenaline hacking up my voice. I swapped a look between the two men. "I can't believe you're both here."

Dominic advanced on us in slow strides, and I fisted the front of his

TWENTY-ONE

work shirt the moment he was within grabbing distance just so I could touch him too. The corner of his mouth tweaked up, warmth from one of his bear-paw hands covering mine, brushing my fingers with his thumb.

"Do you want to go home?"

Waterworks sprung forward all over again at the single fucking notion that I *could* go home. I nodded and fluttered my lashes to gather the tears as I cried, "Yeah." rolling my lips between my teeth to keep from full on blubbering.

Dominic touched his warm thumb to my hot-from-crying cheek, brushing a petal of water away.

"I'll take you home."

I sucked back a big breath, trying to calm myself and get these fucking tears under control. Honestly, how did I have any left at this point?

Swallowing thickly, I closed my eyes and breathed. On one side, I had Dominic. On the other, I had Blake. They were both here, their hearts both thumping beneath my palms.

All I could feel was them.

All I could feel was them and their love *pulsing* between each measured heartbeat.

It was over.

It was over.

"So what happens now?" I asked, sniffling.

Blake was the first to answer. "You go with him out the back. The camera feed on the outside of the house is looping with clear footage."

Nodding, I looked back at him. "What about you? Do you come with us?"

Blake's mouth rolled thin as he diverted his attention to the floor.

"I'll stay here."

My heart *thunked*. "Why?"

The tip of his nose gave a trademark twitch just before he ripped his scorched eyes back up at me. "Because I'm one of the bad guys, Kat."

"No, you—" Words failed on my tongue, head snapping to Dominic with rounded eyes. "You're not arresting him, are you?"

"Kat—" Blake tried to protest, but I shut him up with a glare.

"He's the only reason you're here, right?" Dominic's brows flatlined at the implication. At the fucking *truth*. "He called you and now you're about to take down some of the biggest sex-trafficking assholes in the whole country. Because of *him*. I wouldn't be alive right now if it weren't for him."

Dominic's head angled low, severe stare cutting up at me.

"I would have found you."

"And I would have been dead." Welp, the cat was about to jump outta the bag because the words were already flying out. "Yesterday I had a razor to my wrists ready to do the job and would have if *Blake* hadn't stopped me."

Dominic's eyes nearly erupted from his head. "You *what?*"

I moved on fast, fire singeing each of my words. "You don't know what I've been through here or how I *literally* would not have survived if it wasn't for Blake. He saved me from being beaten, raped, killed, you name it. So I don't accept any answer that doesn't end in some way that helps him."

Dominic went quiet. It wasn't even remotely fair to throw my attempt at suicide in his face so flippantly like that, but he had to know just how *bad* it got and how much he owed Blake for my life.

He and I would talk it all out when we got home—every gritty, gory, gutting detail—but now, it was my turn to save Blake. For *once*, I could give him something back other than heartache.

I could help give him a second chance at life.

And no one had *ever* deserved a second chance more.

Dominic gave a stiff nod after what felt like hours. "I don't have the authority to say with positivity, but I'm sure they can offer him a plea deal."

Relief flowered inside my chest, the blooms airy and delicate. "Thank you."

Another terse nod was all I got from him, his stare rolling with weighty questions I'd have to answer soon. For now, I pretended that upcoming conversation didn't exist and turned back to Blake.

"Looks like we're both getting out," I offered, watching his expression carefully. It hadn't moved just yet, a complexity of smooth and rigid lines.

TWENTY-ONE

His mouth cracked just enough to let out a hollow, "Yeah."

Thoughts were driving behind his shadowed eyes, ones terrified of the transition, ones fretting over logistics, ones worrying if he'd know who he was if he wasn't trapped here.

"I'll help you through it." That brought him back to me, finding me at the center of his mini spiral. My lips pulled into a soft smile to give him something he loved to stabilize him. His eyes fell to it, quieting their commotion. "We'll find a way to reacclimate you from brooding bad boy poet to semi-normal brooding poet in no time."

To that, Blake found a reason to grin too. Just a speck of one, but in the line between his upturned lips, I saw something I'd never seen before in him. Something I used to hate.

Something I resigned to never believe in again.

Hope.

Blake had a touch of it now because, although he was nervous, he liked the idea.

He liked the idea of being semi-normal.

I liked it for him too. I liked it a whole fucking lot. Pictures of him outside these walls flashed across my mind, him laughing in the park, drinking at a bar, writing sonnets beneath a tree and enjoying the bath of sunlight and dance of the breeze because he *could*.

He wasn't looking over his shoulder, wasn't shackled to a life he hated, wasn't anything but what *he* wanted to be. Just thinking about that had my heart swelling up ten sizes too big for my chest.

My heart actually *hurt* because of how happy it was.

What a welcomed fucking change.

Blake and Dominic were staring down at me, and I just couldn't believe it. Somehow, against every odd stacked against us—and there was a fucking mountain load—we were coming out on the other side of this shitshow. We were all safe. We were all here.

We were all *going home.*

Then the bedroom door opened...

And *she* walked in.

TWENTY-TWO

DOM

"Wow, three really is a crowd, hm?"

I realized too late I should have been less surprised to see Heather walk into the room. I froze soon as her overpriced shoes crossed through the door. I hadn't had a chance to organize my thoughts for what I'd say when I saw her again.

My mouth just went dry.

All three heads swung in her direction, each of us likely following a similar thought process. She wasn't supposed to be here, and her presence clearly wasn't serendipitous. Her hair and makeup were done, and the crisp white pantsuit she wore was one I'd seen her wear off to work before—and this *was* work for Heather.

Heather avoided making eye contact with me and swayed her attention to the side, leering down at Kat with a disdainful twist on her mouth.

"How are you still alive?"

Fire sparked with life in Kat's stare, glinting a warning of violence in the shadows of her sharpening emeralds. She became a thing of feral beauty that Heather didn't take seriously; she didn't move back an inch as Kat bared her teeth.

Or when she snarled and snapped her head forward.

Heather let out a sharp cry as Kat's head smashed into hers, tumbling back on her too-high heels while Blake scooped a ferocious Kat up by the waist and set her behind him.

"Okay, Kitten. You've had your fun."

He stayed facing her, his back to Heather and his hands staying on the dips of Kat's waist. She cradled her forehead in her hands, face crinkling adorably.

"*Shit*, that was dumb."

Blake nodded. "Yup."

Despite the fact of there being at least twenty other things in the room that deserved my immediate and complete attention, my gaze wouldn't stop drifting to his hands still holding her waist.

Also—*Kitten?*

Heather stumbled in front of me, breaking my focus with her watery eyes.

"Dom, *do* something. She just attacked me!"

My wife looked to me for help with impact tears gathered in the corners of her eyes, and I stood there staring at her, feeling heavier than I'd ever felt in my life.

How was I supposed to do this? Her betrayal was still so ripe, I felt like I couldn't breathe through the thought of it without wincing in pain.

Meanwhile, she wasn't acting as if there was anything out of the ordinary. This was her norm. Brothels and illegalities and abusing my trust.

None of this fazed her.

My mouth felt like cotton as I unstuck my tongue from the roof of my mouth. "I'm going to go out on a limb and say you deserved it."

"Oh." She pinched her fingers over the bridge of her reddening nose, aggression radiating off of her. "I almost forgot that you're physically incapable of taking my side."

"Your side—?" Anger flashed red-hot up the back of my neck, tinting the edges of my vision. The woman I'd loved for years stood at the center of it, cast in a halo of muddy scarlet. "Heather, I need you to take five seconds to think about where we are right now and why and ask me again why I'm

TWENTY-TWO

not taking your side."

Her eyes rolled in a circle in her head. "You say that as if you'd have taken my side before you found out, which we know is a lie."

"*Heather*," I stressed, my composure slipping. "Focus."

"I *am* focused, Dom." The confident snap to her voice shredded across the room. "Why do you think I'm here? I know we have things to discuss."

I studied the quality of her stare while I had a chance, the stark blue of her eyes a little hazy, but mostly clear cut and acutely attuned. If she knew about the team of S.W.A.T waiting outside or about Ryan, I wouldn't even be able to make out her pupils they'd dilate to such small pin-pricks of rage.

"How'd you know I was here?" I asked, trying to keep things calm.

"The same way you found out I was meeting with Tommy."

Tension screwed up every muscle in my body so tight, it hurt to breathe. "You tracked my phone?"

"Hurts having your privacy invaded, doesn't it?"

Deep breaths.

"I'd say it hurts a hell of a lot more being lied to by your wife for thirteen years."

"One could argue that I kept you in the dark to protect your feelings because I'm a good wife."

I balked, the cadence with which she delivered that line smooth enough to ride the skin like butter. Even Kat behind her threw back her head and scoffed aloud, earning a blistering scowl from Heather.

"Do you think for *one* second you could not force yourself into something that is explicitly between my husband and I?"

"Do you think for one second you could not be a psycho *bitch*?"

Heather twisted to face me again, a look of boredom slacked across her face.

"Really, Dom. Your taste in women has outdone itself."

Absent-mindedly, I curled and uncurled my fists. We were getting off track.

"Heather, what you've done..." I couldn't finish the sentence. "What you do."

Nausea looped around the pit of my stomach as I thought about it all over again. I'd been physically ill the night Ryan and I made the connection between what Tommy said about Heather screwing with my cases to her affiliation with traffickers.

It was shortly after I got off the phone with Blake, and I didn't quite make it outside before what little lunch I had during the day came back up.

Every girl's face that went missing under my watch circled in my head like they were now, acidic bile rising hot up my throat. Every single one of them dead or worse, and my wife the reason why. I spent so much time chasing down a monster not knowing that monster was sleeping soundly next to me in my own bed.

"See, *this* is why I didn't tell you." Heather cocked a hip out and ranted as if we were simply standing in our kitchen. "We were perfectly happy when you were oblivious, and I knew you wouldn't understand even though it's just a *job*. Jobs are material, Dom. You should be able to get over this if I can get over you cheating on me with the help."

"My infidelity is hardly comparable to you selling young women and shipping Kat off to be killed just to be *spiteful*. You did that to hurt me, Heather."

Without a wrinkle in her expression, she said, "No. I did that to save our marriage."

The same exhaustion I'd felt for weeks, months, *years* sunk into my muscles, and it was like I couldn't move. Like I was submerged under miles of ocean and couldn't swim free.

"Our marriage has been over for a long time. You *know* this."

"And yet you never would have even *dreamt* of filing for divorce until she came along." Heather threw a sharp jab back at Kat, then did a double take and paused. "And, *by the way*," she snapped her calculated attention back to me, "I think you need to take a closer look at where your precious girlfriend is standing right now instead of with you."

I looked back to them before I could tell myself not to fall for Heather's game and regretted it the moment I did. His hands were still attached to her waist, and she wasn't making any move to remove them. She'd actually wrapped her little hands around his forearms as if she needed him for balance.

Jealousy wasn't an emotion I was brought to easily, but it sliced down my chest and exposed this barbaric urge to storm over there and shove that asshole against the wall and take Kat for myself.

"Every time I've seen her here, she's been with him," Heather tried to prod my brutish impulse. "The last time I was here, I watched him carry her up to this room with my own eyes, and God only knows how long they were in here. *Alone.*"

Kat's voice came ringing from the back. "That's because I couldn't walk after you brought a fucking psychopath here to *rape* me, and Blake stopped him!"

"You *what?*" I growled, flashes of bright red clashing over my vision.

A heatwave rolled up my body, damp sweat birthing against my skin in milliseconds. Beneath my pores, this *thing* rammed from beneath, trying to break off its shackles and erupt. A beast in waiting.

"What?" Through the sheen of crimson pulsing around my vision, I thought I saw Heather pop one of her shoulders. "I was angry. You had just told me you were in love with her, and I reacted poorly."

That animal impatiently waiting *slammed* forward again, vibrating my whole body.

"You reacted poorly…" I reiterated, not recognizing my carved out voice.

My eyes pried into my wife's, searching out some ounce of regret or a hint of the sweet young woman I fell in love with all those years ago. She couldn't have been all gone.

But the longer I probed, the more apparent it became that the Heather I loved and married had been shed long ago. That version of herself was a coat she wore to trick and romance me as a teenager into falling in love with her.

Now, the coat was gone, and the villain was revealed.

"Dom, we can—"

Heather shut up when I raised a hand in between us. The burden of thirteen years of lies weighed on my shoulders, sitting like cement in my stomach, like lead in my arms and legs. Rising my stare back to Heather's was a feat almost impossible beneath the mass of contempt bearing down on me, but I managed.

I leveled my eyes on hers, sickening myself when I enjoyed the flinch on her face.

What had we become?

"You will never come near me again." Hair on my arms lifted, rising from the chill of my tone. "You will never come near Kat again. And you will never see Maya *ever* again."

Silence ticked on with my threat hanging in the air above us. Heather remained impassive as she processed. Then, her porcelain skin cracked with laughter that she couldn't seem to stop. It bounced around the room, hitting notes that made my eardrums bleed.

"Oh, this is rich." She touched her hand to her chest as if she couldn't catch her breath from laughing. *"I'm* being painted as the bad guy in all of this when the girl you've been going out of your mind to find has been getting her rocks off with someone else!"

"Oh, shut up, you noisy bitch," Kat scoffed.

I lost sight of Heather's face as she snapped around to Kat.

"Careful, Ms. Sanders. Don't you know getting defensive is a sign of guilt? I think you should tell him. Dominic deserves to know that you've been fucking the security guy."

Without missing a beat, Kat quipped back with a smirk and a wink.

"Nope. Strictly fucking your husband."

There wasn't enough warning given to get to her in time as Heather obliterated the scale from collected to murderous so fast, she lunged for Kat's neck before I blinked. Blake reacted with lightning-fast instincts, blocking Heather's attack and shoving her just barely, standing tall and stoic in front of Kat.

I was working somewhere between hating every breath this guy breathed and considering lobbing off my hand before I'd have to shake his to thank him for all he'd done. He clearly wasn't a stranger to protecting Kat, and

TWENTY-TWO

she was as used to accepting his help as he was to giving it by the way she unthinkingly stood at his back to allow him to defend her.

Blindly accepting help wasn't something the Kat that left me knew how to do very well. She was as stubborn as she was infuriating as she was breathtaking. I didn't know what to think of seeing how easily she opened up to it now with someone other than me.

Heather caught herself easily enough, straightening her jacket with a huff.

"Am I to assume you've gone puppy-eyed for this whore too?" She moved on without waiting for a reply from him. "I'm going to go off of context clues and say it was you who brought Dom here, which was a really *stupid* thing to do considering my parents will kill you for it."

Blake set his jaw to the side and back. "I've been ready to die for a long time."

Behind him, Kat stole my focus as she rested her forehead to his back. Undecipherable whispers caught my ears while the subtle change of expression on her word's recipient caught my eyes. It was something so specific and small, no one else in the world would have recognized it.

But I knew that look on his face, and I knew it well.

It was the same one I'd seen staring back at me in the mirror for months as I agonized over my inappropriate feelings for Kat. It was the one I'd been wearing for over a month now, not knowing where she was or if I would ever kiss her again.

It was the look of a man who ached for something he couldn't have.

Heather grabbed the scene again by the reins, flashing my attention to her as she cocked her hip out and reached inside the lapel of her blazer.

"In that case, I imagine my father wouldn't be bothered if I sped up the process."

I saw the horror ignite in Kat's eyes before I saw the gun itself.

Heather clicked off the safety on a pocket pistol I had no idea she owned while Kat screamed, the shriek tearing apart my chest as she tried to claw her way in front of Blake.

"No! *No*, Blake, stop it!" Blake did his best to keep her behind him as she fought tooth and nail to get in front. "She wants me! Not you!"

"You know what?" Heather's voice rang out over the commotion. "She's right."

Then she aimed her gun at Kat.

"I did come here to kill you after all."

TWENTY-THREE

KAT

Down the barrel of Heather's gun, I saw my life—past, present, and no future.

I saw Charlotte's cheeky smile. I saw my mother's eyes. I saw the memory of the first time Dominic and I met and all the love that had followed since.

My life wasn't a great one, but it wasn't bad either.

Despite it being cut short, I think I'd write this life off as a lucky one—which probably sounded batshit considering the gun currently stuffed in my face—but this life had *love* in it. A lot.

Love was hands down the scariest thing I'd ever encountered, gun currently aimed between my eyes included, but you know what's funny?

In the end of it all, I couldn't think of anything I was more grateful for.

Another example of love squeezed his arms around my waist, trying to get me back behind him.

"Kat," Blake warned through gritted teeth.

My top lip parted from the bottom, readying to tell him to shut the fuck up and let me save him for a change when a deadly voice shook the room.

"Heather, drop your gun *now*."

My rounding eyes followed the voice back behind Heather and straight to Dominic.

And to the bigger gun he held aimed at her head.

Heather followed my gaze and turned away from Blake and I, pausing as she came eye to eye with Dominic's weapon.

And she laughed.

Maybe because she was certifiable. Maybe because she knew he wouldn't shoot her. Probably a fucked up mix of both. She might've been motherfucking Satan, but Heather was still the mother of his child, and Dominic's heart was too pure to hurt her.

"Wow." She continued to laugh. "Well, that was unexpected."

Dominic's jaw ticked off center with his trademark indication that he was *pissed*. In fact, he was something so beyond pissed, I wasn't sure there was a categorical name for it yet.

"Heather, I'm serious. Gun. *Down*."

"Oh, please." Her laughter scratched to a stop. "I could blow her brains out right here and now, and you'd hate me for a while but you'd never hurt me. I'm your *wife*."

Barely moving his lips, he said, "I don't know who you are right now."

"I'm the woman who did *all of this* for you. To get this plague out of our lives so they could go back to normal." Blake held me tighter as Heather's glacier eyes fixed back on me, glinting with scorn. "I realize it's inherently cliché to say, but none of this would have happened if you'd never come into our lives. Do you ever think about all the *damage* that's been caused simply because you needed a job as our nanny?"

Honestly?

It was one of the things I thought about most when I laid awake at night. The cosmic domino effect of life was one major mindfuck for a girl on the verge of death.

If I hadn't been fired from Marty's, I'd never have gone on the interview to be Maya's nanny. If the first nanny they hired hadn't flaked, Dominic wouldn't have called me last second to fill in. He and I wouldn't have met. We wouldn't have fallen interminably in love with each other. He never would have cheated, and I never would have been kidnapped.

TWENTY-THREE

Whether I liked it or not, Heather was right, and we four were standing in this room now because of me. Because I got fired and needed a job.

What a shitty origin story.

"If you had stayed away when I told you to, we could have avoided all of this." She so carelessly gestured with the gun, making my insides knot. "You would still be at home with your sister, and your junkie mom would still be alive."

Her brutal truths so effortlessly knocked the wind right out of me as she turned to face Dominic.

"And your life would be calm again. Perfectly ordinary just how you like it."

In a moment split between time and reality, Dominic's eyes shifted over to me. He looked at me in that way that made my stomach flip flop and my whole chest fucking *ache* in that good love kind of way that somehow felt so good. Like my favorite pain ever. We held onto each other through just a look, the whole room melting away around us.

When it all solidified again and Dominic glanced back at Heather, a certain calm had smoothed the strict lines of his perfect face.

"I don't want ordinary anymore. I want the extra. I want the phenomenal, the complicated, the bittersweet, every messy and breathtaking second in between. And I want all of that with the woman standing behind you."

My heart and brain clashed, one happily mooning over such an impassioned declaration while the other was saying, *'hey, cool and all, but maybe not the best thing to say to a woman wielding a gun in my face.'*

And then there was Blake.

His grip on me loosened and then tightened right after, like he honest to god didn't know if he should touch me anymore and also didn't know how he couldn't.

My breathing began collapsing in on itself, too much pressure and tension for my lungs to withstand. I needed to find a way out of here for everyone—everyone except the bitch with the trigger-happy finger.

"Dominic," Heather sighed an exhale. "I think I have been more than patient with this affair, but you still don't seem to understand that it always had an expiration date. Either you got bored of her or I had her taken care of. I just reached the end of my rope before you reached yours."

"You tried to have her *killed*."

"Yes." Heather dragged an irked glare my way. "Apparently she's quite slippery."

My molars knocked together as I held her blistering stare, the seconds pulsing as the bedroom seemed to pick up a heartbeat of its own.

Dominic was the one who snipped it dead.

"Heather, you and I can go somewhere and talk about this. We can. You just have to put the gun down."

"You and I will talk. Plenty. After she's dead and you realize I did you a favor and you *thank me* for keeping you from making the biggest mistake of your life, so you and I can get back to ours."

Exasperation absolutely drowned the man in front of me, brightening his eyes that tore into his wife's. "*Goddammit*, Heather, I don't know any other way I can possibly phrase it to get through to you. We have no life. You and I have *nothing*."

A noise between a screech and growl peeled up Heather's throat, and whether she meant to or not, she pointed her gun at the floor instead of at me.

"We had *everything* before this. I gave you *everything*, Dominic. A beautiful house, a life you could be proud of, the perfect wife on your arm."

"You gave me my daughter," he replied unflinchingly, keeping his gun on her. "That's the only good thing you've done for me."

"You have no *idea* the things I've done for you." She took a menacing step closer to him, not fazed one bit by the potential bullet hole aimed at her chest. "The lengths I've gone to for our marriage, to keep you happy, to keep the peace with my parents who never wanted me with you."

Dominic resecured his fingers' grip on the gun's handle. "I'm sure Ray and Claudia would have been happier if you'd chosen an arsonist instead of me."

"But I chose *you*, Dom. I chose you back then when I could have had

TWENTY-THREE

anyone, and I'm choosing you now. Because that's what a good wife does for her husband *even* when he's been so very bad."

Dominic crossed one foot over the other, moving a step closer to the farthest wall of the room. Heather, like the sun's reflection on the water, moved how he moved.

Her back was completely to me now.

"Heather," Dominic started, low and careful. "I think you need help."

Pressure around my waist shocked me for only a second before I realized it was Blake's hands pushing me closer to the open bedroom door. Oh *shit*. Were we supposed to leave? Was that why Dominic moved?

Heather really only proved Dominic's point by pulling out a laugh from the darkest parts of her soul and shaking her head along with it. "Of course you would go straight for the crazy diagnosis. That's what *all* men do when faced with a woman who knows what she wants. Really, Dom. Do you have to be so stereotypical?"

My heart was in my throat as I listened to Heather's honestly fascinating justification.

Behind me, Blake tried to move me closer to the door, pulling around my waist. Reactionary, I flexed my heels into the floor and rooted myself in place so he couldn't take me anywhere without making a scene.

Heat washed over my ear as soft lips spoke right against it. "I have to get you out of here."

I shook my head against him, and he buried a whispered curse inside my ear. I even felt a brush of his teeth on my lobe as he murmured, "While she's focused on him, we *have* to go. You're not safe."

"Care to share with the class what you two are whispering about over there?" A small gasp ripped my stare back up to find Heather beveled our way with a dirty smirk on her face. "Secrets don't make friends after all."

Behind her, Dominic exhausted my name on a rasp. "*Kat.*"

I met his frustrated glare across the room, fire sparking in my veins.

"*What*? I'm not leaving you."

"Oh, were you under the impression that you were going somewhere?" Heather cocked her head and then her gun, lifting it my way. "Because that would really put a kink in my plans."

"Heather, stop with the fucking *gun*," Dominic boomed, his thick-shaped brows digging together with severity.

"Why, Dom?" She kept her gun targeted at me but swiveled her head to match his stare. "We both know you're not going to shoot me."

The muscles in his defined jaw worked hard, tensing and pulsing on a countdown to implosion. His focus on Heather was almost scary, his steady aim on her even more so.

"If you point that gun at Kat again, I will shoot you… and I will kill you."

Even though I'd had a gun pointed at me twice in the last few minutes, that was the first time my heart started to pound *really* hard. My eyes switched back and forth between Heather and Dominic's gun, each breath more difficult to find than the last as panic expanded a wildfire across my chest.

"Dominic—" I tried, but he cut me off without sparing me a glance.

"Not now."

Frantic energy started bubbling beneath my skin. Now no one wanted Heather to suffer a miserable, humiliating death more than me so I could shoot off confetti cannons around her dead body, but Dominic couldn't be the one to kill her. That would destroy him. *Destroy.*

He'd already been through hell and back because of this woman, and if he was the one to force her final breath, he'd never be rid of her.

Heather's ghost would sit on his chest until she caved it in and he was consumed inside his guilt and regret. If he killed Heather for me, we would have no chance at survival. Her death would haunt our relationship into its grave, and Heather would finally win.

I had to stop this.

"Do you really think you could do that?" Heather challenged Dominic, dropping her weapon to hang at her side, advancing on him. "Do you honestly think you could put a bullet inside the mother of your child?"

Dominic's upper lip curled into a snarl. "Don't do that."

"Do what?"

"Play Maya like a card. This is your mess, Heather. Don't bring my

TWENTY-THREE

daughter into it."

"Oh, now she's solely *your* daughter? Does that mean the scar from my C-section suddenly doesn't exist?"

"No. It means Maya isn't a pawn you can play whenever you feel like you're losing."

"Oh please," she dismissed.

"Or *that*. You either use her to make me feel guilty or you roll your eyes at her and act like you don't care that she exists."

"Because I *don't* care that she exists!" Heather's proper facade glitched out as she exploded, eyes going bug-wide. "Kids were the last thing on my radar, but you wanted a baby so badly it was ruining our marriage, so I put aside *my* wants and gave you a daughter in spite of the fact that I never gave a fuck about her!"

Her eruption leveled the room into complete silence.

My heart stopped, and I was sure Dominic's had too. He looked like she'd just slapped him across the face and told him the world was ending. Maya was Dominic's heart, and Heather just told him flat-out that she didn't give a flying fuck about his heart.

She must have realized just how devastating her blow was, because when she turned her focus to me, a tether had come loose in her eyes, their clarity a little askew.

A little unhinged.

"You know what I see this as?" She carried that slightly manic look back to Dominic. "A fresh start. It didn't come about in the most *ideal* of ways, but every secret is out now. There's no need for more lies or betrayals. We can have a clean slate away from all of this."

"Heather, *stop*." Her name sounded so heavy on his vocal cords, weighing them down and roughing them up.

"No, I won't stop, Dom. You're *my* husband, and as far as our marriage is concerned, your wagon is still hitched to mine, which means you aren't as ready to give me up as you pretend to be."

"I've signed the papers. *You* haven't," Dominic tried to argue, his voice rising with hers.

275

"And I don't plan to! I *chose you* thirteen years ago, and everything is going to be like it was before once she's out of the picture."

"Heather—"

"You may not have the wherewithal enough to see it, but I do. I *see* our future, Dom, and it looks exactly how it did six months ago before the tramp from hell came along, and I am clearly willing to do the heavy lifting to get us there."

"*Heather.*"

"That's what you do for someone you *love*. Do you think you could say the same about some twenty-one-year-old whim of yours? Do you think she loves you like I love you? Do you think *anyone* will love you like I—"

"Heather, *I* don't love you!"

Dominic's shout slashed the air in half, forcing my lungs to gasp for what was left. We four stood in the aftermath, petrified by the tension. I hadn't even realized I'd reached for Blake's hands until the caress of his thumb soothed down my knuckles.

The winter gray of Dominic's eyes might have been the coldest I'd ever seen. His pupils were black ice, skewering her deeper as he slowly—*pointedly*—spelled out, "How could I anymore?"

The shift that came next in the room was palpable, like plates of fate shifting beneath our feet. She repeated his words back to him as if she didn't understand their language.

"How could you...?"

Whether or not he should have, Dominic broke it down for her.

"You lied to me. You tricked me. You used my job against me. You had the woman I fell in love with taken to another state to be sold and killed, not to mention countless young women over the years. You've dismissed and hurt my daughter. I don't believe you even have a heart, Heather."

Whatever lasting sanity she had slipped from her gaze as she screamed. "I have a heart, and I gave it to you!"

I gripped Blake harder as she yelled, wishing like hell I hadn't heard that catch of heartache in her voice. *Real* heartbreak. Dominic must have heard it too—there was no way he didn't.

TWENTY-THREE

Still, it didn't soften his granite expression one bit as he said, "Well, I don't want it anymore."

Right after he said it, everything in the room just sort of... stopped.

All eyes were on Heather, but she wasn't really looking at anything. That slightly ajar look in her eyes from before had now gone entirely AWOL. She was lost. She *had* lost, and I didn't think it was something she was used to. She'd had the upperhand all her life. A winning hand.

Now her hands were empty.

Except for a gun.

I rolled my fingers with Blake's, clammy sweat dampening our skin as my heartbeat climbed. Heather's mouth that was slightly parted closed as if something clicked, a barely registerable twitch happening along her browline. I flinched without meaning to into Blake when she lifted her eyes to Dominic, the hollow pit to them scaring the fucking shit out of me.

She looked across at him for one, two, three beats.

Then said, "You'll thank me later."

A gasping scream rose up my throat as Heather raised her gun back to me.

My world froze. Blake spun me around.

Dominic shouted over all of it.

"Heather—NO!"

The sound of a single gunshot pierced the air and right through my beating heart.

My face got squished into a chest of hard muscle covered by the softest shirt. I knew if I had been breathing, it would have been the burnt scent of cigarettes that filled my lungs. Blake held the back of my head firmly, his other arm slung around my waist to keep me from moving.

To keep me from looking.

Everything behind me was so silent. So *deadly* silent.

I counted twelve frozen seconds going by where no one did or said anything. Aside from the ringing in my ears, it was just quiet. The muscles in my neck strained as I tried to look back, but Blake stopped me, touching his lips to the top of my head.

"I don't think you want to see," he mumbled, tickling my scalp with his warm breath.

The ringing filling the space between my ears crescendoed louder.

Gradually, a sting started festering in my eyes, the dryness of not blinking for a while beginning to irritate. So I did. I blinked, and I blinked again in the cover of Blake's chest. Water of relief coated my lenses, thickening in the corners of my eyes and holding still there.

Then, the water wasn't so much for relief as it was shock.

And the shock burned, burned like embers were falling out of my eyes instead of tears. My neck worked as if it hadn't moved in years as I carefully lifted my head up just enough to see Blake. He let me, pulling himself back only slightly so his gaze could touch mine.

He watched my embered tears slide down my cheeks but made no move to clear them.

"Is she...?" I couldn't force my mouth to work long enough to finish the sentence.

He took his intense stare out to the side of the room and then back to me.

"Pretty much."

Then, the burn wasn't just in my eyes, but in my chest. I supposed not really breathing would do that to your lungs, but it was just so hard to. Honestly, it was hard to do anything under the pressure of shock sitting over my body like a second skin woven of lead.

My brain hadn't caught up yet. I didn't think it knew how to. It wasn't equipped for this.

Not *this*.

As I stood there, something dark, heavy, and malignant crept over my shoulder and dug inside my chest, rooting in my heart. This tar-like thing made a home there, whispering with a viper-inspired slither that it was here to stay.

On feet I couldn't feel, I made the move to turn around and Blake let me. When I finally saw her, had I been breathing, I would have gasped.

Then I would have screamed.

TWENTY-THREE

Heather was on the floor with her back to the farthest wall, legs sprawled out in front of her, arms dangling on each side. One of her hands, from her fair palm to every last manicured fingertip, was painted red as if she'd stuck her hand in a can of paint.

Or grabbed at the bullet hole in her chest to stop the spill of blood staining her expensive white suit.

That hand had fallen limp to her side as the blood continued to spill, letting whatever last drops of life drain out. There couldn't have been much left.

Her eyes were just like my mom's. When I found her dead, that is.

Half-lidded, but staring at nothing. Vacant. Empty skies of thoughtless blue.

It was almost harder to look at Dominic than his dead wife. My heavy eyes dragged away from Heather and started at Dominic's shoes. His wingtips. Then they went up his legs, seeing how his knees were locked and thighs were tight, and made it up to his arms that were still extended out.

The gun he'd just used to shoot his wife dead was frozen in his hands.

The wife he shot dead to save me.

Inside my chest, I barely even noticed that malignant thing priming its claws and sinking them in deeper.

When I finally worked my way up to his face, he wasn't staring at me. Truthfully, I think he'd forgotten I was even there. All he saw with his grief-stricken eyes was Heather on the floor, lifeless because of his bullet. He had as much blood drained from his face as she did.

I should have gone to him, and I would have had my legs been working.

Nothing was really working at this point.

Shock, as it turned out, was a paralytic bitch.

That same logic apparently didn't apply to Dominic as he slowly walked towards Heather. All I could see was the back of him as he carefully knelt down in front of where she sat.

The feeling that I was intruding on their moment was *beyond* expansive, itching at the backs of my heels to leave them alone.

I couldn't, and stayed to watch as he lifted his hand to her face, a ball of sorrow trapped in my throat as he traced his fingers along her cheek as if she was made of glass. A piece of her dark hair was splattered out of place across her forehead, and he gingerly tucked it back into place where she would have wanted it.

She never went anywhere looking anything less than flawless, and death was no exception.

He cupped her face in his big palm, petting the space beneath her eyes while mine fucking welled right over. Was it even right to cry? Was I *allowed* to cry? For him, for Heather, for Maya?

My stupid fucking eyes kept producing tears like goddamn selfish hypocrites no matter how hard I blinked them away. I couldn't go up to Dominic and cry. I couldn't go up to him and be *weak*.

A visual of me going to him and him slapping my hand away and roaring at me to leave him alone barrelled through my mind, followed immediately after by one of him collapsing into my lap as his chest caved in with sobs.

My foot arched to make the move, telling myself that either reaction was fine. Any way he reacted was okay. All that mattered was he needed me. Whether to have someone to hold or someone to blame, he needed me.

A commotion just down the hall from the open door stopped my body in motion.

My head snapped towards it, but in less time than I had to wonder what it was, I was being yanked to the other side of the room by Blake. I stumbled and he caught me, planting me on two barely solid feet and himself just off-center in front of me. I watched his muscles coil up his back and his shoulders pull taut beneath his black shirt.

My slapping heart clocked the newfound tension in his body as he faced the door, terror forming a brand new knot in my stomach.

The commotion coming down the hallway was given a name as she practically threw herself through the door, aged hands clutched on the frame as she stopped.

Claudia's alert-wide eyes started at me, then went to Blake, and finally went towards Dominic.

TWENTY-THREE

And her daughter, still bleeding out on the floor.

She didn't react immediately. She froze for several moments as if her response was booting up, staring at her lifeless daughter against the wall. Dominic didn't even flinch when his mother-in-law came into the room, let alone turn to see her.

Claudia's reaction almost came in slow motion, my breath holding still as it developed. Her eyelids stretched from top to bottom, horror pushing them wide while her coral-painted lips parted as if on a timer, and at the end of that timer came a terrible scream, one worse than any I'd ever heard.

Every wrinkle on her face cracked as if she was a vase and her scream ruptured her from the inside out. The intensity of it shook her—visibly shook her—as she went to cover her mouth with one trembling hand but ended up placing both on the sides of her face as she howled.

Her scream rattled the walls, spreading fast-acting dread from my fingertips up my arms, numbing the extremities, numbing everything except my heart.

It was all I felt, thumping, shaking, catching on fire.

Behind her, the mammoth of a man Sergio came out of nowhere, gun drawn and expression alert. Blake slanted himself at an angle of defense as his counterpart came onto the scene. My eyes dropped to Sergio's weapon, warning bells chiming between my ears to see *another* fucking gun.

I'd just barely escaped Heather's. There was no way I could cheat death twice.

Claudia's screech mangled itself to a stop as she jerked around to Sergio. The sirens in my head amplified to a wail as her head snapped down to his weapon, opportunity passing a dangerous gleam across her stare.

Oh god.

Claudia snatched the gun from his hands, and my heart prematurely stopped.

Breathing. Thinking. Feeling. All of it stopped.

All of me was completely fucking frozen as Claudia swept her eyes over to me, murder a physical manifestation sitting in her waterline. She locked in on her target, breathing heavier and harder, hatred contorting the flesh over the prominent bones in her face.

"*You.*"

Me.

Without another word, she aimed the gun right at my heart.

One last breath swelled in my lungs, and my eyes slammed shut.

Right before the bullet came, I didn't see my life flash before my eyes like everyone said you did.

Instead, I *heard* it.

A blur of Charlotte's laughter, Layla's god-awful singing, birds chirping, babies crying. Dominic's deep-toned confessions of love, Blake's lyrical poetry. Love. Hate. Life. Death. I heard it all. I *absorbed* this language of love composed solely for me. The soundtrack to my life filled my head with music right as the gunshot to end it all filled my heart with dread.

She fired twice.

Half a second later, two more shots rang out.

And then there was silence.

And there was warmth.

I waited for the slice of pain, the fire-hot intrusion of metal inside my body, but it never came. Eyes still closed, I checked in with every clenched part of my body to see if any of them felt the bullet hit, and it all came back empty.

I dared to breathe, filling my lungs with a stolen gulp of air—*and smoke.*

Confusion spliced through my head the moment the familiar scent hit, stuttering my heart as I tested another inhale. The same burnt aroma touched the back of my throat again, and like a junkie getting a fix, I went back in for another whiff until I couldn't stop sucking it down. I breathed him down with huge gulps of relief like I could pack my lungs with his cigarettes and get a nicotine high just from him.

That's why it's so warm, I realized, snuggling in the arms that'd embraced me.

My thoughts were slow-forming as I lifted my head slowly up the front of his shirt, as if I moved too fast, I might wake up and discover I was dreaming. The tip of my nose rode up the hard ridge of his sternum until light shined on the outside of my eyelids, forcing them open and me to look up.

Blake was waiting for me with honest to god *stars* in his midnight eyes, and I lost my breath in him. He pulled the air straight from inside my lungs like he'd done a hundred times before, and I was so willingly breathless beneath him.

Because he saved me. *Again.*

A huff of disbelief caved in my chest pressed to his, staring up at fate's hand-picked savior for Katerina Sanders.

Maybe she really was lucky. *Maybe.*

Peering over his shoulder, Claudia and Sergio were crumpled on the floor, clean bullet holes drilled through their foreheads. Dominic still had his gun aimed up to where they once stood, the magnitude of what he'd done haunting his expression.

A weighted breath collapsed my head back to Blake's chest as I gazed over at Dominic, my heart doing a million laps trying to get me over to him. Devastation carved every line of his handsome face deeper, making me want to run over there and fall into his arms and remind him that we were *okay.*

He was okay. He was alive. Blake was alive.

I, by some sheer fucking miracle, was somehow still alive.

It was enough to almost make a girl smile.

And I almost did.

Then, this sort of wetness seeped against my stomach and stopped any smiling.

Confusion pulled me back, parting from Blake so I could inspect.

Cold swells flushed through my cheeks, drying out my mouth as I looked down at my shirt. My eyes tracked in slow lines over the blotch of dark red staining Zoey's baby-blue shirt over my stomach.

It was a big stain. The width of a large fist.

The cold in my cheeks began to trickle down my throat, filling my lungs with ice as I raised my hand to my stomach. It stopped once or twice on the way, my muscles forgetting how to work or simply not wanting to.

They didn't want to know.

They didn't want to know.

My fingers shook, twitched away from my stomach, fighting to keep from touching my shirt, but I flattened them against it and waited.

Waited for the pain.

Begged for the pain.

Prayed for the pain.

Except there was no pain.

Because the blood wasn't mine.

The blood wasn't mine.

A sharp gasp tore my head up, panic stabbing behind my eyes as I found Blake's. He was already watching me, gifting me a small curve on his lips that made mine quiver. In his eyes, I saw it like I saw *everything* he felt. I *saw* the proof of it, *saw* that he knew exactly what I knew.

"No…" I whispered.

He nodded just once before pain rose up the thick cords of his neck and fanned across his face. A short groan stabbed my heart as it came from him and then, he went down.

"No, no, no, *no.*" I followed Blake to the floor, muttering and panicking as I saw the blood. *His* blood. It was everywhere, slicking up his signature black v-neck, drenching the front of it blacker than black. "*No. No. No,*" I breathed harder, faster, putting my shaking hands over his blood.

"Help!" I screamed, pressing my palms against his stomach, screaming harder when more blood rose through my fingers. "We need help! Somebody, *please. Please!*"

"Kat." His hands appeared on mine, wrapping our fingers in his sticky blood. "It's okay," he tried to soothe, but his strong baritone voice trembled with a weakness that ripped through my chest like a knife on fire.

"*No, it's not!* I mean-yes, *yes* you're going to be!" Lightning flared up my windpipe, striking blind and just so fucking confused as his blood kept pouring out. "You're going to be *fine.* You're gonna be just-just *fine.*"

Whipping my head up towards the bedroom door, I let out a cry that obliterated any sadness I had ever felt up to that point.

TWENTY-THREE

"Somebody, *PLEASE!* I need—" A sob choked my words back, tears escaping over.

"Kitten." My blurry attention snapped down to him as he called my nickname. His nickname for me. It was his. It was *so* fucking his, and he was still smiling at me as he said it.

He was smiling even as he shook his head to tell me no.

"Yes. You're gonna be *fine,"* I argued through a tight voice, but there was so much blood. How could there be so much blood in one person?

Still wearing a curve to his lips just for me, he shook his head again.

"No. I'm not."

"Yes! Yes you are!" More tears slipped down my cheeks at an impossible pace. "You have to be. I-I just need you to be. I just-I *need* you."

"Please don't cry." I only cried harder as he begged me not to, sobbing over him and losing all my air. Tears hung off my chin and splashed his cheeks, giving him some to wear because he didn't have any of his own. In fact, he didn't look even a little bit sad.

Not even a little bit afraid.

He didn't look anything but admiring as he stared up at me as if I was the light he was supposed to go towards.

"Why would you do that?" Hyperventilating chopped each word in half, his blood smeared between my fingers. *"Why?* It's so stupid, so *stupid."*

Blake shushed me, shaking his head in my lap as he brought his hand to me. "I don't want the last thing I see to be you crying," he started, caressing his touch underneath my chin to wipe away fallen tears. "I know I said you're beautiful when you do it, but you shouldn't do it for me."

"Of course I should," I pushed, choking on sobs. *"Of course I* should. How do you not realize how important to me you are?!"

"I do." He nodded softly, stroking my cries to a calm. "I do."

"You can't go," I wept, keeping blurry eyes on him. "You fucking *can't."*

He thumbed my trembling lips, fading black flames memorizing every curve that he'd kissed yesterday. *Just yesterday.*

"God, I'm going to miss this mouth." A hint of mischief tweaked his lips. "Drove me up the fucking wall."

We both laughed—mine wet and his weak.

There were so many things I wanted to say back, but the time was chasing away from us at a pace that was so fucking unfair I wanted to die right along with him.

Suddenly, Blake sucked back a pained gasp, his eyes pinching shut. My palm went to his cheek immediately, holding him in his pain until the twinge of it drained from his face and he leaned into my hand.

"I'm so sorry." I caressed the bristles on the curve of his jaw, crying harder as the light in his dynamic eyes began to dim. "I'm *so so* sorry. You shouldn't have done that. You shouldn't have—"

"There is quite literally nothing else I would rather go out for," he cut me off, his voice getting softer and softer and the seconds getting scarier and scarier. "I didn't do anything good enough to deserve you."

"Same," I whispered in a voice broken beyond repair. *"Same."*

A pain like actual fire had been set inside my chest seared so unapologetically, I knew it had to be coming from my heart. Blake was dying, and he was taking half of my heart with him. He was burning his half off from the inside and taking it with him wherever he was going next.

It had to be Heaven. It *had* to be for someone like him.

"I don't want you to go." I sniffled, face soaked and shaking my head. "I want more time. I want *more. Please,*" I begged, ready to bargain my own soul.

Even as I pleaded with him to stay, he still refused to look sad to go. He was just so fucking focused on me, giving me every blink he had left, every drop of love in his eyes, every breath left on his lips.

"We have other galaxies, remember?" He gave what little strength he had left to drag his thumb across my cheek just once. Once was all he had left in him.

"We'll get it right, Kitten. We'll get it right."

I nodded fast, rolling my wet lips together as the weight of his head grew heavier on my lap. His final moments were gaining on us fast. His eyes were on me for as long as he could hold them open, and I could tell he was struggling and losing the battle. After a few more moments, his eyelids

TWENTY-THREE

closed, cutting me off from the infinite galaxies of ours constellated in his midnight eyes.

Long lashes brushing across my palm still holding his cheek, his breathing pulling softer and fainter. I kept rubbing it, letting him know I was there, that I wouldn't leave him. Ever. Not ever.

"It was worth it, you know." With his eyes closed, Blake smiled one last smile against the palm of my hand and whispered his last words.

"It was all worth it."

Blake passed away in my arms, and I simply held him, not knowing what else to do.

The sobs pushed out of my chest viciously until they turned into literal chokes as I laid my head on his chest, and even though I knew it wouldn't be there, I listened for his heartbeat anyways.

There was such a painful nothing as I laid on him.

He was just dead.

No heartbeat. No lightning in his veins. No smoke in his lungs.

It was just over.

It was *all* over.

TWENTY-FOUR

KAT

"We really appreciate you giving your statement and answering our questions, Ms. Sanders. I know it's been a long and emotional day for everyone."

The man who called himself Sergeant Miller continued to say lots of important things and polite words, but I stopped listening a long time ago.

I'd been barely functioning since we left the mansion.

Yeah. *Left.*

I was out. Free.

It was funny how oxymoronic that word could be.

Leaving was sort of a blur. Lots of blue-coats and officers. Lots of strangers trying to talk to you, touch you, ask you if the blood on your hands and face is yours.

I couldn't tell them it wasn't. I couldn't tell them anything. It wasn't their business to know.

Plus I hated them. Every single one of them.

This time wasn't like when my mom died and I passed out. I was awake for every second of this death—them raiding the bedroom, trying to ask me questions while I was crying, trying to get me to leave the room and leave his body and eventually threatening me to.

TWENTY-FOUR

I screamed at them and lashed out when they tried to pull me away from Blake. Dominic was out of the room by the time they jabbed me with whatever it was that knocked me out long enough for them to bring me outside.

I didn't get to say goodbye.

"Ms. Sanders?"

My eyes were like balls of sawdust in my head, dried out and swollen from all the crying as I lifted them up to the Sergeant across the table. He looked sorry, truly sorry, as his already pudgy face added another chin and he lowered his head in pity.

"I'm almost done, I swear. Just a few more questions, and then you're free to go."

There was that word again. *Free*.

That word was beginning to feel like a joke I wasn't in on, something I should have enjoyed but didn't know the first thing about.

"Now, we spoke to a woman staying at the house who has agreed to go on the record on your behalf—"

"Who?"

Pudgy's eyes widened as I cut him off. He riffled through his papers, pulling a name from one of them. "A Zoey Markez?"

A round face and platinum blonde hair pictured in my head as I inhaled her name, leaning back in the plastic chair, ignoring the creak it made.

"She gave me clothes."

For whatever reason, he wrote that down. "She's agreed to be a key witness to your time there, which'll be a big help. Says you tried to tell her early on that you were there against your will?"

Mindlessly, I nodded.

"Did you interact with any of the other women staying there?"

"Barely."

"When we spoke to them, they all claimed they didn't know anything about the trafficking side of the business."

My eyes rolled back up to him, his goading tactics naked and unpracticed. "They didn't know."

"How do you think that's possible?"

"Because their bosses were really fucking good at lying to people."

More writing. More paper flipping.

"In your statement, and in almost every single statement we got from the women there, you all mention someone named Ray being in charge, but we haven't been able to pin him down. Any ideas where he'd be?"

My empty gut rolled as I shook my head.

We'd been at this for two hours. Maybe longer. I messed with the sleeve of the department t-shirt they'd given me when we got here, twisting the stiff fabric around my fingers. They needed my shirt for evidence.

Because of the blood.

Blake's blood.

They'd also taken swabs of the blood dried beneath my nails and grabbed my fingerprints before a petite woman walked in and told me to take my clothes off so they could photograph any evidence left on my body. To top a humiliating moment off, she then asked if I needed a rape kit done.

Half a day with authorities—the good guys—and I felt more violated than my entire stay at the brothel, auction excluded.

"All right, Ms. Sanders." Pudgy stacked his papers together, tapping them in a neat line on the table. "I appreciate you answering all these questions when I know all you want is to go home after an ordeal like this. Good news is that your story and Detective Reed's match up well enough that I don't see there being any charges brought against him since every shot he fired was justified. These things tend to get sticky when only two people walk out of a room alive, understand?"

I could see him waiting for me to nod or give a verbal confirmation that I understood, but I stayed silent. Rigid.

I didn't understand.

I didn't understand how I was one of two.

I didn't understand being alive when someone else was dead because of me. Three people, actually. Four if you included Sergio.

I was alive and four people weren't. I didn't know how to understand that. Mathematically, it didn't make sense. The problem didn't equate to

TWENTY-FOUR

the result. Ethically, it didn't make sense. One of the few classes I paid attention to in high school was Ethics, and The Trolly Problem said I should have died instead of them.

Four lives trump one, right?

The trolly was coming for me. The *bullets* were coming for me. Just me.

"Those are all the questions I have for now, Ms. Sanders. We'll call you with updates to the case as we get them." The Sergeant stood, so I did the same, knees taking a moment to crack in relief as I stretched out. He strolled in sluggish steps towards the interview door and pulled it open, peeking his head out.

I hadn't moved at all when he ducked back inside, nodding to the open door.

"Detective Reed's down the hall. Same spot he was in when I brought you here."

I lied before.

My stomach wasn't totally empty. They'd given me a cup of water when I got here and another when I sat down to be interrogated. Hearing that Dominic was out there waiting made those two cups slosh around my stomach like the water in the pipes here contained actual lead.

I was at least ten pounds heavier walking out of that interrogation room than when I walked in. The door behind me shut with an echo, sending the noise of my exit down the hallway to the man sitting waiting for me.

Dominic didn't look up. He didn't even flinch.

The water in my stomach gained another five pounds as I saw him, hunched over in a chair that looked just like the one I'd been in for the last two hours, so I knew how uncomfortable it was. His body was too big for it, his long legs propped up so he could rest his elbows on his knees.

His head was in his hands, his perfectly kept hair gone to shit from hours of running his fingers through it.

My feet shouldn't have felt so heavy to go to him.

They should have felt light, floating on cloud nine. I should have been flying towards him after five weeks of missing him, dreaming about him, and even grieving a reality where I'd never see him again.

But I couldn't move. Because of a few bullets hitting the wrong people, my legs had turned to cement.

Moving them was actually an act of sheer will. I physically thought about every step I took down the precinct hall, telling myself to put one foot in front of the other instead of bolting the other way.

Heel, toe. Heel, toe. Don't run. Don't run.

The closer I got to him, the farther the hallway seemed to stretch as if I couldn't keep up with the distance growing between us. It was an effortless distance too, manifesting with ease from the last eight hours, gathering our brand new traumas and laying them down like roadblocks between us.

The real struggle was actually in *closing* the distance. It was like walking through thick, wet, waist-high sand, trudging, fighting, exhausting yourself on the trek alone. My heart was galloping by the time I reached him, pulse throbbing in my temples as I made it through the sand and stood before my ocean.

I'd drowned in this man, and he'd drowned in me.

Now people we loved were dead.

My heartbeat consumed my entire body as I stood in front of him and waited for him to react to me. It was as if my entire body had become one giant heart, pulsing in my toes, beating in my stomach, thrumming in my ears.

Maybe that's all human beings are at the end of the day.

Big, broken, bleeding hearts.

After several moments of waiting and throbbing, Dominic broke his statuesque state, moving his hands to slide around my waist. I watched him do it, forgetting how big his hands were until they were around my whole waist, his thumbs nearly meeting over my belly button.

My body went as he drew me forward until the top of his head met my stomach.

And there he held me. In silence.

It was only a few seconds before the lack of noise began to chip away at my ears, making its way inside my brain to fry it insane. I couldn't say anything though. He needed this.

TWENTY-FOUR

He needed comfort.

But my hands... they didn't know what to do, how to touch him, what would make it better. They felt foreign attached to my arms, robotic even, as they rose to settle on top of his head. Warm relief washed across my stomach, expelling from Dominic's mouth through the coarse fabric of the adopted t-shirt.

The half of my heart that was still alive *thunked*, telling me I'd done good.

So I pet back his mess of hair, pushing my fingers through it because I didn't know what else to do. Was I supposed to talk? Tell him I was sorry he was hurting because he shot his wife to save me? Tell him he shouldn't have done it? Tell him he should just have let me die, and this would have been easier on both of us?

I didn't know how to do this. I didn't know how to heal someone's heart when mine had gone so fucking numb.

"Wanna get out of here?" I asked after a moment.

Without looking up, Dominic nodded against my stomach.

* * *

The sky was unbelievably dark as Dominic and I finally left the Atlanta police station.

It was somewhere past 9 pm, and the jet black stretch above us showcased nothing but the glowing moon. No stars. No planes blinking and flying overhead.

Just the moon.

My eyes started to mist.

It was an immediate reaction, my bottom lip rolling up between my teeth to keep it from visibly trembling when a ball of tears stuck in my throat.

Was that Blake now looking over me, or was that stupid to think? Was he the moon looking in on his withering rose? Or was that just some poetic fantasy I told myself to distract from the fact that he was really in a body bag somewhere alone and dead and *alone*.

So Dominic wouldn't know, I tilted my head so one lonely stream of grief spilled over the side, freezing against my face as soon as the wind breezed by. Neither Dominic or I had moved as we stood next to each other, looking out over a world that was forever changed for us both.

"Ryan and everyone already left."

Dominic's voice almost startled me, sounding rusty against the soft night air.

I gave a slow nod. "So it's just us?"

"Yeah."

Kat and Dom alone in a glitzy city away from home should have meant a boozy night of making love on every surface of a hotel room until I got him tipsy enough to convince him to fuck me on the balcony of it too.

Instead, we couldn't really even look at each other.

"Do we have to go back tonight?" I quietly asked, staring up at the moon. I didn't want to leave it. Not yet.

From my peripherals, Dominic curved his stare down to me, probably wondering why a woman who'd been dying to get home wasn't jumping in the car and starting up the ignition. His attention on the side of my face felt like nails pushing against my skull, trying to get inside my head and spill out what I was thinking.

Instead of questioning me, he simply said,

"We can get a hotel."

TWENTY-FIVE

KAT

Dominic found a hotel a few roads down to stay in for the night, and the lobby looked like virginal saints had taken a stab at decorating it. Everything was white. Stark white counters, couches, end tables, flowers, you name it.

Even the tile flooring was so sickly white, I could see my wearied reflection in it as I waited for Dominic to finish paying for the room.

We drove in silence on the way over here. We rode in silence up to the room. It was only on the third floor, but there were nine whole seconds of stifling silence to fill on the elevator ride up. I counted each one of them. The walk down the hallway to our room was just as quiet, and every second of nothing between us cinched the wires in my chest tighter, stretching them around my heart, strangling it.

Breath could barely make it past my lips the tension between my ribs was so fraught, getting so much worse as Dominic slid the key card in the door. It unlocked, and he held it open for me to go inside first like the unfailing gentleman he was.

Heel toe, heel toe. Don't run, don't run.

Padding inside the room, I was careful not to touch him as I slid by. I think it would have broken my heart to try to actively not touch him if

I'd been able to feel my heart at all. I think it would have broken it twice when Dominic didn't seem to mind or even notice.

The hotel room was just as pearly white as the lobby downstairs, but the lack of color wasn't what made my insides twist. It was what sat in the middle of the room.

The bed.

The *one* bed.

This morning, we would have already been half-stripped on top of it.

Now I was wondering if it would be weird if I slept on the floor.

"I brought you a few things from home." Dominic's voice rode up from behind me just before he appeared next to the bed. "Just some clothes in case you wanted to change."

He sank the overnight bag he'd carried up from his car onto the king size bed, walking away as soon as it was off his shoulders. Unzipping the bag down the middle, I found two of my shirts, cotton shorts, yoga pants, some underwear and a bra of mine too.

My fingers trailed over each piece as if I was touching an old memory, picking up and rolling the royal blue tank top Layla had bought for me a couple years ago around my palm.

These were *my* things. *My* memories.

But they felt different. I felt different.

Mumbling out a, "Thank you," I nabbed the cotton shorts and a tank top, trying not to think about the alternate scenario where I would have stripped Dominic of his dress shirt to wear instead.

On quick feet, I bolted to the other side of the room and sealed my back up against the farthest wall. The tethers in my chest hadn't let up one bit, and since neither of us were talking, all I could hear was how *loud* my struggle to breathe was.

It was uneven, hacked up cuts of air that sounded a hell of a lot like I was gasping for life.

In a lot of ways, I was.

This wasn't how it was supposed to be. This wasn't how any of this was supposed to be. We weren't two strangers of broken paths locked in a hotel

TWENTY-FIVE

room for the night. We were Kat and Dominic. We were the stuff of magic and against-all-odds *love*.

Except all I felt now was numb.

Numb and breathless.

My heartstrings that were wound too tight forced me to look up at Dominic to see if he was looking at me too.

He wasn't.

He was stationary next to a lounge chair in the corner of the room, arms hanging at his sides and gaze trapped on the floor. On nothing. It wasn't even like he knew I was there. If I had to guess by the haunted look captured in his eyes, he was back in that bedroom with Heather, remembering how his bullet drained the life from her face.

I just wanted to get out of there.

"I'm gonna take a shower," I muttered, hoping he heard but not waiting to see as I turned on my heel and disappeared inside the bathroom.

I closed the door shut behind me and nearly fell against it in a mixture of relief and complete fucking exhaustion. The pressure on my chest let up only slightly as I slumped against the door, catching my breath like I'd run miles away from him.

Huffing, I squeezed my eyes shut as my fingers came to pinch the skin between my brows as I thought about how fucked this all was.

I wanted to be able to go out there and grab him and kiss him and drown in him like we'd done so many times before. We were *good* at this before. Even when we tried not to be good at it, our chemistry was fucking heroin and we were inescapable addicts to it.

But now... our systems were broken.

The heroin wasn't making its way through like it used to. Our veins were blocked up apparently, bullets and trauma and shards of broken hearts stuffed inside. Our chemistry wasn't pumping like it used to.

And I didn't know how to make it start again.

Tucking my fingers in my shorts, I pushed them down my legs where they pooled around my feet. The cheap hem of the Atlanta Police Department's t-shirt hit my bare thighs, and I gripped the fabric to rip it off next when a knock at the bathroom door stopped me.

A small inhale ripped my stare right over to it, staring at the—no surprise—white door like it was capable of coming off its hinges and attacking me.

What does he want?

To use the bathroom before I showered? To say he left something in the car and had to go get it? To tell me face to face that he couldn't do this anymore after today? That it was too hard to look at me and not see the blood I forced him to spill?

Cement had found its way to the base of my feet, weighing down each step towards the door. Any pressure that'd released in my chest doubled down as I walked, my lungs barely moving, my head sort of spinning, my skin beginning to prickle.

A thousand tiny stabbing sensations carved their awareness beneath my skin as I reached for the handle of the door, scratching like they were trying to claw at me to stop.

Don't do it. Don't open the door. Don't let him tell you it's over.

But then I was already doing it, twisting the knob and swinging the door wide open between us.

Dominic was there on the other side, holding himself up with his arms high on the door frame and his head hanging low between the peaks of his shoulder blades. Stress tidal waved off of him, smacking me head on, filling my lungs with burning and my eyes with saltwater.

He didn't say anything. He stood there, a fearsome mountain over a riverbed ready to run over. This mountain moved, breathing heavy like it was preparing to collapse, to destroy the eroding river below.

Then Dominic snapped his eyes up, and the crumble began.

The walls of the river shook, falling away piece by piece as the mountain showed its face. Anguish cracked along its once smooth surface, and grief split open its eyes like a whip flaying flesh, bleeding out the agony from the mountain's core. My water ran down the valleys of my cheeks as the mountain towering over me quaked in pain, in torment, in *hatred*.

He hated me. He *absolutely* hated me.

TWENTY-FIVE

Sudden agony sliced down my chest, a whimper falling out as my heart decided to *feel*.

It breached the numbness set in around it long enough to wail, to mourn, to beg for forgiveness from the man currently stripping me bare to the fragile bone with his eyes alone. My knees wobbled underneath the pressure of his devastating stare, breathing going messy, and two seconds away from collapsing to the floor as nothing more than a thin veil of skin and regret.

His breathing ramped up, getting more violent, more aggressive. He was ready to strike and kill, and when he pushed off of the frame and charged my way, my neck bent back to accept the punishment.

Body heat swamped over me, and then so did his rough voice.

"Come here."

All I had time for was a momentary gasp, and then he closed my mouth with his.

Shock exploded behind my eyes, blinding my world to anything that happened before his lips touched mine. Dominic swallowed my gasps and our silence too. He erased our distance like it'd only ever been a mirage. He *owned* me like I'd left his side for five whole weeks, and now I owed him penance for doing such a stupid thing.

I couldn't keep up, moaning when his fingers split into my hair, crying out when he anchored my head back with a merciless yank. The sting in my scalp sparked fresh flames all the way down my spine, pleasure splicing into my pain receptors. Something almost like an itch buried underneath layers of skin started to irritate, making me squirm for another sting.

Or something harder.

Something that could make my stained flesh bleed.

Heat clashed between our mouths as they pulled together and the bathroom became a sticky collaboration of grunts and moans. There was something different about this heat though, different about the way he kissed me and the way I let him devour me.

My back hit a wall, and that same unusual heat blazed down the notches of my spine as they took the brunt of the pain. The heat curled around my bones and sparked fires in my nerve endings as Dominic bruised my mouth and my back all the same while he kissed and mauled and *took*.

Lightning rose in my veins, conducted by the kind of friction Dominic and I were creating. It was a dangerous warmth. A *furious* passion. Love and longing weren't flowing in his blood that hardened his cock against my thigh.

It was rage. His blood was saturated with it.

In the way he didn't let me catch my breath or leave any sweet kisses on my neck before sinking his teeth into it, I *felt* it. His temper was trying to fuck me. His pain was trying to get inside of mine and make me pay, make my hurt a tangible thing he could hear in cries and see in purple fingerprints over ivory skin.

And I deserved it.

Every punishment, every bite, every bruise, I'd take it and encourage him not to stop until my body broke. The itch beneath my skin needed him to keep going until the pain on the outside was loud enough to deafen the pain inside.

I got to watch a cry split my mouth wide in the mirror across from the wall Dominic had me up against as he marked my flesh with his bite again. His dark head of hair was buried in the slope of my neck, attacking my body with unkind kisses while I panted and let him do it.

It was almost out-of-body watching myself moan and my lust-addled eyes roll back in this brilliant cocktail of pain and pleasure Dominic was fueling my blood with. In the mirror, his ass clenched through his black slacks as he worked his hips into mine, prying his stiff cock between my thighs where he'd unleash his attack next.

"I need to be inside of you," he rasped in my ear, dark voice sticking to the side of my neck. I nodded fast, huffing wildly when he picked me up and took me wherever he planned to fuck me.

Surprise lasted only milliseconds when my back connected with the mattress, banished by a cry that stretched up to the ceiling as his cock rocked against my swollen clit. My hands flew to his back, nails sheathing into the sleek material of his shirt.

TWENTY-FIVE

A dangerous rumble vibrated through his chest into mine, rattling my heart right off its loose hinges. Then, he was gone, up on his knees and undoing his belt.

Hooded eyes transfixed on me huffing and spread out for him as he pulled the belt free and undid the button of his pants next. The bed quaked as he knelt off of it, strong fingers wrapping around my ankles and tugging me to the edge.

I went with a sharp inhale, my t-shirt riding up against the material of the bed. Grayed out eyes dropped to my newly exposed skin, dancing over it like ripples on water.

This black lace thong was Zoey's, and if I ever saw her again, I'd have to tell her how much my boyfriend liked it.

His cock strained the perfect outline against his undone slacks, the swollen tip peeking out of the band of his briefs. He took a hand from around my ankle to grab it, squeezing himself through his underwear and allowing his self-control one thorough stroke from base to tip.

A shudder racked his whole body, drying out my mouth and pooling heat between my thighs. Then, the itch reminded me it was there.

Burning. Nagging. Soul-deep.

It pushed me up and crossed my arms over my waist, grabbing and pulling the shirt from my body to expose more skin for him to brand with his rage. Dominic's thick lashes cast a fast shadow over his cheeks as they ripped up, dark eyes drinking in the canvas made for him to mark.

Again, this was a bra he'd never seen, though it wasn't much of a bra at all—a thin strap of black cotton with lacy frills curving against the swell of my tits. It was one of the comfier things Zoey had given me, and Dominic shredded it off in seconds.

Less than. One moment it was there. The next, my tits were spilling free, and he was putting one in his palm and the other in his mouth.

A cry threw my head back, a sting racing hot through my nipple now caught between his teeth. The other one, he pinched and rolled between his fingers as if he could milk an orgasm from me just by doing that.

Honestly, I wasn't convinced he couldn't.

The sensations were building, nerves coiling tighter in my pelvis as he kept up his assault. I began rocking my hips against the mattress, needy to have him fill the place between my legs made for him.

"Dominic," I huffed, folding my fingers through his tresses of hair.

A grunt met me in response, his hot tongue swirling the peak of my nipple as he mumbled around it. "So fucking perfect."

My back arched for him as he sucked my sensitive flesh harder, pushing my tits into his mouth in blind encouragement. The itch was ravenous beneath my skin, so deep down, Dominic's teeth couldn't seem to satisfy it.

I needed *more*, and so did his rage.

"Dominic." I tensed my fingers in his hair, tugging for attention. With a wet smack, his mouth released my breast, eyes glassy with lust fixing on my mouth as I begged. *"Please?"*

The itch was unbearable, like edging against an orgasm but *worse*. So much worse. It was every molecule in my body set on fire with no idea what it took or how much to extinguish it. It was a release I didn't know how far I'd have to dig deep to gratify. Dominic looked as lost in an uncharted version of himself as I was, but he didn't know it like I did.

He wasn't aware of the brand new sheen to his eyes or the unique serration accenting his sharpened features. He was simply lost. In pain. In grief. In all out rage he planned to take out on me.

Without warning, the ceiling disappeared as he flipped me onto my stomach, wrenching my hips up and my ass out. The thong was gone in less time than the bra, ripped down between my knees where it stayed so my pussy was on display like a fucking trophy for the taking.

An unabashed moan scraped up my throat as roughened calluses dragged across my ass, appreciating the naked flesh like a masterpiece he intended to shatter. I propped myself up on my hands, noting haphazardly that he'd never fucked me like this before. Even when he took me in his shower that first night, he'd made sure we were face to face.

Back then, he wanted to kiss me while he buried himself inside of me. He wanted to watch me while I came undone on his cock and got drunk on his name.

TWENTY-FIVE

Tonight, he ripped into me without any warm up.

The fat head of his cock slicked across my entrance, and my entire body got jolted forward as he plunged inside. Pain and pleasure braided together up the walls of my core as he pried my tiny self apart, sinking in without letting me adjust to his size and groaning at the punishing intrusion.

The itch *purred*, delirious for more.

Big hands wound around my waist, gripping for leverage as he fucked me where he stood, and I kneeled lower on the bed like a bitch in heat submitting for more. My cheek was flush with the mattress, hips up high in the air as Dominic bottomed out inside of me, losing volume control with a throaty moan while I yelped and fisted the comforter.

Despite the pain, despite the ungodly stretch, I still heard my breathy voice plead, "*Harder*."

"You want more?" he gruffed, voice carved deeper by desire.

I nodded my heated face against the bed. Another squeak knocked off my lips as he rammed his forward, digging himself belly deep. He did it again and again, thrusting harder, pushing deeper until the room was swallowed whole in a symphony of slapping skin and strangled whimpers.

Every impale got closer and closer to scratching the itch, hurting almost as good as ecstasy felt. Each stab of pain rode higher up my body, my nails digging into the bed so deeply threads started coming undone beneath them. Shouting and burying my face into the linen scented comforter, molten heat was building in my core with every slap of Dominic's hips.

"*Fuck*." I rolled the curse into a muffled thing in the sheets as my head tossed around, bracing my fists around the bedding as his speed picked up. Faint twitches signaled in my toes, leading up my legs to shake my thighs as an orgasm crested.

Suddenly, a shriek flew out of my mouth as my head got yanked backwards, Dominic's fist tangled in my hair. My back hit his chest, scalp crying in a fierce burn as he twisted my neck until his mouth fell next to my ear.

"Are you gonna come for me?" he murmured like a challenge.

I nodded as much as I could, silently willing him to dig his knuckles in deeper. The itch *loved* his force. It needed more of it to go away.

"I will if you keep doing that," I moaned.

"What?"

"Hurting me." I wound an arm around the back of his neck, fingers diving in his hair. "Punishing me."

The almost violent rhythm of his hips slowed to an immediate stop, his wild heartbeat thumping against my back.

"I'm hurting you?" he breathed.

My next exhale sharpened, head shaking against the insult of the question.

"You know you are. You know you want to." My fingers already split into his hair grabbed onto the strands tight. "So fucking *hurt me.*"

I snapped Dominic's head back with a yank of my own, pissing the beast off so he'd give us what we both needed. Maybe he hadn't exactly realized yet in that strict moral compass head of his that hurting me was the only thing that was making him feel better right now, but his body knew it.

His *soul* knew it. My pain was his only remedy, and I'd give him as much of it as he demanded.

Whatever denial Dominic was playing with vanished in the growl that bled from his chest, terrifying the baby hairs on the back of my neck into standing. In the next second, I was falling forward on the bed, Dominic slipping out of me as I tried to catch myself.

My fall transitioned into a spin halfway down, dominant hands clamping down on my thighs like vices and flipping me over onto my back. The bed dipped as Dominic climbed on with me, dragging my body down to hit his thighs, spreading my flimsy legs apart before him as easily as you folded paper.

"Do you want me to hurt you?" The question sounded like a test for us both as he reached down between us, positioning himself at my center. It wasn't until then that I realized he never did finish taking off his pants, just pushed them down.

His shirt was still intact, too.

We both moaned as he pushed himself between my walls again, moving in deliberate, powerful pumps. I let my head fall to the side, riding the slow-build with his question stuck to the front of my mind.

"Yes." A moan caught in my throat, twisting around my next words. "I want you to hurt me."

He cupped beneath my knee, lifting one of my legs over his shoulder. "*Why?*"

"Because I need you to." The new position let him sink to the hilt, popping a fresh cry off my lips. "Because *you* need to."

This time, he didn't make the effort to deny it. He just kept fucking me like a man who hadn't fucked in years, and I kept taking it. The strong imprint of his fingers wound around my upper arms, sealing me back against the mattress as he pushed himself harder.

I couldn't move. With his weight between my legs and his arms holding me down, I couldn't move anything but my head. And I think he liked it that way.

I was an open vessel for him to beat his pain into, and all I could do was take it. It was wrong to slap me, hit me, kick me, and he was too good a man for that. He was too good a man to fuck me like he hated me at one point too, but I'd sullied that golden badge of honor the second his love for me made him put a bullet in Heather.

His goodness was draining right out of his eyes that were feral just for me, *because* of me. My infectious shadow jumped from Blake's body to Dominic's, imposing his radiant light and eating it all up.

The itch in my soul morphed razor sharp, fighting its goddamn best to upstage the stabs of pain radiating inside my heart as I watched the devour happen. Dominic was losing the thing that made him pure because of a decision to save me when he shouldn't have. The vicious shadow of my love inked out the silver-gray eyes I loved so much to something darker than I'd ever seen him wear.

Something almost black.

"*More*," I begged, centering my focus on the itch. I needed it to fucking burn so good, the pain edged out thoughts of his dark eyes and who they reminded me of, bleeding, dying, dead. "*Harder.* Please."

A mangled yelp exploded up my throat as Dominic impaled me so deeply, the headboard slapped the wall and hot pain flashed up my stomach.

"Like that?" Dominic growled over me, his thrusts brutal and endless.

"*Yes.*"

My legs were twitching again, orgasm sitting on the surface but not budging. The itch *screamed* for more, festering beneath my skin where Dominic couldn't quite reach yet. It jumped higher when bones in my arms got crushed by his hands as he pinned me down with every drop of anger thriving in his blood.

It climbed *even* higher when he took one of those hands and made it a necklace around my throat, squeezing like he just might break it. Finally, gasping for breath and counting the dark stars spotting over my eyes, Dominic dropped his head to the slope of my shoulder and sank his teeth in so deep, tears sprouted in a celebration of pain as the itch *finally* got scratched.

My orgasm tore up the length of my body, brutal and unforgiving like everything else about the moment. Dominic groaned and cursed as I froze up around him, stroking himself greedily inside my constricting walls.

My brain scrambled the peak of pleasure lasted so fucking long before it let me go, flooding white hot ecstasy through my limbs that loosened and pulsed. Noises that weren't human or quiet poured out of my mouth as Dominic fucked me through my orgasm, using my body until he was done with it.

"*Fuck.*" He slipped himself out just in time, painting my stomach and chest with sticky lines of his release. He pumped his thick cock in his hand until it was empty, my heavy-lidded eyes watching him do it. Numbly, I thought about how hot that would have been if this all hadn't been so fucked up.

Dominic fell next to me, the bed rocking as he tried to catch his breath. Then the silence was back.

We both let it invade just as quickly as it left. As if it'd been just sitting off to the side, watching us fuck like animals until we were done. Heavy breathing was all there was, and somehow, it made the silence even louder.

TWENTY-FIVE

"Okay, I really need that shower now," I forced out as a joke.

Dominic breathed a small chuckle at my pathetic attempt at humor, softly agreeing. But he didn't look at me. And just like that, the pressure in my chest remounted on my bones.

And it was worse than before.

Rolling off of the bed, I scurried into the bathroom and almost slammed the door shut behind me.

Somehow, I ate up around an hour in the bathroom before I finally forced myself to go back out. The bathroom was so much warmer and safer than out there, the air still muggy from the steam of my shower and no one making me feel so fucking anxious.

The frigid hotel air nipped at my body as I pulled the door open, tying my arms around my waist to hold in some heat. Maybe some sanity too.

Dominic was sitting on the edge of the bed when I got out, bare-chested and sweatpants on in place of his work pants.

Oddly enough, he looked up at me when I came out.

"Hey." An infusion of warmth softened his voice. "Have a nice shower?"

I blinked at the stark change, feeling it tingle between my ribs. "Yeah."

"You were in there a while."

Padding over to the overnight bag for no other reason than to have a distraction, I nodded and said, "Yeah, it felt good."

Which wasn't a lie. The scorch of water *had* felt good. It felt like it was burning off the layer of today, washing the soiled memory of it down the drain for a few minutes. Even a few minutes of feeling like today didn't exist was worth the fire engine-red skin I'd stepped out of the shower with.

I was in the middle of fiddling with the hem of a pair of my shorts when Dominic called my name.

"Kat?"

Shit. "Yeah?"

I didn't turn around, but it didn't matter that I was being defiant because Dominic wasn't in the mood to entertain it. He came right around in front of me, standing in my space until my curiosity broke rank and slanted a look up.

Eyes of melted winter waited for me, their coldfront thawed by regret.

"Are you okay?"

"Yeah," I brushed off. "I'm fine."

Before he could ask me anything else, I made a beeline for the bed, folded back the comforter, and slipped inside. The cold of the sheets was a relished welcome as my bare skin slid along the baby soft linen, nestling my head against the pillow and pulling the comforter to my chin.

Only a few anxious heartbeats skipped by before a creak in the hotel floor boards sounded off and snapped my eyes shut. I tried, and pretty sure failed, to even out my breathing to something resembling sleep as the presence of him washed over me.

The heavy scent of crisp earth knelt in front of me. I imagined him raking his sorry stare over my fake-sleeping face and thinking to himself how such a stupid little girl wasn't worth the sacrifice he'd made today.

"Can you open your eyes for me?"

My heart throbbed up my throat at his voice, eyes doing the opposite of what he asked and pinching tighter. Dominic streamlined an exhale, disappointment no doubt flavoring it as I proved to be the same mess that disappeared five weeks ago. Maybe worse.

No.

Definitely worse.

"I shouldn't have gotten that rough with you," he tried, velvet voice sounding closer.

A cluster of uncomfortable nerves attacked inside my chest, breath shaking as I tried to roll over to escape them. "Dominic, we really don't have to talk about this."

He stopped me mid-roll, long fingers catching beneath my arms and gently bringing me up to sitting. My windpipe pinched to hold back the immature groan trying to pry up my throat as he made me face him. The bed dipped as he sat too, his strong thigh covering my toes so they were stuffed beneath his weight.

Muscles in my feet flexed, stretching out the anxiety at being touched. Trapped.

TWENTY-FIVE

The pressure of his gaze waiting for mine wasn't subtle, but I couldn't take seeing my shadow eating away the light in his eyes again, so I laid my cheek on my folded knees and hugged my arms around my legs. My lashes felt too heavy as I focused on the crumple of sheets next to my feet, trying to find a maze in the messy creases and folds.

Heat wrapped around my ankles when I didn't look up, Dominic's big hands holding me in what small ways he could.

"Kat, today is the first time in over a month we've gotten to see each other, and you won't even look at me now. We clearly need to talk about what just happened."

"I *told* you to hurt me," I argued towards the bedsheets.

"And I shouldn't have listened. I'm not quite sure why I did or why you asked me to, but my girlfriend spent an hour hiding in the bathroom from me, so we're going to discuss it."

"I'm just tired, Dominic." *God*, the lie sounded weak even to my ears.

Calloused palms scratched a sweet sting up the back of my calves as he rode his hands up them, securing his grip beneath my knees.

"Kat, listen to me." Hot breath kissed the top of my head, shivering an awareness of how close he'd come down my spine. "Whenever my hands are on you, whenever I kiss you, whenever I'm inside of you, all I want you to feel is loved. Not hurt. Not in pain. It's my job to make you feel loved and safe, and I'm sorry I failed tonight."

"You shouldn't be sorry." *I deserved it.* "Sometimes sex just gets rough."

"Kat, that wasn't just rough, and you know it."

"Dominic, it's fine. *I'm* fine."

"Well, I'm not."

That did it. My head snapped up, eyes jumping to him to see what had the audacity to make him feel anything less than perfect. I searched around every inch of his face as if hunting down any visible proof of harm to scare it off.

Of course, his face was nothing less than flawless, and then I *had* to finish my inspection in his eyes. Hiding my face in my knees again would just make me a bitch.

My heart wrestled around my chest as I forced my stare up to his, holding my breath for when I inevitably saw the mark of my love shadowing his irises. Neither of us spoke as our eyes came together, mine switching back and forth between his, waiting.

Waiting.

Waiting for the shadow that never showed itself. His eyes were nothing but pools of starlight, burning with intensity just for me.

"I'm not fine, because I've been waiting five weeks to hold you and tell you how unbearable being without you has been, and I haven't done that." My lightning rustled in familiarity. "I'm not fine because, instead of telling you that every day without your smiles or your wicked tongue was worse than the last, I hurt you and made you hide from me." A *zap* split between my ribs, hearing the rolling thunder in his voice. "I'm not fine because all I wanted to do tonight was kiss you until your knees went weak so I had an excuse to hold you close."

My breath wobbled, heart clenching. "You don't need an excuse."

He smiled at that, a gentle thing that curved his cheek up just enough to show me a wink of my favorite dimple.

"Good to know." From the side, his hand came up, lucent eyes watching his fingers as they moved into my damp hair. "Because it's all I want to do now that I have you back. Memorize the curves of your face, your strawberry lips…"

Electricity followed the path of his thumb tracing over my mouth, buzzing wherever he touched in a hypnotized trace. A familiar high doped up my brain as he pet my pouty bottom lip, drops of our chemistry drugging my veins.

The high was hitting him too, drooping his eyelids to half-lidded and amorous, pupils dusted with flecks of longing.

"I don't know that I could have made it another day without you."

His knuckles traced a curve down my cheek, tying heartstrings around my throat.

Thinking about and imagining how much my absence weighed on him was one thing. Seeing it dotted like poison in his eyes was another.

TWENTY-FIVE

"I'm sorry," I whispered, wishing he'd never met me.

A crinkle happened between his thickly shaped brows, probably wishing he'd never let me go.

"I'm sorry," he confessed in low tones, taking responsibility like I knew he would.

We were both sorry. Sorry to have met. Sorry we couldn't stop it. Sorry his thunder had to always chase my lightning.

Right now, my lightning couldn't take it. It couldn't take the sorrowful pits of gray his eyes were or how our limbo sky was coming crashing down on us. It wanted how it was five weeks ago before all of this. It wanted the explosion of neurons and molecules and whatever else our chemistry was made up of.

It wanted him and his thunder, and rising me up to my knees and bringing my mouth to his, I took it.

Dominic made a noise between our mouths that sounded like redemption, and our apologies got erased between moving lips. Our chemistry surged to an immediate high, conducting like the heroin it was all over again and burning up everything else.

I forgot the way he'd thrown me down on the bed earlier as he laid me back like a piece of glass now. I forgot the way we kissed like it was war then as his mouth slow danced with mine now, savoring every taste of me. I forgot the way he once ripped at my clothes as he peeled every layer I had off as if each reveal of my skin was an immaculate discovery.

I forgot the pain, the shadow in his eyes, the malicious itch beneath my flesh as he slid inside of me and made love to me as if we had the whole world to ourselves. The stars were ours, the sun and the flowers, all living for us as we erased the bad and remembered how it was when we were good.

When we were so so good.

Even as Dominic's release was rising after my second, he whispered in my ear that he'd buy me a pill in the morning so he didn't have to leave the bubble of *us*. I nodded and clung to him as he filled me up, moaning his love for me in my ear as he marked me as his.

He kissed the breath right out of me when we were finished until my lungs cried for more. Even then as I gasped for relief, he painted my skin with the love on his lips all the way down to my navel. In layers of sweat and hazy affection, Dominic rolled us over so he laid back and I laid on him, both breathing hard and spent.

In every fucking way.

It wasn't even a few minutes later when Dominic's breathing fell even and deep, and he was out cold for the night.

At least one of us would sleep.

Laying there, I spent the night staring at the wall across from the bed until a burnt orange dawn peeked through the hotel curtains. Dominic's chest was my pillow as I thought about time again. How unfair. How short.

What a mindfuck it could be.

Time had me laying in a bed just like this only twenty-four hours ago. Time had me resting in the same position I was now, a different man's heartbeat beneath my head.

Now that man was dead, and I was here.

Because I stole his time.

I stole his life.

TWENTY-SIX

KAT

"Kat, wake up. We're here."

A sturdy voice climbed inside my subconscious to unwedge my brain from a groggy sleep. Awareness lapped back in slowly, licking at the outskirts of my fuzzy head as I came to. Some sweet-intended pressure around my hand helped lug me out of my sleep, a brush of fingers over my knuckles encouraging me awake.

My surroundings flickered in and out as I rubbed the sleep from my eyes and shifted up in what I slowly remembered was the passenger seat of Dominic's car.

Guilt slashed up my chest and popped my eyes wide open, finding Dominic watching me.

"Oh shit. Did I sleep the whole way?"

The faint bend to his lips said he didn't really mind. "Pretty much."

"I'm sorry. I'm usually not such a shitty road trip partner."

"It's not that long of a drive." The sun bathed golden rays over his face, glinting his roaming eyes into diamonds as he looked me over. "You clearly needed the sleep."

Yeah. You could say.

Spending the entire night stuck in a mindfuck of mortality and guilt wasn't exactly bringing in the Z's. Stifling a yawn, Dominic went out of focus as I glanced behind him outside the driver's window.

The street his townhome sat on looked about the same as when I'd last left it.

Oh, except for the parade of cars up and down the whole freaking thing.

"You were already asleep when my mom called and told me," Dominic started sheepishly, staring at the same line of cars I was. "She sort of threw you a surprise homecoming party."

Cue immediate swell of anxiety.

I tried to smile against the flutter of jitterbugs swarming around my chest. "That was nice of her to do."

Dominic shot me a look to say he knew I was lying but appreciated me doing it. Then he stole his focus back out the window, appraising his home with marbleized tension in his jaw.

If I had to guess, he was just as anxious about going inside as I was.

"I thought the whole drive up what to tell Maya." If his lips weren't moving, I'd have mistaken him for frozen. A stunning statue of guilt. "I still don't know."

Dropping my stare to my fidgeting fingers, I muttered, "Tell her the same thing I told Charlotte."

I didn't look up, but I could feel his gaze swoop back to me. It was heavy as rainfall on my face, drenched in gloom just the same.

"You didn't kill your mother."

The inside of his car filled with the breath I couldn't stop from taking, sucking it down sharp and fast. Attention still on my fingers, I watched my thumb rub the blood out of my knuckles until they were as white as the bone beneath, the itch from last night whispering, *go harder.*

"Actually I did."

A furtive glance up was all I had the courage for, catching Dominic's forehead wrinkle in question and that was it. I unclicked my seatbelt and jammed open the passenger door, practically jumping out onto the street.

Fresh air caressed my face and bare arms, smelling the same as it did five weeks ago. I wanted to say it smelled like home, but the sentiment felt

TWENTY-SIX

fuzzy instead of true, so I let it go. Dominic came around his car to me, walking with an energy that demanded answers without asking for them.

I stopped him before he even could.

"Do you know who's all here?"

That rainfall gaze was still stuck to the side of my face, drowning me in his focus. Thankfully, whether because he knew better or just because he knew *me* better, he dropped it. For now.

"No, I didn't ask."

Dominic fell into stride next to me as I made my way up to his front door, weaving in and out of parked cars. "So we're going in blind."

"Unfortunately."

Before I knew it, Dominic's red painted door was staring us both down. Muffled chatter on the other side droned on as he and I stood immobile, both of us afraid of either one or all of the voices.

For me, it was all. Every single person on the other side of that door terrified me. They'd flag me down, grab at my arm without permission, and ask me what happened, how I was feeling, tell me how lucky I was to have survived when every statistic said I shouldn't have.

My cheeks already hurt thinking about the fake smile I'd force them to carry.

For Dominic, he was just afraid of one voice. One tiny voice he loved more than life itself and the questions about her mommy that little voice would ask.

"Ready?" I suggested, shaking out my tingling fingers.

Dominic was so fucking stiff, his reply the same way. "Sure."

A gulp of fall crisp air went down my lungs in a huge anticipatory breath as I steadied and readied myself for Dominic to open the door. I held that breath in, waiting for him to make the move.

I waited and waited and waited, slowly suffocating on fresh air.

When the pressure piling on top of my chest became too much and I started seeing little baby stars, I let the breath out in a massive puff and swept my face up to Dominic.

"What are you—"

He cut me off with his lips.

They were soft, a little cool from the temperature outside, but that didn't stop them from warming me. Or surprising me. My chest bowed into him as he pressed a hand to the small of my back, drawing me underneath his towering height. He held me firm beneath his mouth, kissing me like my lips were a power source and he needed a jump.

Breath several degrees hotter than the air outside mingled between our mouths as he pulled back, but didn't let me go.

"What was that?" I breathed.

Diamond eyes on my mouth, he hummed, "A kiss."

Smartass. "What was it for?"

A slow-build of weight loaded up in those diamonds of his until they lost all shine and looked too heavy for his head. He dragged them up my face, setting their burden on me.

"I needed it."

"Oh." *Because he killed his wife to save you and it broke his heart, remember?* "Okay."

His strict browline stumbled at the washed out color in my tone, but before he could say anything about it, the front door opened up in front of us.

"Oh!" The strike of a familiar woman's voice turned my neck, Dominic's mother, Meredith, watching her son and I with shocked hands over her mouth.

I'd bet a million bucks she was hiding a smile.

"I thought I heard someone out here!" The gentle twang of her voice dipped deeper as she fought off a glisten to her gray-shaded eyes, the noise wrapping warmth around my ribs like a hug. "Oh, come in, come in!"

She craned her head back over her shoulder. "Everyone, they're here!"

And that warmth washed right back out, icy panic flooding in.

Here we go.

An encouraging squeeze around my waist earned Dominic a grateful glance as we both stepped inside, the whir of chatter now stalling to a silence.

TWENTY-SIX

My favorite.

Ryan of all people was the first I saw, beer in his hands that he tipped up to me when our gazes met. I returned a stiff and awkward nod, not sure what the fuck else to do. He was standing next to an older man that Dominic's mom rushed over to, looping her arm in his and tugging at his shirt, delighted eyes on me as she whispered in his ear.

I gave a small wave, safe to assume I was looking at a version of Dominic twenty or thirty years in the future. His father's salt and pepper hair was still shockingly thick and the sharp cut of his jawline hadn't dulled one bit in age.

The crows feet were actually kinda hot too.

Honestly, if I wasn't in love with his son and this reunion wasn't totally fucking morbid, I'd totally flirt it up with Mr. Silver Fox.

Right as Dominic's dad handed me a polite wave back, a voice shattered the awkward silence.

"Katty!"

A tiny, precious, *perfect* voice that I thought I'd never hear again.

My head snapped up to the stairs where her voice echoed from, heart seizing as I yelled, "Bug?!"

A blur of blonde zipped down the stairs faster than light moved, barrelling her way to me as my heart *soared*—higher than the clouds, higher than Heaven as I pushed through a throng of bodies until there was a path from her to me.

Cheeks rosy with a beaming smile came into view, her bare feet hitting the bottom stair and launching at me.

"*Charlotte!*" Her name fell out of me as I swooped her up, catching her as she jumped in my arms. "Oh my god," I breathed, holding her little body close and trying to convince myself this wasn't a dream.

Stinging behind my eyes threatened happy water works, but I didn't want to cry in front of her. Not again.

"Hey you!" I squeezed my arms around her, never wanting to put her down. "How are you? Are you okay? You're okay, right?"

"You came back!" Charlotte pulled her face out of my neck, ignoring my questions like I'd never spoken. "Did you miss me?"

I traced a knuckle down her sweet rounded cheeks. "More than you could ever know."

She showed me her bright grin and giggled, putting little fingers through my hair and twisting the waves into a misshapen braid.

"You were gone for *so* long, but Mr. Dominic kept saying you were coming back."

"I promised you I would."

Even though I almost broke it at least five times.

"I knew you would too." Her blonde little eyebrow arched up, mouth twisting. "Where did you go?"

Hell and back.

"I just got lost," I told her, smoothing a wild curl back behind her ear. "But I'm back now. Not going anywhere anytime soon."

"Good, 'cause you missed *a lot*."

Booping her button nose, I smiled. "Can't wait to hear all about it."

Behind the framing of her blonde curls, another face in the crowd stepped forward, stealing my focus. My heart did another one of those unkind squeezes that made you feel like you were dying instead of over-the-moon happy.

Setting Charlotte back down, I righted myself with tense muscles locked around stiff bones. The last time I saw her big doe eyes, she was sprawled out on Death's welcoming mat. Because of me. Because they got her instead of me.

By the way Layla produced not a single drop of emotion on her walk up to me, I had a sour feeling that's all she'd been thinking about for the last month.

Mouth pursed tight and big eyes locked on me, she reigned her arm back and—

"Ow!"

I grabbed for my arm, rubbing the sting down from where she'd imprinted my skin with five sharp fingers. A curse rearranged the shape of my lips and readied to shoot off my tongue when it stopped just short of launch, the mist hazing her eyes suspending it.

The first tear of many tears splashed a big wet spot on her cheek.

"You are such a *dumbass*," she croaked.

A wash of vanilla came at me full force as she threw her arms around me, squeezing me with that Hulk strength I forgot she was born with. I would have gasped for air if she'd given me time, but whatever. I didn't care for the next thirty seconds if I had any air so long as I had my best friend squeezing the ever living fuck out of me.

"Don't you ever do anything like that again, you stupid *beautiful* idiot," she cried out her threat. "You got me?"

"Well," I wheezed, hugging her back. "I'm really hoping that was just a onetime kind of situation."

Her laughter blew into my hair, and she wrestled my lungs with another crushing squeeze before letting me go and backing up. A few more people came over after that, some I knew from Marties or high school, some I didn't. Mrs. Sharon was there with Davion and her new baby, giving me lots of love and all the baby snuggles.

At one point there was a line to talk to the girl who'd been kidnapped, and each one I spoke to, I wondered just how many of the dirty details they knew.

About me. About who did it. About who wasn't here because of me.

Layla cut the line short like a good ride-or-die when she could tell I was draining. So many people kept telling me I was so lucky. That was the word they kept using. *Lucky*. I just kept smiling and pretending like I felt it. There were only around thirty people, but thirty people all telling you how you should be feeling and wanting to talk about your trauma was *a lot* of people.

She rescued me with a glass of wine, dragging me to the kitchen for some of the food Meredith had cooked. I filled my stomach with exactly three sips of merlot and two baby shrimps when I saw Dominic with Maya.

My appetite drained out of me like everything else.

He was in the corner of the kitchen, his daughter hoisted up into his arms where she hugged him tightly. Her face was hidden on his shoulder, and his large hand had dwarfed the back of her head as he held it tenderly. His parents stood in front of him, grim expressions drawn on all three faces.

For a stupid moment, I wondered if he'd just told her about Heather.

How he'd shot and killed her mommy to save the nanny.

But like I said, it was a stupid thought. Dominic was too good a father to tell his daughter something so horrible around so many strangers. He'd have to tell her soon though. He'd have to break that little girl's heart because he fell in love with mine.

Setting down my glass of wine, I excused myself to go find the bathroom upstairs even though I didn't have to pee. I only made it about two paces down the hallway before being hit from behind *so hard,* the noise that came out of me was something like a boy getting socked in the nutsack.

Eyes popping wide, I stumbled forward, laying a stabilizing hand on the two tiny arms wrapped around my waist.

"Ms. Kat! Ms. Kat, Grandma told me not to talk to you, but I missed you!"

Oh god.

"Is it okay that I came over?" she asked, chipper and cheery and all the things she was before I left. Before I stole her father. Before I killed her mother.

"Yeah, of course it is." Plastering on a grin up my cheeks, I spun around to where Maya hung around my waist, her head craned all the way back to look at me. "I missed you too, kiddo. You been good while I was away?"

"Yes! Grandma and I had *lots* of ice cream."

Chuckling, I pushed my hands through her mass of ringlet curls. "Sounds like you got a pretty sweet deal. No pun intended."

"What's a pun?"

"Never mind."

She blew past the lack of definition easy breezy. "Did Charlotte show you the pictures we drew for you? We did like fifty to show you when you got back."

"*Fifty?* Man, that's a lot of coloring action."

TWENTY-SIX

"Yeah, we made some for Daddy also because, um, because he was so sad all the time. I think he missed you a lot. Like *a lot*." Maya exaggerated how much she thought her father missed me by dipping her head back and using my waist like a jungle gym to hold herself up.

Her silliness pushed a smile up my cheeks despite it not deserving to be there.

This little girl made me *smile* when all that waited for her from me were big fat tears. When she learned what happened to her mommy and that I was responsible, she'd never smile for me again, so I milked as much of it as I could now because I was just that selfish.

Maya let out a piercing shriek as I dug my fingers into her sides, tickling her into a jumble of squeals and tinsel laughter. We gained ourselves a few onlookers, one set of sharp eyes catching mine from the kitchen.

With a house full of people and chatter, Dominic and I managed to do as we'd always done and only saw each other through the noise. Like tunnel vision to the other. Call it a facet of fate. Call it chemistry on crack. I didn't have a name for it.

All I knew was how my heart quickened with his afternoon rainstorm eyes on me.

"Ms. Kat, do you know when my mommy's coming home?"

I also knew how my heart stopped the very next second.

And how my stomach dropped, and my knees buckled, and the little bit of shrimp and wine wretched back up to sit in bile at the back of my throat.

Sick. I was going to be sick.

Saliva pooled in the sides of my mouth as I dropped my stare down to Maya, heat flushing from the crown of my head all the way down my back, a sticky damp thing of guilty sweat. *So fucking guilty.* She was as wide-eyed as ever staring up at me, innocent curiosity radiating from eyes just like her mother's.

Wires in my head glitched, shorting out my brain with pictures of those same eyes glazed over and lifeless. Those same eyes closed forever. Those same eyes screaming bloody fucking murder at me seconds before the murder was turned on her.

"I-I, um…" Proper human functions went right out the window as I tried to give her an answer. This wasn't my job. This wasn't my place. *Oh god, am I breathing too much or too little? Does she know? Can she tell?* My head clouded with fog too thick to fight rational answers through.

Maya's nose scrunched as I stuttered terribly. Her head ticked to the side, and a bomb of tears jammed up my windpipe, ready to explode all over this nice party and this nice little girl.

"Maya, honey." The maternal voice of a savior swooped in the millisecond before I reached implosion. Meredith wrapped an arm around her granddaughter's shoulders and peeled her away from me, turning her around. "How about you go ask Grandpa when he's going to make those cookies, okay?"

"Okay!" Maya beamed without a second thought and skipped off.

Meredith stayed with me as we both watched her leave, a crippling quiet falling between us. Even after she was out of sight, I watched where she'd been, my brain not working enough to look away or close my mouth or even breathe.

Oxygen was stuck in my open mouth and frozen lungs, sitting stale and useless. Inside my soul, that malignant darkness hissed to remind me it was still there, still lurking and watching me fuck up.

A cool hand slipped into mine, squeezing me back into the present.

Meredith waited for me with knowing and sad eyes, offering up a small smile to the woman who obliterated her son's family.

"How about you go take a break upstairs in Dom's bedroom? I'll cover for you down here if anyone asks."

Still not breathing, I handed her a jerking nod before ducking out of the hallway, up the stairs, and throwing myself in Dominic's bedroom.

The second the door clicked shut, oxygen flooded back in, feeding my lungs that had begun to shrivel. That's all I did for a couple minutes, replenish my starving lungs and keep my eyes closed.

When I finally felt like my heart wasn't seconds away from exploding inside my chest and puking wasn't next up on the list, my eyes flitted open.

Doing a once over of Dominic's bedroom, I came to the quick conclusion

TWENTY-SIX

that he'd done some redecorating since I was last in here. Or just, *decorating*.

Last time, there was just a bed and a lamp. Now, a waist-high dresser stretched across the front wall of it, gray like his eyes and broad like him. The lamp was still next to the bed, but now it sat on a nightstand the same gray as the dresser with a hamper full of crumpled clothing next to it.

The nightstand had a buddy tucked innocently in on the other side of the bed. Mr. and Mrs. nightstands I think they were called. Lying on top of it charging was my phone Dominic told me was released from evidence this morning.

Ryan brought it with him, and Dominic must have brought it up here when I was talking to people.

To charge on the Mrs. side.

My gut picked up again, that damn shrimp rolling around like it still had some kick in it. Steadying an exhale, the back of my head touched the door, remembering the last time I was in here. How goddamn happy I was.

Dominic did that for me. He took all my shattered pieces our first night here and he loved me so hard that he bound them back together. In this very room, he took me from broken to something a little less than. Something a little less lost and a little more found.

The memories I had in this room were pure, *aching* bliss.

I missed that feeling. I missed when realizing how sick in love I was with a perfect man was my biggest setback. I missed the anxiety I *used* to feel that I thought could drown me. No one told me it could get worse, that there was something beyond panic that was so much harder to breathe through.

No one told me *guilt* was so fucking debilitating.

Grief I knew. Grief I *felt*. I lived it, knew the steps to it, wrestled it down every time it came back again. Guilt was new to me. Guilt and grief *together* was a fresh attack I'd never experienced.

Grief was a hole you had to climb out of each time you fell into it. Sometimes the hole was deep. Sometimes it was shallow. Guilt was the torrential downpour beating you down deeper into the hole, slicking up the sides so you couldn't grab on, getting heavier and harder every minute of every day.

The second I left the mansion, the downpour started.

It followed me everywhere I went, bogging me down as I walked out of the hotel this morning, as I rode inside Dominic's car, as I ran up these stairs, as I stood with my back against the door now. It was *on* me like a physical thing I couldn't get rid of or control.

I should have been happy. I should have been *happy* to be home.

But way too fucking many people had to die for me to get here, and I didn't know how to feel happy about that.

A knock at the door behind my back broke the spiral I hadn't realized I'd started going down.

"Katty?" Charlotte's voice came through the wood muffled, the knob turning against my back. "Katty, can I come in?"

"I think you already are, Bugs." A soft smile crinkled my cheeks as she popped her head through, looking around Dominic's bedroom like she'd stepped into a museum.

"You disappeared so I came to find you," she said, still eyeing the room.

My fingertips bent against the door as I pushed it back closed once she was through.

"Well, thanks for checking up on me."

"Why are you up here?"

"Just needed some rest."

She stopped at the bed, turning over her shoulder to me. "Do you not like your party?"

"No, I love it." I pushed closer to her, bumping her shoulder with my hip. "Grown-ups just get tired since they can't stay hopped up on sugar all day."

"Did you have a lot of sugar when you were gone?"

Thinking back to the buffet of donuts and pancakes and pastries, I gave a small nod.

"Yeah. I did surprisingly."

"Were there nice people too?"

When my brain should have gone to the 99% of horrible, not-nice assholes I dealt with over the last five weeks, it went to the 1% instead.

TWENTY-SIX

The exception with black eyes and my infection in his heart.

"Yeah." Slowly, I sank down to the bed. "There were."

Charlotte climbed up next to me, right at my side. "Can I meet them?"

My cheek caught between my teeth as I looked towards the ceiling, shaking my head away from the emotion climbing up my throat.

No crying. No fucking crying in front of her.

I sniffled back the break of tears trying to come out and shifted farther on the bed, taking my sister with me. "Tell me about everything you did while I was gone. I wanna know it all. Don't leave out any details."

She hummed aloud for about three seconds before forgetting what we were talking about and launching into an elaborate story about the first time she met Mrs. Sharon's new baby. I sat there and listened to her animated talking, her voice a sort of lullaby in the background of my broken-hearted thoughts.

Thoughts about Blake and Charlotte, and how well they'd get along.

She could make a friend out of anyone, and he would love her creative side and everything else about her just because she was special to me. I imagined them meeting and talking and laughing.

I sat there and imagined a future that didn't exist, trapped under the weight of a downpour.

TWENTY-SEVEN

DOM

"What the fuck happened to my house?"

My jaw set to the side as we pulled up, the indignance lighting up Kat's voice and the graffiti marking up her front door doing the job. Setting the car in park, Kat jumped out so fast I didn't even hear her unclick her seatbelt, leaving me to catch up behind her as she ran towards her house.

"*Goddammit.*" She shoved her hands up into her hair, the delicate curve of her spine arching as she took in the damage to her place. I came up to stand behind her.

"I haven't been by here in over a month. I had no idea."

But I might have guessed had I thought about it. She didn't live in the safest part of town, and a house gone untouched for more than a few weeks around here usually meant a target for 'street artists'.

"Well, that's gonna be a *bitch* to clean off."

Her arms dropped down, creating a breeze between us. She'd thrown her hair on top of her head for a change today, exposing the smooth slope of her neck more than normal. I rolled my fingers into my palm to stop myself from touching that sweet spot.

TWENTY-SEVEN

Pitching back a deep breath, I nodded her forward. "Don't worry about that now. Let's just get you and Charlotte some more clothes and get back."

My skin had been itching ever since we left my place.

Every empty road we passed or stranger's faces we saw on the sidewalk got my nerves worked up. Ray was still out there somewhere. FBI hadn't been able to locate him, and Archie told me to let it go.

'He's long gone by now, hidin' till the day he croaks,' he'd said.

I wasn't nearly as convinced.

Walking directly behind her, a jingle cracked the cool air as she produced her house keys. I gave a cursory glance behind us before coming back to her and the spot on her shoulder my guilt had been obsessed with.

A shameful bruise in the shape of my teeth was tattooed on the surface of her skin. The discoloration had worsened since yesterday when I first noticed it. What was blue then had bled to a deeper purple now, haloed by splotches of green in her skin.

I'd also found a few darkened fingerprints on her arms from where I held her down.

Guilt raked its talons through my chest when I saw the proof of what I'd done to her in that hotel room. She waved me off last night and told me it was no big deal, but I didn't miss her putting on a shirt with a higher collar when the girls came running into my bedroom asking to sleep with us.

Kat seemed ecstatic about the idea, like she didn't want to spend the night alone with the man who momentarily lost his mind and marked her body. I'd been dying to touch her all morning, but that nasty bruise kept my guilty hands at my sides.

The front door popped open after a little added effort, the noise of wood bending breaking me from my thoughts. We stepped inside, the stench of stale smoke and faint mildew attacking us head on. My nose scrunched against the stink.

Kat was too used to the smell of poverty to react.

"Glad to see this place is still the shithole it's always been." Kat turned around in her home, looking so out of place here despite the fact that this is where she grew up. I supposed flowers came from dirt too. This was the dirt my flower came from.

The floorboards creaked underneath her weight as she walked though she weighed next to nothing. Her collarbone was only a little more pronounced than it was when she left. Same for her ribs when I got a good look at them last night.

It was a happy discovery to see she hadn't lost much weight since being taken.

I was sure *Blake* had something to do with that.

"What's this?" Kat pulled my focus as she picked something up off her coffee table, holding it in front of her scrutinizing face. If I'd had a mirror, I'd bet money I could have seen my blood leave my face as I saw the number card.

An evidence card.

"It's something the crime lab must have left behind last month."

I plucked the number 'six' from between her fingers that had gone stiff, wishing like hell I'd seen it before she had.

Someone was getting their ass chewed out if I ever got off of suspension.

"Oh." Her hand dropped and so did her voice, emerald eyes falling to the couch where we'd found her mother dead. My gut turned to a rock, every breath hurting as I watched her relive the trauma with a new lens.

Things were still sensitive, so she hadn't been willing to give many details yesterday about what she meant when she said she'd killed her mom. Only that her mom didn't die on purpose, and that she would kill Tommy if she ever saw him again.

I told her right after that I'd put a bullet in his knee already.

After looking at me like I had two heads, she pushed up on her toes and kissed me. Hard.

That'd been the last time she'd gone out of her way to touch me since.

"I'll let Ryan know I have it, and he'll bring it back."

"Right." She clicked her tongue. "Because you can't. Because you're suspended," she repeated like she needed to remind herself. My stare dragged down to her shoes where she dug the toe into the carpet. "You shouldn't have gotten suspended over me. You love your job."

TWENTY-SEVEN

Watching her dig herself a hole of blame, I removed the space between us and touched the tip of my pointer finger beneath her chin as gently as humanly possible. Lifting her head up, those eyes that knocked me senseless from the first moment I saw them fixed on me.

"I love you more."

And I would remind her over and over until she got the message loud and clear.

Instead of saying it back or even showing me her smile, she deflected and walked away.

"How's Maya this morning? I didn't see her before we left."

Trying to let her rejection roll off my shoulders, I stuffed my hands in my front pockets and leaned against a wall.

"She's managing. I think she'll probably want to sleep with us again tonight."

Kat only nodded as I thought back to yesterday after everyone left the party, and I had to tell my five-year-old daughter how her mother wasn't ever coming home.

"Daddy, why are you crying?" Maya crawled into my lap, and her tiny hands wiped away the stray tears I'd fought so damn hard to keep in.

"I'm just sad, sweetie. That's all."

"Because of Mommy?"

Sniffling, I nodded. "Yeah, because of Mommy."

She tilted her sweet head at me, trying to connect puzzle pieces too confusing for a five-year-old.

"She's not coming back?"

"No, baby. She's not."

Her big eyes flooded with a wash of tears. "Is it because I was bad?"

"No, no, not at all." I wrapped her little hands in mine, kissing each of her fingers before looking back up into her big wet eyes. "Maya, Mommy loved you so much. You were the best thing she ever did, and she told me that all the time. She would tell me how perfect you were, how smart and sweet and wonderful."

Maya deserved to remember a mother who loved her, even if it was a lie. She didn't need the truth about her now. Not when she was so young, and I still couldn't even stomach most of it myself.

"Can we go visit her in Heaven?" *she asked, hiccuping.*

"No, baby. Heaven isn't the kind of place you can visit."

Teardrops so big I could see myself in them dropped from her eyes. She sniffled as I ran my thumb underneath them, gathering her wet tears from her face.

"I feel sad too, Daddy."

"That's okay, baby. It's okay to feel sad. We can be sad together for Mommy."

Maya dropped to sob into my chest, and I held her tight and rubbed her back as tears of my own dripped down my face. We sat together on her twin size bed and cried for the loss of a woman neither of us ever really knew.

"Okay," Kat sighed, pivoting towards the hallway back to her and her sister's room. "I'm gonna go get enough clothes for, what, do you think a week or so before it's safe to come back here?"

Hauling back a mighty breath, I knew what I was about to say would make her draw claws, but it was a fight we needed to have.

"Kat, I think we should discuss you and Charlotte moving in with us. Permanently."

From where I stood, I watched her body freeze up all the way down to her fingers. The tension was strapped around her voice too as she argued, "Why?"

"Because I don't feel comfortable with you two here."

"This is our house." Defense was already rising hot along the edges of her voice.

"Yes, and you rent it, don't you?"

Seeing where I was heading, she turned to cut me off. "Yeah, so I'm a month behind. I'll just call the landlord. Wouldn't be the first time it happened."

"Except you don't have a job right now, and you shouldn't have to look for one with everything that's happened."

"And you're suspended." A fresh batch of attitude brightened the green of her eyes as they slid my way, as if there was an actual match lit behind

TWENTY-SEVEN

them. "Technically neither of us have a job right now, so I'm not going to put you out for a place to live."

"You wouldn't be putting me out," I pushed back.

The only thing she'd be putting me out of was my misery. I'd become certifiable worrying about her every day if she chose to stay here where I couldn't watch over her.

"Dominic, I appreciate what you're trying to do, but I don't need to feel guilty about you blowing your money on me too."

"Kat..." My focus had fallen off of her before I finished her name and fixed to the floor. The heavy ache that had been in my chest for two days dug bone-deep preparing the words. "Money won't be an issue. Heather's life insurance was pretty big."

Kat didn't respond, and I wasn't surprised.

It was a disgusting thing to say. It would be a disgusting thing to cash in to clothe and feed my daughter and myself with. This entire mess was just fucking disgusting.

"It just makes sense for you two to stay with us. The girls could share Maya's room like they have been, and half of your stuff is already there. I could take care of you there. I could take care of you here too, but it'd be a hell of a lot easier to protect you if you were sleeping next to me."

"Dominic," Exasperation cut clear through her voice. "That's a lot right now."

"It's also smart, all things considered."

"Usually couples don't move in together because it's *smart*," she debated at the wall, her breaths moving a little quicker. She was getting overwhelmed, but this was too important to stop now.

"It's not just smart. I *want* to wake up next to you every morning. I *want* breakfasts with you and the girls each day. In fact, nothing would make me happier."

She blinked over to me, a locked question in her stare.

"Nothing?"

Rolling my mouth together, I shook my head. "Nothing. I want *you*. We would have gotten to this point eventually. It's just a little sooner to keep you safe."

Like I'd hit a nerve, she swallowed a deep breath and took her gaze away again.

"You can't spend the rest of your life protecting me, Dominic." Anxiety was practically running its own circuit beneath her skin.

Loving this woman was knowing all of her ticks, what it meant when she started picking at her lips and when she rolled her fingers into her palms until you were afraid she'd draw blood with her nails—like she was doing right now.

Pushing off the wall, I started towards her. She didn't see me coming, too distracted by her rising panic to realize I was on my way to her until I'd wrapped my hands around her fidgeting fists, bottle-green eyes flashing up to me.

"I can, and I plan to," I told her, rubbing my thumbs across her knuckles. "That's my job."

"No. Your job as a cop is to protect *everyone*."

I slanted my head above her, collecting the sincerity ringing her pupils. She didn't get it. She wasn't just being difficult. She honestly didn't understand it.

"My job as the man who loves you is to protect *you*." My tone softened, thinking about kissing her lips. "Whatever it takes."

Her mouth parted open, and her pouty bottom lip that I was thinking about biting quivered as she showed me the last response I expected to see.

Regret rose to her waterline, and a sting that had nothing to do with Heather ripped a wide cut through my chest. The emotion shredded the whites of her eyes red as she shook her head, taking back her warmth as she pulled out of my grasp.

"We're not moving in," she said as she turned away, cut but not so dry with wet emotion thickening her throat. She went into the kitchen to grab some snacks Charlotte had asked for, leaving me to grapple with the blow of her rejection.

I couldn't wrap my brain around it. All I wanted was to be around her now that I had her back. I wanted Kat almost literally glued to my side so I knew she was safe and because she was my cure to the sadness. In big and small doses, she'd been curing me since the day we interviewed her.

With her humor and sass, her sexy confidence and love, she was the remedy I needed to get through this.

But that need didn't seem to be going both ways.

She hadn't broken down and told me what happened to her during those five weeks away. She hadn't shed any tears and asked me to hold her because of what happened. In fact, she'd built back up her walls that I'd so carefully broken down higher and thicker than ever.

A sudden banging at the front door hacked through the high-tension in the house.

Kat tore a wide-eyed look over to me from the kitchen, and I was reaching for the glock tucked in the back of my jeans before the second round of banging came.

"Katerina, I know you're in there! Open up!"

Her beautiful face creased in confusion as a male shouted through the door, knowing her name and knowing *her*. My fingers tightened around my gun, bringing it to rest in both hands as I nodded for Kat to hide.

I'd only just made the signal when the lock on the front door rattled, the flimsy thing it was busting loose.

A man stumbled in and gave me a target as I aimed my gun fast and precise. Shortly after him, the smell of cheap booze stumbled in right after. My pointer finger stayed hot on the trigger, slowing my breathing as I watched the intruder fumble for his footing.

"God*dammit*." The man cursed at his worn brown boots like they'd done the tripping for him, scuffing them against the floor, unbothered to be mucking up the carpet of someone else's home.

Or someone else's, so I thought.

"Dad?"

Kat's voice came from behind me, ringing with absurdity down every stiffening notch in my spine, pooling a vat dread in my stomach.

You've got to be kidding me.

"What the fuck are you doing here?" she lashed out, going from zero to radioactive like only she could. In my head, I started jumping through hoops, thinking of a way out of this before it got too far.

Before her father said too much and completely screwed me.

He locked his bleary eyes on her behind me, nonplussed at the gun aimed his way.

"Don't take that nasty tone with me, young lady."

Against my back, I *felt* her rage flare up, heating sweat beneath my shirt as she snapped back. "Did you just seriously call me *young lady?*"

"Well, you are my daughter so—"

"I am *not* your daughter," Kat interrupted, her words pointed daggers. "And I don't know why you're here after four fucking years, but you need to get out of my house before my trigger-happy cop boyfriend puts you outside himself."

The word 'boyfriend' tipped off of her lips so effortlessly, a swell of relief burst in my chest. Then, her father's attention cut over to me, and that swell died.

"It was you, wasn't it? The cop that called me?"

I'd never wanted to erase words from a mouth more as I stared down the man who'd given Kat the extraordinary color of her eyes and those daddy issues she loved to tease me with.

Her accusing tone hit the back of my neck like spikes.

"You *what?*"

Shit. Fuck. Dammit.

Noting that her father would have to walk a straight line before he even made his way up to Kat to hurt her, I lowered my gun and turned to her.

"He was the only suspect we had besides Tommy. I was grasping at straws to find you, and with his disappearance and with you being targeted so specifically, it made sense."

"Suspect?" Her deadbeat father tried to interrupt but sank to background music. "Suspect for what?"

"You really thought my *dad* of all people kidnapped me?" Her hands went flying through the air as her temper mounted. "You thought the guy who didn't want to be around me *so much* that he abandoned his whole

TWENTY-SEVEN

family suddenly wanted to reconnect, so instead of picking up the phone, he *kidnapped* me?"

I wanted to throw my hands in the air and beg for forgiveness. "I was taking any lead I had and running full speed with it. I *had* to."

She gave me a look like I'd plunged a knife in her back, and she couldn't believe it was me who'd done it. Under any other circumstances, I wouldn't have been able to believe it either, and I was so goddamn sorry he was here, but I stood by my decision.

If it meant finding her, I would have hunted the son of a bitch down myself and not regretted it for a day.

"This is the guy you're dating?" Her father gave me a lazy once over, obviously missing how my fingers twitched for a hit. Just one good punch. "How fucking old are you, man?"

"Don't fucking talk to him."

The smell of coconut snuck up on me, a vision of dark hair sliding in front of me before I realized it. Her name rumbled in my chest, tucking my gun away so I could pull her behind me.

She slapped my hands away when I tried, holding up a hand that said to back off and let her be my shield. If I hadn't been dead-locked by the tension in my muscles, I might have fallen over.

I brought him here, and she was *defending* me from him. She stood between her father and I like I was a child and he was the big bad wolf coming to eat me, and she'd rip his tongue out and make him choke on it before he got even close.

God love this firecracker of a woman.

"He's the reason I'm here!" her father tried to argue.

"And I'm the reason you're leaving. *Now*."

"Oh, no, I'm not goin' nowhere. It took me a couple weeks to get down here after gettin' your fella's voicemail, but I made it. I'm here, and I been sittin' outside this house since yesterday waitin' for you all."

"Yeah, and drinking your liver to death. Thanks for the concern, *Dad*."

"At least I came." He had the audacity to sound as if he deserved an award for making the trip, and my knuckles had never been hungrier for the taste of blood. He jabbed his weak chin up at Kat. "Where's your sister?"

She crossed her lithe arms, cocking a hip out. "See, that's the kind of stuff you'd already know had you not bailed on your family."

Her father scoffed. "You gonna sing that song all day, baby girl? Because I can fix the tune for you with why I really left if you wanna know so bad."

"I *do* know." Kat steadied herself. "It's because you're a coward. Down to your brittle fucking bones."

"I ain't no coward. Your mom's just a *bitch*."

Every muscle beneath her snow-white skin contracted, and I swore the temperature dropped as cool as outside. My eyes clocked pressure from her fingers repainting her upper arms from creamy to bright red to something whiter than white as she gouged her nails into the skin.

"Don't ever talk about my mom." The structure of her voice was somewhere between shaking and completely flat. It soaked into my chest, drenching my heart for this broken woman.

Her dad rolled his eyes at her, and I regretted it *for* him. "What, she pollute your minds with some bullshit over these years how I was some asshole? I fucking bet she did. Where's the bitch anyways?"

"Get *out*," she seethed, vocal cords shaking, body shaking. Fuck, the *walls* that watched this sorry excuse for a man tear his family apart over the years were shaking in solidarity with her building wrath.

Whether he was too stupid to realize or too stupid to care, he didn't listen.

"I ain't goin' nowhere after waiting two days outside to see my own daughters. You're either gonna tell me where your sister is, or I'm gonna have to find your mother and ask her myself."

"You don't get to see Charlotte!" Kat exploded, hands balling into fists that were only a few seconds away from taking swings. "She doesn't even remember you, and you are reminding me so perfectly well why I am so fucking jealous of that!"

"You watch your mouth with me you—"

He took only two steps towards his daughter, but it was two steps too many.

TWENTY-SEVEN

Surprise flashed across his gaunt face as he tumbled backwards, crashing into the door much more dramatically than the shove I gave him allotted. He jerked his head up at me, whatever shit he was ready to spew dying out fast as I filled my already broad chest even wider, rolling my shoulders back to make him feel as small as he was.

Fear shadowed the sunken in dips of his face as I closed in on him.

"She told you to get out." My jaw flexed, voice thundering like a quietly approaching earthquake. "I suggest you listen."

Her father's stare jumped between mine and Kat's behind me, the room standing in a stiff silence. Looking down at the disheveled, half-drunk man beneath me, I couldn't believe this pile of shit produced gold. No wonder my Kat had trust issues.

A bitter taste filled my tongue as I stared down the man who'd put the first bruise on her heart. One bruise turned to several, and then bruises turned to breaks. A man with as much dignity in his entire filth-stained body as Kat had in her pinky toe had the audacity to steal so much of her worth.

My girl deserved the moon and stars, and I would give them all to her if she asked. I'd climb up every constellation listed in the sky to reach them for her just to prove how much brighter she burned than them all combined.

"This is so fucking dumb." A dark chuckle shook her father's knobby shoulders as he shifted himself back upright. Brushing his hands against his faded tan pants, he shook his head. "Make the long trip out here only to be thrown out of my own home by the daughter I didn't really even wanna see."

My fists clenched in time with the blow he'd shot Kat's way.

If he didn't leave in the next ten seconds, there'd be a body to bury.

He waved a sloppy hand our way, dismissing his daughter for the upteenth time.

"You can keep the house, and your sister and all of it." The tops of my ears were boiling by the time he turned to leave, stopping just before making the exit to fix his eyes on Kat. "I never wanted any of it anyways."

He slammed the door behind him, rattling me and the crumbling house to the core.

A dangerous quiet set in around us, one worse than any shoved between her and I before.

It made it hard to move, hard to speak.

Most of all, it made it hard to feel the woman behind me like I'd always been able to. She was like a ghost behind my back. Ice-cold, terrifying… and fading.

"Kat—"

"No."

She cut me off with one word, clipping my vocal cords. It wasn't even her brilliant temper that had done the snipping this time, but something that made my gut drop and my feet whirl on her.

Defeat had wielded the one word, cutting me marrow deep to hear in her sweet siren voice.

My Kat didn't give up. She didn't know how, and I admired the hell out of her for it.

But she was off. The tiny wrinkle scribbled between her dipped eyebrows as she squeezed her eyes shut was different. Weaker. Every breath she took seemed like a shudder her tight chest could barely get down.

My little lightning was fading right before my eyes, and I knew it was my fault.

"I was only trying to find you."

My whole heart pleaded in those words, begging her to open those eyes so I could see her. Even if the fire in her eyes had a flame with my name burning in it, it was a step better than this. I couldn't make it better if she didn't look at me. I couldn't get behind that Fort Knox mind of hers if she didn't give me the key.

She showed me nothing but her eyelids as my heart pounded harder. Her ivory skin was cracked from beneath, a monstrous pain that hadn't been prodded in years breaking out from beneath because I'd invited it back. Because I'd called it on the fucking phone and brought it here to terrorize an already shattered woman. *Goddammit.*

TWENTY-SEVEN

"I never wanted to see him again," she whispered so low, I thought I imagined it. The guilt splitting my chest in two let me know they weren't invented words, but an admission of hurt so brutal, it stripped her voice of sound. "I *never*..."

Every fiber of my being screamed to hold her, but everything I knew about her told me she'd push me away.

If I hadn't caused this, I could fix this. I wanted to fix this. I *needed* to fix this.

But I ran out of time as she tried to force even one more word to me and failed, turning and going down the hallway instead, closing the bedroom door behind her.

TWENTY-EIGHT

DOM

I waited in the living room for around a half hour to give her time to cool off.

Kat didn't speak to me when she came out of her old bedroom with a bag full of belongings for her and her sister. She didn't speak to me on the car ride home either. We got back to my place, and she walked right upstairs to my bedroom without a word.

Sighing and fighting my urge to follow her, I went into the kitchen instead to make lunch for the girls. Kat loved peanut butter, so I themed the lunch around that—crackers smothered in the sweet and savory spread, apple slices to dip in it, and a few classic PB&J's.

Scribbling a quick note to my mom that we were running low on peanut butter, I stuck it on the fridge in case she saw it and went to the store before I did.

The day I came back without Heather, my parents made the decision to move closer to us. In the next town, closer.

At first, I tried to fight them on it. Now, not even a week into being a single father, and I was so grateful they'd shut my prideful mouth down and put in an offer on a place only twenty minutes away. They say it takes a village, right?

TWENTY-EIGHT

I think that saying must have been invented specifically for when you had the shit handed to you.

Balancing two plates and a bowl, I strode back out of the kitchen to go in search of the girls when the sight of one of them standing by the front door dragged my heart back several steps.

"Charlotte." The bags Kat and I had just come home with were stacked by her feet, upping my pulse. "What are you doing down here?"

Looking down at her purple sneakers, she shrugged one shoulder. "Katty says we're going to stay with Layla."

Dread exploded like white hot confetti all over my insides, sparking pain in about every goddamn place it touched. Turning back towards the stairs, I took them two by two with lunch still in my hands, shouldering my way through the partially closed door.

It smacked the wall as it flung open, either the noise of the door or being caught making Kat jump.

Vivid green eyes that I was a big enough man to admit I'd fallen in love with the very first time I saw them fell on me. My known flight risk kept her feet planted firmly as I dropped a glance to the floor...

And the two other bags she'd packed.

Dread reformed to sludge in my limbs as I set the snacks down on my dresser, heavy gaze trapped on the criminal luggage.

"You're packing," I spoke flatly, hoping this was a nightmare.

It got worse when she replied. "I'm finished."

Dread made the quick-change to horror, dropping a thousand pound brick in my stomach and fucking with the temperature in my body from boiling to arctic cold all at the same time.

Finished. With us?

She took in my reaction with widening eyes, shaking her head fast and probably not catching herself as she stepped closer.

"*Packing.*" The quickness of which she corrected her statement was a brittle crutch. "I'm finished packing."

My gut lightened up, but not much. She was still leaving. Or planning on it.

Now that I'd caught her, I could stop her. I could talk her down from this ledge she was determined to throw herself off of. She was a jumper, but that worried flicker of her gaze said she also knew I was a world class negotiator for all things Katerina Sanders.

She didn't want me to save her, but too goddamn bad.

"Is this because of your dad?" I started.

She drifted her focus away as soon as the question reached her, smashing her eyelids shut.

"*No*," she said forcibly. Like she'd rehearsed the denial.

"I honestly forgot I'd even called him. He never returned it, and then with everything that happened, I—"

"I *know*." Breathing extra hard, she tried and failed again. "No, I-I know—"

Her head dropped into her hands, hiding her face away from me as she arranged her upset thoughts. Shoulders rising, she collected a labored sigh and pushed the words out. "I know I can't be mad at you for it, because I know why you did it, and I can't be mad for it. I get it. I hate it, but I get it."

She was trying.

I'd unleashed emotional hell on her, and she was trying to understand why. For someone with a track record as volatile and rash as hers, that alone meant the world.

"Then why are you trying to leave?"

I made the mistake of thinking she might not notice when I drifted a stride closer since her face was still captured in her hands. It was a thoughtless move, and I knew it the second I did it and saw her flinch.

Of course she felt me without needing to see me.

She was my sixth sense, and I'd never have to wonder again if I was hers.

"I just need..." The heels of her palms were digging deeper and harder against her eyes, worry festering in my chest that she was doing it with too much pressure. "I just need *space*."

"From me?" I asked before the dread could stop me.

Still hiding her face, she was almost too soft to hear. "From everything."

My girl was drowning.

TWENTY-EIGHT

I might've rescued her from a ship taking her under, but that didn't mean there wasn't still water in her lungs. The residual effects of the kind of trauma she'd been through could last for months or even years.

There was only one way to get the water out that bogged down her lungs, and that was to force it out. Knowing Kat, she would hold it in with her lungs burning and screaming until it killed her.

I wouldn't let that happen. I'd work on her until it all came up, spilling out in saltwater horror stories and pain I could erase for her if she just let me.

"Kat, please just talk to me. We haven't talked since you got back about anything that happened. We need to. *I* need to."

It was slowly driving me mad that she wouldn't let me see her. She was using her hands like shields from me, keeping the emotions in her eyes masked so I couldn't dissect them and help her.

I wasn't surprised when she ignored me. "I have to get down to Charlotte."

When she lifted her foot to leave, I heard myself blurting out a question I hadn't realized I was afraid of.

"Is this because of the bruises?"

Finally, her hands fell to show me her bafflement. "What?"

The skepticism chiseled in the furrow of her brow told me I was wrong, but nothing else made sense. "I hurt you, and now you're running away—"

"Dominic, *no*." Passion gripped her voice, and I was a goner listening to every explicit word she gave me. "This has literally nothing to do with that. It wasn't a big deal and you shouldn't feel bad, so *please* stop bringing it up. I *wanted* you to hurt me."

"Why?"

"It doesn't matter why," she exclaimed, emotions running a thin veil over her lovely face. "It's *stupid* why."

"It's not stupid to me."

When she tried to show me her back again, I lashed out to grab her wrist, tugging her into me and bringing us back to basics. My hand slipping up to hold the back of her neck was so familiar, nostalgia warming my chest to remember the feel of her control slipping into the palm of my hand that very first time.

She was so goddamn pliable in my arms even when she didn't want to be, molding her curves to me like rain hitting the solid ground. I did exactly as I'd done back before she got used to her feelings for me, pinching the nape of her neck so she bent right into me, her pouty mouth dropping open as soon as she felt my dominance.

"Tell me why you think it's stupid," I murmured over her parted lips, watching her close and trying not to get hard.

I loved this fiery woman from so many different angles, but this was one of my personal favorites. When she was bowed back beneath me and staring up at me like I had all the goddamn answers she'd ever wanted to know, I loved her with a power that could eclipse the sun.

Though her mouth parted, no words of submission tumbled out. I waited impatiently for the flurry of momentary chaos that stormed her green-field eyes whenever I'd done this in the past, but it didn't come. Instead of open fields, her eyes closed up to strict forest walls, showing me nothing but resistance.

"That's not gonna work this time." Her whisper fanned my mouth, tasting as if sadness was sweetened fruit on perfect lips. It coaxed my own to the surface as she dragged her stare of evergreen around mine, slowly shaking her head.

"You'll just have to let me go."

Her strawberry sorrow dove beneath my flesh, setting off a chain reaction of heartbreak that was full body. The pain originated in my chest, rupturing like the first wave of an earthquake that ripped down my entire being, cracking bones, shifting expectations, obliterating all sense of peace.

I wondered if she could feel my magnitude ten break when her delicate fingers sunk into the meat of my arms just above my elbow as if she was trying to hold me together. She gripped me like we were both falling apart piece by piece, and if she let go, we'd crumble.

I laid my forehead to hers as she held on tight, closing my eyes to match hers.

TWENTY-EIGHT

"Stay with me," I whispered, not above the point of begging. Not even a little. "I just got you back."

"I'm not going far," she tried, fighting to get the words out.

"If it's not right here with me, it's too damn far."

Her forehead crinkled against mine, pulling my eyes open to witness the open break creasing every feature of her face.

She looked like a woman dying for air on dry land.

Against my head, she shook hers. "I can't breathe here, Dominic. It's *so* hard."

"And I can't breathe without you. I've tried too many times, and I always end up suffocating."

My little lightning was a quiet hum for so long, I'd have given a kidney to know what was going on up in that head of hers. I hated hearing that she felt she couldn't breathe here—around me, I presumed—but we could get past it.

I'd alter the fucking chemistry of oxygen if I had to just to help her stay with me.

If she blamed me for bringing Heather into her life, I'd spend the next fifty to sixty years proving how sorry I was. If she was scared of my anger taking advantage of her body again, I wouldn't touch her for as long as it took for her to trust me to be gentle.

Whatever I'd done, I could fix it. I could fix *her*.

Her broken pieces were mine to mend. All she had to do was let me.

Unfortunately the next time she spoke, she'd lost any waver to her fight.

"I have to go."

I gripped her tighter, her eyes popping open to find me as I reached the point where I was ready to drop to my knees for her.

"Talk to me," I rasped, desperation pushing the hard edge of my voice. "Kat, please talk to me."

She took her eyes between mine, and I prayed like a man who'd been devout all his life that she was considering. For a second, I *swore* I saw a slip of the barriers she'd erected since getting home. It was just a glimpse, a momentary falter where she forgot to be stubborn, and the Kat who was taken from me five weeks ago shined through.

She looked desperate, gasping for breath, gasping for help, gasping for *me*.

But a slip of vulnerability was all it was. It was only a second before she caught herself and snapped the walls back up, sealing them tighter than a steel trap.

"I'll text you when we get to Layla's."

She pulled out of my arms and grabbed her bags, nearly running out of my bedroom.

She left without even looking back.

TWENTY-NINE

KAT

"Are you sure you don't want to share the bed?"

"Lay, for the last time, yes. I'm sure. Not my first time kicking it on the floor."

"Lord, I almost forgot how stubborn you were." Her brown eyes rolled with a teasing tweak to her mouth as she laid back against her mattress. Agreeing with a mindless, "Mhm," I shifted around on her carpet floor and the pillows she'd given me to try and get comfortable.

Layla's parents only had one spare room, and I wasn't letting Charlotte be the one to wake up with a stiff spine at five years old.

Distractedly, I remembered her birthday was coming up next month.

Layla and I laid in silence for a while, but I knew it wouldn't last. She'd bombed me with questions as soon as Charlotte and I got here, and I'd shut her down.

My best friend wasn't one to stay shut down for long.

I wasn't tired, but I didn't want to talk either. In fact, if I never had to talk again, I think my mouth would be happy. It was so exhausted with even the thought of explaining my complicated feelings. My tongue didn't have the energy to move, hoping sleep found me instead so everything could just shut the fuck up for a moment.

Every thought and feeling I had was so loud now.

I never thought I'd miss the sadistic silence.

Rolling to my side, I thought about the last time I'd gotten a good sleep, which was the last night I spent at the brothel. I thought I was about to die, and I couldn't remember a better night's sleep.

How fucked up did that make me?

You also still had Blake that night.

Grumbling in the back of my throat, I furiously rubbed my hands up and down my face as yet another intrusive thought fucked with my head.

My thoughts about Blake were constant and overwhelming.

"You okay down there?"

"Yup," I replied curtly. "Peachy."

The mattress squeaked as Layla rolled herself over on it, popping her head over the side to look down at me. "You sure you don't want to talk about your dad?"

"Abso-fucking-lutely."

Remember how Blake used to say that?

Another sigh expelled through my nose as my eyelids slammed shut, wishing I could jump inside my head and strangle my brain. It just needed to stop. Fucking. Talking.

"Okay, so what about Dom?" Layla pressed. "Wanna open that can of worms tonight?"

"Not really."

"Well, we have to talk about *something* that's bothering you."

"Why?"

With only her lilac-tinted table lamp to light the room, the upset in her eyes seemed softer than it probably was. "Because I'm worried about you, ya freaking idiot."

Scoffing, I averted my gaze. "Well, don't be."

"Oh. Okay." My eyes slid back to watch her rearrange her face with sarcasm. "Any other batshit requests tonight, Sanders?"

I showed her the back of my eyes and how high my middle finger could go as I shifted around to lay on my stomach, hiding my peeking smile

TWENTY-NINE

against the pillow.

"Kat, *come on.*" Fingers that I half expected to be stretched with gamma ray green wound around my left arm and forced me back around to where my best friend was already pinning me with staunch focus. "Talk to me. What happened between you and Dominic?"

"Nothing *happened.*"

"Then why are you here and not with him?"

"Is that your subtle way of telling me to get out?"

"*Bitch.*"

"Ow!"

Rubbing where she'd flicked my forehead, I stared up at 'don't fuck with me' umber eyes. "Stop deflecting and being dramatic. I *know* you better than to fall for that. You're hurting, babe. Tell me why."

"I'm *fine,*" I pressed. Except this time, I didn't sound so confident.

In fact, I sounded like a liar.

Layla picked up on it too, resting her head on her folded arm above me, getting comfortable. "Now that that lie's outta the way, why don't you tell me why you're with me tonight instead of the guy who tried to tear apart the world to find you?"

Funny. You'd think hearing about how desperate Dominic was to find me would make my heart soar. Instead, my stomach ached to think what his life would be if he'd never been successful.

"It—" Words stopped, my tongue not wanting to cooperate. "It's just hard. Being around him is… hard," I admitted like a filthy secret. It tasted like one too.

"Like how?"

Inhaling a deep breath and staring at the ceiling, I started, "Like…" and immediately froze, words and air still stuck inside my head. My throat pinched to hold the air as I struggled to find how to describe the feeling.

"It feels like when you're swimming in the ocean and a wave takes you under. You know instinctively that the same wave will bring you back up to the surface, but there are those few seconds under water where you didn't have enough time to grab a breath or close your eyes, and every part of you stings with panic. Being around him now is like those few seconds on repeat."

"Damn." I doubt she'd expected me to be so vivid. "That's heavy."

"It *feels* heavy."

I hated it. So much. This guilt was the heaviest thing I'd ever tried to lift by myself. Every day that I'd been back, the weight of it bared down more and more whenever Dominic was in the same room or when Maya walked around looking so fucking sad.

"I know you're deathly afraid of the word, but you do still love him, right?"

I blinked up at her, trying to be too offended. "Yeah, of course."

I wasn't running away because I didn't love him. No, I'd retired that act in exchange for one *much* more fucked up.

"Then have you tried talking to him about it? Ryan always spouts about how important communication is, and even though I find it really fucking annoying sometimes, I know he's right."

Breathing out a sigh, I sat up on the floor to rest my elbows on my knees and my head in my hands. "I can't."

"Why not?"

"He's got enough baggage because of me. He doesn't need more of my problems."

"Kat." I blinked a look over to my best friend. "That man would hold your dirty panties all day long if you asked him to. Holding a bit of your baggage sort of seems like the thing those big shoulders were built for."

Sighing, I stole my focus back to the carpet. "I'm not putting my stupid feelings on him when he's knee-deep in grief as it is. He's been through too much."

Meeting me, loving me, losing me. Finding me, killing for me, inevitably regretting me.

The weight—the downpour—intensified.

"Um, I hate to state the obvious, but…" Layla pulled my attention again. "What about you?"

I almost fucking scoffed at the thought of me. "What about me?"

TWENTY-NINE

"What about what *you've* been through?" Before I could even finish rolling my eyes, she'd launched into one of her bulldozing monologues. "I know trauma isn't a contest, but baby girl if it was, you'd be winning. First your mom, then I get snatched, then you get snatched. You spend five weeks being trapped. They hurt me, so I *know* they hurt you too. They tried to auction you off like a freaking antique painting an old rich dude wanted to fuck. And all because the guy you fell in love with had a crazy mofo for a wife?"

"Yeah, and he killed his wife to save me," I snapped back. "And how the hell can I bring up how I'm feeling when it's a *direct* conversation back to Heather? How can I talk to him about her when he's in the middle of *grieving* her because of his choice to save me?"

That shut her right up.

Sinking my head back into my hands, I tried and failed to put a muzzle on the carousel of thoughts I'd been riding on lately.

Dominic would regret it.

I knew he would. It was just a matter of time before his good heart cracked.

Eventually, he'd see everything I took away from them when I had no fucking right.

A little girl's only mother. A wife he once loved. Thirteen years of memories they shared and any future ones too. Heather might have been a bitch, a liar, and a shitty wife, but she was still the only mom Maya would ever have, and I took that from her. It was inevitable for Dominic to resent me for taking that from his little girl.

"All I know is you deserve someone to talk to about it all," Layla said. "Even if it's not him."

Subtlety was never her strong suit. Or mine.

"I don't need to talk. I need to sleep until I don't feel like this anymore."

"Well, since I'm not putting you into a coma anytime soon, how about you talk to the only other person who actually has *been* where you were?" Her pointed tone lifted my chin to where she waited for me with creased brows and a serious look. "I know your guard is miles high right now, but if you need someone to understand even a tenth of what you went through, you're looking at her. Heather got me too."

Cue another tidal wave of piercing guilt. "You never should have been involved in this, Lay. I—"

"If you say you're sorry one more time, I'll flick you again."

My apology crashed into an exhale, blowing soft air on my knees as I hung my head between them. I conceded with a nod I hoped she saw but didn't look to check.

"So is there anything you wanna talk about from when you were there?" she pressed.

Blake. Blake. So much about Blake.

He was everywhere inside my head, on the tip of my tongue at any given moment of the day, but I never knew what to say or to who. Dominic was a nonstarter. Meredith had tried to get me to open up, but she wouldn't understand. Plus, in that same vein of thought, who *would* understand what I had to say about Blake?

No one knew him. No one knew us or how we were or what we were.

Star-crossed.

I barely understood it myself, but my chest felt *bruised* by how many words about Blake I'd kept locked up over the last three days. They slammed around, begging to be heard, begging to feel his name on my tongue to trick me into believing for half a second he was still alive.

It was chaos in there, memories of black flaming eyes and blood-smeared hands whirling around in tandem with my lightning as it struck out in grief, struck out in rage, struck out in cries for the loss of lightning in Blake's veins just like mine.

"I met someone while I was there."

The rushed confession dragged a swell equal parts guilt and relief to the surface. It crashed over me, blood tingling in a way that reminded me of the heroin, letting me know that even bringing him up was providing me a small high.

Without sounding surprised, Layla confirmed, "Blake?"

His name coming from her shocked my lips apart, curving my attention

TWENTY-NINE

right up.

"How did you know?"

"I was there when he called Dominic. He gave me food. He gave you your freedom. I kind of suspected there might be more there."

There wasn't a decisive line she was bordering on as she confessed her suspicions about Blake. Her expression was cucumber cool too. I undoubtedly couldn't say the same for myself as I gave her my full attention for the first time tonight as I *begged* for scraps of him.

"Did you talk to him?"

"I talked, he didn't." That sounded about right. My heart *sizzled*. "I only caught him the one time dropping off an orange when I assumed he wasn't supposed to, but when I tried to talk to him, he left without a word."

All her story did was remind me of our first meeting when I found him fixing the lock on my door. I'd also caught him when he hadn't been expecting me to. Except when I ran my mouth at him, he ran his right back. There only lasted mere seconds of our existence together where he tried to ignore me before his lightning recognized mine, and we were fucked.

"Did he bring more than *fruit* to your room like he brought me?" Layla sat up, crossing her legs on the bed as she waited for me with dull amusement.

"He brought me whatever I wanted." Midnight memories crept along the edge of my mind. "Even a cupcake."

"Damn." The curious gleam to her gaze was still frustratingly unclear. "I see you got the five-star detainee treatment."

I debated in silence for all of five seconds before deciding that talking about him felt way too damn good to stop now, no matter what she thought.

"I stayed in his room."

"*Wait*, like the whole time?"

I nodded, remembering James Dean and Marlon Brando on his walls. "Most of it."

"In the same bed?" Shock ripped the mask her suspicion had been wearing right off.

"Most of it."

"*Why?*"

"At first, safety. Then, because I wanted to."

"I'm sorry, you *wanted* to sleep in the same bed as someone who helped keep you hostage?"

"He never *wanted* to keep me hostage," I snapped, biting my temper between sharpening teeth. "He wasn't there because he wanted to be either. Heather's parents trapped him when he was a teenager, and they would've killed him if he ever tried to leave. Plus, he was helping me find a way to escape since my first *week* there. Keeping me hostage was the last fucking thing he did."

Layla threw her hands up in defense, her already huge eyes enlarging. "Okay. I get it."

Her and I blinked at each other without saying a word.

I could feel how hot my chest had gotten in the last ten seconds, molten lightning sitting right up against its surface. I couldn't tell whether the judgment in her voice had been for me or Blake, but I didn't fucking care.

No one said a bad word about him. Not a single goddamn nasty letter.

No one knew him like I did which meant no one could talk about him like I could. He was mine to protect in death, just how I was his to protect when he was alive.

"He means a lot to you," she spoke carefully.

I held a profound beat before correcting. "Meant."

Her thickly shaped brows drew together. "Why past tense?"

"Because he is." My heart numbed preemptively before I said it. "He died."

"Oh, shit. How?"

"Made a dumb decision that got himself killed."

Then came a question I shouldn't have been at all surprised by.

I still was.

"Did you sleep with him?" My pulse stuttered in my neck as she fixed her inquisitive eyes on mine. "And please don't yell at me again for asking. You slept in the same bed as him for a month. I have to ask."

For a moment after my heartbeat dwindled back down, I considered telling her about the kiss. Both of them. But something stopped me from

TWENTY-NINE

saying it out loud, and it wasn't guilt because my lips had been unfaithful or worry for how she'd react.

It was an ownership I felt over Blake now that he was gone.

He was mine and only mine to share if I wanted, and I *didn't* want to. I had only segmented days of memories to remember him by, and I didn't want to give a single piece of him away.

What happened between Blake and I was ours and no one else's.

"No," I answered after probably too long. "He knew I was in love with Dominic."

Maybe Layla had a career in detectiving herself, because she heard exactly what I didn't say.

"So he wanted to sleep with you." A statement. Not a question.

"It didn't matter if he did or not." Which he did, though he'd only come close to implying it that once. "Sex was never on the table for us."

"What *was* on the table?"

I sucked my teeth, quickly correcting her with a disapproving glance. "Not like that. For being in a brothel, we didn't really talk about sex much."

"What did you two talk about?"

A sigh gathered in my lungs, and for a moment, I wished they were filled with tangy smoke.

"Everything else."

Conversations between Blake and I were like a winding creek with no dead ends. We could flow for hours, bending topics, dipping off of ledges and discovering things about the other we never knew, and never found a natural stop. There just wasn't one.

We could have talked until our voices ran dry.

Sex was really the only topic we rarely breached because we were both smart enough not to. Well, most days. One time, I'd been a little stupid and asked him how he lost his virginity and told him I lost mine in a pick-up truck. He'd lost his in a BMW outside a bar with an older woman he'd just met when he was seventeen and drunk.

A few times, he'd been a little careless with his morning wood and neglected to hide it from me as he got up. It would tent the front of his sweats and remind me how big he was.

I honestly think he wanted to catch me looking so he had something to beat off to in the shower.

Which he did. I knew he did.

Lust wasn't what burned between us, but it was there if you'd taken down our barriers. Blake and I were enigmatic together and the sex would have been inspired. There was never a chance of it happening though, so talking about it would have been pouring gasoline on a fire that had nowhere else to spread.

"Kat, I know you said you didn't fuck him, but you two do *not* sound like just friends either."

"We weren't just friends," I agreed shamelessly because *fuck* disrespecting Blake's memory by pretending we were something so simple. "We were…" *Star-crossed.* "Unique."

"Unique like you're in love with him unique?" she challenged.

"Unique like I've never even considered believing in reincarnation, but now I'd bet my *life* that I've known him before."

Now I had her attention, her eyes stretching wide with surprise. My conviction built alongside the passion in my words.

"I didn't have to *try* to understand him. He was just—" I knocked my knuckles that'd closed to a fist against my sternum where I felt his presence the most. "*There.* Like he'd always been there, and I'd just never realized it until I met him. Then we did meet, and it was like… *breathing*," I exhaled audibly, lost to my thoughts of him.

"So, if I'm understanding all of this…" *Good luck. I'm still trying to figure it out.* "You feel like you're drowning around Dominic but like you could breathe around Blake?"

No, *being* with him was like breathing, but I wouldn't correct her.

"Because Blake was fucked up like me. He was messy and emotional and made me feel like I wasn't—" The purple tinted room blacked out as I scrubbed my hands over my face, fighting out the words. "He made me feel like I wasn't spinning out at all fucking hours of the day because he was spiraling right alongside me. It was like if one pissed off gust of wind found

TWENTY-NINE

another and they merged into a tornado that would obliterate everything it touched, but at least the winds weren't lonely anymore."

"But babe, you know that's not what you need, right?" The stable line her tone rode along made my *un*stable head drop back into my hands and my unstable thoughts ask me if I should jump through her window. "That has red flags written all over it."

That time, I kept my crazy mouth shut.

She was right, and I knew she was right. I just hated her for it.

I wasn't so fucked in the head to think that any part of Blake and I was healthy. We survived off of each other like we were equal parts parasite and host. We snacked through our conversations and feasted through stolen touches, and I was sure any therapist with half a brain could have taken one look at us and drawn a big red 'danger' line around us both.

The danger of us wasn't in question. We knew, and it didn't matter. It wasn't enough.

We collided together so hard, it shattered us both, but we couldn't stop. Even feelings that were inherently *good* hurt us when we were together. Happiness reminded us we shouldn't be because we were both trapped and doomed. Affection scolded us for blossoming when it shouldn't have been allowed. Love broke both of our hearts and then stopped his cold.

Blake loved me so much it got him killed.

Dominic loved me so much it tainted his pure heart.

Those two men had almost nothing else in common, but they did share at least one fatal flaw.

Loving me.

"He saved me," I mumbled into my hands.

"I know. He got you out of that hell, but—"

"No." She shut up as my serrated voice cut her off. I didn't look up though. Couldn't. "He *died* saving me."

All curled up on her floor, shivers wracked my body as I tasted the horrible words. Burnt ash and copper blood smeared my taste buds, both of my hands sliding down to cover my mouth to keep it from speaking them again.

Shivers turned to rocking back and forth on her floor, and the next thing I knew, body heat was hugging my side and arms were curling around my off-kilter body. Normally, Layla knew better than to comfort me when I was losing it, but we both knew I wasn't just losing it.

I'd fucking lost it.

My chin shook against my knuckles as I turned them out to press against my lips, the sting of heartache gouging up my windpipe. "He took the bullets that were meant for me." My voice cracked, and Layla held me tighter. "He took them. He grabbed me and hugged me while bullets cut through *his* body instead of mine."

"Babe," Layla blew out against my shoulder where she laid her head. "I had no idea."

Sucking back a ragged breath, the heartache kept pouring out.

"I held him in my lap and he died, and he told me it was worth it. He *died* and told me my life was worth his, and I can't fucking see how that's true."

Wetness splashed my cheeks as I pinched my eyes shut, trying to stop the ruthless images I didn't want to face from flooding through. But it was too late. I saw Blake's magnetic eyes that told me before his lips did that something wasn't right. I saw blood, vibrant and foreboding. Everywhere. All over him. All over me. Our twinned hands covered in it. I saw his pain. His peace. His love for me that painted the last fading color through his eyes.

Moonlight. His love was the color of moonlight.

"You can't blame yourself for that." Couldn't I? "You didn't force him to take those bullets for you."

Cutting my stare to hers, I asked, "Then who do I blame? I have to blame *someone*."

"Fucking blame Heather. She started all of this."

"And I'm the reason she's dead. And her mom and Blake and another guy. If I'm weighing the scales," *And trust me I am,* "one dying instead of four makes a lot more sense."

The weight of her head left my shoulders, twisting my neck to find her staring at me dead on.

TWENTY-NINE

"Kat, you dying makes *no* sense, and I need you to believe that."

A hiccup strangled in my throat as I looked at my best friend, the burn of tears washing my eyes.

"Living doesn't make much sense either."

THIRTY

KAT

The next morning, Layla's mom made a feast for breakfast big enough to feed an entire football team. A thank you, I was told, for saving her daughter's life.

You know, after I put it in jeopardy in the first place.

Charlotte scooped a bite two sizes too big of blueberry pancakes in her mouth, lips already stained blue and cheeks stuffed to the max. Layla helped her father with dishes in the kitchen.

The day was bright and new, and I hated it for being so sunny when I felt so shitty. Sunbeams streamed in through the kitchen window, illuminating tiny dust particles floating in the air that I wondered if I could choke on. The small bowl of fruit sitting in front of me whispered it could do the trick, but death by cantaloupe wasn't exactly dignified.

Not really hungry, I grabbed my still half-full bowl of fruit and stood from the kitchen table. Layla was making a face at her phone when I reached the sink and set my bowl at the bottom of it.

"What's wrong?"

Still scrutinizing her phone in her hand, she shook her head. "You're not gonna like it."

"What am I not gonna like?"

THIRTY

She squished her mouth to the side, flickering her stare up to mine. "Ryan's on his way over."

"So?"

"And he's bringing Dominic with him."

Well, fuck.

My, *'well, fuck'* must have been written on my face because Layla quickly jumped in.

"He just wants to talk to you."

"Then why can't he just call me?" I whined like a baby, crossing my arms over my chest.

"Because he's your boyfriend and he wants to see you." Before I could argue, she sliced me off with a wagging finger, shaking her head and spinning me towards her room. "Go clean up and put a bra on. You have less than five minutes until they're here."

"What?!"

Layla shrugged and pushed me on my way. "Ryan didn't want to give you too much notice in case you split."

Rolling my eyes, I tossed behind me, "Glad to hear he has faith."

What was probably closer to ten minutes later, I came back down the hall with my hair brushed, bra on, and wearing a frown.

I didn't want to do this.

I said I needed *space*. Maybe I'd buy Dominic a dictionary and throw it at his head since he clearly didn't know the meaning of the word.

I spotted Ryan and Layla at the mouth of the hallway, talking in hushed tones. I'd bet my left tit they were talking about me. They both swept their focus my way as I entered their awkward atmosphere.

The air was tight, and I wasn't in any type of mood for bullshit small talk.

"Where is he?"

Ryan nodded his head towards the front door. "He's waiting outside."

A clusterfuck of nerves scurried into place in my gut, not wanting to miss the chance to make me feel like I was going to puke. *Cool.*

"Okay," I sighed on a big breath. "Well. I'll be back."

Just before I picked up my leaden feet to go, Ryan stopped me with an imploring request.

"Just... cut him some slack, okay? He's going through a lot right now."

I sunk my teeth into my tongue to keep from snapping at him. Turned out, I didn't have to because Layla did it first, whacking his chest.

"And you think she isn't?" she accused, glare a daggered point of defense on my behalf. Before the happy couple could launch into a fight triggered by me, I left them behind and didn't stop until I was out the front door.

The breeze hit my face, smelling of freshly cut grass and suburbia. Layla and her parents lived in a quaint little neighborhood, the kind with white picket fences and wood slat swings outside hanging on the enormous oaks.

That's where Dominic was now, leaning against his car under the shaded grace of a massive tree. He pushed off the side when I emerged, stepping out into the sun that serviced his good looks and the bulge of his biceps in a golden spotlight.

My breath caught in a twist of awe and dread. His god-like beauty would *always* take me by surprise. It was his presence that fucking terrified me.

I shuffled down the Montez's driveway, using the bright sky as a distraction. The turquoise bed with pillows of white was just as annoyingly cheery as it looked through the kitchen window.

Save for one muddied cloud poking through the clean sky that I clung to the whole walk down the driveway until I made it right in front of Dominic.

He was the first to speak.

"Did you sleep well last night?"

He sounded genuine as I chewed the inside of my cheek, not bothering to lie.

"Nope. You?"

His silver stare took on a shine that looked rather pleased. Just a little.

"Not really."

"I'm sorry." I aimed my apology at the purple fuzzy socks I'd borrowed from Layla. Maybe I should have put on shoes before coming out. A dead leaf crunched beneath my toes as I rolled them against the asphalt in

THIRTY

distraction.

"You don't have to be sorry."

But it *was* my fault.

Or else he would have said it wasn't instead of just telling me not to be sorry.

So I just nodded and tucked my bottom lip between my teeth, crushing another expired leaf beneath my feet to eat away at the blooming silence.

It was the kind of painful silence that dug itself underneath your bones and burrowed deep enough into the marrow so that each breath you took in the silence felt like a splinter stabbing through your entire body.

That brand of silence was as agonizing as it was maddening.

I was milliseconds away from bolting back inside before Dominic spoke up.

"Do you think you and Charlotte will be staying here another night?"

Slicing my teeth back and forth against my lip, I dug my focus into the ground while I nodded. It wasn't what he wanted to hear, but I didn't have to look up at him to know that.

"Maya really missed Charlotte at bedtime. She asked me if we could Facetime with you and her last night, but I said no. Maybe we could do it tonight before the girls go to bed?"

Fuck, *why* did this sound like a divorced couple negotiating time with the kids? I dug my purple fuzz covered toes deeper into the ground.

"Yeah, that would be fine. I'm sure Bugs would like that."

He thanked me like I was doing him some kind of a favor, and then… more silence. This spell of it didn't last nearly as long, thank fuck, before Dominic demolished it with a blatant sigh.

"Kat, this is ridiculous."

I glanced up. "Which part?"

"You and me acting like strangers when we're the furthest thing from it."

I'd almost forgotten how unapologetically certain Dominic was when he spoke about us. And how it rattled my offbeat heart. There wasn't a crack to be found and bent in his steely eyes as he made his claim about us. There was only the familiarity that proved he was right.

He knew me. He knew every rotted part of me.

It's why he could look at me like I was wilting right before his eyes.

"You were in my bed two nights ago, and now I don't even know what to say to you that won't be a trigger because you won't talk to me," he pressed. "I don't know whether I can kiss you or touch you without you pulling away."

The vehemence driving behind his words pushed me back like a hand on my shoulder, completely contrasting my mumble. "You can touch me."

Dominic clocked the step I moved back with stiff eyes.

"Can I?"

Instead of being able to form the single syllable to tell him 'yes', I pushed back. "Why wouldn't you be able to?"

"Because you're so far away, Kat." Desperation scratched against his formidable voice and carved canyon deep pits in his eyes. "You have been ever since that night in the hotel—"

His words hit, and my eyes slammed shut. "Oh my god, *please* don't bring up the hotel again. *Please*." My hands balled into fists, hot air filling my head. "I can't have the same argument again, Dominic. I can't."

"Well, I'm sorry, but that was the last time you didn't feel like you were miles away standing right next to me. That was the last time, and I *hurt* you."

Irritation jabbed at my sides and popped my voice out harsher than intended.

"You *barely* hurt me."

Proving he was always the calm to my crazy, Dominic's reply was honeyed and soft.

"Barely is too much."

Suddenly, a memory hit me hard and blindingly fast, swallowing me up in a gaping black hole.

"I barely cut myself," I observed.

Blake slid his hands over the back of mine, rolling my fingers closed beneath his. His fists curled warmth and strength around mine, my hands dwarfed beneath

THIRTY

his that I couldn't help but note were a couple shades tanner.

Heavy silence sealed us together, both he and I staring at his hands covering mine. The small but jagged cut I'd made on my left wrist bored back at us, an unearthing of blood barely visible beneath. Blake took a thumb and brushed it across my pathetic excuse for a gash, my speck of red smearing to a soft pink beneath his touch.

The weight of his chin rested on my shoulder. "Barely is too much."

When the memory spit me out, I came to by the welcoming bolts of excruciating panic shooting through my arms, legs, stomach, *everything*. Anxiety fried me from the inside out, every single inch of skin laden with fire-hot pin-pricks that jabbed bone deep.

A whimper fell into my hands as I dropped my face into them, digging my fingers into my eye sockets like I could claw out grieving images of his face.

Blake was everywhere in my head. *Everywhere*. Smiling, laughing, frowning, bleeding, dying.

"Kat, what's wrong?" Dominic's concerned voice stuck out in the middle of my mental collapse.

"Nothing. I just—" *Stop thinking about him. Stop picturing him. Stop. Stop. Stop.* "I just need a second."

"What happened just now?"

"Nothing. I'm fine." *I am so not fine.*

Dominic's displeasure was audible in the collective silence he let linger between us. I imagined him folding his arms across his wide chest and glowering down at me in that intense way he often did.

"How long are you going to keep telling yourself that when you're obviously not? You couldn't be. You're a strong woman, Kat, but you're not invincible."

"I'm not saying I'm invincible. I'm saying I'm *fine*," I grit through gnashed teeth. To prove it, I released my head from my hands and pinned him with a glare straight on.

He wasn't impressed.

"Then why won't you tell me what happened to you while you were gone?" Thunderous eyes switched fast between mine. "Why won't you *talk* to me?"

"Because it's not exactly something I want to relive, and I would think that's pretty fucking understandable," I snapped, feeling my flesh heat and my temper loosen.

"But it's *me*." Dominic pushed his words harder, the distress in his stare brightening. "I could help if you just talked to me. About any of it. I'll take anything at this point."

"Dominic, you can't fix this!" The leaves above us *snapped* in the whip of wind that tore through at the exact same time as my explosion. I fucking loved when the elements felt pissy like I did. "I know you want to, and I know your hero complex is probably dying for me to break down so you can make it all better, but you *can't* make this better. You can't change what happened to me or what's happened to you or any of it. It's just fucking *broken*."

His golden skin paled a shade in the sunlight. "It's not broken—"

"*I'm* broken!" I confessed with force so he'd fucking get it. *I* was the thing that wasn't right. *I* was diseased and infectious to everyone who dared to risk their lives and love me.

Maybe Dominic really was my cure, but I wasn't his. Not by a freaking longshot. I poisoned his life and made him sick in the head, messing with his morals and rewiring his good and pure heart.

Blake might have been my cancer, and I just might have been Dominic's.

My cure stood above me and traced his starlight gaze from my forehead to my chin, sadness draining down his face beneath his skin, sinking his perfect mouth into a severe frown. The dawn of just how fucked up I'd become was painful to watch rise in his eyes. The more he looked at me like I was something to save, the harder it got to hold the heat I could feel sitting in my stare.

It was shaking, and so was I.

When I couldn't withstand the brunt of Dominic's pity any longer, I turned my face out, catching a glimpse of that blackened cloud heading

THIRTY

our way.

The rest of the sky paled as it neared, no longer vibrant or sparkling.

Out of my peripherals, I saw him drift closer, and I let him.

"What happened to you...?" Dominic's whisper was a plea, asking questions he didn't want the answers to. "I go a little madder every minute that passes that I don't know if someone hurt you when I wasn't there to stop them."

You know what would have been cool?

If I could have told him there wasn't anything to go mad about. If I could have taken his agony and banished it by reassuring him that he didn't have anything to fear. It would have been so fucking cool to be able to soothe this man just *once* today.

Maybe I should have just lied to him instead.

"You don't want to know, Dominic." He parted his lips to disagree, but I cut him off with a look of warning. "You might think you do, but I promise you that you don't."

And that was as much as I'd ever tell him about it. He didn't need to know about Mr. Smith and how he probably gave me a concussion after slapping me around so much. He didn't need to know about the devil from the auction who'd put his fingers inside of me while I screamed until blood poured down my throat.

Dominic didn't need any more drops of poison in his life. All he needed to do was focus on healing from the toxins I'd already fed into his system the moment he decided to love me.

When his stoney eyes crumbled to devastated dust, I knew I should have lied instead.

"Someone hurt you." His usually silky voice was a bed of rocks and broken glass.

"A lot of people hurt me, but I got out. Not unscratched, but I got out a lot better than I should have."

"Kat—"

"And you can't reverse it," I cut him and whatever chivalrous thing he was about to say off. "So what good would it do to tell you what happened to me when all that should matter is what *didn't*?"

Dominic was a man built of brawn, devotion, and protection. His blood ran with it all. His muscles were strapped with the promise to defend and shelter. He was bar-none the strongest man I would ever know.

And I was positive he wasn't strong enough to know this.

If he knew what was happening to me at the auction while he was somewhere in the very same building, it would break his sturdy back in ways I was afraid he'd never stand up from again. Dominic always wanted to be the hero, and I always wanted him to feel like he was.

I'd already taken so much from him.

I refused to steal his pride too.

Dominic inhaled a slow, deep breath, letting me see how he meticulously tempered down the violent frostbite that iced his gray eyes and threatened to paralyze the hands that dared to touch me. The wrath hardening his dangerously beautiful face thawed just enough to let his mouth move again.

"At the brothel, you said Blake stopped anything too bad from happening to you. Correct?"

My heart startled, tripping over Blake's name on Dominic's voice.

It didn't sound right at all, like my favorite song had gone out of tune. I hadn't been expecting him to bring up Blake, which was maybe stupid in hindsight, but I wasn't exactly thinking straight or even in zig-zags nowadays.

My head was a warzone, grenades going off left and right without rhyme or reason. One insane thought would strike and another would retaliate, the inside of my skull feeling like one giant festering wound.

There wasn't any deeper wound than Blake's and talking about him with Dominic had every muscle in my body at the ready to strike out in defense.

Carefully, I nodded. "He did."

Relief was nothing more than a strangled gasp in his stare, the emotion competing for air beneath the heavy weight of whatever else Dominic was thinking. The singular storm cloud above us seemed to match the color of his irises as they refocused on me.

He stared a good long while before actually saying anything.

THIRTY

"I'm glad he was there to protect you."

Dominic Reed really was the most handsome liar there had ever been.

I tried not to scoff and roll my eyes. I accomplished a solid 50%.

Dominic jumped right on top of the other 50%. "Why are you rolling your eyes?"

Sighing, I decided I was way too fucking exhausted to have this conversation. All I wanted was to go back inside and sleep until this was all over. Or maybe never wake up.

Never waking up sounded pretty fucking dope right about now.

"Dominic, let's just not."

"No. I'd like to know why you rolled your eyes when I said I was glad he was there to protect you," he bullishly fought.

"Because you're clearly lying!" I almost laughed even when it wasn't even a little funny. "It's written all over your face, Dominic. You don't like the fact that someone other than you saved me from the really bad shit. Which is fine. You're allowed to feel like that. I'm not saying you can't. I'm saying don't lie about being grateful to him. *Be* grateful."

My pointed demand crystalized the ice around his eyes so their glint was *extra* piercing.

"I *am*."

It was possible my bullshit meter was still hitting all-time highs in my expression because Dominic dropped his face closer to mine and the pitch of his voice.

"I am. More grateful than I could ever express. But you're also right. I don't like that you had to rely on someone else to protect you. That's my job, and I think it's rather understandable for your boyfriend to want to be the one saving you instead of some criminal you befriended."

Spontaneous lightning struck a *blinding* fury behind my eyes, setting a vicious wildfire in my blood that came pouring out of my pissed off mouth. "Don't *ever* talk about him like that, or I will walk away from you right now. I fucking swear it."

Some criminal.

Some criminal?

Dominic almost—*almost*—dared to look surprised as I lost my goddamn mind over Blake. Which either meant he had the *bliss* of forgetting who was standing here right now and who was dead in Atlanta with the bullets meant for me buried inside their body, or he didn't see how it mattered to me.

"Fine. I'm sorry, okay?" He watched me for an acceptance that my lightning was still too offended on Blake's behalf to give. My rage was pulsing in my veins, radiating out waves of 'don't fuck with me' in every direction. Dominic had to have felt the waves licking up against his skin as he sighed and sent a hand back through his thick hair.

"Kat." Exhaustion dripped from his husky voice. "I don't want to argue with you. That's not why I came here."

"So why did you come?" I bristled back.

He gave a small shrug, finding me on the other end of his weary gaze.

"I just wanted to see you."

And just like that, I was the asshole.

"I miss you." He pressed on, taking a risk by stepping closer. "I've missed you for five weeks, and I'm still missing you. You're back, and I can finally see you whenever I want, and I *want* to see you. Every day. Every minute. I want you, but you're running from me just like you used to."

The balls of my feet turned electric, trying to convince me to do exactly as he accused me of. I curled my toes into the ground.

"It's not the same," I breathed my pathetic argument.

And Dominic being the hopeful man he was brightened from every angle like he'd swallowed the sun and that's why it'd disappeared from the sky. All because I replied with something other than a diversion. He erased another step between us.

"Then what is it? What's different?"

Everything.

I can't talk to you. I can't confess to you. You can't make everything okay.

"I'm not afraid of my feelings for you like I was back then."

I was fucking *terrified* of the ones he had for me and what other horrible things they'd make him do.

THIRTY

"That's good." He nodded me on, like he was encouraging me to love him. "It doesn't bring me any closer to understanding why you left though. I've looked at it from every angle I can, Kat, and if it's not because of your dad or the night in the hotel, then I can't make sense of what I've done to make you want space from me."

"It's nothing you've *done*," I pressed, feeling my poor mind fraying its edges. It was peeling down the sides of my skull, falling apart, losing grounding.

"Then why don't you want to be around me? I'm hurting. You're hurting. Why can't we make each other feel better?"

"Because have you ever considered that grief isn't *linear*? That what makes you feel better isn't what makes me feel better?" I heard myself shouting, not knowing where the words were coming from that seemed to pour from my soul like they were feeding something starved. "Grief isn't a glove everyone wears the same way. It doesn't fit me the same way it fits you. Grief attacks everyone differently which means the cure isn't universal. It's personal, and you can't get mad because I don't heal like you heal. You just have to be patient."

Or give me up completely.

Give me up.

Please just give up on me.

"Can I ask what it is you're grieving so hard?" His tone wasn't accusatory, but an evenly brushed thing of sullen acceptance. He knew who the thickest layer of my grief belonged to because he was in the room when I cried myself insane over his body.

He just didn't want to ask with words why I was so broken up about Blake.

"Death." I'd never noticed until the word slipped off my tongue how much it felt like a hiss to say. "I'm grieving death, Dominic."

We stared at each other long and hard, that solitary black cloud sitting right above our heads now. Dominic turned back around to his car and yanked open the door, moving on before either of us could do anymore damage to our fragile as fuck relationship.

"I brought a few things back from the house in Atlanta that you might want to look through."

He produced a medium-sized cardboard box that had 'official police shit' stamped all over it. Not *literally*, but it definitely didn't look like a box Dominic should have in the back of his car.

"No one knows Archie let me take these things before they were logged into evidence." *Ah.* "He only grabbed what wasn't important to the case."

The box gave a hefty *thunk* as Dominic set it on the hood of his car, stepping aside to let me poke around. I went over to it, and he stood back as I rummaged through the items, quietly watching as I pulled out a couple ratty paperback books whose fronts were so worn, I couldn't make out the titles. I turned their soft skin over in my hands before setting them down on the hood.

Diving back into the box, my fingers cusped something smooth and latched on.

Digging it out of the mess, I pulled out an ashtray.

I stopped and blinked at it, a funny feeling stirring in my stomach.

Tingles spread through the pads of my fingers that touched the used ashtray all the way up my arm and sprinkled inside my chest. My thumb brushed a stroke over the side of it, breathing growing a little heavier.

Jerking my attention back to the box, I reached back inside and fished out another book.

This one was a hardcover, and it almost slipped between my tingling fingers as I gasped out loud.

A Tale of Two Cities.

"This is his," I breathed in awe, grief burning in the tip of my nose.

"I think most of it is," Dominic spoke behind me. "I asked Archie to give me whatever was his or Heather's from the house, but she didn't have much there, so it's mostly his belongings."

"Oh my god."

Dropping the book he'd read me to sleep with on so many nights, I dove with frantic hands down deep into the box, looking for one thing and one thing of his only.

THIRTY

My lashes were batting away tears that were already trying to fall and paint what was left of him in selfish mourning. Shards of my heart ripped up my windpipe as my breathing sharpened and thinned with desperation. I pushed past his John Keats and his unopened packs of cigarettes, his phone charger and his favorite classic movies, scavenging for anything that resembled black pleather.

And at the very bottom of the box, there it sat.

"Oh my god…" I whimpered again, vocal cords tied tight.

As if it was delicate as dust and could blow away with the wind, my fingers wrapped around the black binding and picked it up. I feathered the tips of my fingers over the front, tracing the face of the notebook like I'd done to him once or twice when he was alive.

His notebook.

I had *his* notebook.

I had his words, his memories, his poetic heart, his blackened soul, all bared on the pages inside. If I didn't want to see the poem about a rose and her lonely moon that sat at the back of this book so badly, I'd have hugged the thing to my chest and never let go.

But my fingers were anxious for his words, opening the cover and flipping all the way to the back. Something rectangular and grainy in color stopped me, bookmarked on the first page of my poem.

Air kicked out of my lungs, the mismanaged organ in my chest *screaming*.

My body went into some type of collapse before I could even touch it, eyes closing shut and knees buckling so hard they almost felt the scrape of the ground. I couldn't touch it. I couldn't even bring my fingers anywhere near the old-fashioned edges of the picture.

Our picture.

I'd forgotten all about it.

Water leaked down the sides of my face as I tipped my head back to the sky, crying up at the black cloud that eclipsed the sun. It'd come out of nowhere and consumed us from overhead, encouraging the rain splashing down my cheeks while the thunder stood and watched.

With a choked cry, I picked up the polaroid picture of us. Blake's notebook got wrapped up in my arm as I folded it into my chest, hugging it hard and giving all of my tears over to our photo.

My cheeks were rosy in it and my smile was beaming, a little too white to be natural as I remembered how fucking bright the flash was. The side of my face was pressed right up against his as I cheesed it up for the lens.

You'd never know I was a victim looking at this.

You'd have no idea Blake or I were both victims. Or that we were made of darkness.

We didn't look it in this picture. We just looked happy.

I remembered what I told him right before the blinding flash went off to capture this snapshot of us. I'd said, *'find your happiness'* because I wanted him to smile for the picture.

And he was.

He was also looking right at me.

The gentle curve to his mouth wasn't aimed at the camera nor was the pleasant sting of his gaze. Even in two-dimension, his black flames sizzled the side of my face where he was pointing them in the photo.

I told him to find his happiness, and he found me.

A sob crashed through my chest, breaking into the air as I clutched the photo that he was meant to have. I *gave* it to him to remember me when I was gone. It wasn't supposed to be the other way around. This was *his*. All of this was his, not mine.

This picture. This notebook. This *life*.

"When he called me, I could hear it in his voice." Dominic's background voice floated over my shoulder, spilling more crazy tears and spiraling me out of my head. "If I didn't already know it by how he looked at you in that room, I'd know it by how he's looking at you in that picture."

There were only my sharp sniffles and wet cries to fill the silence before Dominic asked me the question I was positive he'd been asking himself since back in Atlanta.

"He loved you, didn't he?"

Licking salty tears from my lips, I blinked until Blake was more than a blur of glossy black in the picture. My stare roved all over his face,

THIRTY

remembering how magnificently awe-struck I was when I first realized how beautiful he was.

I hadn't been able to see it at first, then I couldn't *not* see it.

His angelic bone structure. That tiny bump to his nose. Those eyes of goddamn magnets.

He was stunning, and I cried all that much harder because of the beauty I killed.

I clutched his notebook of poems, clinging to it and wishing it was him instead. What was so fucked up about this was how *badly* I needed Blake to be the one to help me through his death. I wanted him to squeeze me in his arms and bury me beneath his sweet smoke and tell me he was okay.

I needed to hear it from his lips that he was okay, and I could be okay too.

Without him, I was still that gust of wind I told Layla about, but I didn't have a partner to spin with. I was just spiraling and spiraling and going fucking nowhere.

When I didn't answer Dominic's question about Blake's love, he asked me one way worse.

"You said something to him that day in the bedroom. It was right after Heather pulled her gun out. He told her he'd been ready to die for a long time, and you whispered something to him. What was it?"

A heavy rale shook in my lungs as I sucked down enough air to hold in and not suffocate. My lips rolled together as I gave a watery blink up at the dark cloud, remembering that moment exactly.

The idea that Blake wanted to die wasn't new to me.

The idea that it could happen, however, was.

For as much as I thought about death while I was there and planned my own, I'd never once thought about Blake's. I'd never considered that he had the ability to die just as much as I did.

When Heather pointed a gun between his eyes that day, the realization hit bullet-fast. In one split second, I realized he was human like me, he could die like me, and how unfathomable a reality without him was.

In the same light-bulb moment I realized he could die, I also realized I couldn't live without him.

"The rose can't live without the moon. She'll die in the darkness," I whispered, maybe not even loud enough for Dominic to hear.

He didn't say anything if he did.

Gingerly, I tucked the polaroid picture back inside the pages of Blake's notebook. "Thank you for this…"

I didn't have anything of his before. Now I had everything.

I had his entire life. In a cardboard box.

Walking back over to his car, I set Blake's notebook on top of the pile and picked up the box. Dominic watched me, mouth thinned and pressed tight.

A long stretch of quiet strung between us before he finally spoke.

"Are you supposed to be the rose?"

At some point, I had to dehydrate myself from tears, right? It seemed impossible as more burned all of my senses, eyes falling shut to keep them in.

"Yeah," I sniffled. "Yeah, I am."

"And you think you'll die in darkness now that he's gone?"

I found Dominic on the other end of a watery smile that was anything but happy, shrugging one shoulder.

"I already am."

THIRTY-ONE

DOM

Good morning. Did you sleep better last night?

I pressed send and set my phone down, sighing away the clench of dread already gripping my gut.

It'd been two days since I'd seen her.

When I went over with Ryan to Layla's two days ago, I'd honestly been expecting to come home with Kat back in my arms and things patched up.

Now I was in an even deeper hell than before.

My phone buzzed in the palm of my hand.

Kat: Did you?

A slight grumble scratched my throat that she didn't answer my question. Stubborn woman.

A few hours. I was hoping you could come over today.

My phone vibrated with a reply.

Kat: Do you need something?

Great, now I *needed* an excuse to see her?

I quickly typed back: **Just to talk.**

My phone sat on the kitchen counter for seven minutes of maddening silence before it buzzed again.

Kat: I'll be there in a bit.

I stared at her words, trying to convince myself to ignore their lack of enthusiasm. After two days of one sentence answers whenever I'd check in on her, I should be sprinting around the kitchen and claiming a victory lap that she was coming over at all.

Ryan came around the corner into the kitchen a few minutes later, beer in hand. Maya had asked him to help her finish her Lego house in the living room.

He nodded my way. "She coming?"

I shrugged and headed for the fridge. "Says she is."

"We'll see if she sticks to it."

"She will." Yanking the stainless steel door open, I threw him a look. "She's not a flake."

"No, she's just putting you through hell," he quipped. I didn't miss the ring of resentment to his accusation.

Popping off the cap of my second Guinness of the day, it clinked on the countertop. "She's *been* through hell. She has a right to feel whatever she's feeling."

"Did she open up about any of it yet?"

Sighing, I downed a swig. "Not much."

Just that someone had hurt her. Or multiple someones. I wasn't sure my blood pressure had come down from the point of boiling since she let on about that fact.

"She's more walled off than when we first met. I keep trying to help, but she's not letting me in."

All she gave me were glimpses.

When she forgot to hide herself or wasn't quick enough to stop it, she gave me flashes of what was going on inside her head.

Mayhem.

It was in her eyes when she lost herself to somewhere in her head that made a frenzy out of them. She'd forget she was so goddamn stubborn and show me a woman who looked like she was screaming for help without a voice.

My chest would ache each time I saw it, but I didn't know how to fix it for her.

I was helpless, and I couldn't fucking stand it.

Ryan pulled out a chair at the kitchen table and lowered to sit. "When do you think you'll stop trying so hard and put yourself out of your own misery?"

I cut a stiff glare across to him. "I'm not giving up on her. She needs help and time, and I'll give her all of that." *Once I figure out what's wrong.* "I didn't go to the fucking ends of the Earth to find her just to give her up because things got difficult. I can work with difficult."

Ryan nodded in silence, but I could see he had more to say.

"What about that guy she was with? She tell you anymore about him?"

My grip around the base of my beer tightened as did every muscle in the top half of my body. As of two days ago, that topic had *officially* become my least favorite.

My mouth touched the lip of the bottle, rushing out the words before drowning them. "No. She just cried a fuck ton when I gave her his stuff."

Ryan piqued a considering eyebrow at me. "Well, the dude did die for her, right? I'd probably shed a tear for him too."

I nodded and tossed back a mouthful of good Irish beer that tasted a little more sour than it did a few seconds ago. He saved her. I didn't. Blake took bullets for her because I wasn't paying attention. All I saw was the woman I spent thirteen years of my life with dead on the floor, and I missed Claudia coming into the room with a gun.

I didn't notice her until the shots had already been fired, and Kat could have already been dead.

"You should have heard her after he was shot." I set my bottle down, thumbing the edge of the label and staring at it. "She just kept screaming. I've never heard her scream like that."

She wasn't even aware when I came up next to her at one point during it and tried to help the paramedics get her off of his body. She just kept wailing and swatting at everyone until they told me they'd have to tranquilize her and I said okay.

I wasn't in any shape to deal with it at the moment.

"Why do you think he did it?" Ryan asked after a moment.

I tapped my pointer finger against the slick base of the glass, watching condensation ride down the bottle. I knew why.

I knew exactly why.

"I went through some of his things before I gave her the box. There was a journal in there that he wrote in. He was pretty skilled with a pen to be honest."

The pages were filled with scribbles of his thoughts and morbid emotions. He was an artsy, feely kind of man, and I probably wouldn't have made it all the way to the back if that polaroid photo hadn't fallen out.

"There was a poem he wrote dated after she arrived there." Jealousy raced hot down my spine the same it did two days ago when I first read it and made the connections. "Pretty sure it was about Kat."

"What was it about?"

I threw back a quick swig before answering. "Love. Unrequited love."

Ryan leaned back in his chair, nodding slowly. "So he was in love with her."

"You love someone, you take a bullet for them," I stated blankly.

I'd have done the exact same thing if I had been paying any attention. If someone had to take a bullet for Kat, a part of me I'm sure was testosterone based wished I'd been able to do it so long as I got to live to tell the story. Now, she had an attachment to a man she'd known for all of five weeks, and I couldn't say anything about it.

She nearly bit my head off for calling him a criminal.

Which he goddamn *was*.

"She clearly didn't feel the same way though." Ryan pulled my attention across the kitchen. "You said the poem was about unrequited love."

I kept my mouth thinned, waiting for the cramping in my gut to subside.

"Wait—" *Fuck*. Clearly, I put up a shitty mask. "Why don't you look so sure?"

Taking my hand from around my glass, I flattened it to the cool counter with a slow-streamed sigh. A rock was in my stomach, slicing me up each time I breathed. Each time I thought about his hands so comfortably on her waist or how she didn't seem bothered to have them there.

How many times had he held her like that?

Where else on her body had he gotten comfortable touching while I wasn't there to break his fucking hands?

"They just looked close." The words burned like goddamn acid to admit. "They looked really close."

The kind of close that took her and I *months* to reach.

Ryan set his drink down out of my peripherals, leaning forward to rest his elbows on his knees. "Well, if he was in love with her, they must have been a little close. Doesn't mean she felt the same way."

I told myself that too.

Then, I'd remember how violently she grieved him or how recklessly she defended his memory. It's how I imagined she'd react if something happened to me. A fire-hot ball of uncontrollable agony and rage that attacked any and everything around her.

It could have all been triggered by how he died. It was entirely possible.

But he wasn't dead yet in that room when she looked at him like he was where she was getting her very next breath.

"You didn't see them together. How this guy looked at her… he *knew* her. She let him in, and she doesn't let anyone in. It took me months of fighting to get where this Blake guy was in weeks."

"Maybe you should have kidnapped her and forced her to spend five weeks with you." His lips peeled apart with an awful laugh. "Maybe that's the trick with her."

"Fuck you, man. There's not a *trick*." Ryan ducked his head in a wordless apology as I snatched my beer up again. "But you're right. I also don't know how much of whatever developed between them was circumstantial."

"You thinking Stockholm?"

"Potentially."

"Dude," Ryan lugged himself out of my kitchen chair and leaned his shoulder against the wall, "I don't think I've ever heard you sound so insecure before. After all the bullshit you went through to get her back, you think she'd give you a little slack."

Yeah. You'd think.

I flipped my life inside out for her only to watch her run right out of it. The second beer was almost empty, and maybe that was the cause for my chest feeling a little extra tight and my lips a little extra loose.

"That's another thing. She's never really acknowledged any of it."

Ryan balked. "Not even a thank you?"

Heat steamed beneath my skin as I mulled over his words. They sat on my chest like a goddamn leech, sucking the blood straight from my heart and brain so stupidity could fall out of my mouth.

"No. She hasn't done anything but push me away and cry over this fucking guy." That thoughtless heat licked up my spine as I settled into my rant. "I don't expect her to fall to her knees and thank me, but I at least expected her to appreciate the extent of what I did to get her back."

My job. My principles. My wife. All gone because of what I did to save her.

She didn't seem to care.

"Hell," I lowered my voice for Maya's sake. "I killed my wife, and she hasn't asked me once about it. The hardest thing I've ever had to do, and she's never brought it up. All she can do is run away from me and cry over another man, and I'm losing my fucking mind here."

The front door slammed shut, stopping my heart cold.

Ryan shot me a look of horror that surely matched my own.

"Maya?" I called, nearly falling out of my socks as I ran around the kitchen counter towards the living room. Her little voice didn't answer my call, and I pushed my legs faster.

My toes crossed the threshold into the living room, heart pulling me back to a full stop. Maya was right where I'd left her, sitting crossed legged on the floor next to a half-built Lego house.

It wasn't her that dropped my frozen heart through my stomach and rolled it onto the floor.

"Kat."

Her name was so hard to force out. My mouth felt like it didn't deserve to say it when she was staring at me like that. Betrayal had burnt up the green of her eyes to a crisp, and she looked so goddamn hurt.

This was bad.

This was very very bad.

"Maya," I addressed, watching with vigilance the lightning storm brewing over viridescent fields. "Go back to the kitchen and hangout with Ryan."

She stood to go, but Kat stopped her with a "wait" as she fished something out of her purse that hung around her shoulder.

Headphones.

She pulled out a stringy white pair and handed them to Maya without taking her flaming focus off of me. My daughter curled the offering between her fingers, and I passed her my phone out of my pocket as she ran my way so she'd have music to listen to. She grabbed it and bounded back to where Ryan had stayed in the kitchen.

Kat waited a grace period of about fifteen seconds before all hell broke loose.

"So, is this what you wanted to talk about?" Her voice. Goddammit, it was *vibrating* in pain. "How you think I'm a selfish, thankless *bitch*?"

"Kat, I didn't mean any of that." This was so bad. Heat burned my face, and I couldn't stop thinking how fucking awful this was. "I know it sounded terrible, and you have every right to be upset, but before this goes any further, I need to make sure you *know* I didn't mean a word of it. I've been drinking, which isn't an excuse. I shouldn't have said any of it."

"Well too fucking late," she snapped with teeth bared. "You said it, and I heard. I *heard* every nasty thing you think of me, Dominic."

"Kat, I *don't* think those things." My head shook as I neared one step. "I didn't mean them."

"*Oh*. So, you're saying you didn't mean it when you said that I don't appreciate what you did to save me?" She came in closer too, one calculated step at a time. "You're saying you didn't mean it when you said I didn't even *care* that you killed Heather for me?"

"No, I *didn't* mean it, and I'm sorry you overheard that."

"Yeah, I bet you are," she shot back with venom that could incinerate.

"Kat, can we *please* take a step back?"

I hadn't thought I was tipsy before, but now my head felt swollen with hot air. I needed to lie down and wake up in a different nightmare. Any would do.

"No, we can't just 'take a step back', Dominic." Anger flamed her cheeks a bright red, something wet glistening in her eyes. "Your cards are all on the table. I *know* now. I know what a shitty person you really think I am!"

"I don't—"

"If you really think that I don't care that you killed Heather, then you clearly think I'm fucking *heartless*." Her words were a whisper as fragile as a cracked glass. "If you think I don't care that Maya won't grow up with her mother because of me..." She trailed off, igniting the silence between her words with an intensity matched in her tormented stare.

"That is *all* I care about," she croaked. "That is *all* I can think about."

"Okay, then you should *talk* to me about these things, Kat, because I had no idea."

She bunched her eyebrows together, parting her lips. "You think that it's as easy as that? Just bring up your dead wife whenever I feel like talking about her and how she's *dead* now because of me?"

I must have shown her the same baffled look as she was giving me as I jerked my head back. "Heather isn't dead because of you. You didn't shoot her."

"No, *you* did, because you had to choose whether to shoot her or lose me."

"*Yes*, and that was my choice to make," I pushed back.

Kat dropped her head into her hands, shaking it back and forth as she mumbled something that got caught in her hands. I paced forward.

"What was that?"

Suddenly, her stare shot back up as she shouted, "I said you chose wrong!"

The confession exploded out of her, blowing her eyes wide and puncturing straight through my chest. It hit me so fucking hard, I almost fell back in shock. It seemed to wind her to clear the admission from her chest, harsh breathing shaking her shoulders and exhausting the barrier she held up between us as it crumbled in a slow shake of her head and one

THIRTY-ONE

heartbreaking whisper.

"You chose wrong..."

In those three words, it all fell together.

Her behavior. Her leaving. Her nonstop tears.

It all clicked in one soul-sinking realization.

"No," I paused long and hard, determined to drill these words into her brain. "I didn't choose wrong. I chose *you*."

Survivor's guilt.

I'd been trained on it, but only briefly. I knew it came when an individual survived a traumatic event and couldn't understand why they lived when others did not. It came with tremendous remorse and culpability, mood swings, inability to sleep, and an obsession with the dead and wondering if they should have died instead.

Why the fuck hadn't I thought of it sooner?

My girl had all the symptoms and had been telling me what was wrong all along, and I just wasn't listening.

But I was now.

"Dominic, you cannot honestly tell me that this was the better choice." She drew her hands up into her hair, clutching the strands against her scalp with pressure that tightened my jaw to watch. "We're fighting, I ca-can't be in the same room as you without feeling like I want to scream, and you said it yourself that I'm making you lose your mind!"

"Because I didn't know what was wrong, so I didn't know how I could help you."

"You *can't* help me," she cried, flinging her hands down at her sides.

"Yes, I can." Nodding, I took a confident step into her and didn't stop even as sharp panic widened her eyes. "I can start by telling you that a life without you isn't one I'm interested in."

"But it *should* be." She bored her gaze into mine with a shocking degree of validity. "You'd be so much better off without me around. We both know it."

"I don't know it." My immediate disagreement deepened the shade of crimson flushing her pale cheeks. Frustration and anxiety were boiling beneath her skin, and I couldn't believe how dense I'd been up to this point.

She was in so much pain I could feel it, actually *feel* it, pouring out of her heart and into mine. It was such a heavy sadness she was crumbling under, a burden she never should have decided to carry all by herself.

"You couldn't be more wrong, Kat. I need you in my life."

"No, you don't." She shook her head fast, sounding so sincere and certain.

"*Yes*, I do. I've spent thirty-one years not knowing you, and even the best moments in those years pale in comparison to ones I know I'll get to make with you."

Kat's eyes widened, and I knew I'd somehow hit a nerve that was about to rupture. "But what about the ones Maya should have gotten to make with her mother? What about those moments that are *gone* because of me? You can't say having me in your life is better than Maya having a mother."

"I can if her mother was a manipulative criminal who had a very dangerous lack of sympathy for little girls."

In Kat's very next breath, she proved just how far gone she was to her vulturous demons as she tried to argue *for* Heather. "She wouldn't have ever done anything to her own daughter."

I'd like to believe so, but I didn't.

"She tried to kill you. I wouldn't have put anything past her."

"Because I stole her husband!"

"You didn't steal me." Another step her way made her retreat towards the door, so I stopped. I didn't want to scare her off. "How I see it, I was always yours. I just hadn't found you yet."

She wore a thin white sweater today, and it got crushed between her fingers as she fisted her hand over her chest. It was as if she was trying to claw her heart right out.

"I wish you hadn't," she mumbled, staring at nothing.

The concept of never knowing her squeezed every last drop of air out of my lungs.

"How can you say that?"

Helpless eyes ripped up to me. "Because then everyone would still be alive!"

THIRTY-ONE

A hand clapped on my shoulder, squeezing the support I needed into me. Ryan spared me a quick glance as he passed by. "I gave Maya some chips as a snack, so I'm gonna get going."

Probably best. This was going to get ugly before it got pretty.

Ryan headed out the front door and left Kat and I in silence. Her eyes like emerald teardrops lowered to my chin, concentrating on nothing but with that look of mayhem she wore so often lately swarming inside them both.

Her lips barely moved as she took a swing at my heart.

"I think I should go too."

She turned to leave, and my feet were hitting the floor before I knew it. I came up behind her as she reached the door, grabbing her arm with one hand and slapping the other against the wood above her head.

"Don't go," I begged, lips hovering just above her sweet coconut hair.

If words could melt bones, that's exactly what mine did to her as she slumped into the front door with a weighted sigh, defeat scenting the air along with her shampoo.

Slowly, she shook her head against the wood.

"You have to let me go, Dominic."

The ache in her whispered words only made me grip her harder.

"I won't," I promised to us both. "I can't."

Gently, I encouraged her to turn around and face me. She allowed me to rotate her body so her back went to the door and her face came right up beneath mine. She was such a gorgeous creature even marked with ineffable pain, and I would have stood there and cherished every inch of her smooth-skinned beauty for hours if she'd let me.

For now, I brushed my thumb along the edge of her cheek, tracing where her tears were about to fall. "I've done way too much to bring you back to exactly where you are now, in my arms, right where you belong."

She pinched her eyelids closed so tightly, the cutest little wrinkle birthed between her eyebrows. I would have rubbed my thumb over that next if she weren't so concentrated on her breathing. It was coming and going in slow pushes, and I wanted to tell her how proud I was for how well she was restraining a panic attack.

I didn't get the chance.

"I don't belong here." My fingers riding her skin froze. She struggled to get the words out, which was a small relief given how difficult they were to hear. The cute wrinkle I was just admiring between her eyebrows deepened, and I already hated whatever she was going to say next.

"I don't belong with you," she said quietly.

"*Yes,* you do."

"Dominic, I have *ruined* your life." Her lashes tore up, bright green flashing with torment in front of me, effortlessly taking up every fragment of my attention. Her eyes were always so fucking bright when she was sad. Right now, they were glowing. "I can't undo that. People that belong together don't ruin each other, and that's all I've done since you met me!"

My arm came up in between us, snatching her hand that I was positive she hadn't realized had gone back to scratching at her chest again. I intertwined our fingers so she couldn't hurt herself anymore, holding on tight and determined to never let go.

"You've done a lot of things since I first met you," I started, switching my eyes between hers, "and ruining my life is not on that list."

The back of her head thumped the door as she let it fall back. *"Dominic."*

"Kat, you can push me away all you want, but I'm not going anywhere and neither are you. We didn't come this far and go through hell just to give up. This will be hard, *yes.* But it's you and it's me, and it's never been easy before. Do you know why that is?"

"Because the universe was telling us to stop before anyone got hurt and we didn't fucking listen?"

"Because," her nostrils flared in rebellion as I chided her from above with a single word. "The things worth keeping should not be easy to obtain. You should work for them. Earn them. If it's so hard, you give up halfway through, then it was never supposed to be yours."

Wood warped with a creak as I eased my weight off the door, bringing my hand that was plastered against it beneath her delicate jaw. I cupped both sides, engulfing her beneath me as I spoke right against her parted

THIRTY-ONE

lips.

"You, Katerina Reigh Sanders, are supposed to be mine, and I am supposed to be yours. That's the way this story is meant to go."

Warm air fanned my lips and chin as she lost control of her breath. It came out sharp and shocked, tasting like her strawberry mouth that I wanted to claim until it was puffy and red how I liked it. Kissing her and dominating her had worked to calm her nerves in the past, but the kind of nerves filling saltwater through her stare now weren't the ones that could be solved with a kiss.

With standing water sitting on the brim of her eyes, she whispered up at me. "Do you know the meaning of star-crossed?"

Ice spontaneously hardened inside my chest, suspending my next heartbeat.

It was hard enough to unfreeze my tongue to answer.

"Yes."

Fresh beads of tears rolled over the sides of her eyes, wetting her lashes as she took in small cuts of air while gazing up at me. "I think that might be us too," she softly confessed as if the realization broke her heart.

I chose very *actively* to ignore how she used the word 'too'.

"I am yours. I know it. I *feel* it. But I've fucked up way too much in this life and you're gonna realize it one day, and by then it'll be too late. The damage will be done, and you'll already hate me for what I made you do."

I smartly slipped my dominant hand back towards the door, pushing the brunt of my rage into the wood, kneading my fist until the skin of my knuckles frayed.

"You didn't make me shoot Heather," I repeated explicitly.

"Yes, I did. You loving me was like my finger pulling the trigger. Just because I didn't physically do it doesn't mean I'm not the reason for it."

Lowering my face to be on level with hers, I spoke low and pointedly.

"You did not kill Heather. *I* did."

"Because you loved me," she pushed back even harder.

"Then that's my Achilles heel, and I'm okay with that."

"But I'm not!" Kat was abruptly missing from in front of me. I spun to find her pacing frantic steps around my living room. "I'm not okay being the reason that people *die*. Four people are *dead*. How am I just supposed to accept that?"

"Those individuals are not dead because of you, and I am so sorry I didn't realize why you were in so much pain before, but I get it now. And I don't care how many times you need me to repeat myself until you understand that what happened in that room is not your fault."

"*Yes*, it is."

"Kat, *no*. Every single person who died knew what they were stepping into by being in that room. Heather knew exactly the position she was putting me in by pointing that gun at you. Her mother and that other security guard worked in the black market, so they absolutely knew the danger they were asking for, and Blake—"

A dry sob crashed through her entire body, nearly taking her to the floor as I mentioned his name. "You and I both know he knew exactly what he was doing when he took those bullets for you."

"Don't you think I know that?" Raw grief bled in from every angle of her eyes, red attempting to ambush their vibrant green. "I *know* why he did it, and I *know* that if I'd never been put in his life that he would still be walking around, but he's not. Because of *me*. Because I am a *cancer* to anyone I meet."

"You are *not* a cancer." My voice cut straight across to her, explicit and precise. "And I'm going to need you to change that type of thinking very quickly because I won't stand to have anybody talking about the woman I love like that, even if it's you."

Surprise flashed her gaze back to mine, popping her mouth open.

A microscopic swell of victory surged through me to watch *something* get through to her. Using the remnants of that triumphant burst, I closed the gap to her one measured step at a time.

"I promise I will use every minute of every day making sure you know how important it is that you walked out of that room. I will tell you every day how strong and inspiring and worthy of every bit of life and love that comes your way you are."

"Please stop," she pleaded in a broken voice.

"I won't," I bullishly denied. "I won't stop until you understand how I see you. How when I looked between you and Heather in that room, I saw my past and my future in front of me, and I made the decision that my past would not destroy my future."

More hot-blooded tears sliced down her cheeks. "You'll regret it."

"No, I won't."

"Dominic, I *know* you. I know your heart, and it's way too fucking good to live with what you did to save me. I have a black fucking heart, and it's all I can even *think* about. All I see when I look at you or Maya is what I took away from you, and that's how you'll start to see me too, I *know* it!"

"Do you know what I know?" Chaos was beginning to scratch a blurry film over her eyes as she started losing herself inside her head again. Determination pushed me a step closer to catch her before she was gone completely. "I know that if I had the chance to do it all over again, I wouldn't do a damn thing differently."

Her eyes bulged as if I told her the house was on fire. *"What?"*

"You heard me. If the choice is between saving you or saving Heather, I choose you every time."

She grabbed her head as it dropped back towards the ceiling, cradling her skull like it would explode if she didn't physically hold it together.

"You can't say things like that to me, Dominic…"

"Why not?"

"Because I don't know what to do with them!" Her hands flung down, guilt howling through her eyes. "I don't know how to be someone who *deserves* to be saved."

My jaw set and clicked. "Then you're just going to have to trust me that you already are."

She shook her head, getting louder and losing her mind's balance. "You're biased and blind, and I am *bad*." Hyper breathing rocked her shoulders as she blinked fast, gasping and slipping away. "I'm *bad* for everyone. Bad for—"

She stuttered, cutting herself off as the thin skin over her throat caved in and hollowed. Her hands flew to clutch her chest, desperation igniting as she fought to find her next breath and couldn't.

Panicked eyes jumped up to me, and I was already charging over.

"Kat, *breathe.*"

A picture of Maya and I that I'd hung up on the wall from two Christmases ago rattled against it as Kat stumbled back, scurrying away as I came closer. Her thin neck was already stretching in need for air, but now she'd taken one of her hands away from her chest to hold out to me to keep me back.

Stubborn *goddamn* woman.

"Come on," I encouraged from afar. "Breathe baby, breathe."

"I ca-can't." She gasped aloud, snapping her head towards the hallway that led back to the kitchen. "I need a-air."

On clumsy steps, she bolted down the hallway where the back door was in the kitchen. My thigh clipped the side of the couch as I made wide strides to catch up to her, quickly righting myself to follow.

I reached the end of the hallway in a halved second, spilling into the kitchen and right behind Kat. She'd stopped running, and my hands went right to her shoulders without thinking if she wanted me to touch her or not. I squeezed her arms in a gentle thank you that she'd decided against running from me.

Then I looked up… and discovered I had nothing to do with her decision.

"Daddy!" Maya chirped. "Mr. Ryan left, but this man came inside and said he's Mommy's daddy. He even had pictures of my birthdays on his phone!"

My daughter beamed up at me from his lap, bouncing happily while I forgot how to breathe. The man holding my daughter in one hand and a kitchen knife in the other tipped his fat head up at me.

"Dominic."

His voice was just as I remembered it. *Chilling.*

"Ray," I spoke.

Heather's father bared his teeth in a smug smile, insanity bouncing off of every one of his sharpened teeth. Like father, like daughter.

THIRTY-ONE

"I sure hope you don't mind that I dropped by. We're family after all, right?"

THIRTY-TWO

KAT

There were only two thoughts in my head at the moment.

One, to keep my expression neutral so I didn't scare Maya.

Two, to get her out of the house before I ripped Ray's entire fucking throat out.

It was funny how fast a person could go from crying their heart out to wanting to shred someone else's clean from their body. Seeing Ray again did the trick.

Him and that fucking knife he held way too close to that little girl's face.

"Maya." Dominic was able to keep all tension out of his voice with how much he was sending into his grip around my shoulders. "Come here, please."

"Oh, no, no, no." Sunlight reflected brilliance off of the blade as Ray waved it around, wagging it back and forth in a casual threat. "I haven't seen my granddaughter since she was a baby. She's staying put."

The imprint of Dominic's panic dented deeper where he held me.

Maya tilted her chin up to Ray, as pure and innocent as starlight. "Grandpa, why are you holding a knife?"

His deadened eyes dropped to her, spieling as if this was some fucked up bedtime story. "Sometimes, grown ups have to use sharp objects to get

THIRTY-TWO

what they want."

"What do you want?" she questioned.

Appreciation sickened the brown of his eyes to a nasty soot black, his mouth's end curling up. "So smart and intuitive." Dominic promised to leave bruises beneath my skin where he held me as Ray fingered one of Maya's curls off her face and sighed, "Just like your mother."

The radiance Maya shone with dwindled as Ray mentioned her mom, but he didn't seem to notice. He was too invested in her ringlet curl he'd wrapped around his fat finger, twisting it around and around.

"I want your daddy to choose."

Maya tweaked her little head at him, not understanding.

But I did. In how Dominic's grip drained of tension and heat, he understood too.

"I lost two people that I loved. The *only* two people I loved." Maya's curl bounced as Ray flicked it away, like a butterfly that'd landed on his finger that he was done admiring. "I'm being rather generous by taking only one away from your daddy."

A frown of confusion deepened on Maya's face. "He has to lose someone he loves?"

"Yes, he does. I lost my daughter and the love of my *life*." Ray's demented cool upended on a snarl as he ranted. Splotches of red sprouted against his skin as his wrath mounted, bending his neck towards Dominic and I. "Let's see how he likes it."

Behind me, Dominic started playing hero. "Ray, that's not going—"

But for fucking *once*, it was my turn save someone.

"It's me." Dominic's hands lost their grip on me as I stepped forward, his fingertips curling in a last ditch effort around my arms before slipping off.

"*Kat—*"

"It's obviously me, so let her go," I finished, bulldozing over Dominic. Pissed off pressure cupped beneath my elbow, yanking me back around. A broad chest and two storming eyes caught me by surprise, Dominic towering over me.

"We're not playing his game."

For a split moment, my brain recognized every place his body was touching mine and realized it might be the very last time. It soaked it in, memorizing his solid heat. Then I jerked back and stumbled away, holding his granite stare.

"It's not a game," I breathed.

I'd lived in Ray's world and under his thumb for five weeks. Games weren't in his interest and neither was mercy. He was here for revenge. We took from him, so he planned to take from us, and if there was one thing Ray was good for, it was following through.

Especially on a threat.

"I don't care what it is," Dominic warred. "It's not happening."

Shaking my head at him to stop, I mouthed, *'Let me get her out.'*

Incredulity ravaged his handsome face as I retreated until the presence of the devil was hot as fire against my back. Spinning around, Ray and his fiendish fucking smirk were right there waiting for me.

"Dominic hasn't given his answer," Ray spoke, twisting the knife so casually in his palm.

"This *is* his answer. Now swap."

He'd picked a particularly large kitchen knife to parade between his fingers. It was trying to steal my attention, and Ray was helping it. Twisting it. Swinging it back and forth. Edging it closer to the curve of Maya's pinked cheek.

A deranged smile was in his eyes the entire time; he was practically tweaking off of the mania he caused. I tried to not let it show, I really did, but my nostrils were flaring like a bull's and I'd wager my face was as beet red as one of its targets.

I didn't take my eyes off of him even as he peeled his fingers from around Maya's arm, holding his hand out as if to say, *'take her.'*

'I dare you', was not far behind, loud and clear as a fucking bell.

My palms got a quick wipe down on my pants before going in. My arms went out to her, and her arms came up for me.

My focus was still laser-locked on Ray as he watched me bend at the knees to grab Maya. She didn't even question it, latching herself around

THIRTY-TWO

me like water to a sponge. Her sick fuck of a grandfather observed the exchange with beady-eyed focus, sending my heartbeat through the roof. I couldn't tell if I was breathing too much or not at all as I snatched her up and stood, hiding her face in my neck.

I wasn't planning to run.

I wasn't even sure what the hell I *was* planning on doing as I spun towards Dominic, but I didn't even get half a step off the ground before a sharp protrusion poked my back.

A gasp bowed my body against the pain and kept my next breath suspended on the tip of the knife poised at the middle of my spine. Dominic went sheet white as he guessed from the rearranging of my expression what was stabbing at my back, one move away from gutting me.

"Put her down," Ray ordered. I didn't even think he stood up to do it. "Tell her to go outside and wait."

I went sinking to my knees fast, desperate to escape the blade pinpricking my flesh. Stupid me didn't think that he'd just move the knife up until the tip was grazing the nape of my neck, tracing a line through my hair.

Doing this goodbye with a kitchen knife trying to fucking french braid my hair wasn't ideal, but here we were.

On my knees in front of Maya, her chin lined up with my forehead as I smiled at her. She was completely calm. Maybe a little confused, but mostly unaware of anything out of the ordinary like it should be.

Looking up at her, I wondered if she and Charlotte would still play together after I was gone.

I think I'd like that. Very very much.

"You're in my top five favorite people I've ever met. Did you know that?"

Maya split a toothy grin across her face and nodded fast, picking up a strand of my hair. "Is daddy too?"

Despite the giant knife sitting at the back of my neck, an unstoppable smile curved up my cheeks. Maya came closer with excitement highlighting her face as I curled my pointer finger towards me. She rushed forward, putting her hands on my shoulders and her ear next to my mouth.

"Don't tell him this," I whispered loud enough for him to hear. "But he's number one."

My eyes went rogue for a stupid second, flickering up at him as soon as the words left my lips. Dominic was transfixed on me, a heart-rending picture both powerless and pained—two things a good man like him should never be.

Thankfully, Maya didn't seem to notice. She was too busy bouncing on her toes as she nodded in promise. "Okay!"

She backed up a step, but not before cutting a playful look back to her father, giggling up a tinsel storm to be in on my secret. She slapped a hand over her mouth, her cheeks a cherry red when she brought her happy face back to me.

My chest—the whole fucking thing—ached so badly. *God*, I was going to miss the shit out of her.

"You know I love you, right?" I couldn't stop myself from stealing another feel of her baby-soft cheeks, running my thumb over one and pinching the roundest part of it.

She twitched her shoulders like it tickled, nodding confidently. "Yes."

"Good." I hoped she never forgot how much. "Now go run outside. Your dad will be there in a bit."

She turned and did exactly that, bolting past her father's legs that were stiff as boards and didn't stop until the front door echoed open and closed.

And then there were three.

Pressure mounted on my ribcage, the air finally allowed to charge with tension so heavy, it felt like someone was holding their steel-toed boot down on my chest.

"She looks just how Heather did at that age." Ray's tone was eerily calm, slithering through my ears as he bowed his head right next to mine. A cringe squeezed the entire right side of my body as sticky breath steamed the inside of my ear as he put his mouth against it. "Do you know what my daughter looks like now?"

Breathing hard and choppy, I didn't hesitate. "I bet dirt and worms are *really* her color."

THIRTY-TWO

A sharpened cry flew out of me, head snapping back as the knife at my nape got replaced by a tight fist, rearing my neck back as he forced me to stand. Pain chewed at the base of my skull as I moaned and came to my feet, squinting my eyes to try and block out the ache.

"You know, it's a shame you never got some manners *fucked* into you," he goaded and growled, a white slice of pain shooting behind my eyes as his knuckles tried to gouge through the back of my head.

"Ray, *stop!*" Dominic boomed in the background, and a glimpse of him rushing forward caught the corner of my vision. I went to tell him to stop, but the cold press of a fine-toothed blade against my neck did the job for me.

Dominic froze in place, and so did my heart.

Which was weird because I thought my heart had gotten used to the idea of death. But then Dominic watching it happen was never part of the deal.

Ray didn't seem worried about Dominic though, confident the knife holding still against my throat would keep him from trying anything.

"I have never met a woman whose mouth is as vile as her face is beautiful. I could have made such a *fortune* off of you, Ms. Sanders." A shiver betrayed my body, wracking the whole thing as Ray ran his grating voice up and down my neck. "If I didn't want to watch you bleed so badly, I'd take you with me as my number one whore when I restart my business, given that you ruined the last one."

"Do you want me to pull out my tiny violin for that sad fucking song?" I seethed between clenched teeth, harsh breathing cutting through.

"No, Ms, Sanders." A sharp breath caught in my throat, his mouth pressing against my ear as he hissed, "I don't want anything but your screams."

Dominic tried gaining Ray's attention back on him, calling his name, but he was engrossed in me and every tremble my body gave him.

"I spoke on the phone with my old friend who wanted to buy you, and do you know what he told me?" My breath ripped into a gasp as the blade's edge indented between the notches of my windpipe. "He described how you *screamed*, how he could feel the vibration of your screams as he dug around inside of you."

A nauseating chill swept through my body, ice burning down my chest as I caught the look on Dominic's face. Like he'd just had the wind knocked out of him.

"Stop," I breathed.

But he kept going, kept making it worse. "He also said you have the tightest young cunt he'd felt in years."

"Shut up, shut up!" I begged, getting louder and desperate.

Ray directed his attention back to Dominic. "I don't need to ask if fucking your nanny was worth it after he described how she felt inside."

A scream clawed its way up my throat as I thrashed in his hold. "Stop it! Stop!"

Dominic couldn't hear that. He didn't need to know. It would crush him. It would kill him. It was *my* burden to bear, not his. Never his. Never—

The press of the knife deepened against my neck, capturing my fight in place.

"You really are a *stupid* girl, aren't you?" Ray's teeth were practically chewing on my ear he was so fucking close. "You don't tell me what to do. *I'm* the one with the knife, and all you are is a piece of meat waiting for me to fucking butcher you. *Got it?*"

Ray's ego-maniac threat went unanswered as Dominic tried to speak, but words fell flat against his tongue. All of my focus was on him and that shell-shocked, sick-to-his-stomach look he couldn't hide.

"Dominic..." I tried his name in a soft attempt to touch him from afar, but it didn't work. Misery wrapped a hand around my throat as pools of realized anguish rose in Dominic's raindrop eyes. It squeezed my windpipe so tight, wisps of words were all I could fight out. "Please. I'm-I'm so sorry. I'm *so sorry*. I didn't want you to know..."

"You said that you weren't..." An onslaught of tears burst to the surface of my eyes as Dominic tried to say the word, but couldn't bring himself to face it.

"I wasn't. Not in that way, I promise. I *promise*." The burn of saltwater splashed my flushed cheek and slipped right down. "But I told you people

THIRTY-TWO

hurt me."

Disbelief was a vivid rift cracking down the middle of his face, exposing the anguish beneath.

"I didn't..." Again, he couldn't finish and breathed my name out in a lament. "Kat..."

Ray hummed beside me, a filthy fucking noise of satisfaction. "I'm assuming you didn't fill him in on much of your time with us?"

My eyes slammed shut, lightning tearing out in the darkness. "Can you shut the fuck up, *please*?"

A husky chuckle resonated through his chest, stark of any drop of humor. "The world is going to be such a better place once I've cut out your vocal cords, Ms. Sanders."

"You're not going to touch her."

The sound of Dominic speaking lifted my lashes, finding him nailing Ray with a vicious glare, furious divots chiseled between his concentrated brows.

Oh no.

My thunder was pissed.

My thunder was pissed enough to say or do something really stupid.

"And why's that?" Ray cocked his head to ask.

Dominic's lips pressed together in a firm line, and then he went ahead and said that really stupid thing.

"Because you're going to take me instead."

"*Dominic.*"

Desperation shocked the stubborn word out of me, needing his hard-lined focus on me.

He didn't give it.

"Dominic!" Finally, his attention was all mine when my fingers wrapped around Ray's forearm and jammed the knife up against my throat. His eyes of starlight exploded with panic, snapping up to me quick. "I'll put this knife in my own throat before I let you die for me. Don't you even fucking *think* about it."

"*Kat.*" Confusion that almost read like betrayal gripped the sound of my name, but it didn't matter. He could feel betrayed all he liked so long as he was breathing.

"Dominic, *no*. No, you don't get to do this for me too." A small sob climbed up my throat and was out before I could stop it, a wet vision of Dominic forming in my eyes. "You've done so much, and you've *lost* so much because of me already, and I can't-I can't let you do this too."

"Kat, there's no *letting* me do anything. I choose who I give my life for."

"I wouldn't survive it!" It was an explosion no one had been expecting, not even me. It widened Dominic's stare as it tore out of me, pouring weakness down my cheeks. Weakness was all I had left. "I wouldn't. I can *see* it. I wouldn't even… make it a few months before I put a bullet in my head I would miss you so much. I *know* it."

I'd go crazy, raving mad with guilt and grief, and a bullet in my brain would be a blessing of silence to all.

"I couldn't survive losing you. I just-I *wouldn't*," I sobbed, weeping so openly for him. "I'm barely surviving as it is, and losing you… I couldn't do it. I-I love you so much, so fucking much, so just *please*… let me do this for you. I am *so* okay with doing this for you."

In fact, I wanted it. I *wanted* death to finally pierce my lungs and steal my breath. The pressure I lived with bearing down on my chest would lift, the pain would evaporate, and I could die with a happy smile on my face knowing I died for someone I loved.

"Dear," Ray's condescension was *pungent*, sticking to the side of my neck as he spoke. "You do realize I'm going to kill both of you, correct?"

My unsteady breathing pulled short, dread freezing my lungs, my stomach, my blood. The only thing that moved was my head as it snapped to face Ray, searching the wrinkles of his face for the lie.

"You said he just had to choose between me and Maya," I breathed, horror rocketing my pulse higher.

"Yes, but in what world would I ever kill the only living relative I have left?" His bloated expression was so thoroughly unimpressed with my existence, taking his attention back out to Dominic. "I'll be taking her with me when I leave. Give her the life you never could."

Dominic's retort was immediate and *throbbing* with murder. "You're not touching my daughter."

"Why? You touched mine and got her killed. I'll do whatever the hell I want to yours."

Realization flowed through my body at a quickening pace, whirling around my bloodstream, building my heartbeat to a frantic pulsing as I twisted and screamed, "Dominic, *run*. Go get her!"

His steely stare switched to me. "I'm not leaving you."

"*Forget* about me! I'm dead already, but you can get her—"

"If he makes one move, I'll remove your larynx to an outside feature of your body so fast you won't even have time for a last breath," Ray threatened like I gave two shits.

"Dominic, go get Maya. *Right* fucking now."

Fury swelled boiling tears to the surface because Dominic so clearly wasn't even considering it, wasn't even *moving*. His stance was immovable, and his concentration was absolutely lethal on Ray. He had that decided look about him that picked my heart up and ran away with it.

I'd seen that look in him before, and nothing good ever came after it.

"Kat had nothing to do with what happened in that room." The thunder in his voice was so powerful, so *confident*, that it terrified my lightning. "She was there only because of me, and she will fight me and tell you it was all her fault, but we both know I'm the one who cheated on your daughter. I'm the one who broke her."

My born-again heart lurched and screeched as I realized where he was leading.

"Dominic, *don't*."

He ignored me, making sure the nail went in his coffin instead of mine.

"I'm the one who shot her and your wife," he finished, breaking a sob out of my sore chest.

"*No*," I cried, petals of tears hitting my flesh and stinging with regret. The air shifted around us three as fate changed course.

Before this, he could have run. He could have *survived*. Now Ray would never let him go.

Sucking back a mangled cry, I shouted, "Why did you say that?!"

Dominic didn't even have the audacity to look *sorry*. He just stood tall and adamant, letting his weakness for me destroy him in the bad kind of way he promised I never could.

"You..." Ray's voice shivered with a degree of feeling I didn't know he was capable of. "*You* killed my daughter? Your *wife*?"

Dominic remained stone-faced as I sobbed, "Dominic, *run*."

"You killed my daughter for this dumb fucking cunt?!"

"*Ah*," I couldn't help but gasp when Ray drove the knife harder into my neck, my skin giving way under the sharp blade like stitches ripping apart. Dominic's eyes bulged out as I imagined my blood sprouted through, the top layer of my skin burning in pain as it split open.

"I thought Blake shot them, but... you?" Ray couldn't seem to comprehend that or how shaky his grip on the kitchen knife was getting. "You killed your own wife to save *her*?"

"And I would do it again in a heartbeat."

Ray was silent for a long time after that. In the quiet, Dominic and I found each other across the kitchen.

And we spoke.

Through the shadows of regret reaching through his eyes, he told me he was sorry it had come to this and that he hadn't been able to do more. In the resilience gleaming underneath those shadows, he told me he would do everything in his power to ensure that if only one of us walked out of here, he would make sure it was me.

In return, I tried to tell him to run, to leave, to get as far away from me as he could. I was his cancer and ruination and he could still live such a full life if he left me now. I wanted him to know how okay I was with dying for him and how thankful I was for his love when I didn't deserve it. I was lucky to have loved him, and this would be my way to say thank you.

In our eyes, it became apparent that we both intended on dying for the other. No matter what it took.

A crack popped in my neck and severed mine and Dominic's connection as Ray twisted my head, bringing bloodshot eyes and a sweat-glistened face right over mine.

"How is it that you get these men to do whatever it is you want?" The wonder cast in his tone said he was honestly curious. "Are you really *that* good of a fuck that these men are willing to lay down their lives for you and kill for you without a second thought? I can't figure any other reason why my daughter's husband and my best security man both lost their minds and lives for you other than your pussy is just that good."

"Gee Ray," I huffed, "almost sounds like you're jealous."

"*Curious* is more like it."

Dominic heard the same nauseating implication that I did, growling from across the room. "I'll kill you before you ever touch her like that."

"And *you*." Ray cut through Dominic's outburst with a knife—literally—switching the blade around to point the tip straight at my heart. "Tell me, do you want to watch her die or just listen to it? I can't decide whether to cut out your eyes or ears or just fucking crucify you and make you watch as I fuck the life out of her."

"God, you are one sick *fuck*," I cursed, spitting the insult up in his face. My tears had dried to bored dust on my cheeks, and I think I honest to god was just so fucking spent on this entire family. I'd escaped them once, and now the head of them had come back from the dead to screw with me one last time, and I was just *so over it*.

"You know what *sucks* for you, Ray? You came all this way to kill me, hoping to get some vengeance out of it, but I honest to fuck don't even care anymore. You would be doing me a favor taking me out of a world where men like *you* get to thrive."

His upper lip twitched. "Is that so?"

I readied a wad of saliva at the back of my throat so I could literally spit my answer back at him, but the sound of thunder rumbling stopped me.

"*Kat.*"

My stare slid over to Dominic on a pull that wasn't even optional. He was waiting for me when I found him, surprising me with what I saw. His gray-eyed storm had come to an unexpected calm, all haphazard emotions collected to a fixed point on me.

"If this doesn't work out how I want it to, I need you to listen to me. Very carefully."

My eyebrows scrunched together. "What?"

"Do you remember the first time I kissed you?" he asked without pause. My only answer for apparently too long was confused silence, so he kept going. "We were in the garage and…" A sweet smile poked happy memories in the dimples of his cheeks. "You looked so beautiful, and you were wearing that ridiculous shirt. I hated myself so much because I wanted to kiss you so badly every minute we were in there."

Yes I was pissed, and *yes* I was drained, and *yes* I was about to get a knife in the neck… but that didn't stop me one bit from melting for Dominic Reed just as his nostalgic words demanded. My shoulders sank and my heart liquified at his feet.

"I remember," I whispered softly.

He nodded almost encouragingly. "Do you remember what I said when I was behind you that day? We were fighting, and my arms were around you. Do you remember?"

My lips touched to ask him what the hell he was talking about. We weren't fighting that day. Not until later, but that lead to the best fucking makeout session in the history of makeouts. It was a day of self-defense, not *real* fighting. When he was behind me, it was to show me a move about—

Oh my god.

"I remember." Holy shit, I remembered.

An explosion of pride burst in his eyes and he nodded, confirming we were on the same page. The page that included a *plan*.

A plan that was going to hurt like a bitch, but a plan nonetheless.

Nerves bubbled up in my stomach as I eyed Dominic carefully and wondered what the hell it was he had up his sleeve. He'd switched from forcing his own signature on my death certificate to a calm so serious, it gave me goosebumps.

Ray tugged on the back of my head, murmuring beside me, "Come on. Even I'm a little curious now. What did loverboy say?"

THIRTY-TWO

Dominic's alert stare flashed just behind us for a fast second before coming back to me, breathing hard with a rigid nod.

Baring my teeth, I chewed out, "Aim for the nose."

Tensing every muscle in my neck, I reared my head forward and slammed it straight back into Ray's face.

Our shouts of pain clashed in the air, his arm loosening so I fell forward while he stumbled back. A hiss sliced up my throat as a white hot invasion ripped apart my skin above my collarbone.

"Now!" Dominic yelled.

A gunshot from out of fucking nowhere broke the chaos in the air, violently *booming* between my ears as I collapsed forward onto the ground.

My hands didn't know what horrible pain to reach for first—my ears, my neck, or my throbbing head. A headache splintered from the back of it, reaching around my skull and grabbed onto my eyes, blinding them as I wailed.

Ringing. So much ringing, over and over and over as I rolled around the floor. Colors and shapes around me blended and blurred into a tornado of confusion as I tried to find a focus and couldn't. Agony *clawed* down the back of my skull, scooping nausea up in my stomach and readying to spill it out.

A numbed touch grabbed at my arms, muffled voices scrapping the insides of my ears, but I couldn't make them out.

My head lolled to the side as my mouth watered, catching in flickering bits the image of a man sprawled out next to me with a chunk of his head missing. Brain and blood and bone all gaped back at me, and suddenly, the twisting nausea wasn't in my stomach anymore.

The benumbed touch on my arms rolled my body over as I wretched, bits of my hair disappearing from around my face as I lost everything in my stomach.

God, the ringing, the pain, the excruciating *pain*. It was still everywhere. Tears leaked down my face as I begged it all to stop. Just stop. *Please stop.* I just wanted to sleep and pass out and die.

Finally, darkness swallowed up the sides of my mind and drowned the whole thing.

I supposed two out of three wasn't bad.

THIRTY-THREE

KAT

I couldn't remember when I'd fallen asleep.

Or really where.

Constructs like time or place didn't really matter to me. I'd happily leave them both behind if it meant I could stay here all day with whoever the hell was stroking my cheek with their fingers made of feathers.

I swear, it was the softest touch, and I wanted to pretend my eyes were permanently cemented shut so they'd never stop.

Until they spoke.

"You've always been shit at faking being asleep," he mused, a dash of humor lightening his dark voice.

A gasp kicked inside my chest, eyes flying open. Saltwater was already stinging inside them as they widened, taking in the pair of black flames hovering right over me that I thought I'd never burn in again. My cheeks were wet before I knew it, and his thumb was on the job, cleaning beneath my eyes and gathering my sadness to take on as his own.

"You've got to stop giving me so many of your tears." His thumb and pointer finger were a wet pinch on my chin, tipping my head up beneath his black palette eyes. "You're going to die of dehydration before your next birthday if you keep this up."

Rebel until the very end, more water spilled over my brims as he scolded me just how he used to. He was so real. Everything about him was so familiar and realistic from the rugged definition to his jaw to the bump in his nose to the scent of smoke wafting off of his dusty pink lips.

But this couldn't be real.

And I hadn't woken up yet, had I?

"I'm dreaming," I whispered unwillingly. "Aren't I?"

He nodded, and it was the saddest fucking thing I'd ever seen. "Yeah, Kitten, you're dreaming."

"That's so unfair," I sobbed, wishing as hard as I could that if I could wake up right now, I could bring him with me. Blake gathered me in his arms on the bed my mind had made up for us, holding me like he used to.

"I know." He pressed a kiss to the top of my head. "At least we have this. We have now."

My fingers tangled in his black shirt, dragging him closer as I cried. "Yeah, but for how long?"

"Not long." A somber sigh tickled my hair as he rested his chin on my head. "You'll have to wake up soon."

Another sob broke through, wrought with grief. "I don't want to."

"You gotta, Kat."

"But that means leaving you again," I fought, remembering how I left him on the floor all bled out and dead and alone. I didn't get to say goodbye. I didn't stay with him until the end like I promised. I let go. The paramedics made me let him go.

The weight of his head left mine, his face carved by the angels coming front and center. "Kat, you didn't leave me."

"I did." Nodding vehemently, I let go of a sob because I never once cared about crying in front of him before. "I did, and I can't do it again. I can't leave you."

Blake brought a hand up to my face, watching his fingertips travel across my hairline, smiling a sad smile. "You were never mine to have. We both know that."

He thumbed another wash of tears away right as they fell over.

"Doesn't mean you had to die," I softly whispered.

His thick browline furrowed, producing his disapproval in deep grooves in his forehead. Warm hands cupped both sides of my face, Blake staring me down with his personal brand of intensity unmatched by anyone else.

"Saving you was the best thing I did with my life. So you're not going to spend any more of yours worrying about me, okay? I'm fine." Slowly, my poet's intensity bled out as he dragged his eyes of sorrowed ink drops across my face, spelling out my heartache without a pen.

"But you're not," he confirmed, knowing without asking.

Lips quivering and eyes watering, I shook my head. "No, I'm not."

And I let go, draining out every drop of misery and weakness in sob after sob because he saw right through me. "I'm not fine. I'm-I'm not. I miss you so much, and it hurts. Everything hurts."

Solid heat pressed into my forehead as he brought his to mine, his hands still covering my cheeks, brushing away my teardrops.

"You know how beautiful I think your pain is, but at some point, you have to find beauty in happiness."

"I don't know how to be happy again," I wept, clinging to his forearms.

"You have to let yourself." His voice was a beautiful melody dipped in sadness, and I never wanted to cleanse my ears of its sound. "It's okay to let yourself feel happy. It's all I ever wanted for you."

Something inside my chest caved in so deep, the pain sunk all the way to the back. A whimper poured out because I knew it was true. All he'd ever wanted was to love a broken girl who wasn't worth it and see her smile in his moonlight.

He was so pure in death, wasn't he? He didn't just look like an angel anymore. He was one.

And not of damnation and ruin like I'd once written him off as. He wasn't searching for salvation anymore. He'd found it. Blake found redemption, and it was... stunning on him.

I tried to smile and be happy through all of this fucking hurt because he wanted me to, but it was so hard, and Blake could see the struggle in my smile. He traced his thumb along it, brushing across my parted lips so lightly.

"Will I ever see you again?" I asked against his finger, watching him as he memorized his flesh against mine. Even in a dream, our touch was electric.

Embered black eyes flashed up to me, his forehead still on mine as he shook *our heads together.*

"In another universe, Kitten."

The gorgeous curves of his face drowned under another swell of tears in my eyes. So this was it. This was goodbye all over again. He was leaving back to Heaven, and I was going back to a life without him.

This was the last time Blake would ever visit me.

"Every time I look at the moon, I'll think of you," I cried.

He seemed to like that, appreciation curling his mouth as he thumbed where I was trying so hard not to frown.

"How poetic."

That, finally, made me smile. It was a frail, broken thing, but it was there, and he touched it like it was the rarest cut of diamond.

"You're my rose, Kat Sanders," he murmured, nudging the tip of his nose with mine. "I'll be seeing you, okay?"

"Okay," I whispered like a promise, nodding against him.

Our eyes on each other, I watched as the midnight in his eyes began to rise to a brilliant dawn, eclipsing all darkness, blinding all of his pain until he was all light, all love, and every bit the angel he was sent to me as.

My angel smiled for me, stealing my breath one last time.

"Wake up for me, Kitten."

My own gasp startled me awake.

I sat up at the waist and immediately regretted it. Pain pulsed behind my forehead, a hiss bringing the heel of my palm to my head. The soft dip of a mattress was below me, the familiar walls of Dominic's bedroom around me. My free hand clenched around the bedding as I panted slightly, heartbeat racing as if I'd been jogging instead of sleeping.

Why the hell was I sleeping in the middle of the day?

The answer might actually have been sitting right next to me as the mattress rocked, grayed-out eyes waiting for and fixing on me. My already throbbing pulse ricocheted as I noticed Dominic there, wondering how long he'd been there, and why he was there, and why he was staring at me like I'd just come out of a coma.

THIRTY-THREE

"How are you feeling?" he asked.

How *was* I feeling?

Sinking my awareness inward, I highlighted the areas that hurt the worst with confusion propelling my voice. "I have a killer headache," I breathed, winded and not sure why.

My hand came down from my forehead, giving a pass against my cheeks to check if they were wet like in my dream. They weren't anything but warm—hot blood running beneath them with *life* and *purpose*.

Blake would be so happy.

Dominic shifted himself so his thigh was against my outstretched legs. He was close, but not so close that I wouldn't have to climb to my knees to properly touch him.

"Do you remember what happened?"

Monochrome eyes were vigilant on me as I cocked my sore head at him and squinted without meaning to. *What happened?*

Pressure mounted at the back of my skull as I tried to think and think until my headache shouted at me to please stop. With a defeated exhale, I pinched my desert dry eyes closed and forced an "uh-uh."

A heated hand laid over my knee, and I decided to say 'fuck it' to my headache. A spike of pain jammed through my forehead as I looked towards the source, but it was totally worth it. Dominic was delivering one of his looks that felt like an embrace, like he was holding me without ever touching me.

"Ray found us," he stated simply. Shock parted my lips. Dominic curved his thumb over my knee as if he could feel my heartbeat kicking with panic all the way down in it. "He had Maya in the kitchen, but you got her out of the house. Do you remember doing that?"

Did I? My thoughts zipped around, trying to find the pieces that fit together.

"Is she—"

"She's safe." His big hand squeezed my knee and cut me off. "Ryan was still outside in his car when he saw Maya come out of the house. She told him enough of what was going on that he pieced it together and called it in. He came around the back with his weapon, saw what was happening, and waited until he had a clear shot."

Shot.

A gunshot.

Bits of memories pried their way to the front as I struggled to remember—flashes of a shiny knife and blood hungry eyes, sound clips of screaming and threatening and begging, sparks of searing hot pain and tearful last moments.

"He got you here pretty good," Dominic rumbled, ghosting his knuckle just below my collarbone. I bent my neck to look down, taking in what I could of the large white bandage sealed against my flesh with clear shiny tape. *Oh shit. I guess he did.*

"The paramedics patched it up while you were passed out and said the cut isn't deep enough to need stitches. Neither is the other one above it on your neck."

My tongue touched the back of my teeth to say that was good, but I couldn't make my voice work. Was it good? Was any of this good? Was it bad? What the *fuck* was the difference anymore?

Dominic mistook my silence as intentional and used it to move the moment along.

"They think you might have a concussion though. They'd like to take you to the hospital to give you a full checkup if you're feeling up to it."

Feeling up to it. In order for that to be true, I'd have to be feeling anything at all.

A block slid in place as my brain tried to absorb all of this new trauma when it thought it already had its fill. It was overflowing now. *Overstuffed.* This was just too much bad shit for one head to successfully hold in without a cranial rupture.

That was a thing, right?

My genes were addictive ones, and maybe I had a secret addiction to trauma. Maybe that's why it always seemed to find me and I had so much of it. I called it bad luck or karma being a bitch, but what if it was really something I *asked for*? What if—

THIRTY-THREE

"Hey." Dominic's voice pierced my rabid thoughts. Blinking up, soft gray clouds were waiting to take me in. "Stay with me. I know this is a lot, and I can already see you getting lost in that mind of yours."

He was right. He was *always* right.

"Talk for me, Kat." Dominic's warm gaze said he was encouraging me, but his stern tone said he was ordering me. "Get whatever is in your head out."

His sharp focus dropped to my tongue as it slipped out to wet my lips. *Words. Say words.*

"I-I'm still trying to process." One sentence, and Dominic lit up like a bonfire. "I'm still trying to remember everything."

"That's understandable. You hit him hard."

Yeah, I was pretty freaking sure I had a nice goose egg on the back of my skull to prove it. Maybe that's what was causing the block. I'd hit my head against that fucker's face so hard, it rearranged the inside of my head to roadblock any triggering memories.

"What were we doing before Ray showed up?" I asked him.

He rolled his lips into a flat line and held a bloated pause.

"Fighting."

Oh. That's right. We *were* fighting. Always fighting.

I heard myself mutter, "I'm sorry."

Dominic seemed taken aback by the apology, thickly shaped brows curving in.

"For what?"

Dry skin unstuck as I parted my lips. "You hate fighting."

And now it was all we did together.

No more teasing. No more laughing. No more whispered sweet nothings. Just ugly fighting.

Dominic reminded me how long and lovely his lashes were as he blinked in a quick succession to recolor his eyes with remorse. His mouth pursed together, attractive lines sprouting on either side.

"Not all fighting is bad. We needed this fight, Kat. I had no idea how much responsibility you'd taken on for what happened or how much pain you were in."

The corner of my bottom lip got trapped between my teeth as he started talking about my pain, and I started getting uncomfortable. This was normally my cue to start panicking and freaking out. I could feel the familiar reaction stinging beneath my skin, ready to rip free.

"I didn't want to tell you," I breathed instead, embarrassed to feel a pinch in my windpipe. "I just wanted to stop ruining your life."

My chin made a move to duck down, but Dominic caught it, the press of his thumb forcing my head back up. "Do you know how much it hurts me every time you say that? How much it pisses me off? Kat, I will remind you as many times as I need to how you are not at fault for any of what's happened."

Searching back and forth between his eyes, there was only one unfortunate conclusion that stood out.

"You love me so unconditionally, don't you?"

My wonder-struck tone pushed Dominic's jaw to the side. "Don't say that like it's a bad thing."

"It's your flaw, Dominic." It always had been. Every unapologetic way he'd ever proven he loved me scattered across my mind, a sweep of bittersweet memories. The wind snagged one from earlier today that I'd forgotten about and brought it center.

My jaw slacked in remembrance while every other part of me *burst* with flames.

"It made you try to trade your life for mine," I started to yell, voice pitching higher and louder as I recalled every second of his self-sacrificing stupidity. "Dominic, what the hell were you thinking?! You have a *daughter*."

"And you have Charlotte," he fired back without hesitation. "And you did the same exact thing for me. Did you not?"

"Because I was trying to save you!"

"And why did you want to save me?"

Fuck, his tone said he was trying to prove a point, and I was already too far off the handle to stop myself from helping him do it.

"Because you're perfect, and you *deserve* to be saved."

THIRTY-THREE

"And because you love me?" he pressed, not like a question, but like a fact.

A goddamn *fact*.

"Yes! Okay?" I pushed up to my knees on the mattress, fighting off my headache and being pissed off that even with the advantage of a bed, this man was *still* taller than me. My chin was tipped up at him, and his handsome face was angled down at me. If we weren't fighting, I was positive our tongues would be halfway down each other's throats.

"I stopped running from that fact already. I *know* I love you. I *feel* it like it's my own goddamn heartbeat. It's not a choice. It's not something that will go away. Loving you is part of my basic function. I love you like I walk, like I blink, like I close my eyes at night to sleep. Automatically and *bone deep*. That's why you *can't* risk your life for me."

Dominic had the audacity to look swept off his fucking feet, *stars* brightening his sky-gray eyes. I wanted to shove him and kiss him all the same because of it.

"*That's* unconditional." He kissed his forehead to mine, gripping my waist. "*That* is how I love you."

"But I'm *flawed*," I forced out through gnashed teeth. "You're like-like, *shit*, what's the name of that famous ceiling painting in Europe?"

He curved thumbs up and down the back of my spine. "The Sistine Chapel?"

"*Yes*. You're like that, and I'm some drawing a toddler with two left hands scribbled down after too much sugar."

"First and for the record, I disagree." My chest sunk with a sigh that blew across his face, and the lovesick lunatic *smiled*. A crooked and beautiful thing that made my heart ache. "Second, you don't need to be perfect for my love to be unconditional."

Fucking *fuck*. This man had a sensible and romantic reply for everything, didn't he?

He was determined to love me, and whispers of my dream of Blake told me to take it. Dominic Reed was my happiness. He was my thunder and my greatest addiction. He was willing to die for me like I was willing to for him, and as much as I fucking *hated* it, he was telling me I had to understand it because that was love.

That was our fucked up fairytale love.

I wanted to take it. I wanted to fall into him and rest for a while before I kept on hating myself.

But I wasn't *just* flawed. I wasn't just a broken girl with lightning in her veins.

I was something unforgivable. Something poisonous, and Dominic deserved to know before signing off on our love story.

Even if it broke both of our hearts.

"I *want* to believe you," I breathed, slowly shaking my head against his. "I really really do."

Dominic squeezed me even harder. "It's *true*."

God, I was going to miss his stubborn love so much after I said this and he left me.

"I'm not just flawed, I'm *bad*."

"You're not—"

"I kissed him."

The even push and pull of his breath across my lips stopped.

A chill overran my mouth without his warm air, freezing down to where my weeping heart tried to hide from the attack of frostbite. It was useless, and the ice consumed it anyway as soon as Dominic drew back.

Then it was all cold.

He didn't ask who the *'him'* was that I'd kissed. He didn't need to. It was chiseled in every hard-bitten line on Dominic's face who the *'him'* was.

Neither of us were breathing. My lungs refused to give me relief from the pain of starving for air, and I hadn't seen Dominic's chest move since he backed away from me. His massive frame was statue-stiff, every visible muscle sharpened with tension beneath his golden skin.

I think I *actually* heard his jaw crack beneath the pressure. Or maybe that was just my heart.

He hated me. He finally, *finally* hated me.

In the strangest way, it was a relief.

"Did you sleep with him?"

"What?" My entire face scrunched up even though he couldn't see it. "*No*, but that doesn't matter."

"It *does*, actually." Each word got shredded through his teeth. "A lot."

"*Why?*"

His eyes were sharp as the knife against my throat earlier as they sliced up to me. "I think it's my turn to ask the questions, Kat."

Confusion pooled in thick behind my forehead as I watched him decipher my infidelity in his head. His eyes had gone cryptic like they used to when we were first falling in love and both of us were trying to figure out how to stop it. I couldn't see his thoughts or feelings, which made it pretty fucking difficult to know why he wasn't stomping out of the room yet or throwing me out of it.

"Tell me why you didn't sleep with him."

The demand was so deep in his throat, it took forever to register in my ears. When it finally did, I was sure I misheard him.

"*What?*"

"If you kissed him, *why* didn't you sleep with him too?"

"Why would you ask me that?" I shook my head, panting harder and heavier.

"*Because* the answer is important, and I'd like it. *Now*."

"Because it wasn't like that with him!" I exploded just like he wanted me to. "I didn't kiss him because I wanted to fuck him, and I didn't fuck him because I love *you*. Everything with Blake was complicated and screwed up and messy, but you know what I get, Dominic? I get messy! What I don't get is *you*, with your perfect love and compassion and understanding. You're stable and reliable, and I don't know what to do with that because I've never had it."

Dominic could be such a stoic man when he wanted to be, and right now, he was as composed as a fucking string-quartet symphony.

"Why did you choose to tell me about this now?"

Swallowing, I found my throat thicker than it was seconds ago. "I was going to tell you when we got home, but then he died and… I couldn't talk about him at all."

"Because you love him?" Dominic's jaw pulsed *and* cracked as he made himself ask the question.

Blake and love in one notion was complex. Knowing you could fall in love with someone if the circumstances were right was a tricky thing to know. But the circumstances *weren't* right, and my heart was already spoken for when Blake and I met.

Still didn't mean I wanted to give myself a forgiving out.

So I said, "In a lot of ways."

"In the same way you love me?" Dominic *immediately* followed up, and my pulse tripped all over itself.

There were only two reasons he'd ask me that.

One, because he was a gigantic masochist, which I knew he wasn't.

Or two, because he already knew the answer.

I wanted to lie. I wanted to give him an answer that would help him hate me, but they would be pointless words, wouldn't they? Convincing either of us that I loved anyone like I loved him was a fool's mission.

"No." If reluctance had ever had a sound, it was that one word. "Not in the same way."

Dominic nodded. A concentrated, deep breath widened his chest, streaming through his nose on the way out.

"Are you telling me this now because you want me to leave you?"

A pinch closed up my windpipe, panic spanning across my chest. The idea was so terrifying it *hurt*. I was physically aching to think about him leaving. My teeth dented my bottom lip to keep it from trembling as I cast my stinging gaze away from him.

"I don't want you to..." I couldn't look at him while I admitted it. It was so fucking weak. So fucking selfish. My arms came around myself, holding what was falling apart. "Um, but... you keep saying I'm good and worth it, and—" Men who thought I was worth it tended to die around me. "I thought you deserved to know why I'm not," I finished on a whisper, sliding my stare back to him.

Holding myself, I gave a shrug of acceptance to him and squished my

THIRTY-THREE

mouth to the side, trying so hard to keep it together.

This was it.

Dominic stared at me long and hard, and I silently and patiently waited for the blow.

I found myself giving him a small watery smile to encourage it.

It was okay. He could shatter me. He'd earned the right.

Dominic's nostrils broadened as I offered the weak smile. Then, without any visible emotion, he started towards me.

"I won't ever be able to fully understand what you experienced," he began, surprisingly steady. "I wasn't there, so I don't know where you were emotionally or mentally or how all of it impacted you, but I know it was a lot. And I know he got you through it."

Alarms started ringing in my head as I listened to the growth of sympathetic awareness ribboning around his tone.

"Dominic, what're you—"

"I *hate* that someone else knows what these lips taste like," he growled, framing my face with his huge hands. My head arched back for him, a sharp gasp dropping my mouth open as he fed me the taste of his undiluted jealousy. "It makes me want to put my fist through every goddamn wall in this house."

My eyes jumped between his, panting harder as emotion started to break through the concrete of his stare. It was a vicious, pissed off, *barbaric* looking emotion. It wanted to punish me for what I'd done, force sorry tears down my cheeks.

For a heart-blundering second, I thought I saw a flash of a blackened shadow skirt behind his eyes.

Then he so very pointedly said, "But he's also the reason you're alive, and I owe him everything for that. He's the reason I'll be the only man allowed to kiss you for the rest of your life. So I forgive him."

My heart inhaled a slow gasp, feeling the build in the air and seeing it in his stare.

"Dominic…"

"And I forgive you," he finished.

Disbelief went off like a cannon inside my mind, pouring out a shocked breath. *"What?"*

"I forgive you." The words made even less sense the second time around. "It wouldn't be fair to hold something against you that you did while you were in a situation I'll never be able to understand because I didn't experience it like you did. You love me. I know you love only me, and that's all I need to know."

A dry sob climbed out of my chest while tears that were plenty wet washed Dominic's thumbs. He caught them all.

"I don't understand," I cried.

"I know you don't, and that's okay. We'll work on it." Through blurry eyes, I sought out even an ounce of judgment in his gaze or voice, but it was all tender—all encouraging and honeyed—and I didn't get it. He should hate me. He should *leave* me. Instead, he gently cleaned beneath my eyes. "I'm not leaving you. Not now, not ever. No matter how much you try to push me away, I won't let you. We're going to work at this every single day, and we're going to *choose* each other every single day."

Pathetic puffs of air were all I had left to fight with. Shaking my head in his hands, I spoke in a tight whisper, "I don't get why you still want to choose me."

"Because," One by one, he picked up my arms that hung at my sides and put them around his neck so I was holding him. So I knew it was *okay* to hold him. He anchored his around my waist when he was finished puppeteering me, piecing us together.

"I happen to love you very much, Ms. Sanders," he professed against my lips, nuzzling his nose against mine. The tears on my cheeks turned to steam as Dominic grazed our parted mouths together, almost kissing me but not quite. "I love you, and I *love* the way you love me."

A whimper pulled free as he dragged his lips over mine, our heated breath fogging up my head and blurring stubborn reminders that I shouldn't touch him as I threaded my fingers through the back of his hair. Silk spooled through my fingertips as I tightened my grip, Dominic's eyes hitting silver with approval.

THIRTY-THREE

"I've never known anyone who loves as hard as you do, and I'm addicted to it." *God*, I'd made him an addict just like me. I ruined him. I ruined his good, clean heart. It was too late to save him from it. The addiction was in the way he looked at me, held me, *squeezed* me. "I need how much you love me."

The word *'need'* hit like an iron fist, caving my chest in with a rattling my breath.

It took me a second to realize the impact was coming from my heart and how it fucking *lunged* at the chance to be something that could help him. He *needed* something from me. All he'd done since I'd known him was help me, and I didn't think I had anything to offer him but poison.

But if I could help him just by how I loved him, what else could I do?

"What else do you need from me?" I whispered up at him.

I'd give him anything. *Anything*.

Something triggered across his silvered gaze, a sweeping clarity brightening the whole thing like sunbeams broke through. His arms tightened around me, and in the next second, he was switching us around so he sat on the edge of the bed and straddled me over his lap.

He gave me leverage and power while gazing at me like he finally found the key to heaven's gate. "I need how much you love my daughter," he spoke straight to my pounding heart.

I lost my breath and dropped my forehead to his, nodding fervently.

"*So* much."

"I need how you protect me." His words were pointed and precise and *drenched* in devotion. "I need that Kat Sanders fire that would incinerate a stranger on the street for looking at me the wrong way."

"What else?" I exhaled, lost in him.

"I need you to stop fighting me."

I sucked down a mouthful of air that felt *and* sounded like a gasp for life before going underwater. The guilty downpour that followed everywhere I went intensified, the pressure pushing down on my chest and buckling my spine as I wobbled on Dominic's lap and whimpered.

It was so heavy. So goddamn heavy.

Let him help. Let him help. Let him help.

Dominic anchored me against him harder, covering both sides of my face as he softened his voice over my lips. "I know why you were doing it. I get it as much as I can. It's another example of ways you try to protect me even if what you think I need protection from is you." A feathered kiss skimmed my mouth, a faint mark of love to try and ease the downpour. He could see it now, couldn't he?

Dominic could see the storm cloud over my head, and his thunder planned to chase it away.

"And you were also right. I can't fix what happened to you... but I thought I could." His throat moved against me as he swallowed with thick difficulty. "I never should have pushed you to talk about it, Kat. I never..."

Leaning back just so, what he learned about me downstairs from Ray attacked the warmth in his eyes, gnawing at it with talons for teeth. His pupils shrunk to pin-pricks, the whites of his eyes blooming with red veins, pulsating and throbbing with nightmares. *Oh shit*, he was picturing it. He was picturing me and what they did, where they touched, how I screamed for him.

Quickly, I ran soothing circles in the rough shadow of his beard, peppering in my own mark of love on his lips. "I'm okay. I'm okay now."

"Please don't comfort me right now." He grabbed my palms from his face, folding my fingers over into tiny fists in his bear-paw hands. "That's not your job. Your only job is to heal."

Heal.

Was I even capable?

My body was crowded with feelings. Each feeling was a stranger with their own language I didn't understand, but they wouldn't stop and I couldn't get rid of them. I was so over-packed, so overwrought that the days honestly felt like one long, strung-out panic attack.

I couldn't breathe. I couldn't think. I couldn't stand on my own.

I was growing so fucking sick of it.

"I'm so tired," I whispered for him, eyes falling closed.

"I know." Pressed together, the low notes of his voice vibrated through

THIRTY-THREE

my chest. "I am too."

With darkness surrounding me and his full-bodied resonance warming and filling my chest, the pressure compacted inside my heart loosened. Dominic melted the pain just enough for poisoned words to drain out.

"I don't know how to be okay again. Every time I feel normal, a thought pops up and reminds me I shouldn't. I laugh, and immediately feel guilty for it. I find a split second of peace and then I start thinking about the auction and what happened there. I want to smile at you or Charlotte or Maya, and before it reaches my cheeks, my brain reminds me of each person who died that one of you loved."

Dominic's thumbs ran comforting circles over my knuckles, encouraging me to keep going, keep letting it all out and letting him in.

"My brain won't let me be happy, and I don't know how to fix it..."

"You keep talking." Soft lips ran across my knuckles, dropping a peck on each one. "We have to keep talking to each other every day, telling each other how we're feeling so we're on the same page."

Silver-gray lifted to me, knowing all my demons, all my weaknesses, all my ugliest parts and proved that love still existed in the darkest parts of ourselves.

Somehow, he still loved me. He knew every single piece of me that I loathed so much I wanted to rip it out, and he loved me anyway. In fact, I think he'd stitch those pieces back intact if I ever got rid of them.

Was that what love was? Knowing the ugly and loving the person anyway? Was love not this perfect fairytale ritual with flawless leads and easy happily ever afters?

Love was allowed to be... messy.

Neither Dominic nor I had to be perfect to love each other so hard the Earth could crack under the devoted pressure of it. He could try to fix me when he shouldn't and I could be something a little bit broken, and our love story was still valid.

For the first time since I'd been home, I *felt* like I was home. The downpour eased so I could breathe, could blink without water in my eyes for the first time in so long. I had shelter. I'd always *had* shelter waiting for me to duck under its cover, but I was too lost to use it.

But Dominic Reed found me. He found me, and he *loved* me. He loved my messy and my darkness, and I loved his willful pride and his light. We corrected the contrast in each other's lives so we could see the beauty of what we were missing.

Holy shit, love wasn't a sickness was it?

It was goddamn clarity.

My thunder traced the rough pad of his thumb down my cheek lovingly. *Adoringly.* "Day by day, hour by hour, we put the pieces back together. You and me. As long as we have each other, that's all we need."

"And therapy," I added, huffing and giving in. "So much fucking therapy."

EPILOGUE

FOUR YEARS LATER

KAT

"God, I hate weddings."

Layla turned to face me instead of the full length mirror, prizing her best death stare. "Your enthusiasm on this blessed day is noted. Now get over here and help me lift this mammoth of a skirt."

"I *am* enthused." Layla wasn't buying it as I strode up behind her, grabbing fistfuls of tulle in both hands. "You saw me at the ceremony. I couldn't keep a fucking lid on it."

She tweaked a smirk and kicked off one of her sky-high heels. "Between you and Ryan, I wasn't sure who was blubbering more."

"Blame it on the hormones, I don't know," I grumbled, cradling the thick skirt of her wedding dress in my arms. The ceremony was over, which meant her stellar but death-trap heels could finally be chucked in place of the badass purple sneaks she'd had bedazzled for the day.

"You can't blame *everything* on the hormones. It's already getting old."

"Your husband's getting old."

Her face bunched up in the bridal suite mirror, eyes going wide. "Oh my god, I have a *husband*. That's so weird."

I dropped her dress back down to the ground. "It's not too late to make a break for it, ya know. We'll steal the limo and be on our way to your honeymoon in Cabo before the fish is served."

"I don't know. Ryan's talking up a big honeymoon sex game." The reflection of her sharp chin jutted up at me. "Can you match that?"

"I can tell you how pretty you are and make sure there's always booze in your hand?" I countered.

She bounced her head from side to side. "Tempting."

Humming, I said, "You want the dick, don't you?"

"It's *good* dick."

"Can't say I didn't try."

Eyes locked together through the mirror, slow, stupid grins peeled up both of our cheeks. Soft laughter tumbled through next, and I wasn't the least bit surprised to feel electricity warming my chest like it did when I was happy.

Happy.

What a thing to be.

"I know I make a lot of jokes, but I really am excited for you two."

My best friend's smile was sweet and soft. "I know you are."

"So long as Ryan doesn't have an attack of dumbass ever again," I muttered, remembered disdain roughing up my delivery.

About two years ago, Layla was in a weird headspace after graduating community college. She literally just mentioned she *might* need some space to figure out the next move in life, and Ryan flipped and thought she was going to break up with him.

So the asshole jumped the gun and did it first.

They only spent about two weeks apart before Ryan realized what an immature dipshit he was and begged for another chance, but the tears Layla cried during those weeks were stained into my heart.

If he ever hurt her again, I'd have his balls in a blender before he could say frappe.

"Why do I get the feeling you're going to threaten Ryan at least twice in your Maid of Honor speech?"

EPILOGUE

Brown eyes slid to mine in the mirror, and I feigned innocence.

"What? You know I hate talking in front of crowds. Threats and inappropriate humor are the only way I'll get through it."

"Oh god, how many dick jokes are in your speech, Kat?" she whined.

I popped a shoulder. "Only six."

Her bangs fluttered as she blew a raspberry, rolling her eyes and trying to seal back a grin. Her slender arm latched around my waist and dragged me up next to her.

I dropped a glance down her dress, resting my head on her bare shoulder. It was a mermaid style, which was a bridal term I needed burned out of my brain after the *seven* different shops she dragged me around to until she found 'the one'. The top was a halter and satin, and the bottom flared out with a dramatic poof.

She was a freaking knockout.

"You should be allowed to wear this everywhere. Ryan about came in his pants when he first saw you walk down the aisle."

"I know, right?" Layla snickered. "And I know you were worried, but I think we found you the perfect dress."

I groaned, wistfully dreaming of the bombshell red chiffon dress she had picked out for me before. Don't get me wrong, this one was nice. I loved the deep green that made my eyes pop like freaking emerald sparklers, and the high slit gave it at least some of the sex kitten vibe I craved. The only *real* difference was the color and fit, since now I needed something that was easy to lift and pee in.

"It's fine," I sighed, looking over my appearance. "Just make sure the next time you get married I'm not five months pregnant, okay?"

Layla pursed her bright red lips together. "Don't blame me. You're the one who decided to get knocked up before my wedding."

I paused, squinting at her reflection.

"Can I blame Dominic?"

She thought it over. "Yeah, that's fine."

"Perfect."

After a few more minutes of makeup and hair touch up, Layla and I made our way out of the bridal suite dressing room and back to the masses. The reception was in full swing, the DJ draping the hotel ballroom with high-energy Spanish beats as she urged the crowd to the dance floor.

Unfortunately, half of the crowd found Layla and I instead in a swarm.

Congrats and compliments and happy tears were being thrown around left and right, and it was only a couple of minutes before I was drowning underneath it all. I hated crowds. I hated strangers. I hated crowds of ass-kissing strangers who had a serious lack of spatial awareness.

Halfway through deciding if I could dip out between Layla's abuela and her handsy uncle, one of the absolute worst things about being pregnant came my baby bump's way.

"Oh, my goodness, how far along are you?" An older woman I'd never seen before already had her liver-spotted hands on my stomach, *rubbing* it like a genie was going to pop out.

Through gritted teeth, I answered, "Five months."

The woman cooed and smiled up at me, her hands still on my belly. "Do you know the gender?"

I shook my head. "We wanna be surprised."

"Oh, but then how will you know what to buy beforehand?" A gleam of worry coated her washed-out turquoise eyes, genuine and totally unsolicited. "You won't know what color to paint the room or what clothes to buy. It's so much easier knowing!"

Clicking my tongue, I tied my hands behind my back so I didn't strangle this woman with her sagging breasts. "We've got kind of a green and yellow theme going for us so it'll work either way they come out."

"Oh, but isn't it *killing* you not knowing what's growing inside of you?"

"Well, I know it's human so that's pretty much the only fucking thing that matters," I snapped with a tight-lipped smile. The woman's stare widened, and she quickly snatched her hands from my stomach.

"Now, if you'll excuse me," I huffed. "I have to go find the bastard who knocked me up."

Now that *really* got a reaction from her, horror stretching across her homemaker face as I went in search of the man half responsible for why

EPILOGUE

every woman over fifty felt entitled to rub my stomach. *Fucking seriously, man.*

I didn't have to look far before I spotted the culprit leaning against a nearby wall in his best man suit, an amused glint in his diamond eyes.

Cocking my head to the side, I bustled up to him.

"You were watching that whole thing?"

"What?" Dominic feigned confusion. "You looked like you were handling it well."

"Yeah, well the next time some stranger comes up and starts rubbing my stomach, you're going to have to prove how much you love me because there *will* be a body to hide."

His eyes crinkled at the sides as he smiled my favorite smile.

"Duly noted."

"Have you seen the girls?" I asked, turning my sights to the lively reception.

Dominic's arms came around me from behind, hands folding together over the top of our baby's bump. The weight of his head rested on my shoulder as he snuggled himself in the crook of my neck.

"Last I saw, they were with my dad, and Charlotte was asking why they couldn't drink the champagne if it was really just apple juice like he told them. Maya was goading her on, of course."

"Of course."

I couldn't believe both girls were *nine* already and about to start fourth grade. I'd heard people say that life goes by in a blink if you're not watching, but I was watching—diligently—and they both had grown up so fast, my head was spinning.

My phone vibrated in the pocket of my dress—yes, my dress had pockets because dresses with pockets fucking rocked—and I fished it out.

"Who is it?" Dominic hummed in my ear.

"Dr. Welsh's office." Today was usually the day of the month I met with her.

Dominic's thumbs ran light circles over my stomach, looking at my ringing phone from over my shoulder. "Are you going to answer?"

Breathing in a sigh, I hit decline and rested my head back on Dominic's chest. Tilting my head up, I offered him a small smile.

"No, I'm okay."

"Are you sure?"

Staring up into those eyes that made me feel loved even when I didn't love myself, I nodded. "I'm sure."

We were both seeing Dr. Welsh in the beginning for couples' counseling and also separate sessions. Dominic stopped going after the first year, but I kept it up once a week until about six months ago.

Once a month was our new norm, and I had her number in case I needed it.

I hadn't needed it though. Not once.

Healing wasn't easy. It wasn't even *hard* like people said it would be.

It was fucking brutal.

The last four years had been like climbing a mountain of uneven slopes and inclines wearing freaking stilettos. The mountain had breakdowns and panic attacks and moments all along the way where I just wanted to lie down and stop moving, stop pushing, stop trying.

But Dominic never let me. He was climbing right alongside me, ready to catch me if I fell and force me back on track. He'd fucking aced therapy. I didn't even know that was something you could *do*, but Dominic Reed had done it.

He conquered the demons that dared to tempt him, and I fell in love with him even more watching him do it. He was so *strong*; I'd never been more sure that someone could hold me still and standing whenever my baggage tried to bring me down.

Sure, it took me a while to accept that blind kind of trust, but we'd gotten there.

Progress, folks.

"Do you think they'd open up the buffet early if I asked nicely?" Pushing to my tip-toes, I tried to scavenge a view of dinner and a weak link in the servers I could drop the pregnancy pity party on.

I just wanted a dinner roll. And maybe an entire rotisserie chicken.

EPILOGUE

"And by nicely, do you mean using the fact that you're pregnant against one of them to get food?"

I scoffed, shaking my head back to Dominic. "This whole 'knowing each other inside and out' really has its downfalls."

His smile lines deepened with a roguish smirk. "If you're hungry, I brought fruit snacks for the girls."

"I don't want fruit snacks. I want *meat*." My hands slipped inside his suit jacket, nails scraping down the silk-feel of his dress shirt and the ropes of muscles beneath. A sound of satisfaction rumbled in his throat, vibrating between our pressed chests. My vision went a bit blurry with an onslaught of arousal, pulsating down between my legs. "I want thick, raw, blood-pulsing *meat*."

The flavor of sweet mint washed hot against my lips, Dominic brushing his mouth against mine. "Are you hungry or horny, Ms. Sanders?"

"Can't a girl be both?" I breathed, pushing to my toes to kiss him.

Getting pregnant wasn't exactly planned.

It wasn't exactly avoided either.

Dominic and I ran through condoms like they were candy. One night, say *oh*, five or so months ago, Dominic reached for the box and there were none left. He rolled back to me on the bed, and neither of us said a word. He just stared down at me with all the love in the world, and I reached up and kissed him. I didn't stop kissing him until he was moving inside of me sans condom, an unspoken understanding fueling every touch and grunt and moan we made.

The sex that night was fucking *inspired*.

The next day, I jumped Dominic in the car on our way home from a PTA meeting at the girl's school. Again, no condom. We never discussed it really. It was one of those things we talked about through knowing looks and through the burn of our heroin chemistry.

We *knew*. We just knew.

"*Kat*." I kissed my name back from his lips, smothering it with my tongue so he wouldn't say anything to make me stop. A victim to his lust just like I was, he groaned and gave in for another panty-wetting kiss before pulling back enough to speak. "These pants aren't forgiving. If you don't stop, the entire reception is going to see how badly I want inside of you right now."

"Good," I breathed, cusping my lips against his. "Then I won't have to keep bragging to everyone about how huge you are since they'll see for themselves."

"I sincerely hope you're joking."

"Let's keep going and find out."

"We can't." Dominic's lips brushed the base of my ear. "Relative incoming."

Shooting my gaze out to the crowd, I spotted exactly what Dominic was talking about coming towards us with long legs and an invasively curious look about her.

"Shit. What's her name?" I whispered.

"Your guess is as good as mine."

Fuck. "She's one of Layla's cousins I think? I know I met her at the bachelorette party, but all I really remember from that night is how many times I had to pull Layla out of bushes."

"She certainly does gravitate towards them when she's been drinking," Dominic murmured in agreement.

The young woman with shiny brown hair was approaching fast, a megawatt smile on her face and her name one *thousand* fucking percent nowhere to be seen in my brain.

Welp. This was about to be uncomfortable.

"Hey girl!" Miss No Name brought me in for a hug, forcing me to untangle from Dominic. He didn't go far, putting himself right at my back with his hands stable weights of warmth on my waist. "You look incredible! You totally have that whole pregnancy glow thing down pat."

She batted me a wink and launched into a fit of silence-filler laughter society taught us about. It was uncomfortable, and so was I. No Name popped her brightened stare up towards Dominic.

"Is this your husband you wouldn't stop *bragging* about at the strip club?"

She cut us another slice of fakely-sweet laughter as Dominic squeezed a reprimand around my waist. Whatever. Totally worth it. His dick was

EPILOGUE

bigger than every stripper's there, and I wasn't shy about broadcasting it.

Tangling my fingers with his at my sides, I leaned my shaking head to rest against Dominic's sternum. "We're not married."

The joy on her face stumbled. *Oh boy.* "I see. Engaged then?"

I shook my head. "Nope."

"Oh." This chick was clearly fighting the urge to blatantly judge. It was almost amusing to watch. Almost. "I guess I just assumed since you're having a baby and all that you were married."

"Yeah, no. Something about having a baby out of wedlock just really turns me on. It's so *sinful*."

The brush of Dominic's face hid in the slope of my neck as he tried to stifle his soft laughter. His breath fanned across my neck as he failed, goosebumps rising and prickling higher as he pressed a gentle kiss to my skin.

Layla's cousin tried to laugh my comment off, but the noise was having trouble making it through her sinking smile.

"Um, so have you two not been dating long?"

"It'll be five years next October," Dominic answered without removing his mouth from my neck.

"*Oh.* So then time isn't the issue. I'm sorry, I just don't get it." She forced out another faux laugh. "You two just seem so happy, and you're having a baby! Why won't you tie the knot?"

Call it a mood swing. Call it anger issues. Call it whatever the fuck you want, but this third degree interview by a woman I was *pretty* sure used her teeth to put dollar bills in a strippers thong had run its course.

"Well, *aside* from the fact that half of marriages end in divorce, I grew up in a broken home and my daddy issues make me a perfect candidate for commitment phobia, and Dominic here *used* to be married. Then his wife tried to kill me." I narrowed my eyes on hers, enjoying how she squirmed beneath my glare. "Does that about answer your question?"

And just like that, Blabbermouth was speechless. Dominic's hands slipped from my stomach up to my shoulders, gently easing me around.

"Would you excuse us?" he chimed, polite as ever.

No Name nodded in a daze, and Dominic turned me around and guided me out of the ballroom. My fingers were stiff they were clenched so tight by the time we reached an area where wedding guests weren't milling around for the hell of it and showing off the booze in their hands that *they* were allowed to drink because *they* weren't creating human life.

Lucky assholes.

"If you're bringing me out here to scold me for snapping at her, can you at least do it in an accent or something to keep me from wanting to bite your head off too?"

A stream of air that sounded humored pushed through Dominic's nose behind me, and I pictured one of those crooked grins of his sliding up his full mouth.

"I'm not scolding you. That woman was incredibly rude." He stopped next to a wall distant from the reception, turning me towards him. "I suppose now that my mom's stopped bugging us about marriage, someone had to pick up the slack."

"Yeah, but you can't knock me up every time someone starts getting pushy," I quipped. "My uterus would implode."

Crisp, clean, earthy notes invaded my senses as Dominic closed in with a devilish ghost of a smile, humming deeply.

"The idea is enticing."

Lord, this man would be the death of me. I had an inkling early on, but the last few years proved it. When you stripped off all of his proper layers, Dominic was quite the primitive man underneath. He wasn't at all shy about staking a claim over me in public or private and got fucking stars in his eyes whenever I did the same.

He always had at least one hand on me if he could manage, and there wasn't a room I walked into that had him already in it where his eyes didn't find me as soon as I entered. We were magnetic, and his attention on me had gone off the charts when we got pregnant.

His testosterone or male pride or whatever it was got a major boner off of getting me pregnant... and it was sort of hot. Like, sort of as in *really* hot.

EPILOGUE

The only way he hadn't 'claimed' me was with a ring on my finger, but he said he was fine with that and—thanks to therapy—I believed him. He wasn't racing to the altar again anytime soon either.

We were on the same page about the whole marriage thing, but Miss Invasive and Judgmental got my anxiety kicking up dust, irritating my sureness. The silken gray tie around his neck was the perfect distraction as I folded it between my fingers, tracing zig-zag shapes in the fabric.

"You don't feel differently about all of that," I braced myself with a breath. "Do you?"

Long fingers came up to ease his tie out of my fidgeting hands. I balled them up at my chest now that they had nothing to grab, and that was where they got squished between me and Dominic as he pressed in close. There wasn't anywhere to look but up, thunderclouds gently rolling through his eyes.

"I don't need a ceremony and papers to know I'll spend the rest of my life with you. You and I have never done things by the book, and while it theoretically should have given me an aneurysm, it's what works for us." I puffed a small laugh and he pecked the tip of my nose. "If you told me tomorrow you wanted to marry me, I'd run out and find you the perfect ring. If you told me you simply wanted to love me until we were old and that's all there ever was to it, I'd smile and say okay. Marriage isn't what I need to be happy, Kat. All I need is you and my girls."

"God, where do you come up with these speeches, *I swear*." My hands started squirming to pat down his suit jacket. "Did you write that one on some note cards earlier and stash it in your pockets knowing I'd probably have at least one anxiety attack today? Come *on*."

"It was a good one, hm?" He quirked a cocky eyebrow.

Fuck, it looked damnable on him.

"Oscar-worthy. Truly. My panties *and* my heart are dropping."

A wicked glint darted across his gaze. "My favorite combination."

Fuck, how was he so hot? My libido mapped out the liquid silver of his eyes down to his kissable pink mouth framed by the manicured beard I was addicted to feeling scratch my inner thighs. It was a toss up between the baby hormones and the raw sexuality Dominic oozed every waking second of the day, but now all I could think about was the deliciously conflicting sensation of his scruff and soft tongue between my legs that made my eyes roll back into my head.

"How much trouble do you think we'd be in if we disappeared for a bit?" I nipped his full bottom lip, swiping my tongue along the fresh bite. Gray storm clouds swelled with hunger and darkened above me, thunderbolts resonating in his husky tone.

"You want to fool around at our best friends' wedding?"

"We did it at their engagement party. I don't see the difference." Memories of that night and how he dragged me into the guest bathroom at Ryan's parents' house to fuck me up against the sink so I could watch him do it in the mirror was added fire to the inferno growing in my core. "In fact, I think we should keep up tradition."

The arch of my throat exposed to him as he lowered his mouth to it. "You are still as insatiable as ever, Ms. Sanders."

"Hey, don't blame me," I panted against him. "Blame this suit you're wearing."

He was a fucking adonis in that thing. The intense gray shade was the exact color of his irises, and if it wasn't his sharp eyes that had my mouth watering, it was how the suit quite literally looked as if it'd been molded around his bulging muscles and the curves of his ass.

His *perfect* ass.

I'd developed a real compulsive habit of grabbing it whenever I wanted that Dominic eventually just accepted. Honestly, what more did he expect from me with a tush like that?

Dominic chuckled against my throat and threaded his fingers through mine.

"Come with me."

Oh *fuck* yeah.

He tugged me behind him, excitement bubbling in my stomach as he brought us down the length of the wide hallway until we reached the end. A pair of solid double doors stood before us, and Dominic cast a vigilant

EPILOGUE

look from side to side before testing the handle and cracking open one side.

He swiveled me an arched look. "Ladies first."

"God, I love how much I've corrupted you."

He sent me a wicked wink that had a direct line to my hormones and hurried us inside the room, closing the door behind. The high ceiling above us was lit in sections, sustaining an uneven glow throughout the secondary ballroom Dominic stole us away into. It was about half the size of the one Layla and Ryan's reception was in and totally barren aside from a few scattered tables and chairs.

Four years ago, Dominic would have gawked at the idea of sneaking into a room that was off-limits. While I do attribute some of his rebellion nowadays to yours truly, his stepping back from the force had a lot to do with it too.

After he was suspended, he never went back.

His old Chief pleaded and apologized, but the damage was done for Dominic. He couldn't unknow how impossible it was to find me between the restrictions and personal agendas and politics of working for the government. His good heart was jaded to the whole thing.

It was actually his old *old* boss, Archie, who suggested he look into police consulting. It allowed him to be a private contractor and choose the cases he wanted to work.

Most of the ones he chose were sex crimes.

Trafficking victims, specifically.

He was a goddamn hero, and I fell in love with him each and every day, over and over again, addictingly and inescapably.

"So..." I sauntered further into the room, sliding my fingertips across the back of a chair. "How much do you wanna bet these walls are soundproof?"

Dominic caught the suggestive smirk I threw him, advancing with the prowess of a starved predator. His movements were calculated, his posture relaxed and confident.

"Were you planning on being loud, Ms. Sanders?"

"Me? Of course not, Mr. Reed. I wouldn't want anyone to catch us."

He reached me, slipping his hands around my middle. "And what exactly is it you think I plan on doing to you in here?"

"Well…" He lowered himself to sit in the free chair, guiding me on top of him with my legs split on either side of his hips. My tits flattened against his hard chest as I ghosted my lips over his. "You have me all alone in a big room, and my dress has a high, easy access slit, so I thought we might… play checkers?"

All I got to see was a glimpse of white teeth beneath a lopsided grin before Dominic called me a brat and shut me up with his mouth. A moan curled up my throat, vibrating between our lips as I melted into him, becoming goo for him to mold and grope and fuck how he pleased.

Impatience being a reliable virtue of mine, my tongue was in his mouth and my hips were rolling against his in no time. He was right too—his pants were *not* forgiving, and the thick outline of his cock was prying to get out of them so hard, I could practically feel every time it throbbed against me.

Needy mewls were sliding off of my tongue and into Dominic's mouth as I fucked myself against him, the pinch of a release stringing together in my lower stomach. His hands were in conflict on my hips, one moment trying to control them and the next, breaking beneath the fabric of my dress and groping the bare skin of my thighs that was all his.

I was all his and he was all mine, and I fucking loved every second of life with this man.

"I think we need to cool down," he mumbled against me, heavy breathing fanning my face.

I was just as winded. "Why?"

"Because there's no lock on that door, and I'm not taking the chance that someone walks in and sees you."

"I don't care." I went back in for another kiss. Dominic caught me, restraining me back.

"I do." He cut me a strict look, and my breath buckled.

Aw fuck, he was serious.

"Then why'd you sneak us in here if you weren't going to completely

EPILOGUE

ravage me until I couldn't walk?" Dominic's laughter touched my puffy lips as he shelved a curl of mine behind my ear.

"Can't a man just want to kiss his woman in private?"

"Your *woman*?" I repeated on a tone of amusement.

Mischief backlit his smirk as his dark brows tweaked up. "Yes, Ms. Sanders. Do you have a problem being my woman?"

Pushing back, I righted my posture with a teasing squint. "That sounds an awful lot like you think you own me, Mr. Reed."

"Only partly." Heat radiated through my baby bump as he placed his palm over it, rubbing it. "This baby I put inside of you gives me a fifty percent ownership over you. Those are the rules."

"Oh." Light dashed inside his eyes as I played along. "Is that how this works?"

My lips came down on his radiant smile as he murmured, "Absolutely."

Did you know it was possible to capture happiness in something as simple as a kiss? I didn't. Not until Dominic showed me how happiness could come in small and big doses, complex or ordinary moments. That was part of our healing. Dr. Welch encouraged us to recognize every blip or stretch of bliss to combat the guilt and the sorrow we felt to prove every day was a mixture of both. No day was pure joy and no day was pure pain.

Even if it was a fleeting feeling of warmth when everything else around you was freezing cold, it proved hope was alive. Yeah, I believed in *hope* now. When Charlotte laughed, I felt it. When I remembered my mom and smiled, I felt it.

When Dominic Reed kissed me, I was *bathed* in it.

My lips swept with his one last time, sweetened and savoring his kiss. Electric butterflies warmed my chest as I eased our lips apart, wisps of love moving between our mingled breathing. His kiss cast a spell over my eyelids, infusing cement into their lashes that made it so hard to open my eyes. I just wanted to melt back into him.

Eyes like a lazy afternoon rainfall were already watching me when I peeled my heavy lids open. He let his head droop back while we kissed, so I had a perfect view of every exquisite inch of him.

"Are you happy?" I asked softly, not because I feared he wasn't. Because I liked hearing it.

The faint lines next to his eyes crinkled as the answer rose up his face. "Deliriously."

The same answer twitched in the muscles of my cheeks, but I barely fought it off. Smiling for Dominic was the easiest thing once I'd learned it was okay to be happy.

And I was. Heart-achingly, impossible to truly capture in a word, *happy*.

"Have you thought of any more baby names?" I asked, coasting the tips of my nails over his beard.

His hands came to rest on my stomach as he breathed out a content sigh. "It's hard. You took the easy part. The first name has all the pressure behind it."

"That's how dibs works. I called the middle name. You get the first. It just has to not suck."

His browline flattened at me, unamused. "Yes, no pressure."

"Come on," I encouraged. "There are lots of great first names that would sound good with Blake."

The second we found out I was pregnant, it was one of the first things I told Dominic. This baby wouldn't have life if I didn't, and giving them a middle name to honor the man responsible for saving us both was such a small way to say thank you, but I think Blake would like it. More than his poetic words could say.

Dominic nodded, focused on my belly. "I'll keep thinking."

"Just nothing like kumquat or Velveeta. I don't want to fuck this kid up anymore than I'm probably going to."

I forced a sharp breath of laughter to cover up the feeling of embarrassment that plunged through my stomach as I heard the self-aimed slight.

Force of fucking habit.

I had a real knack for putting myself down, and I was *working on it*. It was just hard to catch the slip-ups, and without even looking up at him, I knew Dominic was giving me a disapproving glower.

"Kat, look at me." Dammit. The lecture was already in his firm tone, but

EPILOGUE

I did as he said. "You are not going to do anything to this baby but love them unconditionally. I've already seen it with Maya and your sister. You are a *fantastic* mother. I've never been more confident of anything except how much I love you."

My heart skipped a beat, and my insecurity came rushing out in a quiet tone. "I just don't want to disappoint you or this baby."

Adoration eclipsed anything else in Dominic's eyes. "You could never be a disappointment. Of that, I'm also positive."

My heart gave way beneath his words, and he didn't stop there.

"In the last four years, you've gotten your GED and your associate's degree. You put together an awareness program for sex-trafficking while working at the women's shelter, and now you're carrying our baby. You've blown me away every single day that I've known you, Kat. Every single day. *You* are the strongest woman I'll ever know."

"Dominic, if you make me cry again at this wedding, I'm going to be so pissed." But it was too late. My vision was misty with tears that I tried to blink back, not wanting to have to fix my makeup *again*.

"Fine." A tender smile creased his mouth as he cleaned the water from the corner of my eyes. "No more tears. Just kisses."

He laid one on my lips and peppered in a few more when he couldn't stop himself. Between the kissing, and without any effort or panic at all, I whispered against him.

"I love you so much."

My thunder curled his lips into a smile for his little lightning, our perfect storm finding peace at last.

"More and more every day, Ms. Sanders."

THE END

Next Book by Alexandria Lee

That is a WRAP on Dom and Kat! Can you believe it? If you loved those two, I have a feeling you'll love the new couple in my next series even more...

TITLE: There's Venom in Her Kiss

An Enemies to Lovers, Age Gap, Boss's Daughter dark romance

Blurb:

As a boy, I'd developed a likeness for control.
As a man, that likeness had corrupted into an obsession.
Scarlett Avery was the twenty-one-year-old *brat* committed to setting my obsession on fire and dancing in the flames. Literally.
I was an FBI agent, and she was only meant to be a quick assignment. My orders were to chauffeur Little Miss Loud Mouth across the country to deliver to her father—my boss—after her not-so-minor brush with arson. Now, I was trapped in small confines with a woman that made my hands itch to wrap around her pretty neck and squeeze—and what's worse? She wanted me to do it.
In fact, she begged me to break her.
Scarlett Avery was a woman of secrets and sins packaged in a body twelve

years too young for me and completely off-limits. She's my boss's daughter, and I shouldn't think about her wicked smirk or fantasize about ways I could rearrange the pouty curves of it.

I definitely shouldn't give into the dare always written into the green of her eyes, baiting me to hunt her. Destroy her. Punish her.

Scarlett wanted a depraved monster.

But she had no idea how nightmarish I could be.

Releasing July 18th 2022
Pre-order NOW on Amazon: http://hyperurl.co/kfth7g

Want more Kat and Dom?

Haven't had your fill of Kat and Dom and their happily-ever-after yet? I've written a bonus chapter of the night they found out Kat was pregnant! It's got that classic Kat humor, Dom's protectiveness, and of course, some spice ;)

Follow this link, sign up for my newsletter, and enjoy!
https://dl.bookfunnel.com/dq48zzlw66

About the Author

Do you want to keep up to date with me or signed copies of my books? The form for signed copies of the series is below as is my Facebook reader group and Newsletter!

You can connect with me on:

- https://www.facebook.com/groups/1155988098182494
- https://forms.gle/diur5Y1jrxDmeLzJA

Subscribe to my newsletter:

- https://mailchi.mp/d47a710b9325/author-alexandria-lee-books

Also by Alexandria Lee

An **Enemies to Lovers, Age Gap, Boss's Daughter** dark romance available for pre-order NOW!

There's Venom in Her Kiss: Perfect Poison Trilogy Book One.

As a boy, I'd developed a likeness for control.

As a man, that likeness had corrupted into an obsession.

Scarlett Avery was the twenty-one-year-old *brat* committed to setting my obsession on fire and dancing in the flames. Literally.

I was an FBI agent, and she was only meant to be an assignment. My orders were to chauffeur Little Miss Loud Mouth across the country to deliver to her father—my boss—after her not-so-minor brush with arson.

Now, I was trapped in small confines with a woman that made my hands itch to wrap around her pretty neck and squeeze—and what's worse?

She wanted me to do it.

In fact, she begged me to break her.

Scarlett Avery was a woman of secrets and sins packaged in a body twelve years too young for me and completely off-limits. She's my boss's daughter, and I shouldn't think about her wicked smirk or fantasize about ways I could rearrange the pouty curves of it.

I definitely shouldn't give into the dare always written into the green of her eyes, baiting me to hunt her. Destroy her. Punish her.
Scarlett wanted a depraved monster.

But she had no idea how nightmarish I could be.

Dancing with Sin

A standalone epic forbidden romance...

I was a good person who was about to do a very bad thing.

All my life, I had worked tirelessly to achieve perfection. Perfection was in my blood.

All that hard work had earned me my dream job as a professional dancer, the perfect boyfriend, and the naïve belief that perfection was built to last.

All it took was one night. One night to tear down everything I had built until I was left single, jobless, and my heart stained with betrayal.

With my tail tucked between my legs, I drove me and my broken heart to Chicago to move in with my older sister until I was back on my feet.

Little did I know that this was just the beginning of my twist of fate nightmare.

Ethan Black was waiting for me in Chicago as a perfect stranger. A handsome, effortlessly charming, makes-my-heart-beat-out-of-my-chest stranger. I didn't subscribe to the idea of soulmates before him, but now I'm convinced.

The only problem?

He's engaged to be wed to my sister.

Made in the USA
Middletown, DE
14 July 2024

57301394R00254